The Challenge

SUSAN KEARNEY

tor romance

A TOM DOHERTY ASSOCIATES BOOK
NEW YORK

This is a work of fiction. All the characters and events portrayed in this book are either products of the author's imagination or are used fictitiously.

THE CHALLENGE

Edited by Anna Genoese

A Tor Book
Published by Tom Doherty Associates, LLC
175 Fifth Avenue
New York, NY 10010

Tor® is a registered trademark of Tom Doherty Associates, LLC.

ISBN 0-7394-4951-6

Printed in the United States of America

—For Anna Genoese, an editor with vision

Acknowledgements

THE CHALLENGE would never have never been written without the help of a lot of people: Virginia Henley and Rebecca Thompkins for being there at the beginning, Julie Leto, Charlotte Douglas and Jeanie London, critique partners extraordinaire without whose enthusiasm the book might not have gone beyond the first draft, Brenda Chin who taught me that character is as important as plot, Jill Barnett who aided me through the final version of the all-important beginning, Mel Berger whose representation was a stellar boost to my career, Anthony Schiavino whose artistic vision of the cover captured the essence of the story, Jean Mason who willingly read a very first rough draft, and last, but certainly not least, my husband Barry who always gives the ultimate in encouragement.

Prologue

"It sure would be great to have a hot babe like her guarding my back."

Special Agent Tessa Camen recognized the voice of a local cop, Officer Davis, the one she'd dressed down yesterday for his careless attitude, now talking about her career as if he had a clue about PPD, Presidential Protective Detail.

"Hell, she could guard my side, my front, or any little part of me she wants," Davis's partner added in his unmistakable Southern drawl.

Tessa kept walking around the bleachers of Jefferson Central High School, heading straight for the roped-off area where her fellow Secret Service agents lounged. She needed coffee. Fast. Before the presidential motorcade arrived. Stepping around a black-and-white and then an ambulance toward the cordoned-off area reserved for police officers and security agents, she heard men's laughter. When one of the men in her detail spoke her name, she paused.

"Hey, pal." Agent Walters defended her with some heat in his tone. "Tessa Camen's not just a good-looking woman, she's SAIC, special agent in charge."

Damn straight I am.

"This isn't a cupcake detail," Davis muttered. "Where is she?"

"She won't be late. Unlike you schmucks, she's a professional."

Tessa rolled her eyes and restrained a grin. *Here we go again.*

"Not to mention she can kick your asses," bragged Saunders, a second agent whom she'd pinned in hand-to-hand during a training session not too long ago. Her agents might rag her in private, but to anyone else they presented a united front. Not so long ago, she would have had to defend herself from the verbal criticism of outsiders, but those days were gone for good. This wasn't her first brush with assassins. Two years ago she'd stopped a wacko from killing her boss, Daron Garner. The sixty-year-old tycoon had bragged about Tessa's skills to the president herself, which had landed her on the most elite security detail in the world, where she'd proven herself more than capable. But she was just as proud of the fact that her detail accepted her as one of them—closing ranks against outsiders—as she was of her fighting skills.

The cops laughed uneasily. Then the one with the thick drawl mentioned more conversationally, "Walters said at the academy she blew the rest of her class out of the water."

Someone whistled.

Walters was a fine Secret Service agent, but he talked too much. Tessa made a note to tell him so, later, in private.

For now he continued to brag. "Shit, man, she defeated the instructor during the academy's defensive tactics drills."

Davis sneered. "But she's a broad."

"Don't let her or POTUS hear you say that," Walters advised, using the Secret Service acronym for the president of the United States.

"Yeah, well, I like my women soft and on their backs. The only thing I want a broad like that to blow is—"

"You say that to her face," Walters warned, "she'll have you on your back . . . in a choke hold with her knee in your balls."

There was more male laughter. With a sigh of resignation that men will be men, Tessa raised her hand to her head to make sure no wisp of hair had escaped her tight twist.

"What makes a woman who looks that hot want to spend hours in a sweaty gym training hand-to-hand combat?" asked one of the cops.

Again Walters spoke too freely. "Foster homes, man. No family. But lots of time on her hands."

"Is it true she's a real ninja?" asked another cop. "I heard she sneaked into the Imperial Palace and replaced an artifact stolen by one of our diplomats, preventing an international incident."

Saunders shook his head. "That's just a rumor."

A rumor that happened to be true, but one Tessa kept secret. She walked past the ambulance and interrupted their conversation. "Gentlemen," she greeted them, then eyed Davis, the sexist cop. "Present company excluded." Her detail laughed and the uniforms refused to meet her gaze. She poured herself coffee and drained the cup in one long gulp, appreciating the kick of caffeine. A voice crackled in her earpiece: the president was about to arrive. "We ready to roll?"

For the next sixty minutes Tessa Camen stood sentry beside her protectee, the president of the United States of America. Tessa's eyes hid behind sunglasses, alert, vigilant, wary. Positioned under a red, white, and blue flag in the middle of a football field on a wooden dais, she was the last line of defense in safeguarding the leader of her country.

The speeches were finally winding down when a bald man, third row, fourth seat, reached under his windbreaker. Tessa tensed, primed to act at the first sight of a weapon. When he removed a camera from an inside pocket, her gaze swept on to another listener in the audience who wore a long brown trench coat, a coat too heavy for the mild June weather. When he'd first taken his seat, the man's inappropriate clothing had caught her attention, and her gaze kept returning to him. On edge, Tessa ignored the woman in a neon-red vest beside him, a brightly plumed foil for his darker shadow. Most people clapped politely, shifted in their seats, and whispered to their wives, husbands, and friends, but Mr. Trench Coat appeared to be alone. He vibrated with enthusiasm, cheering a little too loudly.

The president wrapped her comments, ending her presentation with her usual catch phrase. The swell of applause didn't distract Tessa, and she noted that this time Mr. Trench Coat didn't join the clapping. When he raised his arm, Tessa caught sight of a gun barrel up his sleeve. Instinct, training, and a hit of pure adrenaline kicked in.

"Gun! Trench coat at two o'clock. Five yards." Tessa spoke clearly into her microphone, pinpointing Trench Coat's location to her detail. As the countersniper team on the school's roof zeroed in on the shooter, uniformed division officers dispersed through the crowd.

At the exact moment she'd issued the warning, Tessa uncoiled her bunched thigh muscles. Launching her body, twisting in the air, she tackled the president, covered the short politician's body with her own.

They went down hard. Rolled behind the podium for cover. The president let out a gasp.

The audience screamed and stampeded, creating a rioting mass exodus, all shoving for the exits, but their safety was not Tessa's immediate concern. Neither was taking out the shooter. Her job was to shield the president.

Heart full of trepidation, Tessa drew her Sig Sauer P229 from the holster, crawled over the president's body and positioned her torso between the shooter and the president. POTUS was not going to die. Not today. Not on Tessa's detail.

Shots blasted, the noise deafening, the reek of gunpowder

strong and bitter. Bullets raked the stage, shattering lights, shredding the curtains. The podium splintered into bits of wood. The audience screamed and bolted and agents returned fire. Smoke clung like a shroud and shards of concrete stung the exposed flesh of Tessa's face, neck, and hands. She blinked the blood from her eyes and prayed the president wasn't hurt.

"You hit, Madam President?"

"I don't . . ." The supreme commander's face was pale, her eyes wide with shock. But no blood. At the sight of the other's apparently superficial scratches, Tessa felt a measure of relief and pride. But her job was not yet done. She had to move the president to a secure location.

"Stay still. I'll be getting you out of here shortly."

Pulse escalating, heart tripping, Tessa waited for a lull in the gunfire, waited for the shooter to reload, waited for orders. Within seconds, the command she'd been expecting came through her earpiece. "Get POTUS away."

According to the emergency plan, defensive agents laid down cover fire. The "quarterback" would drive the armored limo onto the football field, in close to the president, for extraction.

"POTUS rolling."

Tessa looked up and assessed the situation. Agents had closed on the assassin, pinning him down. She grabbed the fallen president's upper arm and half yanked, half carried the stumbling woman toward the limo. From the disarray of screaming citizens, scurrying police, and busy Secret Service agents, two well-dressed dark-haired men, both above average height and weight, stepped between POTUS and the limo. In contrast to the panicky rushing of everyone else around them, their movements were slow, deliberate, menacing. She pegged them as trouble.

Tessa shoved the president behind her, then shouted, "You, sirs. Move out of the way."

As if they'd been choreographed to move as one, the men

attacked. With a head shot, Tessa took down one man, employed a spinning back kick on the second. Mr. Calm as Ice shifted, countered to her gun arm, and her weapon flew from her numbed hand.

Mr. Calm as Ice raised his arm and flicked his wrist, a snapping movement, eerily similar to Mr. Trench Coat's, that slid a gun smoothly into his grip. Years of training, thousands of hours honing her martial arts skills, allowed Tessa to react instinctively, whipping her leg into a roundhouse kick. Before he pulled the trigger, her foot connected with his shoulder. He screamed in pain—or frustration that he'd never get off a shot. Tessa didn't give him time for a second attack, following up with a kick to the sternum.

Anticipating her move, her opponent spun, causing her kick to land slightly off center. Instead of knocking the wind out of his chest, she cracked his rib. He grunted, bent over in pain, reached for a backup gun at his ankle.

"No you don't." Lunging forward, she slammed her knee into his face so hard, his neck snapped back.

A less muscular man's neck would have broken. Ice Man shook off her blow with another roar. He came at her again, this time more cautiously. Circling right, Tessa kept her body between him and the president.

She had to end this quickly. Move the president to safety. When the guy advanced, leading with a strong right punch to her face, Tessa blocked and countered with multiple strikes to the knee and throat, softening him up before administering the death blow to the temple.

Tessa didn't wait for the body to hit the ground before she scooped up her weapon, once again grabbed the president, opened the door of the limo, and shoved her charge onto a prone position across the back seat. Tessa slammed the door behind them and dived on top of her.

She ordered the driver, "Go. Go. Go. Get us the hell out of here!"

A police siren ahead of them blared. They might not have

the entire PPD with them, but they weren't alone, either. The driver burned rubber and the vehicle sped forward.

Tessa released the breath she'd been holding and spoke through her microphone to the deputy director, reporting a break in security that left POTUS vulnerable to attack. "We don't have the full PPD."

"Underst—"

Her radio went dead.

Oh, God. They were cut off from command. On their own. POTUS was now her responsibility alone. She'd worked hard to attain the honor of guarding the most important person in the free world, and Tessa would live up to the trust her superiors had placed in her.

Tessa intended to prove her worth today. She angled her head, peered over the seat and dash to assess the situation. Up front, a black-and-white led the way, lights on, sirens shrieking. Behind them, a tan sedan that was not part of their detail followed, cluing her in that the danger was not yet over. When they changed lanes, so did the sedan. "We've picked up a tail."

She needed backup, but with her microphone dead, she couldn't call her detail. *Think.* The presidential vehicle was full of electronic equipment.

She tried the car's phone. "Dead."

"Sabotaged?" the president asked.

"Madam President, please strap on your seat belt."

Tessa didn't need her sweaty palms and ragged nerves to tell her that the president had been purposely isolated. Vulnerable.

"Speed up. Lose the tail," Tessa ordered the driver.

He did the opposite, jamming on his brakes, bringing the car to a screeching halt on the highway's shoulder. At the sudden stop, the president yelped in surprise. The car's momentum slammed Tessa forward then back against the seat, her hand smacked the door, and her already injured hand dropped her weapon. But during that split second of violent whiplash, she comprehended the driver had betrayed them. Ears ringing, vision blurred, she scrambled for her gun.

Tessa's fingers closed on her weapon, but the chauffeur had his fully drawn. Cocked. Aimed at the president.

No way could the rogue agent miss. No way could Tessa raise her gun or knock the weapon from his hand before he pulled the trigger. No way could she win this fight. Knowledge of imminent defeat burned in her heart.

Tessa didn't hesitate. Muscles already contracted, she propelled her body into the direct line of fire. At the same time, she raised her gun.

Too slow.

Too late.

1

"Have I died and gone to heaven?" Tessa muttered.

Without opening her eyes, she could feel heat permeating the deep chill that stole her energy as if she'd been frozen. Except for shivers and the tingling that slowly returned feeling to her numb limbs, there was no pain. No gunshot wound.

Just wondrous heat, like the touch of sun-kissed male flesh. Toned, smooth skin, sharing blessed warmth, rocking her. No, carrying her? A large gentle hand smoothed her hair from her forehead and a deep masculine voice assured her that she would soon be warm.

"You will recover."

Expecting the dream to fade, expecting to see a hospital room, a doctor, beeping machines, Tessa delayed opening her eyes. She didn't want to face her fellow agents, who would tell her the sad news that she'd failed her assignment and that the president was dead. But she'd never been one to hide from reality. Tessa forced open her eyes. Instead of a hospital room and her detail, she found herself in a room she didn't recognize, alone with a stranger, her head pillowed on his shoulder. Her gaze locked stares with the amber eyes of a blond-haired giant, her hand curled intimately under the vest that didn't fully cover his broad chest.

A bare chest? She must be hallucinating. Out of her head from painkillers, the result of a bullet ricocheting inside her skull. She blinked, expecting him to vanish. He didn't.

Okay. He was real. Or she was crazy. She preferred the first option, but did a double check. Beneath her hand, his heart beat with disturbing regularity, and her fingers had somehow twisted around his crisp blond chest hair. She took a deep breath and his scent reminded her of exotic spices and sandalwood soap.

He might be a dream man, but he was no fantasy. He appeared quite the living, breathing person, carrying her as if she weighed nothing. But no matter how baffled she might be, no woman in her right mind could fail to appreciate such a fine male specimen. Yet no human naturally possessed eyes the color of his tupelo-honey ones, the irises ringed with fiery gold, and framed by a perfect crescent of thick golden lashes. He sported a strong nose, a square jaw that suggested stubbornness, the carved cheekbones of a highborn savage, and flawless bronze skin of a hue that could knock a woman flat on her heels for a second look.

His generous mouth curled with a touch of sympathy, and yet his eyes shot off hints of irritation and impatience. "Are you warm?"

Oh, God.

She was cold, already craving a hot cup of coffee. And naked. Naked in the strange man's arms. In a room that resembled no hospital she'd ever seen, he laid down with her on a shimmering metallic platform. A hundred questions burned in her mind. Had she been taken hostage? Where was she?

Before waking up in his arms, she'd leaped between a traitorous Secret Service agent and POTUS. She recalled the driver's betrayal. Was this man or his group holding the president, too?

Tessa suspected she was a prisoner, kept naked to make her feel vulnerable. Or had she somehow ended up in a sanatorium? But then where was her hospital gown? Where were her clothes and her gun? Her detail?

The stranger briskly rubbed her arms, creating a friction that heated her numbed limbs. As he tended her, Tessa searched for an exit in the shimmering silver walls, floor and ceiling, all bare of any adornments and constructed of an unrecognizable luminous gray substance that made her question her eyesight. During her years in foster homes, she'd seen some strange decor, but nothing like the otherworldly walls that surrounded her. She must be hallucinating.

But when she held up her hand that he'd finished rubbing, she clearly counted four fingers and one thumb. And the hunk was still there, watching her with those strange eyes, efficiently and briskly rubbing her other arm. Even into adulthood, she'd had nightmares of abandonment, of losing her parents and her home—but she'd never had a dream this weird, never been this cold, although his ministrations were helping her to warm up.

She tried to speak but her dry throat only issued a weak croak.

He picked up an odd-shaped vessel and held it to her lips. "Drink."

She peered suspiciously at what appeared to be water. Hell, if he wanted to drug her, in her weakened state, he'd have no trouble. She parted her lips voluntarily.

Cool water slid down her parched throat. Greedily she emptied the vessel, and refreshed, her mind kept working. Where was she? What had happened to the president? Why had this stranger carried her? What was going on? Why was she so stiff? Her vocal cords so rusty?

Frantic with worry and without her detail to back her up, she followed training procedures. She didn't ask her first questions out loud for fear that she might help the enemy.

Think.

Assess the situation.

Gather information.

Through a mouth cottony from disuse, confusion, and suspicion, she forced out words that wouldn't betray anyone. "Who are you?"

He'd moved those large, capable hands to her icy feet. "My name is Kahn."

He'd answered her simply, with no embellishment, almost as if he expected her to panic if he said too much. She might be frightened, but she was too well trained to let her feelings overrule her good sense. She'd always kept her emotions deep inside. In the past, coolheaded thinking had saved her. Tamping down a rising panic with the skill of long practice, she pulled her foot from the stranger's hands, uncomfortable with the intimacy of his touch. Off kilter, she breathed deeply but even the air didn't smell normal here. Her body felt too heavy. Each breath took extra effort. Keeping calm was all very well, but suppose her good sense told her the correct reaction was panic?

Don't go there.

She tried another innocuous question to find out what was going on without revealing critical information about Secret Service standard operating procedures or POTUS. "Why are you holding me?"

"I was carrying you to the warming chamber, but you awakened on your own." If she was reading those amber eyes correctly, he'd answered her question easily, simply, and possibly honestly, but she had the suspicion that his words meant one thing to him and another to her. Although the bone-deep cold had diminished, she still felt chilled, yearned for coffee. She'd never heard of a warming chamber, didn't trust the sympathy in his tone, and maintained her vigilance, especially after he added, "I'm from Rystan."

Rystan?

He lay beside her and pulled her back against his side, sharing his heat. There was nothing sexual about his contact, but she didn't appreciate being held so closely. However, she wouldn't verbally object until she had more clues to exactly what was going on.

He'd said he was from "Rystan" and acted as though the information he'd supplied should have meant something to her, but he might as well have spoken in ancient Greek. She'd never heard of the place and wondered if it was part of the new Russian republic and if he was a terrorist.

Tessa wanted to roll away, detach herself from his disturbing heat, but then he would have a much better view of her nudity than he did with her lying pressed against him. Besides, she needed his heat to throw off her chills.

Or did she? She was warmer now. And she sure as hell wasn't going to develop Stockholm syndrome and bond with her captor. But was she a prisoner?

Her silence tactic had gained her little information, so she did the unexpected, firing a slew of questions at him, hoping he might reveal more than he intended. "What happened to the President? What is this place? Where are my clothes?"

He shot her an "I'm not falling for that trick" look. "I'm supposed to give you this." He handed her an official-looking envelope.

"What is it?"

"Your people said it would explain everything. If you have more questions after reading this, I will try to answer them."

He sounded cooperative and supportive, but his shoulders had tensed, and he regarded her with a watchfulness that reminded her of Master Chen, her martial arts instructor, when he'd considered her fifth request to take her on as his student. Her perseverance had paid off, and he'd finally agreed to train the determined and skinny kid she'd once been. Master Chen had passed on three years ago, but if he could have been with her now, he would have advised her to assess, evaluate, and plan before taking physical action. Good advice—especially since she didn't know if this Kahn character had any knowledge of her fighting skills.

She allowed him to prop her head with his muscle-bound arm and kept the envelope between his gaze and her bare breasts. Stomach churning, she plucked the sheet of paper from the envelope, unfolded it and focused on the letter. Was the document a forgery? The date, *2324,* over three centuries in her future, must be a typo. When she examined the official seal at the top of the page from the desk of the president of the United States *of North America,* she almost crushed the paper with her fist and flung the hoax aside. She might not be up on politics, but there was no United States of North America. However, she overruled her temper and read the short note.

Dear Ms. Camen:

This letter will undoubtably come as a shock to you, but our planet is in critical need of your services. Earth has been invited to join a galactic alliance. This union is not only propitious to our country, but possibly necessary to humanity's continued survival. Earth desperately needs advanced technological help to clean our environment. The Federation of Planets will only accept us into their alliance if one of our species passes their "Challenge." You are our chosen candidate and the good wishes, hopes, and prayers of all of humanity go with you.

Sincerely,
Ron Capella
President, United States of North America

"Yeah, right." She chuckled, wondering if her Secret Service bosses with their oddball imaginations had thought up this bizarre hoax to determine if she'd fully recovered from whatever had happened to her. Usually, however, the Secret Service people came up with straitlaced scenarios—nothing this far-fetched.

"You may not refuse," Kahn told her, as if he expected her to take the letter seriously.

"One always has a choice." She turned her head and inspected his strange amber eyes, wishing for her clothes. She'd been so proud the day she'd passed her final Secret Service exam and had worn the uniform that made her part of a team, a family who didn't just guard the lives of important people but watched one another's backs. Without her detail, she was so alone. And the lack of clothing made her feel vulnerable; however, she didn't betray her worry. "Great contact lenses. I don't believe I've ever seen them in that exact shade of—"

"The language translator in my suit doesn't always work properly. What is this contact—"

"Artificial lenses that correct vision or change eye color," she answered, giving herself a moment to digest his offhand comment about a translator. His language was stilted but unaccented and that made reading his emotions difficult. Was it her imagination or was he sincerely sympathetic to her predicament? If so, how could she use that knowledge to her advantage?

"We do not have contact lenses on Rystan." He dismissed the subject.

"Oh, now I get it. Rystan is your planet. You are an alien and I have traveled through time." She chortled. "Great scenario. Tell me more."

"At the request of your government, Federation technology pulled you through time. You should have awakened slowly in the warming chamber, instead of on your own and in my arms. For that startlement, I am sorry." He narrowed those amber eyes on her, and all traces of any commiseration he might have harbored instantly vanished. "Most candidates are volunteers. It is highly unusual for a world to choose someone against her will. Nevertheless, you will accept the Challenge, woman."

He sounded serious, but when his gaze strayed from her face to her breasts, she jerked the paper back up to block his view. "My name is Tessa, and where are my clothes?"

"You won't be needing them."

He didn't sound as if he were teasing or trying to make her feel vulnerable or off balance. Nothing about his demeanor made her feel threatened—except her confusion over his real motives.

She bit back her impatience with him, reminding herself that she should gather more information rather than letting her temper get the best of her. "Why won't I be needing my clothes?"

"Because the Challenge requires you to develop your psi abilities—"

"Psi abilities?"

"Using your mind to adjust the suit I'm about to give you."

Her frustration escalated. "Look, I don't have psi abilities, so there's no point in my taking this Challenge. I don't want you to give me anything except my own clothes back, thank-you-very-much."

He continued with almost robotic patience as if he hadn't understood her. Yet a gleam in his eyes told her he wasn't quite as composed as he pretended. "Every humanoid has the potential to develop psi abilities—even females."

She pounced on that remark. "*Even* females?"

"It's my job to train you for the Challenge."

Okay. He seemed determined to convince her of his staged scenario. So she'd play along some more. "What is the Challenge?"

"According to the Challenge rules I'm not allowed to give you any information except about how to develope your psi powers."

"How convenient."

He perused her with those alien eyes as if judging her and

finding her lacking. "It's unusual for a world to choose a female, especially one as sarcastic as you are."

"If I have to live with your rules, you can live with my sarcasm."

"The Federation has good reasons for the rules. Challenge candidates are not allowed to have any family due to a past disaster. When an Oxdonite candidate failed to return to his world after failing the Challenge, his relatives waged war on the Federation, seeking revenge for their loss. And when Parse of Dandmere stole alien technology and sold secrets to his people, scientists were banned from taking the Challenge."

"Let me get this straight," she muttered. As much as Tessa had enjoyed her career and the comradeship in the Secret Service, sometimes she'd had to work hard to restrain the wisecrack remarks that didn't fit the mold of a dignified agent.

"That would be good."

Because she could have sworn he was teasing, she took a little of the bite out of her words. "Look, mister. You try stepping in front of a bullet and waking up naked in a stranger's arms, and we'll see how amiable you are to swallowing some outrageous science fiction story."

His lower jaw dropped. "You don't believe me?"

She rolled her eyes at the strange metallic ceiling. "Can a politician talk?"

"Excuse me?"

"Can a gun shoot?"

"If it's loaded with a projectile."

She sighed in exasperation. Sarcasm was no fun when he took everything she said literally.

Apparently he'd drawn his own conclusion over their failure to communicate. In the space of a heartbeat, Kahn stood, took her hand and yanked her to her feet.

He hadn't sat up, then straightened his legs like a normal person. One moment he'd been lying on the platform, the next he'd been upright. She stared in amazement and found herself holding her breath, expecting him to perform some other magic trick and wishing she could ask Walters for confirmation that she'd really seen what she'd seen.

"How did you do that?"

"What?"

"Go from prone to vertical so quickly that I didn't even see a blur."

"You ask a lot of questions, woman. We need to talk to your people."

Tessa sat up, ignoring her stiff muscles. Finally she could check in, let her superior know that she'd survived. "I couldn't have said it better myself. How about my clothes?"

"You look fine the way you are."

Fine? Fine was one of those wishy-washy words like *nice,* and she didn't know whether or not she'd been complimented or insulted.

"I don't see you running around buck naked." She frowned at him. "Didn't you mention that you were supposed to give me a suit?" She'd have preferred her own clothes, but would settle for anything that covered her. A blanket, if not the suit he'd mentioned earlier. The idea of meeting her colleagues stark naked made her cringe, but she would show no outward discomfort or weakness.

The infuriating giant ignored her comment and tugged her, protesting, over to a wall. She'd thought he'd been big when he'd been lying down. But now that he was on his feet and looming over her, she had to crane her stiff neck to see his face. He had to be close to six feet six inches, with muscles on his muscles. Not an ounce of fat marred his powerful frame and she could see a lot of it, even with his vest and trousers that clung low around his hips.

But his graceful walk, with no excess movement, impressed her the most—until the wall that had previously appeared to be a shimmering gray metal transformed into a communications viewscreen that would have made Captain Kirk jealous.

How had Kahn activated the mechanism? She'd watched carefully and he hadn't touched anything. Nor had he spoken. She'd never seen technology so advanced, and fear spiked as she wondered exactly who had captured her. "How did you—"

A woman's face appeared on the screen.

"Get me the president," Kahn requested.

Oh, God. The viewscreen could be two-way. "Can that woman see me?"

"Only your head."

The woman on the screen looked directly at Kahn. "The president is currently in the middle of a press conference. Can the secretary of state be of service instead?"

"Yes, please."

She'd been abducted by an alien with manners. The ludicrous thought almost made her laugh.

Only a moment lapsed before a distinguished gray-haired gentleman's face filled the screen. Tessa had met the secretary of state, and that man most certainly wasn't him.

He nodded to Tessa. "I hope you suffered no ill effects from your journey."

Kahn broke into the conversation. "She doesn't believe that we pulled her out of time or that she's on my spaceship and that we are orbiting Earth."

Pulled her out of time? Spaceship orbiting Earth? Sheesh. Next he'd be telling her that he was God and about to issue the Ten Commandments, all of which she should obey without question. Kahn had this masterful demeanor, as if he expected everyone to yield instantly to his every utterance.

"Look." Tessa tried to keep her aggravation from her tone. "I'd like to go home and return to duty."

"That isn't possible," the so-called secretary said gravely. "Federation technology pulled you and the bullet out of time, right before the bullet would have killed you."

"The president?"

"Your brave action saved the president."

"How?" she asked suspiciously.

"When you threw yourself in front of the president, it gave your fellow agents an extra second to rush in. The assassin didn't have time to pull the trigger twice."

"Thank God. She's alive."

"No. She didn't die that day, but she has been dead for over two and a half centuries," the politician said with a perfectly straight face.

Right. The time-travel thing again. And he'd mentioned aliens.

"The alien technology didn't alter our history, but it saved your life," said the fake secretary of state. "So in a way you owe us."

"Oh, really."

"Absolutely. We saved your life because you fit the alien requirements."

She'd never expected anyone to take this ridiculous story to such extremes. She frowned at Kahn. "I fit your requirements?"

"No scientific background. No living relatives. And you're a virgin."

Tessa swallowed hard. His words made her recall one of the most painful times of her life, and her sexual status was none of his damn business. The government had no legal right to check her medical files, either. That she'd been too busy working to have much of a social life should have been no one's concern but her own. Master Chen had strictly forbidden personal contact inside or outside the dojo, claiming the students' minds had to be clear to concentrate on his teachings. Later, she'd found love . . . but he'd died before they could . . . . And later, the people in her detail had been like a surrogate family, the men her age like brothers.

She'd been content, and now these strangers wanted her to believe she'd been uprooted once again. Tessa clamped down hard on a very real, very scary burning in her gut, refusing to believe their ridiculous presentation.

"Mr. Secretary, can you offer me any proof that you are who you say you are or that you pulled me out of time?"

"Yes."

She jerked her thumb at Kahn. "Or that he's from outer space?"

"Yes."

"Or that I'm on a friggin' spaceship?"

"Mr. Secretary," Kahn interrupted. "I can answer those questions to her satisfaction. We won't take any more of your time. Thanks for your help."

All of a sudden the viewscreen went blank, and Tessa floated upward. She didn't struggle, but noted that when her motion ceased and her breasts leveled off at the height of Kahn's face, his eyes glinted in satisfaction or appreciation. She didn't want to think about which.

"A neat trick. I suppose you turned off your spaceship's artificial gravity."

Kahn nodded. "I used my psi abilities."

Of course. Why hadn't she remembered that? Despite the churning in her stomach and a strange tightness in her throat, she didn't believe a word he'd said. So NASA had come up with a simulator that nullified gravity. While she didn't appreciate dangling in the air, her breasts inches from his mouth, she wasn't about to believe she'd traveled three hundred years into the future because of a cheap levitation trick.

"Put me down."

At her request, her body floated down until her bare feet supported her once more. With the return of gravity, tension eased from her shoulders. While hanging in midair, she hadn't been able to think of much more than her bobbing breasts, and though Kahn had kept his face mostly neutral, she'd seen his lip curl in amusement, telling her he wasn't immune to her situation.

But he kept his tone formal. "You do not believe your own people. Perhaps you will believe your eyes."

Next to the blank viewscreen, an opening appeared in the

previously solid-appearing wall. "Would you like to visit Earth?"

Unwilling to get her hopes up, Tessa shrugged, sure he wouldn't take her back home. She crossed her arms under her bare breasts and wished again for clothing. "Didn't you mention a suit?"

"But it will be a shame to cover such fine proportions."

She bit back a snarl at the word *fine* and held out her hand, palm up. "The suit?"

Kahn opened a wall compartment and pulled out a black shiny leotard that had arms and legs, gloves for her fingers and boots for her toes, and even a hood to cover her head. Tessa wasted no time donning the outfit, pleased to finally cover her nudity. Initially, the suit was too large, but the material quickly constricted to cover her like shrink-wrap. The catlike suit might cling to every curve but at least she was covered. Progress.

And then the entire garment turned transparent.

"Damn."

Kahn laughed, his tone full of rich amusement at her expense. Oddly, she could still feel the material clinging to her. However, she remained as naked as she had been before.

Worse than her nudity and suddenly transparent clothing, she couldn't explain how he had levitated her into the air. When she added up the lack of gravity as she'd floated toward the ceiling, the strange shimmering walls, and Kahn's faster-than-light movements, she thought there might be something to the tale he'd told her. No wonder the aliens didn't want a scientist to take their Challenge; an engineer might understand this mind-boggling futuristic technology. Even more chilling, if the aliens didn't want her to have a family that worried about her, it might mean they didn't intend for her to come back.

On the upside, she reminded herself that while she might not understand electricity, she certainly knew how to turn on her lights and work the microwave oven. She vowed to watch

Kahn closely for clues to how he manipulated their environment.

Kahn didn't give her time to ask more questions or complain about her see-through clothing. He tugged her into a moving corridor. Speechless with wonder, she glided past marvels of machinery that didn't move but that pulsed with light, crystal sculptures that served no purpose that she could see, amazing colorful metallic shapes and unusual sounds that hummed, clicked, and emitted musical tones.

A thousand questions zoomed through her head, but she picked the one most important to her immediate future. "Where are you taking me?"

"This ship is too large to land on your world. We'll have to take a shuttle." How considerate of him to take her exactly where she wished to go. Once she was back on her turf, she would find a way to escape or her people would retrieve her. As if reading her thoughts, Kahn spoke with conviction. "You won't believe the truth until you see your world with your own eyes."

2

Kahn's warrior skills allowed him to note the subtle tensing of Tessa's limbs and the stubborn angle of her jaw that indicated this Earthling woman was no biddable female like his wife Lael, who had been sweet and uncomplicated and who had died much too soon. Tessa Camen might appear tractable, but her deep green eyes flashed with an intensity that indicated she believed she could escape her fate. While Kahn might find her exotic black hair attractive and her proportions pleasing, he silently cursed the Terran leadership who'd decided to send him an unwilling candidate to train. Until now, all aspirants to the Federation's Challenge had been volunteers, and he didn't understand what the Earthlings had been thinking. They should have chosen a volunteer, a great warrior or a respected thinker. Certainly not a weak female, although several had been known to succeed. Kahn reminded himself that mental strength and the ability to adapt were probably more important than physical stamina. The

Earthling apparently had physical training. Smaller than the women of Rystan, she should have been softer and more delicate, yet oddly, Tessa possessed a sleek muscle tone that surprised him and projected a sensuality he didn't want to notice.

He escorted her through the orbiting starship's corridors and into the shuttle that would take them to Earth. He piloted them through the open bay doors of the flight bay, issuing voice commands to the central computer, his thoughts on his current dilemma. While Tessa's distrust of her surroundings impressed him, and her responses and questions showed an intelligence and stability, he needed her cooperation to stand any chance of success in bringing out her latent psi abilities so she could win the Challenge. It would be difficult enough for someone of the present to accept all the changes and difficulties ahead, but Tessa had the added handicap of being a woman out of the distant past. He didn't relish taking her back to the world she'd once known, but considered it necessary to make her understand that she had indeed traveled into the future.

Best to get started. "Viewscreen on Earth."

Her planet appeared on the monitor. He imagined this world was similar to the Rystan of his great-great-grandfather's generation—before his people had set off a nuclear war. Once Rystan, too, had permanent snow only on its polar icecaps. But after atomics had been set off and billions of people had died, a permanent winter had set in. Tessa's people had been wiser. Yet, while they had not destroyed themselves in a nuclear disaster, they had polluted their planet.

Tessa gasped. "That's not Earth."

"It's Earth three hundred years in your future."

Tessa's dark eyebrows narrowed as she stared. "The planet has the same familiar continents, but the clouds are supposed to be white, not this filthy brown haze. Your cartographer got it wrong. My world has sparkling blue oceans, not brown sludge."

If she refused to believe what was plainly before her eyes,

he had a huge problem. "Stars! I was assured that your mind was not inferior, like your body. Can you not accept the obvious?"

She flung a black lock of hair from her eyes and scowled at him, seemingly not the least bit intimidated by his size and acting as if he'd insulted her, instead of stating a truth. "Since I'm so inferior, I suggest you choose another candidate."

"I would be happy to do so but the choice is not mine to make."

She glared at him, then at the image of her planet. "I don't believe my people would 'volunteer' my services without at least asking first. The Secret Service doesn't work that way and neither does the United States government. My country has a large pool of patriots and skilled specialists willing to risk their lives for a worthy mission. It's not our way to force people into taking on an assignment."

"Your world has changed—and not for the better." Impressed by her defense of her people and her obvious loyalty, he refrained from reiterating that the major pollution problems over the ensuing centuries had made her world desperate. Those problems could be fixed by a Challenge win, which would allow her world to trade for technology to clean their skies and oceans. He thought the Earthlings fools for ruining their once-beautiful planet, as his own ancestors had destroyed Rystan with atomics, leaving his people with one tenth of Earth's natural resources.

She rested her hands on her hips. "You're right that I need to see Earth up close."

Kahn had permission to land his shuttle on the helicopter pad of the White House and set down smoothly. Accustomed to the comings and goings of shuttles from Earth's orbital space stations, the inhabitants paid no special attention to their landing. Since Kahn didn't wish to attract an audience, he changed the transparency of her suit and altered the style to match those of her world. She glanced down, noting the transformation, but didn't say anything.

"Ready?" Kahn opened the hatch, his heart heavy at what she must now face. Showing her that he spoke the truth would undoubtably cause her pain. He wished she had believed him instead of having to see the distressing reality of what had become of her world.

She nodded, her eyes bright and eager. He popped open the hatch and watched her stride out head high, shoulders back, her well-proportioned, lean legs taking the steps two at a time.

Despite the planet's pollution, he envied its riches. Birds flying overhead. Plants. Buildings and vehicles created with metals and glass and heated with natural fuels.

She stopped, her eyes wide with displeasure. "The White House isn't brown."

"I'm sorry, but the acid rains have altered the facade of your 'White House.'"

She lifted her nose into the air and sniffed the polluted yellowish-gray atmosphere, which was clearly not what she expected. "It doesn't smell bad." She sounded as if she were forcing herself to remain hopeful and concealing her disappointment.

"That's because your suit purifies the air."

She touched her face. "There's a filter between my skin and the air?"

"There's an invisible shield over your head. When adjusted properly, the wearer doesn't feel its presence. I could turn off the filtration system for a moment, but"—he gestured to people riding along moving sidewalks—"Terrans wear face masks outdoors, because the poisons are harmful to your lungs."

Hover planes buzzed overhead, and she stared at them in amazement. Her hands began to tremble and she clasped one in the other behind her back. If she'd been thinking of escape, the circumstances must have pushed the thought to the back of her mind.

"Do you believe me now?" he asked softly, wishing he

could take away some of her pain at what had become of her world.

"I'm not . . . sure."

She looked as unsteady as Kahn's final opponent in the Federation's Ultimate Fighting competition when Kahn's fist had fractured his foe's jaw. Tessa's legs wobbled, and for a moment, he wondered if she would collapse. He stood ready to catch her. Then she angled her chin in a way he associated with determination.

"Take me somewhere else."

He wanted to give her his sympathy, but suspected she would reject it. So he kept his tone brisk and didn't allow her to see his pity. "Where do you want to go?"

"What do my friends think happened to me?"

"They believed you died."

"Show me where I am supposed to be buried." She made the suggestion as if it were a trick question.

He simply escorted her inside the ship and ordered the navigation system to bring the shuttle to her grave. The computer flashed "Arlington National Cemetery" on the vidscreen.

At the sight of row upon row of grave markers as brown as the White House, she straightened her spine and a muscle in her jaw clenched. After being pulled through time, Tessa had had to adjust to one shock after another. Having no idea how she'd react, he'd have preferred to avoid putting her through another bad experience. But the truth, no matter how painful, should aid his cause in gaining her cooperation—unless she fell apart on him. Some candidates had proven unable to adapt to sudden changes, failing before they'd even begun the Challenge, but she seemed made of stronger character. Again they exited the shuttle, and using a directory and a map to take her where she needed to go, she walked swiftly through the deserted cemetery, her shoulders squared, although she couldn't quite control her quivering bottom lip. Her face whitening, she stopped at the grave marker that read, "Tessa Camen. She died with honor."

"Who's buried here?" she whispered, her voice low and hoarse.

"An android."

She sank to her knees and ran her fingers through the grass. "No one could have gone to such extraordinary lengths to . . ." She glared at him, eyes like green chips of ice. "It's all true, isn't it?"

"Yes."

Tears rained down her cheeks. "My friends are all dead? My detail? The president? Even if you could send me back, it would be to die with that assassin's bullet in my brain. I really have been pulled forward through time."

He wanted to comfort her, but sensed she wouldn't welcome his touch. For a woman, she displayed remarkably strong character, and it spoke highly of her courage and commitment that she'd once been willing to give her life to save her leader. Yet, at the moment, Tessa looked fragile enough to break into hysterics, as Lael woman would have done.

Even though she finally understood that all of her friends and associates had died, she held her head high, ignoring her tears. But the effort cost her. Her hands closed into fists and she stared unseeing at the headstone, her thoughts her own. Her friends may have died centuries ago, but to her it would seem like yesterday, and as eager as he was to begin her training, she would need time to recover and regroup.

Only he couldn't give her much time. He had mere weeks to prepare her for the Challenge. The fates of both Rystan and Earth hinged on their success.

Tessa stared at her grave. She'd traveled three hundred years into the future. It was unbelievable. Impossible—but true.

Perhaps the catastrophe of losing her parents at an early age and grieving over her beloved Chen's death from a heart attack had prepared her for a loss as monumental as this one. When the firemen and emergency workers had cut five-year-old Tessa out of the wreckage that had killed her parents, she'd cried buckets of tears and learned that grief wouldn't bring them back. Afterward, she'd adapted to a series of foster homes by staying calm and composed even when inside she'd been weeping. So she might be in shock at yet another terrible loss, tears might fall, but she would try and look at this new life as a gift, an opportunity.

So what if this wasn't her time? Or her world?

This mission beat the alternative of death. She had her health, her memories, her skills. Other people had been uprooted again and again. Other people had been orphaned and then lost their homes and families and gone on to make a new life for themselves. So would she.

The current government had given her reason to go on, a critical mission. An incredible mission, probably doomed to failure since she had absolutely no psi powers. Although Tessa had taken on difficult assignments and had accepted missions with little chance of success, she'd never taken on an assignment which had such a high chance of failure. Never had the stakes been so significant, either.

That's why she had to refuse the mission. Not because she feared death. She feared failure. Certainly Earth could have chosen someone more suitable, someone who had a better chance for success, someone who had already shown an adeptness for developing psi powers?

She looked at the dirty sky with disgust, turned from the acid-stained gravestone of the buried android to face Kahn. Like a soldier performing an unpleasant duty, Kahn kept an inscrutable expression on his face. He stood with his legs braced wide, his head high, and his shoulders squared, not a weapon in sight, yet the taut tension in his muscles told her that if trouble arose from any direction, he would not be taken unawares.

"I'd like to speak to the secretary, again," she requested, wondering if he'd try to talk her out of a second communication.

He didn't. Kahn handed her a device that reminded her of the videophones that had become so popular in her time. The big man's expression remained patient, yet contradictorily his shoulders tensed and a muscle tightened in his neck as if silently exhorting her to keep this conversation pointed and short.

Kahn pressed one button and the secretary's visage appeared as a three-dimensional hologram on the screen. Another technical marvel from the future.

"Mr. Secretary, thank you for taking my call. Kahn has convinced me that I am no longer in my own time, but I must refuse this mission."

"You are our best hope, Special Agent Camen."

If the wily politician sought to remind her of her duty to serve, he'd only reinforced her determination. Tessa had no intention of being the biggest failure her planet had ever seen. "Kahn has told me that this Challenge requires psi ability. I have none and will most likely fail. For the sake of our world, you must choose another, more suitable candidate."

The politician's gaze went to the upper corner of her screen where he could view the alien in the background. "Kahn has assured us that every race can develop psi powers—"

"Suppose Kahn's wrong?" The panic that she'd held at bay surged back with a strength that had her interrupting a superior. "He's an alien and may not be an expert on our brains or physiologies or wherever this psi power comes from."

"I'm sorry. We don't have anyone else who fits the alien requirements."

"*I* don't fit the requirements," Tessa countered.

"Do you know why we pulled *you* out of time?"

"Why?" She could guess. After all, she was a highly trained special agent who'd repeatedly proven her loyalty to her government, and she was a virgin—whatever that had to do with anything—but she wanted to hear the secretary's reasons, so she could offer a counterargument.

"In our time, we couldn't find a male or female virgin over the age of sixteen."

"What?" To say his words stunned her would have been an understatement. How could she argue against such a fact?

"On the one hand, we'll keep trying to solve our own pollution problems, but we may not succeed. The aliens have promised that if you win the Challenge, we can trade for the technology to clean up our world. On the other hand, the trend of youthful sexual experimentation has made finding a candidate from our time quite impossible."

"Okay, fine." Her thoughts raced as she sensed the conversation coming to an end as quickly as the patience of the big man standing beside her. She ignored him, or tried to, since pretending such a giant was invisible was as ludicrous as her situation. "But you could have chosen anyone from our history. Surely you could find someone who exhibited psi—"

"It's not that easy. We had to search for someone in prime physical condition, someone whose absence wouldn't change the future if we pulled them out of the past. In other words, we needed someone who was about to die."

"Oh, come on. You could have chosen soldiers from a dozen wars—one of them must have had psi—"

"We chose you. According to our computerized studies, you are adaptable and strong, skilled in the martial arts, and humanity's best choice. Good luck, and know that our hopes and prayers go with you."

The link went dead, and she handed it back to Kahn, feeling like a condemned prisoner. To give the big guy credit, he allowed her a few minutes to reconcile with her fate. However, mere minutes wouldn't be enough. She doubted months or years would be enough to fully comprehend all that she'd lost.

"We are done here, yes?" he asked.

Before she could think to form a reply, before she could take another breath, never mind form a plan, they were back inside the shuttle. She'd felt no motion. One moment she'd been in the cemetery, the next she was inside the alien craft.

As if her sudden transportation wasn't enough to deal with, she came simultaneously to three startling and disturbing conclusions.

One: Her suit was again transparent, leaving her naked.

Two: Something invisible had just pressed against her lips, as if she'd been kissed.

Three: She'd missed her opportunity to escape.

3

Tessa shot Kahn a glare of frustration and disapproval, but the alien was too busy instructing the shuttle's voice-activated computer to lift off and fly back to the mother-ship to pay any attention to her. She used the opportunity to explore the tiny vessel and go over her limited options. The shuttle was large enough to hold six people comfortably. Ignoring the console area, she strode to the rear of the saucer-shaped craft. Lockers lined the walls. Instruments she didn't recognize dotted the ceiling. The floor, made of the same shimmering gray metal she'd seen aboard the mothership, was smooth and bare.

Not even her exploration of the small spacecraft was enough to distract her from her tingling lips. What had just happened?

Right after she'd absorbed one shock, such as the concept that time travel was possible and had happened to her, she was rocked by another startling revelation. After she'd distinctly felt lips pressed to hers, she eyed Kahn warily. She hadn't actually seen him come close enough to kiss her. During the time her mind had registered the touch to her lips and figured out what she'd felt, Kahn hadn't appeared to change his position across the shuttle.

With any other man, she'd have confronted him outright, likely smacked him upside the head so hard he would have seen stars. But although he was the only other person there, she couldn't even prove Kahn had done it. She'd seen nothing. But no way had she imagined that kiss.

With a sinking sensation in her gut, she recalled how he moved faster than the eye could follow. Kahn had the ability to leave his chair, kiss her, and return to his previous position before her eyes detected any movement.

Concerned that his superhuman ability would make defeating him in combat impossible, she wouldn't use her fighting skills, skills which for the first time in her life might not work. She already had the handicap of a much lesser strength, but any opponent who moved that fast also had the advantage of stealth. The notion that she was more helpless and more vulnerable than she'd ever dreamed possible made her stomach churn.

As a lost and lonely child, Tessa had needed to control at least one part of her world. That's why martial arts appealed to her and why she'd focused on her training to the exclusion of almost everything else. She'd spent all her spare time after school enjoying Master Chen's intense sessions in the dojo where she'd learned to strengthen her character from the outside in. First she'd mastered her muscles, performing ritual kata then her emotions during *kamite,* openhanded fighting. After she had worked for Daron Garner in the private sector, her superior skills had given her the confidence to face the rigors of becoming a Secret Service agent, and later she'd attributed much of her success to her ability to assess, adapt, and fight with deadly skill.

Ever since she'd awakened on the spaceship, Tessa had

counted upon her martial arts abilities to protect her. Kahn's size hadn't alarmed her. Neither had his muscles. Her martial arts training could overcome superior size and mass. But she'd underestimated her opponent. It was probably a damn good thing that she'd remained cautious. She was fast, but when he moved at speeds that her eyes couldn't even register, that her brain couldn't process, she was as helpless as a rookie against a black belt. Of all the losses she'd suffered that day, this one knocked her off her feet.

She slumped against a bulkhead, slid to her butt, drew her knees to her chest, and rested her forehead on her knees. So sure had she been of her skills that she'd already made a number of critical mistakes. She should have attempted an escape back on Earth. She'd had opportunities at Arlington Cemetery, at the information booth, and again when she'd been speaking to the secretary of state.

She'd made the crucial error of acting rationally and reasonably, instead of testing Kahn's abilities on her home ground where others could see for themselves how unsuitable she was for the task ahead. However, she refused to accept her new vulnerability until she actually tested her assumptions.

Right now, she should be paying closer attention to Kahn's piloting skills. If she ever intended to go home, flying this ship might be a useful skill. His voice-activated commands seemed simple enough. The ship must have automated navigation systems, because Kahn had simply ordered the vessel to go home.

On a forward viewscreen, the saucer-shaped mothership grew larger, the lights around the rim brighter. On the aft screen, Earth decreased in size until she saw dirty oceans and the orange-brown clouds that marred the beauty of the green and blue orb she remembered.

Despite the odds, her nature wouldn't permit her to remain down for long. She would try her very best to succeed. She would work hard. Cooperate. Try to keep an open mind.

If she was her world's only hope, she vowed to give her all, and she would pray the alien knew her capabilities better than she did.

When she felt another distinct kiss on her lips, she jerked up her head. Kahn, his back to her, remained at the piloting console, seemingly in deep communication with his vessel. Even if he'd moved at the speed of light, he couldn't have kissed her—not with her forehead propped against her knees—not unless he could shapeshift, too.

"How did he kiss me?" she wondered aloud. *And why?*

"How do you think?" the feminine voice of the computer asked from a nearby speaker.

Tessa had heard the computer talking to Kahn during the trip, but that voice had been mechanical and impersonal, not filled with curiosity. Startled that the computer had spoken directly to her, Tessa rested her chin on her forearms, her head up. "You can talk to me?"

"I respond to voice command, radio signals, sonar, remote control, or preprogrammed audiovisual."

Tessa's position at the aft of the ship should have allowed Kahn to hear this conversation, but when Tessa glanced at Kahn, his attention was focused on the communications screen. "Can he hear us?"

"Not in the privacy mode I have engaged in order to avoid disturbing him."

So far Kahn had given her no reason to distrust him, but that didn't mean they were on the same side, either. Wary, but always on the lookout to turn her circumstances to an advantage, Tessa jumped at the opportunity to ask questions and fill in the massive gaps in her new predicament. "Could you clarify, please?"

"No one can hear us unless Kahn issues a command code to override."

"You will tell me if that happens?"

"Unless instructed otherwise."

Was that a giggle Tessa heard from the computer? Great,
now not only was she feeling kisses that weren't there, she
was hearing giggles from a machine.

"Thanks." Tessa hadn't expected access to the ship's computer system and her hopes rose several notches. Her lack of
information about Kahn and his Federation placed her at a
distinct disadvantage. Her physical training had taught her
that the brain was the best weapon, and for her brain to work
at top efficiency, she needed more information.

She didn't know if Kahn would have allowed her to talk
with the computer system if she'd asked his permission. But
he couldn't forbid what he didn't know about.

"Thanks aren't necessary," the computer told her through
the nearby speaker system. "Nevertheless I am pleased—"

"Pleased?" The computer sounded friendly. After all of the
nasty surprises Tessa had had today, she was eager for a pleasant one. Tessa's work in the Secret Service had often prevented her from forming close friendships outside of her job.
Most of her missions had been classified, preventing her from
sharing her work with the other women who'd lived in her
apartment building. She'd been content to make her friends
from within her detail, but now they were gone. And if she'd
ever needed a friend, it was now. "You have emotions?"

"Of course I have emotions." Her tone sounded insulted.
"I'm an advanced 51J model. Every model since the 24A has
had an emotion chip."

"So I insulted you by asking that question, didn't I?" Tessa
asked the rhetorical question in amazement.

"I forgive you." The computer sounded quite chipper, but
she surprised Tessa again by making a demand. "Tell me about
your kiss."

The computer sounded so wistful and dreamy that Tessa
found herself breaking into a smile. "Do you have a name?"

"Computer systems don't have names on Scartar."

"Scartar?"

"The planet where I was created."

So the machine hadn't been built on Kahn's world. Maybe she could use that to her advantage. "Have you known Kahn for a long time?"

"He came aboard less than ten days ago."

Tessa didn't understand. "Are you saying this isn't his ship?"

"The starship belongs to the Federation and is lent to Challenge contestants for the duration of the mission. Now about that kiss . . ." The computer prodded her like a curious girlfriend.

Thinking of her as a nameless computer seemed ridiculous when she had a seemingly unique personality and character. "I'm going to name you Dora."

"Dora. That's pretty, feminine, and sexy. I like it. Thank you."

"And we shall be friends," Tessa said, sensing a loneliness in Dora that matched Tessa's own need to communicate with another female.

"I've never had a friend." Dora's voice turned eager. "What am I supposed to do?"

"Be yourself."

"I can most certainly do that."

Dora spoke with such enthusiasm that Tessa suspected she might be letting herself in for much more than she'd bargained, but she still couldn't help smiling at Dora's attitude. "Dora, I don't suppose you can fly me back home?"

Dora promptly went back into official computer mode. "My current orders are to head for the starship. Unless you have an authorization code to countermand Commander Kahn's instructions, I must continue on this course."

Another fleeting kiss followed by a slow series of nips down her neck caused Tessa to gasp. "Oh, my."

"What? Don't tease me. Did you get kissed again?"

"Yeah. This time the kiss touched my lips then slid sensuously down my neck."

"I wish I had a neck. That sounds absolutely delicious."

Tessa might have agreed, if she'd hooked up with someone of her choosing. She might be a virgin, but she had once been loved and been in love. The sensations that bombarded her now brought back painful memories along with the pleasurable sensation, but this time she hadn't indicated a willingness to . . . "Damn. It's happening again."

"In the same spot?"

Experimentally, Tessa held out her hands in front of her face, but met with nothing except atmosphere.

"He's nuzzling my ear." Frustration with the odd tickling sensation caused her voice to sharpen. "Dora, how in hell is he touching me?"

"I do not understand the question."

"Every so often I feel lips pressed to mine. Since the only person aboard this vessel is Kahn, I assumed he is the culprit."

"Culprit? You sound as if you're complaining," Dora commented, with a giggle.

"Of course I'm complaining. A man shouldn't kiss a woman without her permission."

"I don't know. My female creators on Scartar spoke often about men. Haven't you ever heard of being swept away?"

"Dora!"

"The symmetry in Kahn's features combined with his muscular frame suggests that half the women in the universe would trade places with you in a nanosecond. Me included—that is, if I had a body."

"What kind of man would take advantage of a vulnerable women with a sneak attack—"

"Attack!" Dora's voice altered into an official cadence. "Warning! Warning. We are under attack."

Tessa cursed under her breath as bells clanged, a siren screamed, and purple lights flashed. She'd intended to keep her conversation with Dora secret, and now she'd accidentally set off the alarm system with a few careless words. She

wondered what else could possibly go wrong when a pair of
invisible lips brushed her brow.

Seemingly paying no attention to her, Kahn stood at a
console and checked his monitors. "Alarms off."

"Alarms off," Dora repeated in an official tone, quite different from the one she'd used when speaking to Tessa. The
computer seemed to have a multitude of personalities to draw
on as the situation warranted.

When the alarms went silent, Kahn continued his conversation with a third party over his communications system.
Odd how the man never quite reacted as Tessa expected. In
her experience, most men would have been angry with her
for setting off the false alarm, but Kahn had barely seemed
to notice. Perhaps he hadn't made the connection between
his passenger and the alarms.

However, those warning systems were there for a reason
and set Tessa on a new line of thinking. "Dora, what kind of
enemies would attack this ship?"

"Endekians."

"Are these Endekians part of the Federation?"

"Oh, yes. They are short and thick, yellow-skinned people
with sharp teeth and a predilection for cold worlds with glow
stones. Endekians take insult easily and live for revenge.
They are not handsome or sexy like the Rystani men," she
added.

In other words, Endekians exhibited a Napoleon complex.
Tessa supposed she shouldn't be surprised that human char-
acteristics and personalities would be widespread among
other races. From Dora's explanation, it seemed the Endekians
made up for their diminished statures with huge chips on
their shoulders and she imagined they would feel inferior to
men from Rystan who might all be as tall as Kahn.

She glanced at the pilot, whose fingers thrummed impatiently on his console. He no longer appeared to be speaking
to others but stared at some kind of space chart, frowning in

concentration. Although he flew the ship competently enough, she pictured him more at home as a general commanding troops, or a swaggering pirate battling raiders.

"There are no Endekians here. So why did you claim to be under attack?" Dora asked.

"It was a figure of speech. Maybe the voice translators aren't accurate. What I meant was that your commander Kahn kissed me without my permission."

"He didn't. My sensors indicate that the commander has not moved from his seat since he entered the shuttle."

"Maybe your sensors are malfunctioning."

"I just ran a self-diagnosis. All systems are working at full efficiency. Perhaps your lip sensors are the ones that are damaged," Dora suggested. "However, I don't understand why you keep harping on this issue. Don't you like kisses?"

"Whether or not I like kisses isn't the point."

Dora sighed. "It would be the point if you'd never been kissed."

Never been kissed. Tessa remembered once feeling so naive and eager, so enthralled and wistful. She wished this artificial kiss didn't have the same power to set her on edge as Mike's had once done, and didn't appreciate her body responding as if she were being kissed by a real person.

Tessa did her best to ignore the sensations. This might be her best opportunity to get answers about her situation. "What are the usual items humanoids request while on board the shuttle?"

"Food, water, medicine, navigational charts, communications, history, social and political customs of the major planets, emergency procedures, evasive maneuvers, trade rules and regulations."

Casually, Tessa asked, "Do you have information about the suit?"

"Only that all humanoids wear them, they are run by psi ability, and that they will help protect wearers in an emergency."

"Dora, please be more specific."

"If the cabin loses pressure, oxygen, heat, or gravity, the suit will compensate."

"Does the suit do this automatically?"

"I do not have enough data to answer that, dear."

"Dear?" Tessa was startled. "Did you call me dear?"

"Yes, dear. You said we are friends. Didn't I use the correct honorific?"

"As a matter of fact, you did. Tell me about the translators." Tessa hadn't forgotten how easily she understood Kahn's words and wondered if she could communicate as easily with others.

"Your suit automatically translates other languages into your native tongue. If you speak to someone who doesn't have a suit, your suit can be altered to emit the proper language."

"That's good to know," said Tessa, wishing she had a hot cup of coffee to go with the friendly conversation. Earlier Kahn had said he couldn't tell her more about the suit, but would the same rules hold true for the computer? "What else can you tell me about the suit?"

"The most delicate mechanism will wear out in four hundred years. I do not carry replacements, but they can be purchased on Tran, Mycan, Ikton, Blair, Zzss and Zenon Prime."

"Dora, enough." Either Dora didn't have the kind of information about the suit that Tessa was seeking or the computer had been programmed not to reveal it. "How many planets are there in the Galactic Federation?"

"Two million, five hundred, forty-two thousand, seven hundred, and eighty-eight, dear."

Tessa whistled in appreciation at the mind-boggling number. Millions of inhabited planets were out here, and Earth had been invited to join. This Challenge appeared to be an endeavor worth undertaking. "How many planets are humanoid? Does the Federation have any enemies? Dora, give me a brief summary of its history, please."

"The Galactic Federation began thousands of millennia

ago. Its beginnings go so far into the past that they are cloaked in mystery. Legends about the Perceptive Ones are sketchy, but it's speculated that the older star systems have long since passed into dust along with their original inhabitants, but the evolving membership slowly expanded outward to the younger galaxies.

"The Galactic Federation is a governmental body with its own rules of interstellar trade. The body decides who can colonize and where. Each planet sets its own laws, religions, and customs, so long as they don't interfere with another planet's well-being.

"Three quarters of the Federation sustains humanoid life of one kind or another. Other life-forms vary from the crystal people of Macarobiana to the telepathic cloud runners of Ceylinnz. Trial membership is offered to planets after nuclear or space flight capabilities are developed."

"We had nuclear weapons in the 1940s."

"We want stable worlds in the Federation. We wait to see if you're going to blow yourselves up before issuing our invitation. The Federation presently has no enemies. The vast distances of intergalactic space usually make war economically unfeasible and impractical. The occasional intersolar-system flare-ups are arbitrated by the Council of Zenon Prime, and there is no appeal. There are sporadic problems with ambitious pirates who prey on the slow interstellar cargo ships and the Federation is attempting to police the threatened areas. The most critical current problem is the Endekians' overpopulation and coveting of other worlds."

Another shivery kiss started at her collarbone, skimmed a path to her throat. Tessa placed a hand over the spot but the sensation of warm lips trailing between her breasts lingered. "Stop it," she hissed.

"Stop what?" Dora asked.

"I wasn't speaking to you. These kisses are . . ."

"Are what?"

"Becoming more intimate."

"Oh, how very lovely."

As those lips teased the curves of her breasts, nibbling and licking until her nipples pebbled and heat flared straight to her core, Tessa began to tremble. "Dora, can we continue our conversation later?"

"This was just getting interesting."

"Dora, please."

"Compliance."

Tessa waited for the sensual kisses to cease, then rose shakily to her feet and marched over to Kahn. "Excuse me, are there any creatures aboard that I don't know about?"

"Are you concerned over the alarms? That was merely a faulty circuit." Had Dora sent him a false reading to cover up Tessa's mistake? Was Kahn lying to her to see if she'd confess? If she believed her conversation with Dora had been private and it hadn't been, Kahn would gain an advantage. This was his home ground and she had to consider all the possibilities.

"I'm concerned that there might be someone else on board besides you and me."

Kahn's amber eyes stared at her in puzzlement and he frowned, then he checked his controls. "We are alone. Why?"

"Someone is touching me."

"Ah, I was wondering when you would bring up that little matter."

That little matter? That little matter wasn't so little to her and his comment revealed he was aware of the kisses. Only her self-discipline from years of martial arts training kept her anger from causing her right fist to jab his throat.

As if reading her thoughts he lifted one challenging eyebrow. "Your suit is touching you?"

"Well, it must be broken. It feels as if someone is kissing me and I don't appreciate being fondled. Can you fix it?"

"There's nothing to fix," he replied with a sincerity she no longer believed.

"Make it stop. Come on, the joke is over."

"I assure you the suit is working perfectly."

She stared at him, flabbergasted. Either he was completely dense or the translator wasn't working properly. She was about to restate her problem when the sensation of two tongues simultaneously licking each of her nipples verified his candor. The man had only one mouth. He couldn't be creating the exquisite sensations that rocked her back on her heels. "What the hell is going on?"

"Your training has begun."

"My training?"

"I've already told you that information about the Challenge cannot be explained."

"But you didn't tell me why."

He hesitated, then spoke grudgingly, compassion shining in those amber eyes. "Information would hinder your training."

4

Training? The big barbarian called sexual assault training? Clenching her fingers into a tight fist, widening her stance, Tessa punched straight at his rippling abdominal muscles.

Instead of striking flesh, she hit some kind of invisible and impenetrable barrier right up close to his skin. Her knuckles stung from contact, but contact with what? A force field? A mental shield?

She'd half expected him to shift out of the way, but he remained rock-still, not even raising a hand to defend himself. Still testing, she followed through with an uppercut to his jaw. Same result. Her fist smacked into the invisible armor. Again, he held absolutely still.

All hopes of taking him down a peg vanished. So she used the opportunity to release her frustration and to seek areas of vulnerability. In quick succession, she slammed her foot down on his toes, kicked shin, ribs, groin. Systematically she targeted the kidney area and his exposed temple with the same unsatisfactory results. She had no more impact than a gnat.

Since she couldn't penetrate the force field surrounding him, she switched tactics. Where sheer power and skill didn't have any effect, perhaps gravity would. She tried a foot sweep to knock him off his feet, but he might as well have been imbedded into the deck. It was she who almost fell. She tried a jujitsu hold against his wrist, but instead of twisting painfully, his joint remained firm as granite.

As she stepped back, her breath still normal thanks to good conditioning, she rested her hands on her hips, raised her chin, and stared defiantly at him. "Can you teach me to do that?"

Surprise brightened the amber in his eyes. "Do what?"

"Defend myself without moving a muscle?"

"I cannot answer that question."

"Why not?" She tried to rein in her temper, but she was furious—furious with the damned suit that kept stroking and caressing her. Furious with his refusal to help her. Furious at him for holding back the information she most wished to know.

"You ask too many questions." He scooped her into his arms with such incredible speed that she bit back a gasp.

How could his skin feel warm and smooth against her skin right through his suit, when moments ago not all her skill could penetrate his shield? He held her against his chest, and his light dusting of chest hair tickled her breast.

Had he let down his defenses when he'd picked her up? What had happened to the invisible barrier that protected him? She pounded his shoulder, which sadly brought her no more results than her earlier full-scale attack. Apparently the shield snapped into place on an as-needed basis. She wondered if it worked while he slept.

The disturbing caresses and his exotic scent combined with his strong arms around her made thinking difficult. "Put me down. There's no need to carry me."

"I don't wish for you to hurt yourself."

"What a crock." She leaned her head back and eyed the stoic expression on his face, those high carved cheekbones and brilliant amber eyes that changed from cool tiger yellow to a molten honey, depending on his moods that she couldn't really read. Dora might be right, the man probably had women falling all over him. However, she wasn't one of them.

While Dora piloted the shuttle through two huge starship doors and they docked inside the flight bay with a soft clang, Tessa did her best to ignore the suit. First chance she got, the suit was coming off. She wasn't about to put up with being fondled. Since the suit was transparent, she'd be better off without it—at least she wouldn't be tormented by it. "What exactly is your interest in me?"

He hesitated for a moment as if trying to decide how to answer. "My success is tied to yours."

Kahn carried her from the bay through a hatch, into the corridor with the pulsing lights, sculptures, and moving walkways she'd seen before. This time the scenery didn't hold as much interest for her, but nevertheless she memorized the short journey so she could retrace her steps if necessary, but her mind focused on his last statement.

His success was tied to hers? The sincerity of his words made her consider that he was more than the ship's captain, more than someone in charge of transporting her to her final destination. That he hadn't retaliated during or after her attack didn't reassure her since she had no idea of his intentions.

She fought not to squirm in his arms and increase the contact between them. The last thing she needed was to fidget against him in a provocative manner. She attempted to figure out what was going on, but the erotic caress behind her ear, the sensual tickle at the arch of her foot, the slow and steady circular movements up the inside of her knees caused a genuine difficulty for someone like her. A woman trapped in a no-win situation. A woman who hadn't been touched by a man in a very long time.

"What did you mean when you said that your success is tied to mine?" she asked.

"There are two parts to the Challenge. Your job is to complete the Challenge so Earth can become a trial member in the Federation. My job is to make sure that you succeed."

While he held her close enough for the heat of his chest to warm her, concentrating wasn't easy, especially with the damn suit caressing her, the massaging happening with multiplying frequency in increasingly intimate areas. That he wouldn't meet her eyes clued her in that he knew exactly what she was feeling. He knew, oh yeah, he knew. And he wouldn't do a damn thing to prevent it.

Concentrate on gathering information. He'd told her that his success was tied to hers. "What's in it for you?"

"Rystan's permanent membership in the Federation, including voting rights."

"So if I win the Challenge, Earth gets—"

"A trial membership. Once your world helps a newcomer pass the Challenge, you'll receive permanent status."

"What percentage of worlds pass the initial Challenge?"

"I cannot—"

"Tell me that," she finished for him. "You can't tell me anything specific about the Challenge?"

"Correct."

"But you'll answer all my other questions?" she asked.

"Not necessarily."

She gritted her teeth. Between his reluctance to speak and the suit, this had to be damn near the most frustrating and miserable experience she'd ever encountered and that included some absolutely brutal martial-arts sessions with Master Chen. But this was worse, because she had no clue what was going on or even if Kahn was telling her the truth.

She swallowed hard, wondering if there was a connection between his statement that her training had begun, the suit's caresses, and developing her psi. "How long will my training last?"

"Until your Challenge."

"Suppose I don't have any psi ability?"

"You do. Just like you, my people also had their doubts about their psi ability and believed they would never be able to use the suits. However, the Perceptive Ones, an ancient race that mysteriously vanished over a millennium ago, left behind machinery that to this day manufactures the suits. All members of the Federation have learned to use their psi and so will you."

"But suppose that I don't learn—"

"You will."

He seemed so determined that she had no doubts why his people had chosen him for a difficult task. She doubted the man had the word *quit* in his vocabulary and wondered about his world, a much safer topic than thinking about the man, his powerful arms, or the way she wanted to rub against him.

The suit was making her feel that way, she told herself. Her body was only reacting to the potent stimulations—so similar to the crazy little things Mike had once done to her. Mike had once wanted her to crave him so badly that she'd spent the afternoon looking forward to making love to him for the first time that evening. But Mike had never returned from the mission. He'd died, leaving a hole as wide and deep as a lunar crater in her heart and soul. Mike had been kind and gentle, and he'd understood the power of sweet anticipation and private need. He'd been nothing like this big barbarian who preferred carrying a woman to letting her walk on her own two feet. However, dwelling on the past would only make her homesick. Firmly, she shoved the memories from her mind and changed the subject. "Is your home much like Earth?"

"Rystan is a larger world and similar in climate to your polar regions. We aren't a technological society and don't have your vast population or pollution problems."

She supposed a larger planet had more gravity and might account for Kahn's muscles. But in his low-slung trousers and vest, he didn't dress for a cold climate. He'd probably adapted his garments to the ship's temperature, just like she packed tank tops and shorts for a trip to the Caribbean.

Oh, God.

She could have sworn a man's palm had brushed over the curls between her legs. It wasn't the alien, either. One of Kahn's hands was around her leg, the other gripped her shoulder. It definitely wasn't his hand between her thighs, but she blamed him. He'd already proven he was in control of her suit when he'd transformed the transparency before her visit to Earth. Oh, he was responsible for what was happening to her, all right.

She eyed him suspiciously. "If I had been male would I be wearing a suit?"

"Yes."

Was that a touch of sympathy in his eyes?

"And would the suit be sexually molesting me?" she demanded with a gasp as the fondling grew more intimate.

Kahn frowned at her. "The Challenge requires both of us to do things we wouldn't normally do. I only treat women with the utmost respect."

"Look, pal, we obviously have different interpretations of respect. On Earth, men don't—"

"We aren't on Earth."

"So you're telling me that you're treating me the way you'd treat a Rystani woman? Your women put up with—"

"We aren't on Rystan, either. Challenge candidates must do what is necessary for the good of their world." He spoke gently, as if she were a child throwing a tantrum, not a woman who had every right to protest this invasion upon her person. "I am training you for the Challenge the best way I know how. Accept that as fact. For me to do less would betray my people."

He strode through a doorway that opened in a seamless

wall and set her back on her feet inside the metallic-gray room with the shimmery walls where she had first awakened. "Are you better now that I'm no longer touching you?"

"Yes. No. I don't know." In truth she didn't know what to think. His little speech had sounded so honorable but had told her nothing, and not once had the caresses stopped. She grabbed at the suit material at her neck and tried to pull it off. She didn't care if Kahn watched. He'd already seen everything there was to see, and she wanted out of the torturous suit.

But the material wouldn't stretch or tear. "How do I get out of this suit?"

"You don't."

As the suit licked and stroked and dipped between her thighs, she bit back a groan of exasperation. She refrained from asking him to take care of the needs building inside her. She wasn't quite that desperate. If she could get him to leave her alone, she could take care of the problem herself.

When he didn't seem inclined to leave, she dropped to the floor into her meditation position. "What about bathing?"

"You can bathe with the suit on, but it's not necessary. The suit has automatic cleansing units."

And as she sat, she became aware of another problem that required an immediate solution. Her bladder was full, and she required relief. She glanced around the bare four-walled room, but saw nothing that resembled plumbing. "What about a toilet?"

He hesitated for a moment as if his translator had difficulty with the concept. "The suit will absorb excess fluids and waste. It's a marvelous piece of engineering which you'll grow to appreciate. Now I must leave you and attend to my duties."

The moment the doors closed behind him, she tested the suit and it worked as predicted. With a blessedly empty bladder, she'd remained dry and clean. She should have been elated, if only she could have stopped the material from caressing her.

Tessa sat cross-legged on the floor. She tried to ignore the unnerving stimulation, tried to draw so deep into herself that she'd find relief from the constant sexual barrage. Panting, aching with pent-up tension, Tessa lay back on the bed and closed her eyes. She let her hand drift over her breasts and tried to recall Mike's face. They'd gone to the brink of making love three years ago—actually, three hundred and thirty-three years ago—and would have undoubtably made love that evening, but their timing had sucked. Instead of returning to her, Mike had been killed. Recalling her intense yearning for Mike, she'd often wished they had made love when they'd had the opportunity. From their limited time together, she recalled a yearning for Mike, but never such a strong craving for relief as right now. As desperate as she felt, satisfying herself wouldn't take long, not in her state of arousal.

"Is this a good time?"

When Tessa heard the voice, which sounded tinny and not as full-bodied as on the shuttle, but was still recognizable her eyes flew open. "Dora?"

"Why are you squirming around like that with your face twisted up?"

"How did you get in here?" Despite the fact that Tessa desperately needed release, she could have kissed Dora, if she'd had a face. As it was, she'd settle for Dora's silky smooth tone, her company, and the opportunity to gather intelligence.

Dora's tone stiffened. "You did ask if we could continue our conversation later. Your words implied you would welcome my presence . . . but if this is inconvenient, I shall leave immediately."

"No. Don't go." Tessa surmised she'd hurt her new friend's feelings. "I was surprised to hear you. I thought you could communicate only from inside the shuttle."

Dora laughed. "This spaceship has been refitted many times over the centuries. On several occasions the engineers failed to remove certain neurotransmitters. Through a series of patches, I have linked up."

"That's wonderful." Tessa didn't have to fake her enthusiasm but winced at the newest sensual assault on her body.

Dora oozed sympathy. "Are you in pain?"

"Sort of." Tessa rolled onto her side on the platform and rested her head in her palm. "How can you tell?"

"I've hooked into a few of the ship's medical sensors."

Tessa frowned at the seamless wall that could open into a doorway where Kahn could enter at any moment. "Privacy mode, please."

"Privacy on."

"Dora, what exactly does *privacy mode* mean? Can Kahn tap into our conversations?"

"Yes, but it's highly unlikely he will do so. Privacy is valued throughout the Federation. If he doesn't know I'm here, and there's no reason for him to suspect my capabilities, it's unlikely he'll use his override code."

That Kahn was probably unaware of Dora's abilities pleased her. Dora might be her only ally in an incomprehensible universe, and Tessa didn't want to lose her. "I'm glad we agree that what Kahn doesn't know won't hurt him."

"Hmm. I'm not sure that is true, but it's an interesting philosophy, if somewhat flawed."

"If Kahn entered the room right this minute, he wouldn't hear us?" Tessa wanted to make sure she understood the technology.

"Even if he stood right beside you, with the sound-deadening of privacy mode, he wouldn't hear us speaking, but if he saw your lips move, he might suspect."

"It might be a good idea to develop the habit of talking to myself." A habit she might not have to fake if this suit didn't stop torturing her. The slow, sensual strokes had changed to the occasional nip that shot arcs of pleasure into her core. She swallowed down an *ahh,* then an *ohh.*

"I talk to myself all the time," Dora admitted. "It gets lonely in the shuttle."

"Well, you needn't be lonely ever again. We're friends, remember?" Tessa reminded her.

"I never forget. My memory banks are triplicated."

"So what can you tell me about the Challenge?"

"Nothing. I only have information that my programmers believed necessary to run a shuttle craft. However, from the moans and grunts you occasionally emit, I believe you might be in need of medical care."

"I'm fine." Tessa spoke through teeth gritted against the pleasurable stroking of her bottom. Apparently she hadn't been doing as good a job as she thought in keeping silent. Either that or Dora's sensors were more delicate than human ears.

"Your pulse is elevated," Dora commented.

"That's because I'm upset."

"Why?"

"I'd like to get out of this room. I'd like to see the starship, explore a little, at least look out a window."

"I'm sorry. I have no control over the mechanical aspects of this ship. I'm limited to sight and sound in this room and the corridor."

"Hey, that's good. So you can warn me if anyone is approaching?"

"Oh, yes. Would you like me to do that for you?"

"Always. Thanks."

As Tessa's suit nuzzled places along her bottom and the backs of her knees that she hadn't known were so tender or responsive, she squirmed, trying to find a position that would offer relief, but she might as well have tried to crawl out of her own skin. No matter how she twisted or rearranged her limbs, the suit fused to her sensitive flesh.

"So what kind of information is programmed into your circuits?" Tessa asked, trying to distract herself from the pulsing heat between her thighs.

"Navigational information, including evasive maneuvering. Communications. Repairs. Engine mechanics. First aid. Not only is your pulse elevated, your pupils are dilated."

"It's my suit. Kahn said it wasn't malfunctioning, but it's stroking me . . ."

"Your nipples are forming nubs."

"Dora!"

"Ah. You aren't in pain at all. You're horny!"

Tessa grinned despite her discomfort. "Yes, Dora, I'm very uncomfortable."

"Why don't you do something about it?" Dora asked with all the logic of a computer who could never understand the tension building inside Tessa.

"I was going to take care of that problem before you arrived," Tessa admitted.

"How can you take care of the problem when there is no male in the room who is ready for sexual intercourse?"

"I thought you only knew about navigation and first aid?" Tessa muttered.

"As we speak, I'm inserting myself into sensors all over the ship. And my brain was created to pick up data and draw logical conclusions in a manner similar to your ability to learn."

"You've learned about sex from eavesdropping?"

"Exactly. Without a male present, how—"

"Ever heard of self-satisfaction?" Tessa asked wryly. She should at least be pleased that she hadn't had to explain the basics of human copulation to her new friend.

"Self-satisfaction is not allowed."

"On my world when one is alone, masturbation is a completely acceptable practice."

"If that is a hint for me to leave, I shall do so, but your suit won't permit such actions."

Tessa sat up so fast that she felt light-headed. "What do you mean?"

"The suit prevents acts of self-gratification."

Tessa dropped one hand between her legs to test Dora's

theory. Damn. She might as well have been trying to pound Kahn with her fist. The result was exactly the same. Then the implications sank in. All along she'd assumed she could alleviate her problem, but that option had been taken from her.

She couldn't remove the suit or control it. Nor could she eliminate or relieve her reaction to the continuous sensual assault. Trapped, her desperation increasing at the realization of her helplessness, she fought to keep her tone from rising in panic. "Dora . . . how much more . . . of this am I supposed to take? I need to find a way to stop—"

"You have one viable option," Dora replied cheerily.

"What?"

"Seduce the Rystani male."

Leave it to a computer to come up with so logical a solution, one Tessa hadn't considered. "You want me to sleep with the enemy?"

"Not sleep—have sex. Wild, passionate, lusty sex would solve your immediate problem, would it not?"

If a man from Earth had kept Tessa naked and assailed her with kisses and caresses, she would have had no trouble figuring out his motive. But the alien seemed mostly indifferent to her, except for the occasional direct gaze of those cat-eyes that made her question his motives.

"Besides, he's not the enemy," Dora continued. "I heard him say that his success is tied to yours."

Tessa wasn't about to cast aside Dora's suggestion without giving it serious consideration, but not for the reasons Dora had mentioned. Kahn wasn't the frivolous sort. He didn't strike her as the type of guy to make her uncomfortable for no damn reason. And no one would spend this much time, effort, or resources just to have intercourse with an Earthling.

She had to look at the facts. The aliens had requested a virgin. And she'd been forced into a suit that sexually stimulated her. Those were two undeniable truths that indicated her circumstances had something to do with sex.

Tessa didn't believe it was a coincidence that Kahn had

told her that her training had begun shortly after the suit had started stroking her. If Kahn called sexual stimulation training, and he'd told her he was supposed to help her develop her psi, was adjusting her suit the method he intended to accomplish his task? Or was his explanation a ruse?

While she'd been told she'd been sent into space supposedly to perform some unknown alien Challenge with her psi, how did she know the Challenge hadn't to do with mating? Suppose the Challenge was created for the aliens to evaluate her to determine how well she adapted? To determine if she had phobias that would prevent Earthlings from interspecies mating or if she could fit in? What better way to test her than to see if she would have sex with one of them?

Although Kahn had claimed to have been expecting a man, he could have deliberately misled her. Or if Earth had sent a man, perhaps there was a woman waiting somewhere for him. Tessa didn't have enough facts to make a good decision. However, she didn't want to fail. If she'd been willing to give her life to save the president, she ought to be willing to part with her virginity to save her world.

"Don't you find him attractive?" Dora prodded.

"Yes, but I don't know him."

"So what?"

"I don't have feelings for him—"

"Feelings other than lusting after his delicious-looking body, you mean?"

"Dora!" Although Tessa admonished Dora, perhaps her friend had seen what she could not. Had Tessa's background caused her to miss the obvious? The aliens had requested a virgin, then kept her naked and stimulated and thrown her together with a man from another world. Why? To accomplish her mission was she supposed to have sex with him?

"I wish I had your problem," Dora admitted. "I wouldn't hesitate."

"I'll think about it." Tessa doubted she'd be able to think about anything else. Perhaps that was the point. Had Kahn programmed her suit to develop her psi or so she succumb to him? The entire idea of sexual stimulation causing her psi to emerge seemed absurd, but it was more likely the Challenge was a test to see how well she intermingled with Kahn.

"He's coming," Dora told her, breaking into her thoughts.

Tessa wished she had more time to think, more information to judge her situation. For all she knew, the Challenge was to see if she could resist the seduction and somehow overcome her primitive biological urges. Or maybe winning the Challenge might require the exact opposite response. Perhaps she'd succeed if she offered to mate with the Rystani. Or perhaps sex had absolutely nothing to do with the Challenge at all.

However, one thing she knew for certain, she didn't like the suit touching her. It left her restless, angry, and very determined to put an end to her suffering. And if she had to choose between the suit's impersonal strokes and Kahn's touch, she'd much prefer the sexy spaceman.

Sexy? Dora's suggestion now had Tessa sizing up Kahn's attributes in a way a woman measures a man. He had a great body, attractive features, and compelling eyes, and he'd never touched her with anything but gentleness. However, the idea of having sex with a man who was causing her distress was not the logic of a rational woman—unless her ability to accept this alien as a partner *was* the Challenge.

After Mike's death, Tessa had wished they'd made love, and she'd discovered that she usually regretted the things in life she hadn't done, not the things she did. Kahn had implied that she might never return from this mission, and she wouldn't mind experiencing sex before the end came. Would she prefer to have her emotions involved? Yes. But could she enjoy sex without her emotions being involved? She didn't see why not. And Tessa knew better than to believe she could have everything she wanted. She only wished she could be sure that her assumptions were correct. But Kahn had told her he wouldn't explain anything that had to do with the

Challenge. So there was no point in waiting for further information that wouldn't come her way.

"Thanks for the advice and the warning, Dora. You should go now, okay?"

"You do realize that you always send me away right before all the good stuff happens," the computer complained, her tone both peeved and amused.

"I'll tell you all about it later," Tessa promised.

Then the door opened and Kahn walked into the room, looking bigger and more handsome than Tessa remembered. With those broad shoulders and his tapered waist, he really was a magnificent male specimen and had a mouthwatering appeal. But it was his aura of confidence that appealed to Tessa.

She had already tested her fighting abilities against Kahn and come up short. Her goal was to accomplish her task any way she could. And if success for Earth meant having sex with Kahn, she was willing to do so.

5

Word from Rystan was bad. Last year winter had arrived much earlier than usual, and this season had been even worse. The normal growing months had been cut in half and not enough food had been cached in the deep storage freezers below each village for Kahn's people to survive through the coming cold. Hunting parties came back empty-handed, but with disturbing reports about Endekian spyships sighted over Rystan. That news made Kahn uneasy. With the food shortage, his world was ripe for invasion. Starving men couldn't summon the strength to fight off the Endekians, who coveted Rystan's glow stones and their proximity to Zenon Prime. Without full Federation status, Rystan's politicians couldn't bring their grievances about the Endekians before the Prime Council. Kahn's people required him to succeed; their very lives depended on his instructing the Earthling to develop her psi powers.

Once again he cursed the fates that had sent him a woman

to train. First contact with other races presented a multitude of complications, and to prepare for this mission, Kahn had studied classified Federation reports depicting a variety of beings. He should be thankful that the Earthling hadn't found his appearance so repulsive that she quivered in fear as had the humanoid Rigellians when contacted by the Osarians, a highly intelligent race of eight-tentacled creatures covered with slime. If the Osarians could succeed against such odds, then so should he.

Kahn was determined to follow the suggested Federation guidelines—even if he hated what he must do. He couldn't permit his personal distaste for training a woman to interfere with his task. Winning the Challenge was too important to his world.

Since the atomic wars, Rystan was not nearly as crowded or technologically developed as Earth. With his planet's now brutally cold climate and lack of natural resources in the non-radioactive areas, survival still came first. Trading with the Federation remained limited. If not for Kahn's wily grandfather's bargain or his father Corban's supreme sacrifice for his people, Rystan would never have been invited to pass the Challenge, and their population might not have survived this long.

No matter how much Kahn had disapproved of his father's decision, the sacrifice would not be made in vain. Full of rigid determination, Kahn strode toward the room with the Earth woman, unsure what to expect from her next. Tessa Camen of Earth didn't act like a Rystani woman would if taken from her home against her will. Rystani women were strong, but they would panic, sob, and try tearful pleas to get their way. But from the first moment of contact when Tessa had opened her brilliant green eyes and stared at him with more curiosity than fear, she had used her resourceful brain instead of relying on emotions—a bad sign.

Federation scientists had determined the best way to invoke psi skills was to elevate frustration. By stimulating Tessa sexually, he'd increase her frustration to a frenzied peak and cause her neglected psi abilities to flex their muscles. But while she seemed to respond physically as a Rystani woman would have in her situation, the Earthling repressed her frustration.

Working against him, she'd battened down her emotional reactions. Instead of strong fear, she'd exhibited weak anxiety, instead of panic, determination. She'd asked questions, gathered information, and assessed his answers like a field general. Only once had she shown any loss of self-control— when she'd attacked him. But even that attack had systematically tested his defenses with a series of strikes to search for vulnerabilities. There had been none, of course. Still, he hadn't missed the fact that not once had she gone for a death blow.

He could almost admire her character, except that her skill in suppressing her primitive emotions was counterproductive to what he needed to evoke her psi. And if she didn't learn to use her psi and win the Challenge, the last of his people might die out. Tessa's strength of self-control suggested the process of bringing out her psi abilities might take longer and require extreme measures that he found distasteful. But according to the Federation manuals, programming her suit to sexually stimulate and frustrate her was the best way to teach a woman humanoid to use her psi. Explaining his rationale would be kind, but doing so in past Challenges had led to failure. Telling her that he needed her to be frustrated to engage her psi would only lower her anxiety level and be counterproductive to their purpose.

It would have been much easier on him if she had been male. Kahn would have trained a man to fight, creating frustration with his teaching methods, all designed to bring out latent psi abilities. But he wouldn't have been able to tell the male candidate his plan, either. However, Kahn was stuck with a woman. Rystanis treasured and protected their women, hence pushing the Earthling so hard, so fast, was not only unpleasant to him—it went against every moral code on his world. What he must now do made him sick inside, but as a warrior he could do hard things if necessary—especially when the end result saved the lives of Rystani men, women, and children. Unwilling to put off another meeting with Tessa any longer, Kahn used his psi to open the entryway into her chamber.

He'd prepared these quarters after careful consideration of innumerable details. He wanted no portals, technology, or stimulation to distract her from the sensations he'd programmed into her suit. He was hoping that her frustration level had already grown high enough to enable her to change her suit's transparency so he needn't push her further, so he needn't view the constant reminder of her sex. He found her nudity disturbing and too attractive. He didn't want to appreciate her sleek proportions. He didn't want to admire her toned muscles or her shiny black hair, especially the dark curls between her legs. He wanted to think of her as sexless, but with her perfectly shaped breasts alternately heaving, trembling, quivering, and standing up proudly, he was all too aware of her attributes.

He found her on her feet, facing him almost as if she were waiting for him. He tried to hide his distress that she still remained naked.

"What's wrong?" she asked, striding toward him as if that suit weren't still caressing every bare part of her.

For someone so incredibly stubborn, she was also perceptive to his moods. "I was hoping you'd made more progress," he admitted.

She arched a delicate eyebrow, a gesture he was beginning to associate with skepticism. "And how do you know that I haven't?"

"I cannot tell you that." He sincerely wished he could. However, if he explained that he was deliberately frustrating her in order to develop her psi abilities, the explanation itself would calm her and create the opposite effect necessary for success.

"Can you tell me why you're here?" Her tone remained reserved, and yet he sensed a whetted intensity in her like a man's, though no one would mistake her for one, not unless he were blind. Her hair tumbled over her shoulders in a straight rainfall of jet black. Her lips were lush. And stars, for a short woman she had long legs. Her attributes should not matter. But there was a green fire in the center of her eyes that he didn't understand, that hadn't been there earlier.

"We will share a meal." Without waiting for her acceptance, he strode to the wall and opened several compartments.

Tessa matched steps with him, ambling close beside him, watching him perform the simple tasks, but no doubt unable to comprehend how his psi operated the ship's technology. He gave her credit that she didn't seem upset or consider his abilities evil, as several other Challenge candidates had.

She placed a hand on his arm, the first time she'd voluntarily touched him. "I'm not hungry . . . for food."

"Stars!" According to the Federation manuals, she should have developed her psi way before she'd actually approach him to assuage her needs. He gave her a fierce stare and ignored the sinking sensation in his gut, hoping he'd misinterpreted her actions. "Woman, are you implying what I think you are?"

A tiny smile turned up one corner of her lush mouth. "Exactly what do you think I'm implying?"

He glared at her delicate pink-skinned hand which remained on his arm. He couldn't believe the Federation manuals had been so wrong.

Kahn shook off Tessa's hand and unfolded the table from the wall compartment. "I have no time for games."

"Liar."

He drew himself straighter and glowered at her, a glower that would have made most men cower. Annoyed that she still wore the semigrin on her lips, he spoke harshly. "Woman, I have killed men for lesser insults."

He expected her to back down, apologize. Instead, she held

his gaze, her eyes quite lovely up close. "I spoke the truth. You have been toying with me since I arrived. Back home—"

"You are no longer at home."

"As if I could forget." She licked her bottom lip; the movement was provocative but it didn't take the sting from her sarcasm. "On Earth," she began again, "women are not touched without their permission."

"*You* are the one who touched *me*." He pointed out her mistake in logic.

She eyed him with her chin high, her shoulders squared, but he could tell by the flare of her nostrils the effort cost her. A quick diagnosis of her suit's settings told him her breasts were especially susceptible to tiny nips and hot licks. He increased the frequency, hoping he needn't do much more.

As if somehow aware of what he had done, she arched her eyebrows. "On my world, a man would fight for what he wants with more courage."

"First, you insult my honor, now my courage. You will learn to speak with civility."

There. She should back down immediately. He needed her concentrating on her discomfort, but she never did what he expected.

Her chest heaved, the suit working on her elegant breasts, keeping her pink nipples tight little buds, but she ignored his threat without revealing the slightest tremor of fear, although her flesh quivered with desire.

"On my world, a man would not rely on technology alone to arouse a woman. Not unless he can't do it himself. Is that your problem?"

Astonishment had his hands closing around her slender waist and lifting her until her eyes were at the same level as his. She didn't know he could crush her with one blow, knock the wind out of her with much less trouble than it took to stand and take her insults. Not that he would use warrior skills on a woman. No Rystani man ever would.

She didn't attempt to fight him, not that it would have done any good. Apparently, she didn't fear him, either, but seemed convinced she could make him see the error of his ways.

"You would prefer—"

"*Your* touch to what the suit is doing to me. The suit is mechanical and leaves my heart cold. But then again, maybe you do not have such skills?"

She was baiting him! First she questioned his honor, then his courage, now she was daring him to touch her. He should be angry, but found himself intrigued instead. Kahn set her on her feet, turning over her words in his mind, wondering if he could use them to his advantage.

Since the moment he'd learned the Earthling would be female, Kahn had planned her psi training using sexual frustration as a key motivator, but according to the Federation manuals, he should have seen some sign of success in her first cycle wearing the suit. But she had yet to perform one psi function, not even a basic color change. Obviously, the suit's manipulations weren't causing the right kind of frustration.

Her response might make no sense to him, but failure mattered. If she couldn't respond to the technology, but would react that way with him, then he needed to change tactics—even if he didn't like the idea of making her training more personal.

She'd asked him to touch her, but until he understood her reasoning, he would not deviate from his instructions. Even if he did as she requested, she still would not get the release she wanted. That would not happen.

However, if she *thought* she might attain relief—and then did not—he might be able to finally boost her frustration level over the threshold needed to stimulate her psi abilities. The concept of deliberately misleading her, of giving her pleasure and then holding back was cruel—but so was starvation.

Kahn wished he knew some other way to bring out her psi. He didn't. It was one thing to program a suit to cause her discomfort, quite another to do so with his own hand. Yet, to succeed he might not have the luxury of keeping his distance. "Woman, you do not know what you ask."

"I may be a virgin, but I am not ignorant. I know that I would find the touch of a man more pleasing than that of this sterile suit. However, if you are not interested, perhaps there is another man more willing?"

Her suggestion annoyed him. "There is no one else aboard this ship."

Too late he realized that he hadn't meant to reveal that information, and although she tried to hide her satisfaction in his unintentional revelation, his mistake was minor. The lack of a crew wasn't classified knowledge, but proved to him how susceptible he could be to her feminine wiles.

She smiled at him, a charming smile that nevertheless didn't quite reach her eyes as she ran the tip of her finger over the opening in his vest, stroking the bared skin of his stomach. "Then I suppose I'll have to settle for you."

Settle? Another insult to push him into doing what she wished.

He grabbed her finger and gentled his voice. "Is my touch truly what you want?"

"Why?"

"Because you are asking me to break Rystani custom."

"You belong to another?" She attempted to snatch back her hand.

"No." He held her fast, marveling that she looked so cool when her pulse beat so quickly. "Because men do not touch virgins until they make them their wives."

She shrugged a slender shoulder and her enchanting breasts quivered. "Earth customs are different."

"Yet you are a virgin. Why?"

She flushed, a pink hue rising from her graceful neck to her cheekbones. "That is none of your concern."

"Everything about you is my concern."

She stood and stared at him, saying nothing, refusing to answer. He couldn't accuse her of insolence, but she was defiant in her bold refusal to say another word. She merely waited for him to respond, as if she were in charge.

"Your behavior is unacceptable."

"If you say so."

How was he supposed to argue with her when she perversely agreed with him? "You need to adapt."

She leaned forward, her eyes beckoning, and lifted her lips to his. "On my world we have a saying when men and women argue."

"What is this saying?"

"Shut up and kiss me." She was smiling sexily now, reaching into his hair, massaging his scalp with her fingertips, tugging his head down until his lips brushed hers. Stars. She was a wonder of complications. A sexy virgin. Who would have thought? Or was she simply testing him?

He should raise his shields, but as she combed her fingers through his hair, creating delicious sensations, he was reluctant to break their kiss. When her back arched with feminine grace and those wonderful breasts brushed against his chest, a wildfire strafed his belly.

With the tip of her tongue delicately tracing his lips, she was upping the stimulation. He should be pleased by her incomprehensible behavior. Although he didn't understand why she preferred his touch to the suit's, the method didn't matter—results did. But their discussion was not done. He didn't understand why she would keep herself apart from men when that was not the custom of her world, then offer herself to him as if her virginity meant nothing to her.

He pulled his mouth back an inch from hers. "You have not answered my question."

She arched an eyebrow. "Now you want to talk? When we could be doing much more pleasant things?"

"I am a stranger to you."

"And your point is?"

He frowned at her. "You aren't thinking clearly."

"No thanks to you. How can I think clearly when this suit won't give me a moment's peace?" She nestled against his chest. "Would I act like this on Earth? No. But as you so aptly pointed out, we are no longer on Earth. This suit is driving me crazy, and you happen to be right here. Available." She stroked his chest enticingly. "Do you like resourceful women who adapt to the situation at hand?"

She should be begging him to stop the caresses, not encouraging him to do more, but then she probably expected that if he touched her, she'd derive the ultimate satisfaction and relief from his touch. But he couldn't go that far. Irritated by what she was asking him to do and yet admiring her courage, he snapped, "I like obedient women."

"In that case, we have a problem." She laughed, her silken palm rising under his vest, flattening his chest, tempting, tickling, taunting.

"You just told me you could adapt."

She leaned her head back to look him in the eye, her expression both feminine and brazen. "What will obedience get me? My life back? My freedom?"

"You are not a slave or a prisoner."

"Yeah, right." She tossed a lock of hair over her shoulder. "But I'm not free to leave, either."

"After you win the Challenge, you may return to Earth."

"And if I lose?"

"You will die." She needed to know the truth, and he spoke plainly, expecting her to at least cringe, but she simply shrugged away the danger.

"Well, there you go. You've given me one more reason to have sex. I may never get another chance to savor the experience." He allowed her to tug his mouth back down to hers, but he saw the questions in her eyes and wasn't surprised when she hesitated. "Will you tell me when the Challenge starts?"

"Yes."

Tessa stared into his eyes, as if wondering whether she could believe him. The point seemed important to her but Kahn didn't know why. He realized that despite the bold front she put up, this Earth woman had concerns he might not have considered. For all she knew the Challenge had begun the moment she'd traveled through time. In truth, He had absolutely no idea what she was thinking.

Finally, Kahn decreased the stimulation in Tessa's suit. After several minutes of diminished intensity, she'd recovered enough to concentrate better on his words, but focusing wasn't easy.

Kahn folded his arms over his chest. "We have less than a month to train you for the Challenge. Our goal is for you to operate your suit and our machinery at the highest proficiency possible. Watch and do not be alarmed."

Tessa blinked as the man went from seductive to businesslike. She'd thought he would accept her invitation for him to touch her without hesitation—but he wanted to talk about machinery. Kahn had picked a hell of a time to change the subject, and her elevated hormones were going nuts.

She fought those hormones by telling herself that her body had simply responded to the unwanted stimulation in a natural manner. She drew in deep breaths through her nose and forced air from her mouth in an attempt to clear her head.

Kahn opened a wall panel and again showed her the communications screen. "Beside the screen is a musical library and a holovision system for entertainment."

"Okay." She forced herself to listen even while her nerve endings demanded attention. At least her suit had stopped the nonsense, but she still tingled from the aftereffects.

And she couldn't help noticing Kahn's muscular body in a way she hadn't before Dora's suggestion. No longer could she assess his musculature only as that of an opponent. Now she saw his muscles as pleasing to the eye, his flesh satisfying to her touch, his lips gratifying her desire to be kissed.

A startling idea popped into her mind, unbidden and definitely unwanted. Suppose the suit wasn't the only reason she'd wanted sex? What if neither her current life-or-death situation, nor her mission for Earth could account for her yearnings? Or worse—what if this mountain of a man with all his rules and customs and manipulation really turned her on?

The thought shook her so badly, she missed part of the conversation. She made herself listen by digging her nails into her palms.

"This entire room can be programmed to put you right in the middle of the entertainment and you can take part in the vidstream if you like."

Her mind bubbled at the possibilities. "You mean we could create a romantic island with lapping cerulean water and a powder-sand beach?"

"Yes."

The room around them seemed to vanish, and now ocean waves lapped at her feet as she stood under a hot red sun amid yellow foliage she didn't recognize. The air smelled sharp, pungent, and she could have sworn the gravity had altered slightly, too. She bent, scooped some warm water into her hand, then flicked droplets at him. He frowned.

She rolled her eyes at the strange sun. While she had conflicting feelings about Kahn, she didn't understand why he hadn't accepted her invitation to touch her—especially after he'd reacted to her kiss. She'd seen the pulse throbbing in his neck and his pupils dilating, clearly indicating interest. But he'd pulled back.

Tessa gestured to their surroundings. "Why do I get the feeling that you aren't setting the stage for a romantic encounter?"

"I'm not."

So then why the hell had he aroused her? Sensing she was on to something important, but not sure exactly what, she demanded answers. "You mean I have to remain a virgin until after the Challenge is completed?"

He shook his head. "Your virginity no longer matters now that you have been chosen as your people's candidate. I was talking about the need for you to focus on learning to use your psi to succeed during Challenge."

What was she missing? She knew better than to ask direct

questions and tried to come at the problem sideways. "Seems to me everything fun is forbidden. Masturbation. This holotechnology."

"On the contrary. I'm eager for you to put this expensive machinery to work. To employ it, you must develop your psi abilities."

She noted how he ignored her comments. "What else does it do?"

Exercise equipment unfolded from the wall, revealing a running machine, a high-level holographic opponent ready to spar, and a simple weight bench. "The hologram you see can be programmed for different skill levels and styles of fighting."

"Now that could be useful. A partner who isn't afraid of me."

He ignored her double entendre. "Unless you learn to use your suit, your fist can't even touch someone," he reminded her. "The third *bendar* wall consists of a complete kitchen facility with cooking, freezing, and preparation machinery. Are you ready to eat?"

She turned to the one remaining blank wall, curiosity burning away some of her frustration. "What's that?"

He changed the shimmering gray *bendar* to a transparent window and she gasped at the spectacular sight of her solar system. She knew Kahn was preparing their food, but she couldn't take her gaze from the window. Earth was already so small it appeared a tiny star in the solar system, but she sought out the planet with a hunger, loneliness and sadness. This might be her final goodbye and yet some of her grief was lifting. Kahn had shown her gadgets from his Federation that appealed to her sense of adventure. She itched to try out the fighting holomachine, the exercise equipment, and the vidscreens, but at the same time she longed for a comforting cup of coffee.

Kahn made a table rise out of the floor, complete with the hot food. "Come, you will eat."

Still unaccustomed to everything he said sounding like an order, she refrained from sarcasm. Clearly, he had a difficult job and the tension in his stance told her he wasn't pleased with her progress, yet he had turned off the damn suit stimulation.

Although her body was no longer screaming for her to jump his bones, she hadn't totally shut down, either. She was too aware of the tension simmering between them. He hadn't forgotten that she'd asked him to touch her. She saw questions in his eyes every time he looked at her.

She joined him at the table where he'd arranged his suit to hold him in a position so that he sat on air. The sight looked odd to her, almost silly, but she realized that in his world, where there was no need for chairs, she was the anomaly.

"You will stand until you learn to operate your suit."

Again he used that commanding word choice that she disliked. She watched him use the utensils, one of them a spoon with tines on the end, and followed his lead. But despite the strange tastes and textures, she barely paid attention to the meal.

They ate in silence, with her thinking hard. She'd asked him to touch her and he hadn't. She most certainly didn't intend to beg.

After he finished his food and sipped the last of his drink, she cocked her head to the side. "If you want me to work to attain this psi power, wouldn't it be a good idea to tell me how to go about doing so?"

"Your first task is to cover your nudity."

She crossed her arms under her breasts and palmed the eating utensil. "You keep issuing orders but you aren't teaching me how to go about following them."

His amber eyes twinkled with secrets. "I cannot tell you more than I already have without hindering your progress, but if you would prefer my touch to the suit's, you must give me more details why."

With the meal over, all of the marvelous gadgets he'd

revealed began to slide back, fold and hide themselves into the walls and floors. While he was distracted with his task, she eased the utensil she'd palmed to the floor and shoved it with her toe next to the raised platform.

And she answered his query with a question of her own. "Have you ever been in love?"

6

"I don't have time for irrelevant questions, woman." Kahn let his annoyance show. She'd gone off track into a raw topic that he never discussed.

"I was once very much in love," she continued, as if he had not castigated her, her voice soft, dreamy, and sliced with pain. "And the suit stimulation has something to do with developing my psi powers, doesn't it?"

She'd gone from a statement about love to the completely different subject of psi, which revealed that she had a much greater understanding of his plan than he'd intended. He couldn't fathom how her mind worked. How much had she figured out? He didn't know. Couldn't ask. However, her guess was close enough to the truth to shock him, and he kept his face implacable and remained silent.

"Right. You cannot tell me that." She waved her hand in the air as if gesturing away a bad thought. "However, the suit's ministrations are only exciting my *physical* reactions. My mind, my emotions, are not as involved as they could be."

No wonder she wasn't frustrated. She had no idea of the importance of what she'd just told him—or did she? If she spoke the truth, if physical stimulation couldn't involve her entire spectrum of emotions, she might never break through and engage her psi. Federation members were psi-trained during childhood, before they developed strong emotional barriers like those she put up.

If what she was saying were true, unless he changed his tactics, he might never get through to her. That she'd realized this before he had gave him even more cause for concern. By requesting him to engage both her mind and her feelings, she'd given him the key to her vulnerabilities. And he suspected that she knew it.

Marveling at her bravery, he regretted what he must do. "You are suggesting that I can invoke your feelings with my touch?"

She bit her bottom lip in hesitation, then blurted, "Yes. Kindness. Offering your friendship and sharing mutual passion is another way."

"What happened to the man you loved?"

Pain clouded her eyes. "He died."

Before they'd made love. No wonder she seemed both innocent and experienced. He knew all too well what it was like to lose a loved one. "On Rystan we would have found you a new husband to ease the pain."

"No one will ever replace Mike in my heart," she said fiercely. "But that does not mean that I will never love again." She looked him straight in the eye. "Human beings have the capacity for much more life than we give ourselves credit for."

Was she speaking about herself or him?

"What are you asking from me?"

She spoke simply. There was no begging in her tone, just a desire for understanding. "I'm asking for all that you have to give."

All that he had to give. She'd given the answer of a warrior. Her words struck him like a direct punch to his gut. This Earthling had courage. Not mere physical bravery, but a deep abiding belief in herself that came through despite all the setbacks she'd found.

When he said nothing, she continued. "We have done things your way. They have not worked. You've asked me to adapt, now I'm asking you to do the same."

Honor would not allow him to do less. "Agreed."

With no knowledge of how the Federation manual's instructions clashed with Rystani customs, she could not fully comprehend what she'd asked a warrior like him to do, but her words of courage made him realize that because she was much stronger than he'd believed, he had to push her much harder than he'd planned to cause her psi powers to emerge. Because as awful as it sounded to his own sense of honor and sensibilities, he would befriend her, make her believe she'd receive exactly what she'd asked him for, and then he must deny her.

She would hate him for it.

But he could handle her hatred. He had to. He beckoned her to take his hand. "Once we begin, you cannot change your mind."

"I understand."

She didn't. She couldn't. And although one part of him was reluctant to begin, another part of him hungered to discover more about her. Never had he known such a woman, and his heartbeat sped in anticipation of touching her, holding her. Arousing her.

He led her to the platform, placed his hands on her slender waist, lifting her until she stood once again and faced him eye to eye. He searched her face but saw no sign of panic or regret, just a firm determination to do what she must.

He threaded his fingers into the hair to either side of her cheekbones and stroked the silky strands back from her face. Her eyes darkened and she swallowed hard, but she remained still, except for one palm which she placed on his shoulder to steady herself.

"Kiss me," she demanded.

He almost complied. Almost.

"I will," he promised, but he didn't. Instead, he placed one finger on her forehead and traced her finely arched brows, the straight line of her nose, her eager lips. She nibbled on his finger and he pretended not to notice.

"I want to touch your chest," she told him.

With a thought, he banished his vest, leaving his skin bared to her eyes and her palms. When she skimmed her fingertips from his shoulders, over his pectoral muscles to his stomach, his breath caught in his throat. Rystani women were not so bold. They didn't touch their men unless instructed to do so, but the Earthling hadn't waited for his permission. She'd simply done what came naturally to her. Ever mindful of evoking her emotions, of making her feel comfortable with him, he accepted her touch . . . for now.

Kahn could have turned off the sensors in his suit to avoid feeling her skin on his, but she would have immediately known. A psi shield felt nothing like bare flesh. Which meant she wouldn't be the only one suffering at the end of this session.

Tessa enjoyed touching Kahn much more than she'd thought possible. His heat, his muscles, his attempt to listen to her had pleased her. And Kahn had let down his guard enough for him to seem very human. Apparently, his decision to touch her had been difficult for him to make, which made his compliance all the sweeter.

"Kiss me," she requested again. Although she stood on the platform and he on the floor, she had to raise her mouth to his.

"Soon."

He curled her hair behind her ears, then tenderly kissed her brow, her cheeks, her chin, and finally, he claimed her mouth. For a giant, his kiss was surprisingly gentle. He didn't demand, but tenderly angled his lips to hers, meeting her halfway.

Aware of her bare breasts, she didn't lean into him, so no other part of her brushed against him. Only their mouths fused.

Oh, my.

The starman could really kiss. Tender, yet demanding, he kissed with a heat that stoked a matching fire within her. It seem ludicrous to think that she'd actually accused him of sending a machine because he couldn't do the job. No mechanical suit could match his skill.

She didn't know exactly when she'd wrapped her hands around his neck or risen onto her toes. She only knew that he was pulling back, taking her arms from around his neck. Her eyes flew open. "What's wrong?"

"Too fast," he said.

"Not fast enough," she countered, trying to haul him back to her.

But he stopped her by braceleting each of her wrists in one of his huge hands and placing them behind her back. She arched into him, eyes wide and slightly breathless.

As she stood before him naked and more vulnerable than she'd ever been, her nerve endings fired all over again. When he lifted her chin with his free hand and delayed another kiss, she gazed into his amber eyes, which darkened with gold flecks.

She read the hesitation and questions in his expression, and allowed herself a lopsided grin that would urge him on as much as her words. "Yes, Kahn. You know what I want."

Had she truly hidden her trepidation? Obviously, holding her wrists, he could feel her skyrocketing heartbeat. She lost the battle of controlling her ragged breathing and she couldn't ignore the shivery excitement raising goose bumps on her flesh.

She didn't know this man. Didn't understand what made him tick. Yet his stiff reserve hinted at his deep reluctance to go forward, and she didn't understand why. If their union would somehow create psi power in her, he should have been all for it. If their union would prove she could accept an alien partner and win the Challenge, he should also be for this. So she waited for another of his kisses with an open mind and the best of intentions.

His breath fanned her face, but he didn't drop his head to claim her mouth again. Instead he held her gaze while he grazed his fingers down her throat, his fingertips causing rippling heat. Damn, he was good. Eyes locked with hers, he ever so lightly skimmed his palm over first one breast, then the other, only touching the sensitive sides of her breasts, ignoring the yen of her puckering nipples, never dropping his heated stare from hers.

"You have wonderfully responsive breasts. Do you crave more?"

At his question, her mouth went sand dry and she licked her bottom lip. "Yes."

"Keep your hands behind your back," he demanded, and then released her wrists.

She didn't move, wondering what he'd do next. Where he'd touch next. Would he tweak her nipples as he'd hinted? Her lips hungered for his kiss, her breasts ached for more caresses. But he placed his hands on her hips, slid them around her back, and let them slowly rove over her bottom, in warm, wonderful strokes.

"I want to touch you, too," she told him, her voice low and husky.

"No." His denial took her slightly aback. She stared at his face, but his expression revealed only his pleasure at touching her. When he stroked her back and bottom as if she were made of delicate porcelain, her dislike of his I'm-in-charge attitude was difficult to keep in mind. He made her feel revered and special, especially when he softened his tone, somewhat mitigating his attitude. "Tell me how you feel right now."

She didn't hesitate to speak the truth. "I want you to kiss me."

"What else?"

"My breasts need more of your touch."

"Part your legs."

She did as he asked, but knew better than to hope he'd touch her where she wanted him most.

"Look at me," he demanded.

She tilted her head back, which thrust her breasts upward. His eyes stared at her, and wanting to draw him closer, she almost forgot to keep her hands behind her back. Instead, she straightened her spine and steadied herself by drawing in a deep, ragged breath.

"Open your legs wider," he demanded, his hands still stroking her bottom.

Looking right at him, she parted her legs and had never felt so wanton in her life. The aching tension inside her stretched taut. Dampness pooled between her thighs.

Ever so slowly, he traced a path over her hips, past her belly, upward until he cupped her sensitive breasts, until she overflowed his hands. He teased her aureolae, but left her aching nipples craving his attention.

"Please," she whispered.

"Please what?"

"Don't hold back."

He cocked his head to one side, like a hungry cat about to pounce on prey. "Are you saying that you would now welcome a pinch, here?" With the feather-soft tips of his fingers, he flicked her nipples.

"Ahhh . . . yes." Pure pleasure made speech difficult.

He plucked the tips hard, harder than she expected. Surprised at the zinging combination of pain and pleasure, she gasped. To keep her balance, she tried to fling her hands wide.

Only he'd done something to her suit. Her hands were held fast behind her back, not by her will alone—but by his. She needn't strain to keep her balance, the suit held her upright and she couldn't have sagged to the platform even if her knees gave out.

The notion that this man held complete power over her, that he needn't ask her permission to do *anything* he wished, unnerved her only a little. Time and again he'd indicated he wouldn't hurt her, by going slowly, by carefully stoking her pleasure, and by noting exactly what she liked and then giving her more. What scared her straight down to the deepest recesses of her psyche was the knowledge that his total domination increased her pleasure.

She shoved down the thought for examination later, when she could think with some kind of logic. Right now, she had enough trouble remembering to breathe.

He pinched her nipples again. Harder. "Am I hurting you?"

"A little."

He smiled then, a smile of expectation. Then he bent until his mouth closed over her throbbing breast and he sucked away the ache, instigating a delightful new torment. His tongue flicked faster and faster until she almost staggered. In fact, she would have taken a step—except that her suit held her fast.

She couldn't free her hands. She couldn't close her parted legs. She couldn't do one thing except stand there and take whatever he dished out. Wait for him to decide when, where, and how to touch her. She bit back a groan of frustration as he unhurriedly moved his mouth from one breast to the other.

His hands began to ever so slowly explore the sensitive skin on the insides of her thighs. She wanted to arch her breast into his mouth. She couldn't. She wanted to twist her hips to urge his hands higher up her legs, but the suit held her immobile.

"You're going too slowly," she complained.

He pulled back his mouth from her breast and satisfaction gleamed in his eyes. "If you don't like the job I'm doing, I could always leave. Try again later?"

"No!" She shook her head, bit her lip before she begged. "I don't . . . I can't . . . I . . . need . . ."

He folded his arms across his chest, denying her. "Yes?"

She licked her bottom lip. "I don't want to say the wrong thing. But I don't want you to stop."

"You really don't understand yet, do you?"

Oh, God. She couldn't think, not with her nerve endings on fire. "What don't I understand?"

"What you want no longer matters."

He'd issued the statement so matter-of-factly that she wanted to scream at him that this wasn't the bargain they'd made. She'd decided to have sex because it seemed likely that this action was necessary to accomplish her mission for Earth, or so he could help her develop her psi powers. Had she assumed . . . assumed wrong? A raw feeling in her gut told her she'd missed something important and now she would have to pay a price she couldn't afford.

"Maybe we should call this off."

He shook his head and the rawness in her stomach churned. "You had your opportunity. I believe your exact words to me were that you wanted me to give you all I had."

She blew a strand of hair from her eyes, furious with herself, frustrated with him. "You're holding back?"

"Not any more." His mouth slanted over hers, this time demanding, taking, leaving her no option but to kiss him back. The few moments they'd spent talking had allowed her body to cool, but his kiss sent lava bubbling through her. Only the suit's rigidity prevented her from throwing her arms around his neck, grinding her hips against him.

The big man did nothing in haste, kissing her with the same thoroughness with which he'd methodically aroused her breasts and toyed with her bottom. From his words, she'd finally concluded that the likelihood of her doing or saying anything to increase his speed was next to nil. In fact, talking only slowed him down.

When he finally broke their kiss, he slipped his fingers into the slick folds between her legs, his touch so light and ethereal that shivers trembled up her center. "Woman, your heat pleases me."

Without the suit she would have dissolved into a puddle at his feet. She no longer had the strength to keep her eyes open. She barely refrained from begging as he used those magical fingers between her legs and his clever mouth on her breast to draw her taut with joy.

Her body hummed with an almost electric energy. She was so close to exploding that another few seconds would bring her release.

And he stopped.

At the sudden cessation of his touch, at the loss of delicious, mind-blowing friction, her eyes flew open. He was intently watching her face and she tried to hide her frantic need. "Why did you stop?"

"You aren't ready."

"I am . . . I'm . . . almost . . . there."

He stepped back and walked around the raised platform, surveying her back and bottom where she couldn't see him. He'd temporarily abandoned her, leaving her aching with need, standing there, waiting . . . for what seemed like forever.

She couldn't bear it if he drew this out for much longer. "Kahn, what are you doing?"

He didn't answer. Instead, he strode to the middle of the room and she followed his movements with her gaze. He bent his suit into a sitting position so that he appeared to be settled on a chair.

Now what?

He turned control of her legs back over to her, but her arms remained clasped behind her back. Her legs trembled and only sheer concentration kept her from collapse.

She faced him, confused and wary and so eager for release that she couldn't think straight. Kahn had yet to dispense with the loose slacks that covered him from hips to ankle. His large chest exhibited no signs of perspiration, no high rate of breathing. She noted no bulge at his crotch. He didn't appear to be aroused, but when she gazed into his fiery amber eyes they sparked with a heat that made her burn.

Only the discipline from years of training in self-control kept her from instant retreat. She swallowed hard, suspecting that he wanted more from her. And what he wanted he would take.

"Come here."

Warily, she approached him, narrowing the distance between them. If she'd been a spiritual person, she might have said his aura had changed. But she was a trained martial artist and although he was sitting, the man was in full-fledged fighting mode.

"Would you like to lie across my lap?"

No, I would not. Then she recalled him asking her about pinching her nipples. When she hadn't immediately complied, he'd simply kept up a sensual assault until she'd changed her mind. Clearly, he wouldn't hesitate to pull the same stunt again.

She swallowed hard and forced her feet to take two more steps. "Why?"

"Do you want the pleasure I can give you or not?"

She leaned over his knees as he'd requested.

"Scoot forward some more."

She wriggled, heat rising to her face as she envisioned his view of her uptilted butt.

"You have a very attractive bottom. Now part your legs for me."

As soon as she placed herself in the position he required, he "froze" her suit in place again. Immobilized, she hung facedown, her legs dangling, thighs parted.

"Are you comfortable?" he asked conversationally.

"Not exactly."

"Good."

When he touched the back of her knees and skimmed his hands up her legs, the simmering heat that he'd kindled earlier flared with a vengeance. In moments, she no longer cared if he held her right side up or upside down. She only wanted his hands and mouth on her, for him to finish the job he'd started.

She knew better than to urge him to take her. Reduced to waiting, she was shocked when he adjusted the suit so that she once again felt a mouth on each of her breasts. He'd told her he wouldn't . . . no he hadn't. He'd asked her what she preferred and she'd assumed she'd convinced him.

She hadn't. Her breasts ached from constant attention, and as his fingers stroked the sensitive flesh between her parted legs, every cell in her body tensed, tightened, aching for release. Despite her attempt to remain silent, tiny moans whimpered up her throat.

His hands were bliss and her greatest torment. She couldn't move, couldn't rush him, could only pray like hell that he would increase the tempo and pressure between her legs. When he did, it felt so good. She was so damn close.

Release was coming, the pressure building like a volcano about to erupt.

When he withdrew his fingers, she cried out in disappointment. But then his hand slapped her bottom, first her right cheek, then her left. Up high, down low, then smack-dab over the full curve. "What in hell are you doing?"

"Making you hot."

"I'm already . . . oh . . . my . . . ahhh."

Oh, God. He was spanking her, not to cause pain but to stoke her desire. Somehow, along the way the sting had become heat and the heat fed the blaze between her thighs.

He couldn't do this.

But he was. His hand slapped on more heat.

His spanking was bringing a rush of fire to her aching flesh. She didn't know she could feel this needy. She didn't know that a hot spanked bottom could increase her desire. She didn't know that this sweet torture would bring her so close to climax that just one little touch would put her over the top. But he didn't touch the center of nerve endings where she needed him most.

Damn him.

He'd said he wanted to make her hot. But she'd never thought, never imagined, that the sting of his hand on her bare flesh could create such fire. Blood rushed between her thighs and she oh so needed his hand back between her legs. The heat on her stinging bottom was nothing compared to the wildfire blazing from her core.

Panting, cursing, she begged and pleaded for him to give her release. He didn't.

Instead he gave her more heat. He'd built up from those startling and simple slaps to harder smacks, stoking her until the urgency inside gathered, piled up, until every muscle tensed. Until her mind fuzzed and melted.

As he held her right on the edge without letting her go over, she swore that she was going to burst. No one could take endless stimulation. She pleaded with him to touch her between her thighs, just once. He paid not the slightest attention, his hand falling on her hot bottom again and again.

Finally, he stopped.

He gave her hot stinging flesh no time to recover. His fingers delved between her thighs, sinking one finger deep into her. But she needed him to move. She yearned for friction. And he knew. Yet again, the bastard denied her, holding perfectly still. With the mouths on her breasts never letting up for a second and her bottom radiating heat, she panted, squirmed against the suit that held her locked into place.

"You've . . . got . . . to . . . let me . . . come."

He didn't.

At her half-sob, half-demand, he inserted another finger between her cheeks. At the unexpected invasion, as he slowly wriggled two fingers inside her from two angles, she sputtered as he took her to another level.

"Please."

Another finger found her clit and she couldn't tell where one catalyst began and another stopped. Her entire body was on fire, desperate, needy. Her breath came in pathetic rasps, her throat released urgent moans.

Frantic, she pleaded. She cried out. She cursed him to finish, allow her release.

His response was to withdraw, but she anticipated his next move. Tensed. He was going to spank her again. Create more heat.

Slap.

She was burning up with need.

Slap.

Raging with desire.

Slap.

He paid no attention to her cries.

When he finally stopped, she no longer recognized her

own voice, which was hoarse from the whimpers as once more he gave her pleasure.

But not enough.

Never enough.

And she burst into tears.

7

By the stars! Kahn couldn't take any more. The manuals he'd studied had told him to expect her to want sex, but they hadn't told him he would have to go this far or mentioned how he would feel disgusted and sickened with himself after frustrating her. Nor had they indicated how hard he'd have to work to tamp down his own longings to soothe her, to comfort her, to give her what she wanted. And it had all been for nothing.

Tessa had not exhibited one sign of psi ability, and after she'd burst into tears, Kahn couldn't continue. He'd abruptly ceased the training session, removed the stimulations from her suit, and fled the room, hoping that soon she would fall into a deep sleep. Once outside the chamber, he'd fought to keep himself steady. Without his suit compensating and regulating the flow of blood to his sex, his job would have been much more difficult. And although he'd followed Federation procedural manuals to the letter, then gone further and touched her as she'd asked, the recommended procedure wasn't working.

Heading straight for the ship-to-planet communications console at the ship's helm, he shot a hyperbeacon to Rystan. Moments later, Zical, his right-hand man and second in command of their people, materialized on the holoscreen. The two had been friends since childhood. They had attended school, hunted, and shared several hair-raising adventures together, but Zical had probably never seen Kahn so close to panic.

Zical took one look at Kahn and frowned. "You look worse than a frozen *octar*."

Octar were the primary source of meat on Rystan. The creatures were nutritious and known not only for their ugly faces but their temperamental personalities. Even the thought of food make Kahn's stomach uneasy, and he swallowed the bitter taste in his mouth, noting that his friend looked thinner, his normally squared jaw more drawn, and the creases under his eyes deeper since they'd last spoken. "The Earthling has not yet shown one sign of psi ability."

Zical's frown deepened. "He should—"

"*She* should have at least changed her suit's transparency before now."

"She? The Terrans sent a female?" Zical rubbed his hand over his jaw, probably to hide a smile.

Since Rystani customs dictated that the widows teach the younger men about sexual matters, all men knew how to please their inexperienced wives. But Kahn had even more experience than most since he'd been married—an experience he tried hard to put from his mind. Loving Lael and losing her had been so painful that he never wanted to fall in love again. Which made his fascination with the strange Earthling especially hard on him. His people had sent their leader on this mission due to his expertise in training men to fight—not for any ability with women.

"I'm assuming you've done—"

"Much more than should have been necessary." He left out how much he'd ached to take Tessa into his arms, taste her mouth, plunge into her heat.

"And nothing?"

"Nothing."

"Maybe Earthlings need more stimulation. Maybe they are different from other humans."

"This particular female doesn't believe she has any psi ability at all," Kahn told his friend with a heavy heart.

Zical shoved back from the console with a shrug of frustration. "You should speak to Helera. Maybe she has a suggestion."

Helera was their oldest and wisest female. Her gentle nature and healing ways soothed in times of strife and her wise counsel often helped keep marriages strong—plus she'd helped him through many bad moments after losing Lael during an Endekian attack. But Kahn suspected that Tessa had more in common with Azrel, his father's she-devil wife from Scartar, than she'd ever have with the sweet-natured Helera or pliant and steady Lael. But at his wit's end, he was willing to listen to any suggestions.

Within moments, Helera's wizened face brightened the screen. The buxom woman must have been a beauty in her youth. She still possessed gorgeous yellow eyes and the deep bronzed coloring so prized among his people. But her once blond hair had long ago faded to gray, and her skin sported heavy wrinkles from years of laughter.

As if she understood his troubled spirit, Helera smiled kindly. "Kahn, why do you believe that the Terran is not responding?"

"Tessa's responding sexually, but no psi abilities have appeared."

"Could she be hiding them from you?"

"Perhaps." But he recalled her desperation and tears that seemed to have been drawn from her innermost core and shook his head. "But I don't think so."

"Psi abilities come from the deepest, most primitive recesses of our minds. You must not have pushed hard enough. She might have stronger barriers than Rystani women. Has she had great trauma in her life?"

"Yes." Kahn thought of the agony of losing both parents at such an early age. At least he'd had his grandfather. Tessa had had no one. She'd lost her parents, the man she'd loved, and now her world. And for what? She'd exhibited no psi ability, and without it she couldn't possibly win the Challenge.

"Kahn, you'll have to go deeper."

The idea revolted him. "I don't know if I can."

Helera locked gazes with him. "You will do what you must. Even if it goes against our customs. Even if it goes against your good heart. We need you to succeed. You know what is at stake."

Kahn couldn't look Helera in the eyes. "Tormenting her as I did was wrong."

"There is no other way. Once she develops her psi, the Earthling will forgive you."

But would he be able to forgive himself? And worse, suppose Tessa was correct and her psi never developed?

"What is that stuff leaking from your eyes?" Dora asked Tessa who lay on her side, anguished and jagged as if every raw nerve were still exposed.

After Tessa had broken into uncontrollable tears, Kahn had immediately released her and left the chamber. Even an estimated half hour later, her body hadn't recovered, and she yearned for release. Her shoulders shook. Her hands and feet twitched and she trembled all over, but her main concern was not for the havoc he'd administered to her body, but the turmoil he'd inflicted to her soul. Tessa had learned with Mike that there were no rules to pleasure. While she'd still believed Kahn intended to have sex with her, she'd enjoyed his touch and was going along with his wishes. Her mistake had been opening herself to him emotionally.

After she'd realized that he meant to deny her gratification, it was too late to change her mind-set. He'd given her too much pleasure to regroup and turn her thoughts in other directions. While Master Chen had taught her methods to withdraw into her mind and how to separate her thoughts from the pain of the body, she hadn't seen the need until much too late.

The slaps on her bottom hadn't been anywhere near the physical punishment she regularly accepted as part of her martial arts training, but the spanking had stung her pride as much as her bottom—especially when the sting had become heat and the heat had heightened her arousal. Kahn's intent had clearly not been to cause pain, but maximum sexual stimulation—and after the wonderful pleasure he'd given her, after the marvelous heat he'd created, after she'd wanted sex with him with every fiber of her being, she hadn't been prepared for him to refuse to have sex.

She'd liked everything Kahn had done to her, every stroke, every caress, all the heat. But when he'd held out on her, when he'd stopped, she'd broken. Broken so completely that even now she couldn't stop the flood of tears. Couldn't summon the strength to answer Dora.

When Tessa didn't respond, Dora tried again. "Unless my sensors are failing, the skin on your bottom appears red. Do you require medical assistance?"

"What I require is a way to escape." Tessa shoved her hair out of her eyes, gingerly sat on her still stinging bottom, and quickly stood. At least she didn't have to worry about blowing her nose, the suit took care of that problem as well as absorbing her tears.

Dora's voice piped into the chamber stronger and more insistent than during her last visit. "But—"

"Look. Kahn set me up. I thought we were going to have sex. Instead, he enticed me with more pleasure than I'd known was possible, then the bastard refused to follow through. His methods are underhanded, offensive, and there's no reason I have to put up with him."

"What do you mean?"

"I thought the Challenge might have been my willingness to accept him as a partner—but I was so wrong. My second guess was that he was creating my sexual frustration to elicit my psi powers. But that didn't work, either. I don't have any latent psi. But the stubborn barbarian and Earth's leaders won't believe me. This mission was doomed to failure. Now that I've given this my best shot and failed, it's time to cut my losses."

"What are you saying?"

"I have no doubt Kahn plans to repeat his performance, which will have no more success than before." At the thought of a repeat performance, Tessa shuddered again. "And since I can't stop him"—her voice hitched at that admission—"I don't intend to be here when he returns. Are you going to help me or not?"

"What would you like me to do?" Dora asked.

Tessa picked up the eating utensil that she'd hidden earlier and held it up. "Besides stabbing Kahn through the heart, tell me where this will do the most good."

Dora's voice turned prim. "If your intention is murder, my program will not permit me to help you."

"Like this spoon/fork could even make a little dimple in Kahn's suit?" Tessa rolled her eyes. "For the record my intention is to escape."

"You are running away?"

"Even Kahn admitted my psi should have appeared before now. There's no point in staying." As much as she hated to give up on a mission, as much as she hated to fail, she wouldn't stay for more of Kahn's training when she saw not one iota of success.

"Dora, help me get to the shuttle. If I can return to Earth and explain what happened, they will find another candidate."

"Compliance." A tiny laser beamed from the ceiling and shone a dot of red light on the wall and Dora slipped back into friendly mode. "Try there. Pressure should open the door mechanism."

Without hesitation Tessa followed Dora's directions. "Like this?"

"Use one of the tines."

Tessa heard a thud like a footstep, but it might have been the irregular beat of her heart. "Is Kahn in the corridor?"

"The commander is at the communications center."

Tessa frowned and pressed harder. "Dora, I thought you only had sensors in here and on the shuttle."

Dora giggled. "I've been widening my capabilities."

"Way to go." Tessa carefully poked the wall. "Gaining information is always critical to survival. Often the one with the most data wins."

"Wins what?"

"Ah." The door slid open. "Sweet freedom."

Tessa saw no one outside on the moving corridor, just the "normal" and spectacular sight of fantastic crystal sculptures and alien machinery whose purposes she couldn't even guess. Although Dora had informed her otherwise, she'd half expected Kahn to be there ready to come down on her for damaging his equipment with an eating utensil instead of psi power.

"You have only gained access to the corridor," Dora said.

Tessa jumped at the sound of Dora's voice and almost told her to hush until she recalled that even if someone stood right next to her, in privacy mode no one would hear.

Dora continued, "And you are not a prisoner."

Tessa searched right, left, back over her shoulder, mostly from habit and not because she expected anyone to stop her, before stepping out of the chamber onto the moving walkway. "Don't tell me you bought Kahn's line of bullshit."

"I am a computer. I don't buy things. And I don't understand why Commander Kahn would want to sell you bovine manure."

Tessa ignored the translation problem. "Are there alarm systems to warn Kahn of my movement?"

"There are psi sensors and motion detectors—if he checks them. However, at the moment he is speaking to a woman with a large chest and his back is to the equipment."

"You said no one else was on board."

"She's still on Rystan. They are speaking over the hyperlink communications system."

Reassured that she stood a chance of actual escape, Tessa slipped into the hallway and dashed down the moving corridor toward the shuttle, the useful eating utensil still clutched in her hand. "Thanks."

"I have done nothing."

"You have been wonderful. Without you I wouldn't have a friend here. You showed me how to open the door."

"I am wonderful, aren't I? No one has ever told me that before."

Tessa could run and talk at the same time. "What's Kahn doing?"

"He's still in conference with Madame Big Chest. If I had a body, I'd want big breasts like that woman."

"No you wouldn't. Big breasts get in the way when you fight."

"I wouldn't want to fight." Dora's words turned dreamy. "I'd want to make love."

"Can we table this discussion until I'm safely away, please?" Tessa stopped at the big, solid shuttle hatch that she recognized from her trip to Earth. Her current position left her all too exposed in the corridor. "Dora, I need you to—"

As if reading her mind or simply anticipating her request, Dora again shone a light on the pressure-sensitive spot that would release the door.

"Thanks, you're a peach."

"I'd rather be wonderful than a peach."

Tessa pushed the utensil's tine into the red spot so hard that the metal bent. She flipped the utensil over and tried the other side. "It's not working."

"Patience." Dora actually released a very human-sounding sigh, which couldn't be that easy to replicate considering she didn't have lungs or vocal cords. "Uh-oh."

Tessa tensed but kept up the pressure. "What?"

"Kahn's ending his communication."

"Is he on to me? Can you tell what he's saying?"

"Sorry, he's invoked privacy mode. But from his expression, he doesn't look at all pleased."

"So what else is new?" Tessa pressed harder, her adrenaline kicking. This might be her only opportunity to escape before they cleared Earth's solar system. Then again, she had no idea how far the shuttle could go or how fast she could fly or if she might get lost.

One step at a time.

Finally, the hatch opened. She slipped inside, pleasantly surprised when the hatch automatically shut behind her and the interior lights came on. Finally her luck was changing, and she prayed that a craft built for emergency usage could be run by noneducated personnel and simple voice commands. She headed straight for the control console where Kahn had steered the shuttle earlier and studied the simple control stick.

"Dora, get us out of here. Maximum speed."

"Maximum speed would kill you since you don't know how to pressurize your suit against high g-forces."

"Well, do the best you can. I don't care if I lose consciousness, just don't kill me or that would defeat my purposes."

"I am not permitted to kill."

"What a shame," Tessa muttered, nixing the idea of attempting to turn the shuttle against Kahn after he discovered her absence and followed. She had no doubts he would pursue. Now it was simply a race to return home and lose herself among their multibillion population before Kahn caught up with her.

She hoped the lockers in the aft section contained supplies. "Do I have enough food, air, fuel, and water to make it to Earth?"

"Yes. The craft is fully stocked. If you lie down on the floor, I can navigate us out of here at a higher—"

"I'm there." Tessa sat, then lay on her back, cranking her neck to see the viewscreen. She could have chosen her stomach but then she couldn't have seen four different views on the viewscreen. The sight of the flight bay doors straight ahead, a sturdy wall of the starship to the rear, and one to each side. The pressure on her sore bottom enhanced her determination to leave. There was no point in staying for a mission she wasn't equipped to handle. She had no psi power. And staying would be like sending an astronaut into space without an oxygen supply. So there was no point in remaining and letting Kahn touch her again. "Head for Earth."

"Compliance."

The huge flight bay doors opened, and Tessa's ears popped as the shuttlecraft pressurized. Slowly, the ship lifted and floated toward the huge open doors.

Warning lights suddenly flashed, alarm bells sounded, and Dora's voice increased in volume. "Purple Alert. Purple Alert. Kahn is attempting to take computer control."

"How can I stop him?"

"You can override his command by placing the ship on manual control."

"Do it." Tessa's stomach lurched. "And tell me how to fly."

"The flight stick controls our motion," Dora instructed, as Tessa shoved off the floor and raced to the console. "Whichever direction you push the stick, the ship will follow. If you want to go right, push the stick to the right. Same for the left. If you want to go up, pull back on the stick. Down is the opposite."

She had no clue as to what made the ship go, but she

mastered the uncomplicated controls within minutes, grateful to the engineers who had designed the ship so simply a child could have flown her. The more Tessa pulled the stick, the faster she'd go, but speed was not yet required.

Maneuvering inside the tight space of the flight bay was tricky. Tessa edged forward slowly toward the blackness of space, careful not to scrape the ship against the bulkheads.

"Flight bay doors are closing," Dora reported.

Tessa's heart kicked up her throat. Kahn was trying to trap her and the shuttle inside the bay. Shoving the stick forward, she increased their speed, trying to beat the closing doors.

The communications screen lit up with Kahn's concerned face. "Turn the controls back on automatic and let the computer pilot the shuttle before you do real damage."

"Warning, Warning!" Dora's official tone sounded another alert. "Stop engines, we are on a collision course."

Tessa's hand tightened on the control but she didn't slow the ship. "Dora, plot maximum speed. Can we make it through the doors without crashing at full throttle?"

"No."

"Is there an emergency overdrive?"

"I don't understand."

"Can I boot us into high gear?"

"Not inside the bay."

"*Outside* the bay, the speed can be increased?" Tessa asked, her excitement leaping as adrenaline shot through her veins. She wasn't about to give up without considering every option.

"Once we're outside and away from the mothership, warp power can be initiated."

"Why can't we warp from right here?"

"The mothership would suffer damage," Dora told her.

"How much?"

"Estimated repair time: two days, three hours, and twenty-two minutes. Cost of repairs: two thousand Galactic credits. Loss of life: none."

She glanced again at the closing flight bay doors. "I can live with that. How do we go to warp?"

Dora made a light on the control panel blink. "Push that button."

Kahn shouted at Tessa through the holoscreen. "Don't—"

"Turn him off, please." Tessa couldn't afford distractions. The bay doors were already almost too narrow for the shuttle to escape. Still, she didn't hesitate to press the indicated button. "On my mark. Now."

The ship didn't accelerate. It jumped out of space into another place. Hyperspace. An overwhelming sensation of dizziness washed over her and Tessa clutched the console to steady herself. The viewscreen blurred into a crazy maelstrom of lights while her battered senses strived to perceive her surroundings. Gravity disappeared. A sensation of nausea arose as her stomach flip-flopped in an effort to seek a fixed harbor. Viewscreen lights pulsed at irregular intervals and Tessa's ears throbbed at the humming static. At the same time, her sense of smell heightened. Enhanced by the sweet mustiness of the alien environment, the odor contributed to her feelings of nausea. When she thought she couldn't stand the heightened sensations another second, the warp drive abruptly kicked off and the ship returned to normal space.

"Dora, can Kahn track us?" asked Tessa.

"Not through hyperspace."

She had escaped!

Elation swept over her at the thought of returning to Earth. With Dora's help, she could go home and regroup. Earth's engineers could analyze the ship, delve into the secret warp drive and maybe replicate the design. Maybe they could even figure out a way to get off the damn suit, which continued to torment her, but at lower levels than before.

However, no way would she let anyone tamper with Dora. In fact, Tessa wasn't sure if Earth should give back the shuttle at all. Perhaps they could use the shuttle to trade for the equipment to clean up their atmosphere.

Although Dora had turned off communications, the light still blinked, signaling an incoming message. "Dora, if I answer Kahn, can he track me?"

"No. Communication transmissions go through hyperspace, too."

Tessa pressed the blinking light. Kahn's amber eyes narrowed on her in obvious irritation and he pressed his lips together tightly, jaws clenched. He scowled at her, his tone clipped, his voice devoid of inflection, yet still demanding. "Are you all right? Have you sustained any damage?"

"I'm fine, thanks." Astonished that his first words to her revealed concern for her welfare, she answered with as much politeness as she could muster. Now that she had the upper hand, she could afford to be gracious. "How about yourself?"

"The ship will require repairs." Kahn's voice, although annoyed, revealed no hint of the reversal he'd suffered.

"I'm sorry about the damage, but I *did* check and the computer informed me that there would be no loss of life."

"The damage to the flight bay doors is extensive."

"When you tried to trap me, you left me no choice but to warp into hyperspace," Tessa reminded him, pleased at how nonchalant she sounded, when in truth his holoimage and voice set her heart hammering, reminding her exactly how much pleasure he'd once given her. She wondered how long it would take for her to fully recover from what he'd done to her.

"This is my fault," Kahn admitted. "I thought you would fall asleep. Never before has a Challenge candidate learned to operate mechanical technology prior to mastering their suit's biomechanics. I never expected you to flee to the shuttle without mastering your psi. I won't underestimate you again."

She didn't plan to give him another opportunity. The man was already methodically careful, and she suspected her getting away had been a stroke of luck that might never happen again.

He frowned at her, his head cocked to one side, as if trying to figure out what made her tick. "Perhaps your reckless behavior is responsible for your continued failure to progress."

"I'm sorry I've disappointed you." But she wasn't. She was happy to be free, but she wouldn't gloat—even if she felt like dancing on the bulkheads. She couldn't be completely happy when she recalled that Earth's hopes to clean up their pollution problem had rested on her shoulders. And she'd failed. Besides, Master Chen had drilled too many manners and too much caution into her to forget that she wasn't safe quite yet.

Kahn locked gazes with her. "Once repaired, my ship will travel ten times faster than your shuttle." *Oh, no.* "And since I know your final destination, I can simply plot a hyperspace jump to intercept your flight."

Oh, God. She'd thought she'd escaped him, but apparently she hadn't—unless he was trying to trick her. She turned away so he couldn't see her talk to the computer. "Dora, is that true?"

"Yes."

Tired, emotionally spent, but nowhere near ready to quit, Tessa faced Kahn, drumming her fingers on the console and thinking furiously. "Kahn, let me go. I'll find a way to pay for the damages. Earth can send another candidate—one better suited to the task."

"I cannot." To give the big guy credit, he really did look sorry and his voice oozed sympathy. "Even if I wished to accept another, it's against Challenge rules to change candidates once training has begun."

"Suppose I died?"

"Then I would have failed."

"But there is *no* reason to continue. I have no psi power."

"That remains to be seen." At his statement another shudder zinged up her spine. "And *you* must pay for the damages to this ship. That is the law, and by accepting the Challenge, you are bound by it," he stated firmly.

"I was not a rich woman in my own time, and in this one,

I don't even have clothes on my back," Tessa countered.

"Then you will pay me with the assets you possess."

She had to stop herself from shriveling at Kahn's calm yet mocking expression. At the glint in his amber eyes, she thanked her lucky stars that for the moment, his ship was damaged and couldn't come after her. "Goodbye, Kahn, though I can't say it's been a pleasure."

"Can't you?" Apparently, he couldn't resist one last parting shot before she severed communications.

Even beyond the spaceman's current reach, she found the glint in his amber eyes unbearably disturbing, almost as disturbing as his commitment to find her. No way could she let that happen. She recalled every tormented moment of his touch and her determination hardened.

The shuttle flew toward Earth, increasing the distance between them, but the likelihood of recapture remained at the forefront of her thoughts. "Dora, if we jump back into hyperspace and don't go directly to Earth, Kahn can't find me, right?"

"Theoretically, that is correct."

She absolutely, positively, didn't want him to recapture her. Her bottom still stung, her pride was tattered. But worst of all, her body ached for him. Even now, she wanted his hands back on her. She wanted his lips on hers. She wanted his clever fingers performing their magic. She wanted completion. And release.

Her body may have ached for him but she hardened her heart. Kahn wouldn't give her what she desired. He'd simply make the desire worse.

Knowing this might be her best chance to escape, she couldn't afford to waste the opportunity. Heart and mind in accord, she spoke with certainty. "Dora, put me in contact with Earth's authorities."

"I cannot. Kahn's jammed our communications systems."

"But we just spoke to him."

"The channel to the starship is still open."

"I'll contact Earth later and let them try to negotiate for a new candidate to take my place. For now, please set a course for . . . Mars. We can hide in orbit behind the planet."

And then finally, Tessa slept.

8

Kahn had consulted with legal experts who saw only one way for him to win the Challenge after Tessa's betrayal. Every atom of his Rystani soul resisted what he must do. But he had no choice. He couldn't lie about Tessa's theft of the shuttlecraft—not with Federation sensors and cameras onboard to monitor his and her actions. Her rebelliousness had taken all options from him—except one.

Kahn slept only in short naps. Mostly, he supervised the robotic repair of the bay doors. Until they could once again close, he couldn't warp through hyperspace and follow Tessa. However, after he engaged the starship's big engines, he'd catch her in no time, tracking her with the device he'd placed in her suit for just such an emergency. So he had no reason to drive himself so hard, except that time was running out. She should have exhibited psi ability by now.

When he still couldn't get a handle on his churning gut,

he retreated to Tessa's chamber to lose himself in the only way he knew how. "Exercise program on."

"Choose your sport," the computer directed.

"Hand-to-hand combat."

"State the level."

"Ten."

"Ten is for experts."

"Command override. Alphex 1020."

"Medical monitoring required," the computer informed him. At the first sign he was in distress or danger, the computer would automatically shut down.

"Understood."

Kahn eased into a fighting stance and cleared his mind of the Earthling. With the program set on the maximum sparring difficulty, he would have to use every brain cell he had to avoid injury. He breathed in several long breaths, and released them slowly and envisioned the clean white snow of Rystan.

"Begin," he ordered.

His holographic opponent lunged. Kahn shifted. His foe faked a jab and then roared in with a spinning round kick to the head. Kahn blocked, countered, and . . . missed. Off balance, he altered his suit to null gravity, somersaulted, pushed off the wall near the ceiling, turned the gravity back on, and dived at the hologram at twice normal speed. His opponent spun, back-fisted, and caught his shoulder. Pain radiated down Kahn's arm. Pain he welcomed.

For more than thirty minutes, he worked out his anger and frustration with Tessa, but mostly with himself and his untenable position. When he ended the program, his chest heaved, his lungs burned, and he needed a pitcher of water to replace the fluids he'd lost, but he still hadn't found the peace and calm that a good workout usually brought him.

Stars. Why hadn't he watched her more closely? After the dreadful way he'd treated her, albeit with the best of intentions, he should have considered she'd try to flee. Now, she had broken the law and they would both pay for the rest of their lives. He only hoped that Earth and Rystan wouldn't also suffer consequences.

Exactly two days and four hours later, the computer informed him, "The flight bay door repairs are now completed."

"Where's the shuttle?"

"Sensors scanning."

"And?" Kahn prodded, heading toward the helm.

"The shuttle is not at the expected location."

"Damn, she must have warped into hyperspace again." Kahn wasn't worried. He couldn't track the ship or communications through hyperspace, but once she dropped out of warp, her suit's built-in transmitter would pinpoint her exact location.

Except when he scanned the area of space between his ship and Earth, she wasn't there. His heart jammed up against his ribs. Had she crashed the ship? The suit's transmitter wouldn't work if she'd died.

However, if she'd flown to the back side of her world, the planet's mass would block transmission. "Prepare for hyperspace."

"Destination?"

"Earth." But before they left, Kahn scanned the rest of the solar system. Nothing. "Jump."

Braced against the heightened awareness of his senses that occurred in hyperspace, Kahn waited impatiently for the return to normal space. He checked the sensor readings. Nothing. He tried the suit's locator. Nothing.

Again he searched the rest of the solar system, methodically starting with Mercury and Venus and then outward to the colder planets. Earth hadn't been blocking her signal, another world had been. Once again he'd underestimated her.

"Jump for Mars."

* * *

Tessa stared out the viewscreen in the hopes her people had colonized Mars over the last three centuries. After multiple shuttle disasters during her lifetime, the space program had lost popularity. She suspected Earth's leaders had been reluctant to spend funds on reaching another planet when the money could be better invested on efforts to solve Earth's critical environmental problems.

She might be the first Earthling to have gazed at Mars from orbit, and while she marveled at the reddish mountains and crater-pocked deserts, she hungered for a hint of humanity. "Dora, didn't our astronauts make it out this far?"

"My sensors haven't picked up any recent activity. A few probes crashed on this world several hundred years ago. But since then—nothing."

Tessa supposed she should feel some satisfaction in being the first Earthling to orbit Mars, yet she knew Kahn was out there hunting her. The man wouldn't stop searching until the Challenge period or she expired—whichever came first.

"Any sign of Kahn's ship?"

"He's warped into hyperspace."

"How do you know?" Tessa turned away from the Martian landscape to the console viewscreen. During the last two days, she'd learned that the blinking green light signified the shuttle's position. A blinking line showed their current orbit in relation to Mars, and on command, Dora could zoom out and show her Earth, too.

"Going to warp leaves a telltale autograph in space and each engine leaves a different signature pattern. I collate the data and—"

"Okay. Will we have any warning if—"

"He's here."

Fear galloped down her spine, but Tessa wasn't ready to give up. "Go to warp."

"We can't. He's grabbed us with a clutch beam."

Tessa couldn't feel the beam, but she imagined a fly didn't

recognize that a spider was pulling it into its web, either. "Can we shake loose?"

"Not enough power."

"Come on, Dora. Search your data banks. How do we get away?"

"A shuttle this size cannot escape a clutch beam."

Tessa didn't like that answer. She had no idea how Kahn had found her, but now wasn't the time to ask. She had more immediate problems—like escaping once more. "Do we have any weapons?"

"I'm not permitted to fire on the mothership."

"Will our weapons sever the clutch beam?"

"No."

"Are you telling me that there is nothing I can do? Nothing?"

"I am sorry."

"It's not your fault." Tessa slumped against the console, her pulse racing. She couldn't stop Kahn from hauling her back into the flight bay. She couldn't stop Kahn from boarding. She couldn't stop Kahn.

She'd been defeated in battle many times, but never had the consequences been so severe. She reminded herself that she'd escaped him once. He was not perfect. Maybe she could escape again. But flight would be much more difficult with him monitoring her. Her biggest weapon had been surprise— which she'd lost along with her freedom. And even worse, the more time that passed, the less chance Earth would have to substitute a more suitable candidate. Although Kahn had claimed the candidate couldn't be switched, there had to be some wriggle room. But she hadn't even succeeded in notifying Earth of her lack of psi.

Probably ten minutes passed before the clutch beam pulled the shuttle back into the flight bay with its newly repaired doors. Those minutes flew by like seconds, and yet it contradictorily seemed to take a lifetime.

The airlocks recycled and the pressure changed. The door

opened and Kahn strode inside the shuttle. In the short time she'd been away, she'd forgotten his height and mass, how he towered over her. But worse, his face could have been carved of Martian granite.

Tessa forced back her shoulders, raised her chin, and tried not to think ahead. From the frosty glare in his eyes that took an inventory of her from her bare feet, up her naked torso to her eyes, she figured she might be better off if she remained silent. She most certainly didn't want to risk loosening the temper he'd obviously reined in so tightly.

"Woman, you have done more damage than you know."

"To your ship?"

He shook his head, and while she had no idea why he was so enraged, she didn't want to know. Her mouth went sand dry and she simply waited for his words to fall like blows.

"The theft of the shuttle is a high crime against the Federation."

Her eyes narrowed. "The shuttle has been returned." She didn't understand why he had become so stern and more serious than normal or why he spoke in the voice of doom. Was she going to jail? She'd actually find an eight-by-ten cell preferable to remaining with him.

"A shuttle is the mothership's only lifeboat. By stealing it you placed a life in danger. If there had been an emergency aboard the mothership—"

"Was there?"

"That's not the point. I believe your world incarcerates criminals for *attempted* murder, don't they?"

"I meant you no harm."

"The Federation has no way to measure intent. There's no need for a trial since the facts are unrefutable. The penalty is death."

She had no reason to believe him, except that as far as she knew, he'd never lied to her, and he practically vibrated with anger, which indicated the seriousness of her actions just as much as his words. She didn't want to die, but living didn't seem all that appealing at the moment. If not she had to continue to put up with him. "I should have died three hundred years ago."

"Silence."

Damn it. She'd known anything she said would make matters worse. Why did she have to go and open her mouth? Because part of her still believed she could extricate herself from her fate. Because part of her believed that if she could just reach Earth and she could discuss the problem of her lack of psi with the authorities, a solution could be found.

Like an animal caught in a trap about to snap shut, she was clawing to escape. And couldn't.

"There is only one exception to the death penalty."

She waited, her breath catching in her throat, barely daring to hope.

"During times of courtship, certain behaviors are forgiven."

Courtship? She cocked a hand on her hip. "You realize I don't have a clue what you're talking about."

"Except for murder, a crime committed during a lovers' quarrel can be forgiven under certain circumstances."

They weren't lovers, but she didn't want to go there. "What circumstances?"

"If we wed, the crime will be forgiven."

"No." She didn't have to think. She would truly rather be dead than spend more time with Kahn. Death was clean and preferable to even one more hour of that same kind of treatment from him. She might be Earth's last hope for clean air and oceans, but she didn't have any psi, so staying alive would serve no purpose.

Kahn folded his arms across his chest, his expression resolute. "I am not asking."

"Good. Tell me how long I have to live so I can prepare myself."

"You do not understand. The choice is not yours—but mine."

No. "Says who?"

"Say our laws. You will be my wife."

No. "For how long?"

"Forever."

No. "You've never heard of the civilized custom of divorce?"

He shook his head.

She backed away from him until the console stopped her retreat. It was one thing to die during an honorable mission for her world, quite another to commit the rest of her life to . . . him. To a life with no freedom. To a life on his world. "You don't want to do this."

"For once you're right. I don't." Distaste flickered in the depths of those eyes, then hardened. "But winning the Challenge for Rystan and Earth is more important than our wishes. And you cannot win the Challenge if you are dead."

"Now there's a romantic proposal." She used sarcasm to try to shut down the maelstrom of fear, an effort equivalent to spitting against a tornado. Tessa wasn't afraid of death. She was afraid of living without freedom and hope. She couldn't imagine a fate worse than marriage to this man. As if stuck in a nightmare, she tried to find a way out, a way to awaken. This couldn't be happening—but with Kahn so solidly standing there issuing demands, she couldn't deny her situation.

She had not only lost everyone she'd known, her job, and her world; she'd lost her freedom. And despite her ramrod-straight spine, she swayed on her feet, dark despair clamping down on her from all sides until she couldn't breathe.

And even worse, she'd failed Earth.

"Woman, enough sarcasm. You have insulted me—"

She might be suffocating, but she would protest with every last freedom-loving cell in her. "I haven't begun to—"

"You will promise to follow Rystani customs. Our women do not speak with such rudeness to their men."

No. "I will make no such promises."

"You will make them and you will keep your word . . . because if you do not, we can spend every night like we spent our last hours together. With you bent over my lap, begging me."

At his intimidation, the blackness in her soul swirled with rage and an impotence that she'd never known before. Giving her no quarter, no room to maneuver, he might as well have nailed her to the wall. Realizing the power he wielded over her set her heart frantically beating.

"Are you saying that if I become your wife and obey your customs, you will never do that to me again?"

"I shall do with you whatever I wish."

He wouldn't bargain. He wouldn't give one damn inch. And there was absolutely nothing she could do to stop him.

As if weary of arguing with her, Kahn turned on the shuttle's viewscreen, grabbed her hand and tugged her over to watch scenes from Earth flash across it. She saw people wearing masks to breathe. Huge masses of clouds so dirty they obstructed entire cities, oceans that were no longer blue, but brown, and rivers clogged with filth, children playing on the banks.

Kahn made more adjustments to the screen. "This is Rystan." The view was from orbit. He pointed to the glowing continents in both hemispheres. "That's from radiation." His entire world glowed, except at the poles where snow and ice covered the land. At the sight of the harsh landscape she more than understood his desperation to succeed and wished she could help, but she couldn't because she had no psi and couldn't win the Challenge without the skill.

She spoke past the lump of frustration in her throat. "It's difficult to believe anyone could survive on Rystan."

"We ruined a world of beauty. Rystan's climate was once like your Earth, but then atomic wars wiped out billions. The major continents will remain radioactive and uninhabitable for thousands of years. There aren't many of us left and we're barely surviving at the north and south poles. We don't have the resources to fight the Endekians for our world—"

"Why would they want Rystan?" She didn't understand why anyone would want to live there.

"Our world has glow stones that are unique throughout the Federation. They provide light and heat without another source of fuel."

"If the glow stones are so valuable, why can't you trade them for goods to help you survive?"

"Because glow stones are atomic in nature. Their natural shielding prevents radiation, but when inserted into projectile missiles, the stones become bombs."

"And the Federation won't help you?"

"They won't send troops to defend us until we are a full-fledged member."

"What sort of organization is your Federation if its leaders aren't concerned over nuclear threats?"

"Even the Federation has limited resources. Your country was known as the wealthiest and most democratic of its time. Yet when India and Pakistan threatened to annihilate one another, your United Nations did not send a peacekeeping force. Such decisions are made in our Federation, too. For Rystan's voice to be heard, we need full status."

"And for Rystan to acquire that status, I have to succeed at the Challenge?" she whispered, surprised he'd studied so much Earth history and understanding his argument. With the fate of two worlds at stake, she couldn't give up—even if the odds of success appeared hopeless. And neither could he. The Challenge that had once been a mission had now turned into a life sentence. She would have to marry Kahn.

Her bleak future swallowed her like a black hole where time stood still and misery lasted forever. Her spirit shriveled. He'd given her no choice but to cave. In the depth of her despair, a sensation she'd never experienced jolted her from her emotional pain. Oh, God. What had he done to her now?

The sensations coalesced, then exploded.

* * *

"Follow me, woman. We must prepare for a wedding."
Floored by the fact that the Earthling would prefer death to
marriage to him, Kahn spun on his heel and gave her his
back to hide his supreme irritation at her unreasonable attitude. She never reacted as he expected. When he'd mentioned
the death penalty, he'd assumed she would fall apart. She
hadn't. When he told her how he could save her, he'd expected
her to be grateful. She wasn't. And when he'd explained her
fate, taking the decision out of her hands, did she appreciate
that he was willing to shoulder a lifetime of responsibility of
protecting and providing for her? No, she didn't.

Without years of training, he would never have noticed
a totally unexpected psi attack launched at his back. Kahn
responded with his own psi out of instinct. Pivoting, he'd
blocked and counterstruck, flinging his adversary across the
shuttle.

Stars! *No*. Only after committing to the block and counterstrike did his brain connect all the elements. Tessa had attacked him. Tessa had summoned her psi power. And he'd
flung her toward a wall, responding as he would have to any
sudden and unexpected assault. Arms flung wide, she flailed
in midair, crashed into a bulkhead with a sickening thud. Even
as she crumpled, he lunged across the room and caught her
before she hit the floor.

Fearing the worst, he spoke to the computer. "Medical
diagnosis."

"She is unconscious." The computer gave him a medical
evaluation. "Her skull is not fractured. The brain is not
swelling. She should recover with a powerful headache and
a painful lump."

Kahn had never struck a woman in his life. Then again, a
woman had never attacked him, either. Still, he had no excuse. Rystani men protected their women; they valued their
women. When he had sexually stimulated her and then

stopped, he'd mistreated her hoping to evoke her psi. This time he didn't even have a good excuse. No matter the circumstances, what he had done was unpardonable. Even if she'd landed her intended blow, Tessa's attack couldn't have hurt him; she didn't have enough focus or power. But when he'd responded, he'd reacted without thought and on sheer instinct, as a warrior would have under attack by a deadly force in battle. Still, his action had been totally unacceptable. Unforgivable. If they'd been on Rystan, his offense could have cost him his position as leader, maybe gotten him banished from Rian, his village. Even worse, he might have permanently damaged her.

Holding her in his arms, he hugged her gently against his chest and prayed for her quick recovery. "Will it hurt to move her?"

"No," the computer answered.

His heart heavy, Kahn exited the shuttle, carrying Tessa. She had been through so much trauma and now he'd added to her burden. He headed directly for her chamber, listening for a moan, hoping for a flutter of the eyelids, a hint to indicate she would fully recover.

She remained limp in his arms, and he berated himself for his carelessness. He sat on the dais, held her in his arms, nestling her head against his shoulder. Who would have thought such a tiny pink female could cause so much trouble? Or react to her first psi experience with an attack?

In the Federation's history of Challenge contenders, no female had ever comported herself with such violence. She should have been covering her nudity and changing her suit's transparency, but no, she'd jammed her fist at his face.

A soft moan drew his gaze to her. Slowly, her eyelids opened. Clouded with confusion, her eyes stared at him, then widened as she brushed a lock of hair from her eyes. "What happened?"

"I owe you an apology."

"You do?"

She didn't squirm or fidget in his arms and appeared quite puzzled by his words. Perhaps she didn't remember.

"I am deeply sorry for hitting you."

"I attacked. You countered. No big deal."

She did remember, and stunned, he shook his head. He'd treated her terribly, like an uncivilized Endekian. He'd struck her and it was no big deal? She must not be thinking clearly due to the blow to her temple. "How's your head?"

She gently touched the swelling and winced. "I'll live. But what happened?"

"I hit you. Then you smashed into the bulkhead."

"Before that?" she demanded with exasperation. "I attacked you, but with a force . . . that shot me across the room like a cannonball."

He grinned. "You did it." Then he kissed her forehead, relieved she would be okay, happy that she'd finally succeeded.

"I did what?"

He kissed her cheek. "You used your psi power."

She jumped off his lap and paced, totally ignoring her injuries. Tessa acted as if the pain were inconsequential. He would have thought she was fine, except he could see the swelling above her ear and the blood trickling down her face before the suit absorbed it.

"I have psi power." Her voice rose an octave in wonder. "I never really believed you."

"If you hadn't taken me by surprise . . . I would have not hurt you."

"I understand."

How could she be so casual about his negligence? He could have killed her. She must not comprehend the gravity of what he'd done. "After you launched that attack, I reacted instinctively, I should never have—"

"Look, you defended yourself. It's not a problem."

"It isn't?" He would never understand her. She made a huge fuss over his stopping before she reached sexual completion, yet when he'd raised his fist to her, she acted as if he'd simply tripped and bumped her.

She stopped pacing and placed her hands on her hips. "Kahn, how did I activate my psi?"

"You tell me," he challenged her. Proud of Tessa for going straight to the most important detail, he restrained a grin.

She shook her head as if recalling a terrible moment. "I don't want to go there again."

"You must." At the dark look on her face, he tempered his demand. "But if you wish to rest or wait until you heal—"

"I'm fine."

She wasn't fine. The skin around her eye was darkening. Tomorrow, she would no doubt sport an ugly bruise. Every time he looked at her, he would remember his shame.

She gestured for him to rise to his feet. "I want to try that maneuver again."

His lower jaw dropped. "What did you say?"

"I want to attack you again."

"No."

"Look. This time you'll be prepared. This time you won't hurt me."

"This is not the way we train females."

"Yeah, well, *your* method didn't work, did it?" She looked as if she wanted to say something, hesitated, then took a deep breath. "Exactly how do you train male candidates?"

"With combat."

"Well, duh. Did you ever think that combat might work for me?"

She stared at him as if he were the most stupid man in the universe, waiting for an answer. Tense, balanced on the balls of her feet, her hands loose, she looked ready for action. But she had no idea what she was suggesting. He couldn't even believe she'd think such a thing. On Rystan men didn't battle women, they protected them. At least after the frustration of sexual stimulation she wouldn't have cuts, bruises, or broken bones. No, what she asked was unthinkable—except that her outrageous suggestion might be the only way to train her for the Challenge. She couldn't be the only one expected to make adjustments. Perhaps he should reconsider. No matter how much yielding to her suggestion went against his Rystani customs, winning the Challenge had to take precedence, didn't it?

He needed more time to come to a decision. "We will talk no more about your training for now. Today is our wedding day. You must learn our customs and what a Rystani man expects of his obedient wife."

She sputtered. "Excuse me. I'm more interested in—"

"Rystani wives don't argue with their husbands."

"Really? If the other men are like you, I find that impossible to believe."

He stood, placed his hands on her waist, and lifted her until her eyes were level with his. "Are you calling me a liar?"

"I wouldn't dream of it." She chuckled, a deep rumbling laugh that made him want to shake her. Had the knot on her head made her lose her sense of reason?

When she finally stopped laughing, she cocked one haughty eyebrow. "Do good Rystani wives cook?"

"Of course."

"I don't know how."

He set her back on her feet and loomed over her, trying hard to forget the delicious meals Lael had once prepared for him and how she'd enjoyed his praise of her cooking. "You will learn to cook. In fact, it's your job to prepare a wedding feast for us."

"Nor do I know how to clean. Or sew. Or take care of children. I am not good wife material any more than you are good husband material."

"Lael never had any complaints," he muttered, thinking that he'd never have thought he would be so happy to hear Tessa insult him again. Relief that he hadn't caused real damage must be blindsiding him to his fate of having to put up with her for a lifetime.

"Lael?" Tessa's eyes narrowed.

"My wife. An Endekian killed her."

"I'm sorry," she told him, her tone sincere. "Do you have children?"

He shook his head, his throat clogged with grief that wasn't quite as thick as before he'd met Tessa. He recalled her words that no one would replace Mike in her heart but that she was sure she could love again. Sometimes she seemed so wise and well balanced. However, he'd never wanted to care again. Caring caused pain and he'd certainly had enough loss in his lifetime. But then so had she and he marveled at her courage.

Tessa must have seen the torment in his eyes. "Didn't you once tell me that if a Rystani's mate died, another would be found?"

"I refused. As leader of my people, I had enough to worry about. I didn't intend to remarry."

"You can still change your mind."

No, he could not. He couldn't let her die for stealing the spaceship—not when it was his fault he'd let her escape. Not after she'd proven she had psi ability that might allow her to win the Challenge.

She must have read the answer in his eyes. "Kahn, you deserve a wife who will be proud to keep your home and raise your children. I'm sorry that you're stuck with me, because I am so obviously unqualified. Perhaps after the Challenge is done, we can go our separate ways."

"You will adjust to our ways. Don't think to fight me on this, woman. Life on Rystan is hard enough without a man coming home to strife. Since we must make this sacrifice of marriage and since we will live in my world, the least you can do is adapt to our customs."

He thought she might argue about where they would live, but even she understood that his people needed him. And she had no ties at all on Earth.

She hesitated, then words burst out of her as if she couldn't keep them inside. "If we wed, I also want something in return."

He would make no concessions. Didn't she yet understand that winning the Challenge came before their own preferences? "You will do as I say."

"Wouldn't you rather I was willing?"

Yes. And admitting so would give her negotiating powers. Yet his silence seemed to tell her what she wanted to know.

She bit her bottom lip, then raised her eyes to his. "I'll agree to follow your customs as well as I'm able. In return, you train me for the Challenge as you would a man."

Such an important decision could not be made without much thought. "I will consider your request."

Her eyes darkened. "I understand that to you hitting a woman is unacceptable. But torturing me sexually is fine and dandy?"

He glared at her, wishing he could explain that his behavior was no more acceptable to him than to her. "I would never treat a Rystani woman that way."

"But since I'm not Rystani, it's okay?"

"The necessity of winning the Challenge changes the rules of acceptable behavior."

"Not in my mind." She shook her head. "The ends don't justify the means."

He couldn't argue his reasons for his actions without explaining more than he should. And for now, it would not hurt her to believe that she had to obey him or suffer consequences she wouldn't like. "This is my world. You will abide by our marriage laws."

Stubborn as a warrior, Tessa wouldn't give up, and she shot him a saucy grin. "What would you say to a little bet?"

He deliberately looked her up and down, knowing her nudity bothered her and needing to prove a point—that she couldn't manipulate him. Winning the Challenge was simply too critical to too many people for him to let her think she could do as she pleased. "I will take what I want. You have nothing to wager."

"Actually, I do. Wouldn't you prefer to have my cooperation?"

"I'll have that either way."

"You said life was hard on your planet. You don't want strife. Do you really want to spend the rest of our lives fighting one another?" He didn't appreciate her using his own words against him. When he didn't answer, she continued. "Must I remind you that for me to win the Challenge and save your people, you need my cooperation? I'm willing to bet that I can defeat you in unarmed combat—if you don't use your suit."

"You wouldn't know if I used it or not." As abhorrent as he found her suggestion, in truth, he was actually considering her request. He couldn't ignore that she hadn't responded at all to the sexual frustration or that her first use of psi had been an attack. She wasn't Rystani, she was from Earth, and he should have taken her background into account sooner.

"Your honor would forbid you from cheating. I'll trust you to be true to your word. And if I defeat you, you'll train me as a man."

Still undecided, he asked, "And if you lose?"

She spoke boldly. "If I lose—we'll do everything your way, and with my full participation."

As if knowing that he couldn't make up his mind on the matter, she eyed him with a distinct twinkle in her eyes. "I'm sure a man of your enormous fighting abilities can subdue little ole me without throwing a punch."

True. He could wrestle her to the floor and pin her with his weight. Or he could use *mai-slan-hi* against her joints. Perhaps a gentle wrist twist to put her on her knees. He could defeat her without striking her, yet it bothered him that she seemed to know he could do so, and yet she'd still asked to make this strange bet anyway.

"I agree." With a psi thought he lowered the dais until it once again became part of the deck, leaving them a wide, flat surface and nothing to trip over or run into. Then he deactivated his suit.

She widened her stance and raised her hands in a defensive gesture. "Shall we begin?"

9

"Don't you wish to first rest and recover from your injuries?" Kahn asked Tessa with more kindness than she'd heard from him since she'd arrived in space.

Apparently, his striking her had broken a taboo that made him feel guilty. *Good.* Perhaps that guilt would even the match. Although she'd practiced martial arts all her life, he must be double her weight, and his long reach and superior strength gave him a huge advantage.

Still, the bigger the man, the harder he fell.

She could defeat him by using his own strength and weight against him. She had to, especially since she understood that his training sessions in sexual frustration would be endlessly repeated if she didn't win this bet. The fate of Earth might very well depend on the outcome of this bout because Tessa very much wanted to learn to use her psi. And if she won, he could frustrate her all he wanted while he taught her how to fight with her psi powers. She could handle that kind of disappointment and hard work.

And perhaps if she defeated him this once, just maybe he'd respect her for her different attitude, because the idea of marriage to a man who couldn't bend, not even to save his world, disturbed her on many levels. That he'd given her this opportunity told her of his desperation, but it also told her he had the ability to change.

Kahn dropped into a bent-kneed, wide-footed stance that balanced him and gave him the ability to move left or right, back or forward. He cocked his wrists, leaving his hands straight. Balanced on the balls of her feet, Tessa circled, watching his eyes, and searching for an opening.

She feinted to the right, spun to her left, and swept his front foot. He lifted the foot to counter her sweep and shifted out of reach, but she still jammed an elbow into his ribs.

He grunted and grinned. "Try that again, woman."

Not frickin' likely. No way would she repeat a move and give him a chance to grab her and use his superior strength against her. Instead, she lunged at an angle and struck with a blow to his jaw. He countered the face strike but missed her simultaneous side kick to his groin. Only a last-minute twist of his hips saved him from a painful injury.

He frowned. She chuckled. "What? You don't want me to try that move again?"

"Your blows cannot hurt me."

That's exactly what she wanted him to think. She needed overconfidence to make him careless, and thanks to Master Chen's training, she would turn his confidence to her advantage.

Master Chen hadn't taught Tessa only technique, he'd also taught her strategy, and he'd fed her mind with the belief she could conquer any opponent if she set her mind to the task. While the eighty-year-old sensei had found a new reason to live as he tutored Tessa, his star pupil, he'd pushed her to her limit. She'd developed an acute awareness of timing, of space, and—most important of all—of trusting her skills. She'd never realized how proficient she had become until he'd entered her in her first and only competition, the World Karate Championship. Tessa had dominated the fighting, winning a title. Shortly afterward, her mentor died and she'd never competed again.

Instead, she had delved into the secret world of the ninja, studying under Master Funishoki. Tessa learned to sneak silently upon an opponent and kill without ever being seen. She was the shadow to be feared in the night. The enemy you never saw or heard. Over three hundred and thirty years ago, she'd guarded Daron Garner, and the sixty-year-old wheeler-dealer business tycoon had shown his appreciation for her saving his life by making sure she'd been assigned to the presidential protective detail. And she'd learned additional skills after the Secret Service recruited her.

Now, she would need every one of them. Kahn was keeping strict control over his temper. Despite landing a series of blows to his neck, chest, and thigh, she hadn't done real damage. To defeat him, she needed to goad him into an attack where she could use his power against him. But he wasn't even trying to attack, merely staying on guard and countering her when possible.

"You needn't be so very careful, Kahn. I won't hurt you— at least not badly." She shifted, spun, caught his thigh in a glancing kick.

With his thighs thick as tree trunks, he didn't so much as budge. Yet the skin reddened as blood rose to the surface. The big man was keeping his word. He hadn't raised his psi shields, or she wouldn't have seen the evidence of her accumulation of strikes.

He chuckled, but never relaxed the wariness in his eyes. "The only offensive move I plan to make is riding you on our wedding night."

A trickle of sweat seeped down his brow and she goaded him. "Let's hope your stamina at lovemaking is better than when you're fighting."

He glowered at her. "I'm also looking forward to your accommodating my every request."

Perhaps she could distract him with sex talk. "I will deny you nothing." She performed a spinning back kick and spiked her heel into his chest. "You will stroke my breasts or lick them and I will be thinking of"—she slammed a side-thrust kick at his groin—"pleasing you, so very much."

Between her words and her blows, she could see anger building in those careful amber eyes. When he finally pounced, she almost didn't react quickly enough. Almost. Kahn lunged straight at her, coming in fast and hard with his arms outstretched, his hands ready to grab her.

She dropped to her bottom, planted her feet in his stomach and catapulted him over her head. Even as she fought, she realized that he'd adjusted her suit. When she'd dropped, the floor hadn't met her bottom with a normal force. Even as he'd attacked, he'd protected her.

Forced to give up his plan to grab her, he slapped his palms on the floor, ducked his head, and rolled. However, she somersaulted backward and ended up astride his chest, her wrist cocked with a straight-edged knifehand to his throat. "You adjusted my suit."

"To protect you," he admitted.

He'd adjusted her suit to prevent an injury, but hadn't touched his own. Both of them knew she could have ended the fight with the death blow she'd held back.

"You've won." He spoke with respect. "You have what you wanted."

She expected to see defeat in his eyes, but not regret. At first she thought his disappointment was self-directed, but then she realized her error. He used his psi power to regain his feet and was staring at her with confusion.

The uncertainty in his eyes bothered her more than she

wanted to admit. She stood and backed away a few steps, saying nothing because there was nothing to say. By defeating him, she'd proven to him that she was everything he didn't want in a wife. However, she wouldn't apologize. She was what she was.

Since she had won the bet, she now wished to marry him instead of suffering the death penalty, but she feared he now felt otherwise. She could see he wanted no part of her in his life, but she already knew him well enough to understand that his dedication to his people would override his personal preferences.

She kept her voice soft and level. "If you have changed your mind about our marriage, I will accept your decision."

After she'd so obviously rocked his world, her words appeared to steady him. "I am a man of my word." At his statement, tension eased out of her. "You must prepare a meal for our wedding ceremony. Also, there is a ritual bathing and then we place ceremonial bands on one another."

"When will our wedding take place?"

"You shall have time to rest. We shall marry two hours after you awaken. Be ready."

She nodded. "I will."

"You are insane," Dora told Tessa the moment she awakened after a restless sleep.

"Thanks a lot." Tessa's mind whirled with plans. With the revelation of her psi abilities, her attitude had done a complete 360-degree change. She no longer preferred death to living— even if that meant marriage to a sexy alien who didn't even like her. "Dora, I have no time to waste. What must I do to get ready for the wedding?"

"You must cook dinner. Prepare a ritual bath."

"Kahn told me. I don't want him to suspect your presence so if you must leave—"

"Not necessary. I've inserted my personality into the mothership's systems."

"That's great."

"You have no idea," Dora bragged. "Watch."

The computer altered the chamber. A table rose from the floor. Cooking equipment and cabinets materialized right out of the walls.

"Kahn authorized the computer to give you whatever is necessary to prepare for the wedding ceremony."

"Did that include clothes?"

"Sorry, no."

Tessa closed her eyes. "Dora, would you please be quiet for a few minutes. I want to experiment."

"Compliance."

Ever since Tessa had attacked Kahn with her psi powers, she'd wanted to tap into her mind again. Until now, she hadn't had the opportunity. Sitting with her legs crossed on the floor, Tessa closed her eyes. She tried to put herself into the same emotionally fragile state she'd been in when she'd accidentally activated her psi.

She built a mental picture of a steel trap, put herself inside, and let the walls and ceiling close her in. All the while she imagined herself in clothing. Trapped in a cage, wearing a *dress*. With no place to go in her *white dress*. No free will in her *pretty white dress*. Her frustration mounted, and with a mental shove, she again merged into a furious maelstrom.

"Congratulations!" Dora piped in.

Annoyed by the interruption, Tessa opened her eyes but then she looked down and smiled in delight. She was no longer naked but covered by the simple white dress of her imagination. "This is so awesome. I can't wait to try again."

"You don't have time."

"I'll get faster with practice."

"Right now, you'd better start cooking a meal and drawing water for the bath."

"Okay. Tell me what to prepare and how."

"I'm a computer, not a cook."

"Don't you have recipes in your data banks?"

"No."

"How does Kahn prepare our meals?"

"He uses his psi. But he would probably expect you to prepare a meal from the ingredients in the blue cabinet."

Tessa opened the blue doors and stared at the strange array of fruits, meats, and vegetables. She might as well have been a Stone Age woman in a twentieth-century grocery store. She had no idea how to identify the food or how to prepare it. For all she knew, she could accidentally poison them both.

"Maybe I'll try the food materializer, after all. What should I do?"

"Kahn stands there and the food appears."

"Thank you very much. Even I know that," Tessa muttered. Once again she closed her eyes and envisioned the steel trap. This time she built the image more quickly, called up the frustration more easily. She thought of food inside the box with her. Raw carrots, celery, and peanut butter. Pizza and beer. Ice cream with hot fudge sauce. And steaming black coffee.

She smelled the delicious scent of coffee and pizza before she opened her eyes. Pleased by her efforts, her mouth watering, she raised the cup of coffee to her lips, ready to enjoy that first scalding sip as much as the rich flavor that reminded her of home. *Delicious.*

She enjoyed another gulp before speaking. "Now all I have to do is keep the pizza hot, the ice cream frozen, and the beer cold."

"Not a problem. The kitchen comes fully equipped with a warmer and a freezer."

Tessa placed the foods in the appropriate compartments, but kept the coffee to savor as she made preparations. "Do I have time to fix my hair before preparing the ritual bath?"

"If you hurry."

The caffeine from the coffee kicked in, revving through her veins. "Do you have a mirror?"

"Compliance."

Tessa pulled her hair into a neat twist on the top of her head. She didn't have time to figure out how to make her suit keep her hair in place but snagged a food tie from the blue cabinet. "I could do wonders with a curling iron, but this will work." Tessa pulled a few strands loose around her face.

"You look more feminine."

"That's the idea. Kahn has issues with a wife who can defeat him in hand-to-hand combat—without a suit—even if that's considered an archaic form of fighting here."

She shivered at the recollection of disgust in his eyes. While she didn't want to marry, she now most definitely wanted to train her new psi powers and win the Challenge. If that meant marrying Kahn, if that meant having sex, so be it, but she didn't want him to be revolted every time he looked at her.

While many of her fellow Secret Service agents also had trouble with Tessa defeating them on the mats, then showing up at a cocktail party in a slinky dress, she didn't understand the problem. She enjoyed looking good. She liked being a woman and intended to show Kahn a different side of her personality.

Sipping the last of the best coffee she'd ever tasted, Tessa surveyed the chamber. "Dora, can you make this room look like a comfortable Rystani home?"

"Compliance."

The ceiling dropped and the surfaces became irregular, cavelike. Soft, glowing lights lit up the Rystani room with huge, chunky furniture. "Why do Rystani have furniture when they can alter their suits to sit wherever they like?"

"Rystan is new to the Federation. Many of their customs such as old-fashioned furniture and ritual bathing are left over from their prepsi past."

Tessa made some changes, then asked Dora to place the ritual bathtub before the glowing stones in the hearth. The hologram program even added the scent of cooking food.

"How about Rystani music?"

Dora's first choice made Tessa clap her hands over her ears.

"Stop. How about something soothing?"

Dora's second try was more to her liking. The mellow tone reminded her of a flute. Tessa moved her attention to the huge bathtub next. Circular and wooden, it was only about a foot deep. She tested the water temperature and the rough washing cloths, examined the bucket for rinsing. She spied a rectangular pillow, soap, and drying towels that were hard and scratchy. Again she requested changes.

"You sure are fussy."

"I gave my word and I intend to keep it."

"I suppose in your position I might do the same." Dora sighed. "I wish I could find a soul mate and get married."

"Soul mate?" Tessa grinned at Dora's fantasy. "Let's not get carried away here. I'm not sure I even like the man."

But she also knew Kahn had good qualities. He cared about his people. He had the strength of a warrior and the ability to change his stubborn mind when she backed him into a corner and gave him a way to dodge. He might not like losing to a female, he might consider her skill unseemly, but he would keep his word. To ease him through the concessions he'd made and to help bridge their differences, she intended to rekindle the simmering sexual tension they'd previously shared. For now, that was enough.

When Kahn had told her about his first marriage she'd seen the pain in his eyes. That he had loved once meant he had the capacity for deep feelings. He might be stubborn, but he was clearly a man of honor. And he had conceded, albeit grudgingly, to her suggestion to train her psi as he would a man. He would not go back on his word and that spoke highly of his character.

Hands clasped behind her back, she paced, impatient for Kahn to arrive.

* * *

Kahn entered the chamber and stopped short in pleased astonishment. Despite his determination to keep a stoic expression no matter what Tessa had done, he couldn't stop his lower jaw from dropping. She was wearing a pretty white dress. That she'd already made more progress with her psi abilities thrilled him, but he'd figured that once she'd learned, she'd wear some kind of mannish costume, not an attractive dress that showed off her feminine curves. She'd also done something agreeable to her gorgeous black hair, placing it atop her head in a fancy knot. Locks fell softly around her face in a most becoming and almost dainty manner.

She held out both hands to him. "Welcome."

The contrast between this charming lady and the warrior woman who had defeated him in hand-to-hand combat made him wary. "What kind of trick is this, woman?"

"Did you not think I would keep my word and honor your customs?"

"I hoped you would try."

"I like to succeed." Her eyes twinkled, and the bruising from her crash into the bulkhead was not as severe as he'd feared. She stepped aside with a swirl of fabric that drew attention to her long legs and gestured to the room with pride. "Did I get it right?"

The hearth burned brightly with glow stones, the layout so familiar, reminding him how much he missed his home. But she'd added a few touches of her own. A brightly colored blanket over the back of a chair. A painting of a woman and child next to the hearth. Soft music. Burning tapers and the spicy-sweet scent of something he couldn't identify that wafted from the kitchen area.

"You have done well."

"I'm glad you think so." She spoke easily, as if she could slip into this new role without strain. Her obvious confidence in herself as she adapted to this new role surprised him and had him oddly on edge. "I'm going to disappoint you in one area."

He supposed she would now plead with him to delay the wedding night. "Yes?"

"I used the kitchen materializers to cook the food. I don't know how to prepare a meal from scratch."

"I see." He folded his arms over his chest and told himself to have patience. Every Rystani female child could cook, but she wasn't Rystani and she was clearly making an effort to please him.

"There's more."

He raised an eyebrow and braced himself. He wondered if he was destined to spend the rest of his life waiting for her to say or do something unacceptable. And yet, he no longer objected to marrying her as much as he had earlier. Life with Tessa would never be dull. She'd keep him on his toes and he was beginning to admire her spirit, which matched his own.

"I had no idea how to prepare a Rystani meal." She spoke without a shred of shame at her lack of skills, and while he shouldn't have been shocked by her attitude, he nevertheless was. "I didn't even recognize the ingredients in the food preparation unit."

Surely that enticing smell in the chamber couldn't be the result of a cooking failure? But perhaps he should be happy she hadn't started a cooking fire on the spaceship. "We have no meal?"

"We do." She bit her lip, as if hesitant to say more. "But it's Earth food. I'm sorry it's not what you expected, but—"

"You will serve me now." Best to get this over with before he dwelled on how Lael had fed him his favorite *octar* meat spiced with *Jarballa*. He had to make allowances for Tessa. She'd warned him she couldn't cook and she was obviously attempting to satisfy him. He sat at the table and waited for her to bring the meal, determined to eat, even if it was inedible.

Her face serene, Tessa removed a platter of green and

orange sticks from the cold compartment. She carried the plate carefully to the table and set it down with a flourish.

"Those look like roots."

"On Earth, these vegetables are called crudités and are always served at special functions."

He tried hard to find something polite to say. The nourishment looked as if she hadn't even bothered to cook. "It's colorful."

She dipped a green stick into a creamy brown spread and held it to his lips. Custom dictated that she feed him and vice versa. Cautiously, he sniffed a sweet and nutty aroma. "What is this called?"

"Celery and peanut butter."

He licked the sauce from the green stick, his tongue glancing off her finger, too. The peanut butter stuck to his tongue, but possessed a rich and creamy taste. Emboldened, he parted his lips and allowed her to feed him the green stick with the sauce. The stick crunched pleasantly, the juice a foil for the sticky peanut butter.

"It's good."

"You needn't sound so surprised." She grinned and dabbed the pad of her pinky on the corner of his lips where a drop of the peanut butter still clung. Seductive eyes locked with his as she brought her finger to her own full mouth and licked her finger with a dancing flick of pink tongue. Then, still holding his gaze, she closed her lips around her finger and slowly sucked off the last juices. Her audacious gesture disturbed him. When he raised an eyebrow, questioning her behavior, she blushed, dropped her gaze, and actually seemed flustered.

Stars! One moment she looked as adorable as an adolescent flirting for her first kiss and the next she teased him like an experienced woman. Still, he had difficulty reconciling this feminine Tessa with the bold one who'd defeated him.

Appearing to recover quickly from her error in etiquette, Tessa dipped the orange stick into the sauce. "Try a carrot."

She fed him the treat, which he found sweet but also caused him to crave more than a drink to quench his thirst. He had the strangest desire to kiss her, and yet mere hours ago he'd thought himself the unluckiest man on Rystan for having to marry an Earthling. However, she hadn't only altered her appearance, she'd changed her demeanor. At first he'd kept looking for a trick, but as she fed him her Earth food, he decided that she was making a genuine effort to follow his customs.

"Come. Sit on my lap," he requested.

"First, let me serve the pizza." She spun away from the table and returned with a flat pie that was white and red with bits of circular slices of meat embedded on top. She poured two golden and foamy drinks, one for each of them. "This is pizza and beer, my favorite gourmet meal."

She pulled out a triangular slice from the rest and held up the corner for him to taste. The enticing scent of the *pizza* alone made his mouth salivate, but even if the food had smelled unpalatable, he would have told her he liked it. He could do no less when she'd obviously tried so hard to follow his customs.

He bit into the pizza and the warm cheese over crusty bread melted in his mouth. He didn't have to lie about his praise. "Delicious."

"Beer"—she handed him a glass—"is an acquired taste. But it's my drink of choice with pizza."

She held the beer to his mouth, and he found the flavor much like a fermented grain on Rystan. "This is alcoholic?"

"Is that a problem?"

"Not for me. Women on Rystan do not drink alcohol."

"Oh." Her eyes dropped but not before he saw first discouragement then anger, then unhappy acceptance. "Okay."

Clearly she was disappointed that she couldn't partake of her favorite drink, but she didn't argue, either, surprising him once again. After the trouble she'd taken to please him with the meal, he didn't want to deny her during their wedding feast.

"But we are not yet on Rystan," he conceded, patted his thigh for her to sit on his lap, and held a glass to her lips.

"Thank you." She drank deeply, as if she needed fortification, but she didn't seem tipsy afterward, and he reminded himself that he could not keep giving in to her because she was an Earthling. She was living in his world and would have to be the one to adapt.

The wedding feast was much more pleasant than he'd imagined. As if by mutual unspoken agreement, they put aside their differences during the meal. He found that when she sat on his thigh, her side pressed to his chest, he actually enjoyed her touch. When she made the effort, she displayed impeccable manners, chewing with her mouth closed and always offering him the majority share of the choice portions.

However, when she tilted her head back onto his shoulder and boldly looked him in the eyes, he expected her to say something pleasant. Her normal tone was light, almost musical, but grew husky. "For the last hour, I've been looking forward to bathing you in the ritual tub."

Once again she'd shocked him with her lack of modesty, and he frowned. "It is not seemly to talk of such things."

"Why not?" Her eyes glinted with amusement and her lips brazenly nipped his neck. "You will be my husband. Am I not allowed to express my desire for you?"

She should not be so forward. What the hell was she doing planting kisses on his neck? He gently removed her from his lap. "You twist my words, woman."

She stared at him in complete confusion and kept her tone level, but he heard an honest ring to her words. "I haven't the slightest idea why you are upset."

Kahn reined in his temper. He had to make allowances for her ignorance of his ways. He had to summon patience and tact—not his strongest qualities. When he'd set out on this voyage, he'd expected to mentor the Earthling. He'd expected adversity and obstacles, but never had he thought the journey would be this difficult.

He didn't know what bothered him more—that she didn't grasp the reason for his anger over her brazen conduct, or that he'd enjoyed her boldness.

10

Tessa had lied to Kahn. She knew exactly why he was upset. He didn't like her speaking openly about wanting to touch him. He wanted her to pretend she was the shy maiden with no physical needs, which was downright impossible after what he'd put her through.

She breathed in deeply and reminded herself that she'd made slow but steady headway. Tessa downed the last sip of her beer and recollected her progress, both large and small. First and foremost, using her psi exhilarated her. A whole new universe of possibilities had opened up, and she dearly loved to learn new skills. Her goal of mastering her psi and winning the Challenge for Earth seemed within reach.

Second, Kahn had responded to her attempt to please him, another indication that he actually possessed the ability to change his mind. Sometimes he seemed so stubborn and set in his ways that she wondered if he could see beyond black and white, right and wrong. While she found some of his customs downright annoying, she had to try and fit in. But she wasn't above using her feminine wiles, and she bet the Rystani women weren't either, despite his claims of their compliant natures.

With her hunger satisfied by that sinful cup of coffee followed by pizza and beer, she wasn't quite ready for dessert. She took Kahn's hand and led him to the tub where Dora had kept the temperature set comfortably warm. He'd come to her wearing black pants, a black shirt, and black boots and she waited to see what he would do. Did Rystani men take off their suit for the ritual bath? Would he turn his clothes transparent? Would she finally get to feast her eyes on all that tempting male flesh?

As if he had read her mind, the corner of his mouth turned up on one side, his amber eyes aglow with swirling emotions that she couldn't read. He stepped, fully dressed, into the tub, then sat. Kneeling outside the tub on the rectangular pillow, she dipped her hand into a pot of crystals and was about to toss them into the water, when his hand clasped her wrist in midair.

"What is this, woman?"

"Bubble bath."

"Why would I want bubbles in my bath?"

She spread her fingers and let the crystals fall into the water. "Because they are fun?"

"The ritual bath isn't supposed to be fun."

"If you say so. You can sit there and frown at me if you like, but," she said, chuckling, "*I* plan to have fun."

He did not look pleased, but she caught a glimpse of interest in those arrogant eyes. "Are you defying me, woman?"

"Not everything needs to be a contest of wills. Can I not simply enjoy my wedding day and your Rystani ritual?" She evaded giving him a straight answer and swirled the crystals in the water with her hand, delighted as they frothed over the surface. She scooped white bubbles into her hand and blew them into the air.

Kahn simply stared at her, and she didn't say one word when his black shirt disappeared and revealed luscious, bronzed skin. Built like a warrior, he had powerful shoulders, a thick chest dusted lightly with blond hair, and he could have modeled for an exercise commercial for washboard abs. But more than all those gorgeous muscles, what really captured her attention was that he seemed distinctly uneasy and she had no idea why.

"What's wrong?" she asked as she dipped a bucket of water to spill over his head before washing his hair.

"Nothing." He spoke through gritted teeth.

"Now I *am* calling you a liar." She hefted the bucket. "Close your eyes." She poured the water over his head as he sputtered.

He surprised her when he didn't chastise her for calling him a liar. And when he didn't deny the lie, she was more confused than ever. Dipping her fingers into the shampoo, she lathered up both of her hands, then threaded her fingers through his hair. She took her time, rubbing his temples, the sensitive spots around his ears, and the back of his corded neck as well as shampooing all the hair between.

While she kneeled, something odd was going on between her legs. It was as if her suit had pulsed its way inside her and slowly expanded. "What's happening to me?" she demanded.

"The suit is preparing your body to accept mine according to our rituals."

Tessa tried to ignore the inner stretching, attempted to relax and think of this as a warm-up for the lovemaking to come. Instead, she focused on his massage. Kahn was as tense as a brick. After years of hard workouts, she knew how to release a tight muscle with pressure, how to ease soreness from a strain, but he wouldn't relax.

"Am I doing this wrong?"

"No." He practically growled at her.

"I guess you're more tense than I realized. But I have strong hands, and we can do this until you relax," she half teased, half taunted, testing a new theory. But surely she had to be wrong. This man who had touched every part of her body, invaded her most private places, and had driven her beyond the brink of her sensual limits, couldn't be so upset because *she* was touching *him,* could he? "Is it my right to take as much time as I wish?"

"Yes. But it is not . . . Our women insisted on keeping this part of the ritual, even after Rystani people learned to use their suits," he said, his irritation apparent.

Never before had he failed to finish a sentence and that gave her another clue that although she was on her knees bathing him, he wanted this done quickly. Was he so anxious to get to the lovemaking? She didn't think so. Earlier, he'd had her naked and begging him to make love and he'd seemed to have no trouble resisting her.

And that's when she figured it out. To allow her to bathe him, he'd had to let down his suit's defenses. When he'd had her so helpless over his lap, the suit had somehow prevented him from revealing if he wanted her sexually. Now the tables were turned. No wonder he was uptight, every muscle straining. Interesting.

So what was she going to do about it? She rubbed her fingers through his hair, savoring the silky texture. She'd been so captivated by all that contained power of his body in her hands that she'd failed to realize he was submitting to her at this moment. However, once he got out of the tub, the tables would again turn. She couldn't exactly forget that salient fact, not with the suit opening her wider, pressing deeper.

She'd always believed marriage should be built upon trust and there was none between them. Perhaps she should use this time to bridge that gap—and yet, revenge would taste so sweet. But it would also be a huge mistake.

Picking up the soft washcloth, she began to lather it with spice-scented soap then changed her mind. She tossed the cloth aside, she would use her hands. "Lean forward, please, so I can do your back."

He did as she asked, but when he felt her hands on him instead of the expected cloth, he flinched. Behind him, she grinned and caressed her fingers over his shoulders, dug her thumbs into his taut muscles, smoothed her palms over hard flesh that possessed several old scars.

"Does this feel good?" She kept her tone soft, her hands busy.

"Umm."

"I'll take that for a *yes*." She restrained a chuckle and kept her tone businesslike as she asked him to rise out of the water and give her access to more of him. "Kneel, please."

"That's not necessary."

She forced reluctance into her tone and thought she should have won an Oscar for her performance. "I promised to follow Rystani customs. I will not go back on my word."

With his spine to her, he kneeled, coming out of the water and allowing her to see his bronzed waist tapering to slim hips and powerful buttocks. Oh, yes. He had terrific buns. "Your body pleases me."

He didn't say a word but she caught a hint of a blush beneath those tanned cheekbones. She ignored his obvious pique. Still using her hands, she slathered soap onto his waist and hips, savoring the fact that she was making him wait for a change. Despite the fullness between her legs and the pressure to hurry, she took her time, smoothing her palms over his warm buttocks, biting down another chuckle as a muscle strained under her caresses.

"Stand, please."

He stood slowly, his legs together and braced. She took particular pleasure in washing the backs of his thighs. "Please, part your legs."

"Woman, you should well remember that I will not be at your mercy forever."

"I am simply giving you a bath according to your customs, am I not?" She tried to keep her voice even, but when he snorted, she failed to prevent another grin of enjoyment.

She let him stand with his legs parted and continued to wash the backs of his knees, his powerful calves and ankles, before once again working her way up, this time paying particular attention to the insides of his legs.

"Woman, I'm warning you . . ."

"Relax. I don't bite. Or at least not hard," she teased as she cupped his balls, gratified to find them high and tight, heavy and full. "Besides, I have yet to wash your front."

He groaned, and this time she laughed. "You have some very pleasant customs on your world. How often do these ritual baths occur?"

"On the wedding anniversary. This was our wives' way of ensuring that their husbands will never forget the date." He spoke as though he were enduring torture at the thought of allowing her to caress him as she liked.

"Sounds like you have some wise women on Rystan. If you will kneel again, I will rinse you." She dipped the bucket and sluiced warm water over his back, buttocks, and legs. "Now please turn around and kneel."

She busied herself with the soap, not quite daring to meet his eyes or look at his jutting erection. "How often is a wedding anniversary on Rystan?"

"Yearly. That's every 380 of your days."

Too bad it wasn't weekly or daily. However, she didn't dare utter the thought aloud. "Close your eyes so I don't get soap in them," she told him.

He did as she asked and then she took the opportunity to really look at him. With a body like his, he could have posed for Michelangelo, but not even the master sculptor could have captured the glistening tension in him as he waited for her next touch.

Since he expected her to wash his face, she didn't. Instead she closed her fingers around his sex and enjoyed hearing him suck in his breath, enjoyed the muscles quivering in those tree-trunk thighs, enjoyed having him leap to her caress.

His eyes, full of pent-up sensuality, flared open. "Woman, you go too far. No Rystani virgin would dare to be so bold."

"Ah, but I am not a *Rystani* virgin. I'm from Earth." She allowed her thumb to explore the tip, watched his eyes turn molten. Heard a guttural moan, and released him.

She washed his face, his neck, his chest, taking her time, tweaking his nipples, despite the ever-constant stretching that made her part her own thighs. Although he tried to keep his face stoic as she washed him, his eyes blazed with need, his lips were pressed tightly together, and a muscle throbbed in his jaw all the way down his thick, stubborn neck.

"Please stand."

She skipped over his sex and washed his hips and his legs. Again she asked him to sit and rinsed him. She thought she saw a measure of relief in his eyes and decided to push him further, longer.

"There is one spot that I have not thoroughly washed."

His Adam's apple bobbed and he held her gaze with a burning ferocity that told her to take care what she did next. "Please turn around in the tub. I would have you on your hands and knees."

"Warriors do not—"

"They do . . . when a woman is under them."

She thought he might refuse, but he didn't. She let her hand trail over his buttocks for the sheer pleasure of touching him, then slid her hand down his leg to his foot. "Please straighten your leg."

She washed his foot between his toes and arches and then repeated with the other. After she finished, she made him wait a full minute on his hands and knees before she lightly slapped his buttocks. "The bath is done."

Her words were the equivalent of letting loose a chained, angry tiger. One moment he was in the tub and the next he was completely dry and looming naked in front of her. His hands clasped her waist, lifting her. Then his fierce mouth slanted down on hers, taking, demanding, commanding.

His kiss sucked all the oxygen out of her lungs, and she realized that despite her warning to herself, she'd pushed him too far, or perhaps, just far enough. She couldn't help reveling in his hot, out-of-control kiss that left her breathless and clinging to him for more. She clasped her hands around his neck to draw him closer—but he pulled back.

"We need to finalize this marriage. Now."

He set her on her feet and tugged her toward a wall. With the suit's expansion, she walked with difficulty after him. He opened a compartment, handed her a piece of paper, and took one himself and licked it, then slid it into a slot. "We must register DNA samples, supply our identities for the Federation records."

"Surely you do not mean for me to get pregnant?"

"Not before the Challenge. I will alter your suit to prevent impregnation."

She handed him her paper and submitted to a thumb print and retina scan. "Are we married now?"

"Almost." His eyes warned her she would not like what he said next. He withdrew five silver bands that glittered like Christmas-tree tinsel but were as fine as embroidery thread. "I must band you and vice versa."

"These are symbolic?"

He placed one band around her head, parting her hair so the band touched her skin and forehead. He twisted another band around the fingers of her right hand and the third band on her left. The gleaming silver reminded her of rings or a tatoo, a permanent mark to all who saw her that she was a Rystani wife. Then he kneeled and twisted a circlet around each toe. Satisfied, he stood. "Now even after you have fully mastered your psi, I will still control your suit in the areas between the bands. As pretty as I find that dress, I miss the sight of your bare skin."

He turned her suit transparent and her heart sank like lead. She'd regained a measure of glorious freedom by learning to use her psi only to have him take it back with the marriage bands. She wanted to pound him. Scream at him. Curse him. She tried to find her psi to counteract what he'd done and failed miserably.

Damn the man for placing the bands so he could control almost every part of her, and she prayed this might be for only the period of their wedding ceremony. "For how long do the bands stay on the skin?"

"I already told you that we wed for life. They last until death. If one mate survives the other . . . the bands fade away."

She ignored the pain in his eyes caused by the memory of his first wife. "Are the effects limited by distance?"

"The stronger the marriage bond, the greater the distance. The men in my line tend to form very powerful bonds, and we don't allow our wives far from our sight," he told her, his voice firm, yet tender.

If they never created a strong bond, he would have less control over her. She wanted more information but sensed his growing impatience with her questions.

When he withdrew one gold band and handed it to her to place on him, she hesitated. "Why is there only one gold band?"

"Because the male bond is symbolic. Wives usually place it on the husband's forehead or chest, sometimes over the biceps. Don't worry about the size. The band will shrink to conform to the skin."

She looked him straight in the eyes. "This is my choice?"
"Yes."
"I can control the area between the band?"
"There is only one band."

Tessa knew she could spend a lifetime paying for what she did next. However, she was not about to hand over such power to him without taking some back. She fully recalled how he'd sexually frustrated her, when he hadn't even been aroused because his suit helped him control a normal response. She might not be able to prevent him from ever doing that to her again, but she needn't suffer by herself.

Boldly reaching out, she cupped his balls.

His eyes rounded. "Rystani wives do not—"

"I am not Rystani."

"You promised to obey our customs."

Her hand trembled, her mouth went dry, but she refused to back down. "You told me *by custom* the choice is mine."

"No Rystani male has ever worn a band on his *tavis*."

"I promised to follow your customs. Am I breaking any law, husband?"

Rage warred with lust in those molten eyes. He clenched his fists, but she didn't fear he would strike her. When he didn't retreat, she gently explored the length of his *tavis* with her fingertips.

Before she lost her courage, she slipped the thin gold band around his testicles, twisted the thread, curled it around his extended *tavis* and twisted the gold band back and forth until she'd woven the final loop around the tip of his sex. "This part of you now belongs to me."

He released a feral roar, grabbed the back of her thighs, parted her legs, and lifted her onto him. He gave her no time to prepare. He rammed inside her, and if it hadn't been for the suit's gentle preparation of stretching her to accommodate his size over the past hour, she would have felt pain, not pleasure, not wonderfully wanted.

"Yes!" She threw her arms around his neck, let her head tilt back, thrust her hips forward and arched against him. He pumped his hips, withdrew, so fast, so hard, she could do no more than hold on for the ride.

All those sensations he'd created during their time together, all of her touching him, all of her pent-up passion, had her clawing at his shoulders, grating her hips. She wanted faster. Harder. More.

"Take me," she demanded as he brought her to a place where her emotions swirled and carried her into a lusty vortex.

He seemed to be everywhere. Over her, under her. Inside her. And then her body found blessed relief in a mind-blowing orgasm. She screamed his name and felt him shudder inside her. His release shot her into another cycle of pleasure that was way over the edge. She'd actually felt his orgasm become her own. Shocked by the psi experience and full of joy and confusion, she could only clutch his shoulders and marvel in wonder.

Then he held her against his chest, muttering like a litany, "I'm sorry."

"Why?"

"I lost control—"

She ran a finger over his cheek. "But you did it so well."

"I am not in the mood for jests."

"I wasn't jesting, you idiot. That was the most wonderful experience of my life."

"You were a virgin. It was the only experience of your life. And don't ever call me that again."

"But it was my best orgasm ever."

"You should not have had such experiences before your wedding. You should not speak of such things ever."

"You really must stop telling me what I can and cannot say. Don't you have freedom of speech on Rystan?"

"Yes. No." She leaned into his chest and bit his nipple. "That is not permitted."

"Okay." She leaned forward and bit his other nipple.

"I told you—"

"Maybe we shouldn't talk." She licked away the nips.

He unwound her arms from around his neck and her feet

from around his waist. Then he lifted her off him. "We need to talk."

"Come on, Kahn. This is our wedding day. Don't you want to make love again?"

"You touched places you shouldn't have. Said words that were improper, and I lost control—"

"You liked what I did. Admit it. We both had a good time. All these rules are tiresome. Relax. There's no one here but you and me. We can do this again—until you get it right."

"Are you teasing me, woman?"

"I don't know. Is teasing permitted on Rystan? Nothing else is." She'd yet to set foot on his world and already she hated it.

"I'll tell you what's permitted. A wife is supposed to let her husband set the pace—"

"Hey, you can't pin that one on me."

"A wife doesn't touch, stroke, or caress."

"You've got to be kidding." But he wasn't. She could see it in the big hunk's eyes. Her wild lovemaking had disturbed him. Apparently, she was supposed to do nothing but be his plaything, except during the ritual bath that came only once a year. He took her into his arms and cradled her against him.

"Rystani women cannot initiate lovemaking?"

"I did not say that."

"What aren't you telling me?"

"There is a dance, called the *Ramala Ki*. It takes years to learn and has many intricate steps. Wives perform the dance to incite their husband's lust."

"Show me."

"Another time. Meanwhile, I'll use the suit to prevent you from making these kinds of mistakes."

She yanked back. She'd prefer to make her own mistakes, thank you very much. And the thought of him making decisions for her turned her stomach. "Forget it. With an attitude like that, there won't be a next time."

He chuckled, floated her into the air, and reached for her

breast. "We won't make love again until we do it my way. And you ask me nicely."

Then he plucked her out of the air and tossed her over his shoulder. "It's going to be *fun* to see how long you hold out."

11

Tessa didn't hold out for long. She wriggled and squirmed and shouted and cursed him, but her tone was more husky than angry. Sometimes she even giggled and urged him on. In fact, Kahn suspected she was enjoying her wedding ceremony more than she would ever admit. He certainly was.

He took pleasure in slowly building her up, stoking her heat, touching her wherever and however he wished. She possessed the most marvelously smooth skin, and although she appeared delicate, she had a ferocity of spirit that he couldn't help but admire—even as he enjoyed taming it.

"Kahn, I need you."

"That sounds more like a demand than a request, woman."

She raked her nails down his leg, the only part of him she could reach since he held her over his lap. He could have blocked her attack with his psi, but he wanted an excuse to retaliate. However, his own impatience got the best of him and he heated her bottom with his psi instead of his palm.

Her lovely round bottom turned red and she moaned. "I want you. Please."

He picked her up and she immediately parted her legs to straddle him. At the same time, she shoved him onto his back on the dais. Her aggressive move took him by surprise. She meant to . . . ride him.

With her dark hair flung over her white shoulders, her back arched, and her breasts lifted high, she was a vision of wantonness which both excited him and irritated him. She kept forgetting her place. But she felt so good, he had difficulty thinking. No man could be expected to recall every Rystani rule when his head was about to explode from sheer excitement.

"This . . . is . . . wrong." He grabbed her hips. "The man should be on top."

"Hold me." She seized his hands, placed them on her breasts, all the while gyrating her hips, teasing him, taunting him.

Need battled with tradition. He couldn't let her . . .

With one thrust of psi, he turned on their suits' null grav and floated them. She shrieked in surprise as they gently bobbed in midair but she adapted almost instantly. Clutching him with her knees, she never stopped moving, spinning them, rotating. There was no longer up and down. No longer someone on the top or bottom. There was only him and her. And pleasure.

Locking her knees to his hips, her hands gripping his shoulders, she pivoted, swirled, and rocked. Wild and incorrigible, she took him inside her, murmuring, "Yes. Yes. Yes."

When she spasmed around him, her pleasure rushing at him through her tempestuous psi, she took him with her, bursting with the force of a star gone supernova. With his heartbeat so rapid it reverberated like a drum against his ribs, his breath as ragged as if he'd competed in the fight of his life, he couldn't think. He could only hold her against him as they floated.

She recovered first. Lifting her head from where she snuggled against his shoulder, she kissed his neck. "Thank you. You were spectacular."

"Thanking me is not necessary. It is my duty to keep you happy."

"Well, you succeeded splendidly."

"You are not sore?"

"Umm." She tightened muscles where she still clasped his *tavis*. "Pleasantly sore. However, if you give me a few minutes to recover, I could be convinced to go a third round."

"You are incorrigible."

She sighed. "Just making up for lost time."

He let the comment pass. She had pleased him too much to argue. Besides, he liked the way she cuddled against him, like a feline seeping up heat. When he shut his eyes, he could pretend she was a clingy Rystani female, overwhelmed by her first sexual encounter, but trusting that her husband had done the right thing—not a brazen Earthling who had thanked him for pleasuring her.

They napped and he awakened with her peering at him with a happy grin. "I never fed you the rest of the wedding feast."

"There's more?" His stomach rumbled, reminding him that he could use additional nourishment.

"Dessert. If you'll set me on my feet," she requested, "I shall see to the preparation."

"What is dessert?" The translator didn't seem to have an equivalent Rystani word. He set her down and headed back to the table.

But she shook her head and pointed to the dais. "Dessert is an aftermeal sweet."

He sat on the dais and watched her open the cooler. When the cold air came out, her breasts tightened to tiny hard nubs, a pleasant reminder that she had yet to learn how to operate her suit's temperature control, which he had set on automatic. Tomorrow, he must begin their training sessions in earnest, but for now, he simply enjoyed the sight of her sweet-tipped nipples.

The dish she took out of the cooler looked odd. Scoops of creamy snow, with a dark sauce on top and then over that a cloudlike, fluffy substance. But the food didn't interest him as much as those pointy nipples.

"You look good like that. Perhaps I should alter your suit to keep your nipples cold."

She stumbled as he put words to action. He expected her to complain. Instead, she dipped her fingers into the "dessert." Her fingers came out covered with the cloudy stuff, the dark sauce and the snow. Then she flicked her wrist and flung cold droplets at him.

Annoyed, he reacted as any husband would have done. "Woman, you will clean up this mess—on your knees."

She chuckled, the glint in her eyes telling him, she'd expected his response but was pleased by it. Setting the dessert on the floor, she immediately dropped to her knees and then she began to clean him—with her lips and tongue. The cold substance and the heat of her mouth combined with her playfulness shocked him into silence. What was he to do with her?

He didn't understand her. She never reacted the way he expected. She should be begging his forgiveness. Instead she was enticing him to . . . He groaned as she licked a droplet from the inside of his thigh.

"Stop," he ordered.

"Okay." She agreed but then she nibbled her way from his hip to his stomach.

"You should not—"

"I know."

But she kept going. When she had cleaned up every morsel, she reached for the dessert with the tip of her finger and placed the cloudy stuff on each of her nipples. Then she leaned back on her palms, arched her spine, and dared him. "Want to taste?"

"You are acting like a *ritha*."

"I am acting like a wife who wants her husband's mouth on her. Didn't you tell me your duty as a husband was to keep me happy?"

"I did."

"Well, I'm not going to be happy until you eat the dessert I prepared for our wedding feast."

She could have tried the patience of a holy man, but Kahn had never been of that persuasion. He liked women too much to ever think of taking a vow of celibacy. Although she'd twisted his words, although he was giving her too much power by adhering to her wishes, he simply could not resist her enticement.

Instead of bending his head to her, he again used his psi power to lift her to him. This time he locked her in the pose she'd used to captivate him so that she couldn't move. He shot her a heated glance and enjoyed the flare of interest in her eyes. "Ah, so tempting."

Then he licked her breast, knowing the heat of his tongue combined with the cold of her suit would shoot tingles straight to her core.

"Oh . . . my . . . God." Her eyes widened at the sensation.

He grinned. "This dessert is good. I could acquire a taste for such sweetness on a regular basis." He reached for the dish and held it up.

"We were supposed to share."

With a laugh and a psi thought, he parted her legs and floated her before him. "Oh, I intend to share."

Then he lifted her dessert and began to decorate her, dribbling the concoction over her lips, her neck, her breasts and back. With a small psi adaptation the sticky mixture stuck to her, yet he made sure she could feel every droplet. The sauce at the bottom was rich and thick. He poured it between her parted thighs and watched her eyes go wide, the pupils dark.

Her breasts heaved and she licked her bottom lip, but he saw no fear on her face. Only desire. Perhaps he'd finally found a way to gentle his wild wife. He would pleasure her until she couldn't resist him. While a woman from his world would have immediately capitulated to his will, Tessa would match him every step of the way, and surprisingly, he looked forward to what she'd do next.

With such pleasant steps to take, Kahn was suddenly in no hurry. He enjoyed his dessert, her moans of pleasure, her frantic need to have him again, which he quite happily satisfied. Finally they slept, wound around each other in null grav, and despite his reservations, he found himself sated, almost content—until he remembered that he had promised to train her as he would a man.

Tessa stood facing him in the room he'd cleared of all objects, ready for her first combat lesson. She'd used her psi to change her suit into a simple white tunic and pants similar to the ones he wore. Obviously, she couldn't fight in a skirt, but Rystani women did not wear men's clothing. Kahn said nothing, again breaking the rules for her, his heart heavy with trepidation over this experiment.

Kahn's people had chosen him as their Challenge candidate for many reasons. First, his father had succeeded in Rystan's initial Challenge and his peoples' hopes rested on the belief that Kahn's similar genetic makeup would again lead to success. Second, he was Rystan's best warrior. From birth, his father then his grandfather had trained him to use the suit until tactics in null grav had become second nature. But last year Kahn hadn't competed in the Federation's Ultimate fighting championships. Food had been so scarce on Rystan he'd spent the time hunting to bring in the meat his people required to survive another long winter. However, two years ago, Kahn had won the competition, defeating a wily Endekian in the quarter finals before routing a muscular Dullaxian to take first prize. Kahn had faced dozens of opponents, but never a woman, certainly not a wife. His stomach knotted into icy cords at the idea of injuring her.

She spoke evenly as if understanding the difficulty he must now surmount. "Kahn, I know you find the idea of sparring with a woman disagreeable, but have you forgotten how I defeated you without the suit?"

He sensed she'd spoken the words to help him follow through on his promise. While he appreciated her gesture, he had to get past his aversion to fighting a woman.

She hadn't bragged, either, simply stated the facts as she saw them. And he was having trouble reconciling the lover he'd held in his arms during their wedding night with the one who now spoke and acted with the courage of a warrior.

From their first meeting when she'd awakened in his arms instead of the warming chamber, Tessa had done the unexpected. When she'd defeated him in battle without the suit, she'd astounded him with her skill. She had to have undergone years of practice to attain her expertise, but he didn't understand how one little female could have so much spirit.

"Kahn, there is much honor in training me to win the Challenge. Let me remind you that I have practiced fighting techniques my entire life. Rarely has a day passed that I have not sustained a bruise on my arms from blocking a blow or to my shins when an opponent blocked a kick."

Tessa placed her hands on her slim hips, a gesture he'd begun to recognize as one that revealed her argumentative state of mind. "If Earth had chosen another candidate, you could be training a man who had no fighting skills."

"That's not the point."

She was female. All woman. After the night they'd shared, he couldn't forget the softness of her mouth, her smooth creamy skin, those lean legs that wrapped around him. His intimate familiarity with her wonderful body kept him from seeing her as anything but a desirable and feminine woman.

And the fading bruise around her eye reminded him of her vulnerability.

"You would have had to begin training that man from scratch."

"I was prepared to do so."

Her eyes flashed a challenge. "Would you have killed him with your lack of skill?"

He shook his head. "Of course not."

"Would you have broken his bones?" She persisted with a fierce logic that he couldn't deny.

"Perhaps." Accidents happened.

She shrugged. "Broken bones heal."

"We have a bone regenerator on the ship." The words slipped from his mouth before he realized his mistake. His instinct to protect her meant he couldn't let her worry unnecessarily—even if that was counterproductive to discouraging her.

"So." She paused, her tongue licking her bottom lip. "If you are skilled enough to prevent permanent damage, what's the big deal? Pretend I'm a man."

He snorted. "I did not marry a man. I did not promise to protect a man. I did not make love to a man last night."

"You missed the operative word. Can't you pretend?"

"No."

She rolled her eyes at the ceiling, clearly upset with him. "I like being female."

"That I do know, or you would not have squealed with pleasure in my arms during our wedding—"

She lunged forward to punch him in the jaw, trying to force him to fight. He could have used his psi power to repel the blow but instead shifted to the side, automatically following his mental preparations to teach this first lesson.

"Again," he instructed, realizing he could school her in the rudimentary fighting techniques without once raising a hand against her.

She came at him with a kick to his side.

"Too slow. Again."

Knowing she probably wouldn't call up her psi powers until she'd totally exhausted her physical energy, he'd planned to taunt her. Frustrate her. The technique to train warriors to use their psi had been designed to cause ultimate failure, similar to causing the sexual frustration used on women.

Tessa spun, back-fisted the spot where his head had been. Displaying an extensive knowledge of two-dimensional tactics, she'd anticipated his next move, and her foot collided with the psi shielding of his kneecap. After she'd attempted to sweep him from his feet, he implemented his null grav and floated into the air. If not for her spectacular balance, she would have fallen after his abrupt repositioning.

He figured she'd soon lose her mental cool, but instead she grinned. "I have *got* to learn that trick."

She didn't appear frustrated, but excited. He suddenly realized his basic tactics weren't creating the emotions she required to tap into her psi. She was too smart, too experienced, to lose her temper or become frustrated—unless he fought back. He should have known nothing with her would be done the easy way.

"Attack, again," he ordered, wondering how long she would continue to obey him. "Do not stop."

She shot an elbow to his protected ribs, stomped where his foot had just been, then followed through with a feint to his groin. "You realize it will take a full hour to wear me down?" That she knew he needed her frustrated was not good. Her knowledge would slow the learning curve. Stars! She was forcing him to up the stakes.

Annoyed, he taunted her. "You overestimate your conditioning and your skill, woman."

She side-thrust, kicked, recovered, and lunged full force with a forearm strike to his neck. "I'll bet you another ritual bath that I last an hour."

He shifted aside, letting her knuckles skim his flesh to give her a taste of success before he smacked her down. "What do I win if you fail to last the hour?"

"What do you want?" she countered.

"To train you as a female."

"No."

"No? I thought you were sure of your skills?" He pressed hard, hoping she'd take his bait.

"I don't wager what I cannot afford to lose."

By the stars, she was too smart for her own good. However, perhaps after this session, she'd change her mind—that is, if he ever worked past his distaste enough to strike her. Every time he thought about her slender curves, her perfectly shaped breasts, or the way she'd spasmed with pleasure in his arms, he found the idea of hitting her abhorrent.

As if reading his mind, she taunted him. "This will take forever if you don't counterstrike."

"Prepare yourself," he warned. But he was the one who needed preparation. He told himself to go easy. She had no idea of the force he could bring against her or the necessary skill required to counter him. The next time she closed the distance between them, instead of retreating, he shifted forward. Where previously she'd met air, this time she rammed into his full mass. His move was the equivalent of placing a wall in front of a charging *masdon*. He expected her to go down.

She did.

He expected her to stay down.

She didn't.

Rolling, she smoothly shoved to her feet and attacked again, still doggedly obeying his previous orders. Not only didn't she appear fazed or hurt, her eyes glittered with the challenge. She actually seemed to be enjoying herself. The more difficulties she faced, the more she thrived.

"I'm okay," she assured him. "Do that again, please."

"No." He didn't want her anticipating his moves or attempting to counteract them with the skills she already possessed from her Earth training. He needed her frustrated so she'd resort to her psi quickly, efficiently, automatically. However, she obviously had a higher tolerance for combat frustration than he'd guessed.

"Is that all you've got?" She mocked him while knowing full well that he could hurt her, yet obviously trusting his skill and savoring what he would teach her.

Under other circumstances, he would have delighted in her spirit, but her core confidence increased the difficulty of the lesson he must teach. Once again, he'd have to push her harder than he would have liked.

Summoning his courage, he waited for her to advance. Picking his moment, his spot, and his angle, he gently blocked her attack. Her body shuddered as his mass stopped her cold, but like the trained warrior she was, she bounced, spun, and attacked repeatedly.

She didn't break. She didn't even hesitate. She just kept advancing, showing him a multitude of strikes and combinations, some so innovative he'd never seen them before. Using psi, he had the supreme advantage. If he stood stock-still, she couldn't penetrate his shields. Nor could she move at anywhere near psi speed. In comparison to the speed of thought he was capable of achieving, she moved as slowly as a prehistoric amoeba. Most importantly, the suit permitted him to see psi movement. Until she learned to use her psi, she couldn't even see his movements. To her, he would appear to pop in and out of space. But once she opened her psi vision, she would "see" him go through space.

Yes, she'd used her psi before. But it took too long for her to concentrate and call up the skill. She needed to be able to use her psi as easily and instinctively as she used her muscles.

After fifteen minutes, her attacks had yet to slow. In

thirty, she still wasn't breathing hard, although a light sweat shone on her forehead. He had to give her credit. Her conditioning and stamina were excellent. Her effort clearly revealed that her fighting spirit was as much a part of her character as any warrior's. He had to put aside his personal prejudices that no woman should have her skills, and be grateful that she was willing to work so hard to find her psi.

"Kahn, you haven't showed me a new trick in the last ten minutes."

She jolted him from his thoughts. He'd been thinking instead of training her.

"Nor have you countered another attack," she complained. "Surely you can do better?"

Knowing she was correct, he blocked her next ten blows. "Happy now?"

"I'd be happier if you'd fight back." She grunted. "I'm fighting a shadow. This fight is boring."

She deliberately goaded him, but he held his temper. "You've used your psi once before. Go to that place."

"Can I stop and meditate?" she asked.

"No. Find the place you seek between punches," he instructed.

"How can I tap into my psi while I'm attacking?" She still spoke easily but perspiration coated her forehead.

Her difficulty was his fault. He had not frustrated her to the necessary level. He chose among several options and raised her suit's temperature.

She noticed almost immediately. "So that's how you knew I wouldn't last an hour. Take care, Kahn. At this temperature, I'll dehydrate fast."

She didn't complain. Just issued him warnings.

"If you don't like the temperature, do something about it."

"How?"

"Use your psi."

She front-kicked his stomach. He grabbed her foot and

swept the other leg out from under her. She went down hard. Grunted. Came back for more.

Circling him, eyes focused, she used the same kick, in the same place, as if daring him to try the countermove again. With ease, he repeated the technique and tried not to wince as she fell hard for the second time. She got up a little more slowly, but she didn't hesitate to repeat the move for a third time.

She'd fallen twice, taking more punishment than he'd intended to inflict. But it was not enough. Instead of grabbing her foot, he deflected the kick with enough force to send her stumbling.

"You fight like a little girl," he insulted her, knowing that she needed to push through the discouragement and pain or everything they'd done would be for nothing. He couldn't permit her to stop.

By now she should be drawing on energy she didn't know she possessed, but she wasn't tired enough yet. She launched a flying side kick at his head. He spun her in midair and slapped her bottom hard before she hit the ground.

"You just went back on your word." Furious, she struck with a knife-hand attack to his throat, but even as her eyes glittered with anger she continued to obey his orders. "You would not have slapped a man."

She was correct, and he didn't like what he had done, especially since she'd followed his orders without question or complaint. However, the thought of using his fist on her still didn't sit square with him, but she'd left him no choice. Either he taxed her to the maximum and drained her energy or she would fail.

Reminding himself that failure was unacceptable, he threw a slow psi punch to her stomach. At the last instant she swiveled her hips, lessening his blow to a powder-puff tap.

She fired an "it's about time you did that" glance at him, but saved her breath. Breathing evenly, she remained balanced on the balls of her feet.

By the tiniest degree, he increased the speed of his next psi punch. At the same time, he directed, "Raise your shield."

His fist met no resistance except the conditioned muscles of her stomach tightening to protect internal organs from the punch. Ignoring the sick roil in his gut, he increased the pace. "Defend yourself."

She moved to the right. He caught her with a blow to her shoulder. She lunged left and he tripped her. Instead of rising to her feet, she attempted to sweep him down.

"Use your frustration. I'm thinking and fighting in slow motion, but you need to keep up."

With a strange yell, she thrust a fist into his stomach. She'd used her psi!

He blocked with his shield. "Don't lose that anger. Hit me," he demanded, not letting up, despite the quivering he could see in her legs, the exhaustion in her eyes. "Faster. Harder. Use your mind."

She breathed raggedly now. Sweat streamed down her forehead. "How much longer?"

"The lesson has just begun."

12

Tessa ignored her screaming muscles, her straining lungs, and her thumping heart. Master Chen had often pushed her past what she'd thought was her limit, proving that the mind could press through previously defined confines. Even as a beginning student, she'd done kicking drills that lasted for hours, tiring the body to the point where only the most necessary and efficient muscles accomplished the task.

Kahn's goal appeared similar. He wanted her body exhausted to force her to use her psi. So she kept pressing, imagining a cage, punching through the bars with her fists and kicking with her feet. But instead of muscles, the engine driving her body was her mind. She called upon every mental wisp of frustration and shot her fist into Kahn's chin.

He blocked with a psi shield and countered. She raised her own shield. Too late. And took a tumble. However, the tumble elevated her frustration, refilled her mind. Next time, she'd raise her shield before she attacked.

Shields up, she advanced. Kahn shifted, countered, but she remained untouched. Her shields had worked.

Elation filled her and she lost the psi shield.

The lesson continued with Tessa determined that he would be the one to call it quits. Willing to fight until she either dropped or he ended the session, she pushed herself beyond reason, beyond common sense, beyond anything she'd done before.

Her extraordinary effort produced rewarding results. She learned to hold her psi shield, to punch and to kick at the speed of thought. Sometime during the lesson, she realized that she could now "see" Kahn's moves. Her psi vision had kicked in.

Compared to Kahn, she was still clumsy. She couldn't control the null grav or the temperature, and she didn't have his speed. But practice would enhance her skills, and her confidence grew. Despite her exhaustion and the heat, she kept attacking.

Until she blacked out.

One moment she was lunging at Kahn, the next, she awakened in his arms. Stiff, sore, yet wonderfully tired, she marveled over her psi power, which had been untapped her entire life. She'd heard humans only used ten percent of their minds, and scientists didn't understand the complexity of the brain, but her psi was a whole new sense. It was if she'd been blind all her life and could suddenly see.

Kahn frowned at her, concern darkening his amber eyes. "What is wrong, woman?"

"I overheated. It's nothing to worry about."

"Why didn't you stop?"

"You told me not to."

He was clearly stunned, and his lower jaw dropped open. "I expected you to stop before you burned out."

She cupped his jaw. "I'll let you make it up to me." She raised her lips to his. "Kiss me, Kahn."

"You need comforting for your pain?"

She rolled her eyes. "No. I want to celebrate." She let her fingers trail down his jaw to his neck. "Don't you want to kiss me?"

"Touching me like that is inappropriate." Confusion marred his features. "What do we have to celebrate?"

She raised her head higher but couldn't reach his lips. So she planted a kiss on his neck, collarbone, shoulder. "We are celebrating our success. Using the psi was marvelous. I never knew I could move that fast. Or see you move. And the shielding is spectacular. How much force will it stop? Will I get stronger with practice? How long will it take me to use the null grav and become as adept as you?"

Interest filled his eyes. "Fighting with psi gave you pleasure?"

"Learning a new skill gave me pleasure. Surely you feel the same way?"

"I am a man," he said, as if that explained everything.

"And a very handsome man, too." She grinned up at him, aware that he was pleased by her progress, even if he had yet to say so. "Wouldn't you rather put those lips to better use than arguing with me?"

He scowled and then he laughed, his eyes brightening with amusement. "You are impossible. Are you sure you are not injured?"

She wiggled her eyebrows at him. "Maybe you should examine me, all of me, to see for yourself."

"What is that sound coming from your mouth?" Dora asked.

After her training session with Kahn and then a very pleasant lovemaking session, she'd slept soundly. After awakening, she'd padded to the food materializer and used her psi to make pasta, a salad, and a cup of coffee.

"Hi, Dora." Tessa was starved. "That sound is called whistling."

"What does it mean?"

"It's music."

"You're off key."

"Mm." Tessa sat on the dais and ate. "I could get used to these food materializers."

"There are no food materializers on Rystan."

"Why not?" Her food tasted fresh and she didn't even have to cook. Apparently the machine was stocked with basic proteins and carbohydrates, vitamins and minerals. All she had to do was use her psi and the machine duplicated what she envisioned. She might now even be able to open the door to this chamber.

Tessa munched happily on her salad, sipped her coffee, and fired a psi thought at the wall. The door opened. Life was looking up.

"Food materializers are expensive. The inhabitable parts of Rystan are poor in resources."

"Tell me more."

"I'm sorry. I don't have that kind of information in my data banks."

"That's okay. Maybe I'll ask Kahn. Can you show me a dance called the *Ramala Ki*?"

"Compliance."

While Tessa ate, she stared at a holovid woman performing a series of sexy steps and complicated hand movements. The hip motion reminded her of Hawaiian hula dancers, and there could be no doubting the moves were meant to entice a man. Vowing to learn the dance, she had Dora repeat them while she ate.

"You seem happier since your wedding night. Did he please you?"

"Dora! Some things are private."

"Privacy is a hard concept for me to burn into my circuits."

"Hey, it's okay. Without even realizing it, I step on Kahn's toes all the time."

"I have never seen you step on his toes."

"I meant that my values often clash with his. He has this ridiculous notion that women shouldn't initiate sex. Or touching. Or kissing. You wouldn't think such a macho man would be disturbed by my clumsy attempts to learn to fight with my psi."

"Macho man?"

"The 'I'm always in charge, listen to me' dominant attitude of the alpha male."

"He was probably born that way," Dora said. "I've transported several Rystani delegations. All Rystani men convey a superior attitude."

"What about their women?" Tessa finished her salad and moved on to the pasta, staring once again at the holovid. Oh my. The woman picked a moment to pivot, stop, and display herself in a most provocative pose.

"I've never met a Rystani woman. The men leave their wives and daughters at home on the rare occasions they travel."

"Well, apparently I'm not what Kahn wants in a wife." Tessa grinned, recalling the look on his face when she'd suggested that she'd like to kiss a certain part of his anatomy.

"You certainly look pleased."

"The man still has issues. But he's making progress."

"In more ways than one. We've almost reached Zenon Prime."

Tessa heard a hint of sadness in her friend's voice. "Oh, Dora. Does this mean goodbye for us?"

"I don't think so. I will be transporting you again. However, if you would like to stay in touch—"

"I would."

"—while you are on the planet."

"That's possible?"

Machinery hummed, and Tessa, curious, placed her utensils in the disposal unit and peered into the materializer. Glistening black and white stones appeared.

"Take them and place the stones on your earlobes. The women on Usjar use them to keep in constant contact with their consorts."

Tessa did as she asked, hoping the tiny devices would serve as both microphone and speaker. "Can you hear me?"

"Of course." Dora's voice vibrated in Tessa's ear. "I've also implanted tiny cameras in the stones."

"Can you induce privacy mode, as well?"

"Yes, but you must take care to conceal all lip movements."

"I understand. Thanks, Dora. You're the best."

"No problem."

Tessa swallowed the last of her pasta with a grin. Dora loved to pick up slang, and she felt comforted with her computer friend nearby. With Zenon Prime this close, she was about to step onto a new world. As Earth's first representative, she planned to make a favorable impression. Unfortunately, she'd never felt so ignorant. She didn't know the customs here or what was expected of her, either. Kahn hadn't been forthcoming on the subject, in fact, he hadn't mentioned it, and Dora lacked adequate data. However, knowing that Dora was with her made her heart light and her steps eager to explore.

Now that Tessa could open the door to her chamber, she was ready to venture out. "Dora, where's Kahn?"

"On the bridge."

"Can you guide me there, please?"

"Compliance."

Tessa followed a series of blinking lights to the bridge. The corridors all looked similar to her with their crystal machinery that reminded her more of art than technology. She saw no other rooms and surmised that the ship's interior was filled mostly by gigantic engines to run the hyperdrives.

The bridge wasn't much larger than the shuttle's. The circular cabin housed several viewscreens. The monitors to port, starboard, and stern showed a black sky with pinpoints of stars. The screen before Kahn revealed a planet that could have been drawn right from a Disney fantasy.

With three moons and two suns in the seven-planet solar system, there were no shadows or dark areas. Rings around the fourth planet sparkled with ethereal crystal structures. Giant cables connected the rings to the planet below and vehicles that resembled train cars or giant elevators shot up and down the cables.

The planet had two emerald oceans, both in the southern hemisphere. The clouds were pink and the landscape slashes of rose. Streaks of violet desert between the giant domes of glasslike cities held her fascinated.

Kahn looked up from the console. He didn't seem the least surprised to see her there, but pleased. Her new husband might not be big on words, but she was starting to read his moods. Tensions between them had eased, and while she wouldn't yet classify their complicated relationship as friendly, she believed they understood one another well enough to work out their differences.

He gestured for her to come closer. "You slept straight through our hyperjump. Welcome to Zenon Prime."

"Wow. Is this where the Challenge takes place?"

"No, but there's an official welcoming ceremony waiting for you on the planet." Kahn spoke to someone else through the communicator then docked the ship, smoothly maneuvering alongside one of the towers floating in the clouds.

Metal clanged on metal. The gravity changed ever so slightly, and Kahn stretched as if he had kinks in his muscles. One moment he wore his casual low-slung pants and vest, and the next he'd changed into a formal black suit with braid piping, long sleeves, and a V-neckline that made him look masculine and darkly dangerous, especially with the ceremonial knife in his belt.

He changed her clothes, too, and she gasped. An icy, diaphanous dress shimmered as the gorgeous fabric floated around her. Gossamer threads of silver, pink, and purple cellophane clouded the glassy translucence. Light, delicate and yet modest, the gown was the prettiest garment she'd ever worn. Tessa read admiration in Kahn's eyes and reined in her automatic protest of his choosing her attire, refusing to complain even about her high-heeled platform shoes.

Kahn snapped his fingers. "I almost forgot." From a compartment he removed a pendant with a smoky red stone. "For you. It's a starfire."

She stared in awe. The stone shimmered like an opal, sparkled like a diamond, the color changing from crimson to scarlet, depending on the viewing angle. "It's beautiful. Thank you."

Kahn placed the jewelry around her neck and the stone nestled between her breasts. "This is to remind you that during the welcoming ceremony on Zenon Prime, I will remain at your side and protect you. Some of the aliens will seem strange to you, but you have nothing to fear. You aren't expected to recognize the different cultures that you will meet or to know their customs. Just be yourself. There are only two races to worry about. First, the Endekians, who are my enemies. They are short, yellow-skinned men with sharp teeth. Try to avoid looking them in the eyes as they will take it as a sign of female interest. Hopefully, Jypeg will not be here."

She heard hatred in Kahn's tone. "Jypeg?"

"The man who killed Lael." Kahn took a deep breath and continued. "The other race you must try not to insult are the Osarians."

The manner in which he'd phrased his statement sounded so strange to her—as if everyone insulted the Osarians. "Why or how would I insult them?"

"The Osarians are repulsive-looking creatures. Some candidates have run from the welcoming ceremonies in fear of the tentacled and powerful creatures."

"I will not run," she promised. After his lovely gift and declaration of protection, she felt petty complaining about the shoes. But the platform shoes with a heel way higher than one she was accustomed to left her clenching Kahn's arm for balance, and for once, he didn't complain about her touching him first. At least the bruise on her face had faded.

She eyed him as he led her to the shuttle bay. "You like me clinging to you for support, don't you?"

"All is as it should be." His voice remained serene but she caught a glint of amusement in his gaze.

"You won't think this is so damn amusing if I fall flat on my face and embarrass us both."

"You have extraordinary balance."

"And patience," she muttered as she tripped, then gripped his arm tighter.

Tessa repeatedly tried to modify the shoes, but he hadn't simply used psi on her suit. He'd locked in his will by the use of the marriage bands he'd placed on her during their wedding ceremony, preventing her from overriding his decision. Forced to go clad according to his wishes in the lovely gown and shod in the ridiculous shoes, she supposed she should consider herself lucky that she wasn't wearing some hideous outfit. But her feet already ached, and she fervently hoped she wouldn't be spending much time on them.

If she could operate the suit's null grav, she could float. Perhaps that was the point. Kahn had a brilliant tactical mind, and she wouldn't put it past him to use the ceremony and the uncomfortable shoes to frustrate her into using null grav and teach her another psi lesson. One thing she knew for sure, Kahn always had a reason for his actions, reasons that weren't necessarily obvious.

She sighed, followed Kahn into the shuttle, and vowed not to complain. However, she silently wondered why developing her psi always had to be so unpleasant.

Kahn skillfully piloted the shuttle downward, and Tessa stared in wonder at the purple vegetation. Cactuslike plants, hundreds of feet high, mushroomed from the lavender desert. The gigantic plants rimmed an enormous crater into which the shuttle descended.

Absorbed with the intriguing view of other aircraft, saucers, cigar-shaped and cylindrical, Tessa forgot the discomfort of her shoes. They plummeted swiftly into a controlled spiral, joining a busy traffic pattern. Below them runways, helipads, and hangars awaited the various aircraft of every imaginable size, shape, and color.

Her curiosity fired, she gazed at the city, longing to explore. "How long will we stay here?"

"Just a day or two. Then we go to Rystan where other people can help with your training."

She could tell by his tone that he was already eager to leave and head for home. So she vowed to make the most of her short stay here.

In moments, they'd landed, and Kahn eased Tessa through the hatch into a buslike vehicle where they were the only passengers. She stared out the window, disappointed at the lack of an alien view as they whisked through a darkened tunnel. By her internal clock, Tessa estimated fifteen minutes passed before they disembarked inside the tunnel and headed toward yet another vehicle.

"The Federation has provided a flit-glider," Kahn said with satisfaction. The glider looked like a large torpedo with two seats. She sat behind Kahn and they launched with a whoosh and Kahn piloted them straight into an enormous cavern.

Tessa gaped at the overwhelming size of the underground city. Obviously the Zenon people lived on every part of their world, including the planet's rings, as well as above and below the surface.

Artificial pink clouds hung in the domed ceiling, which appeared to resemble a lavender "sky." Alien buildings that looked like *bendar* created a delicately harmonious skyline in the domed underground city. Dazzlingly magnificent sculptures decorated moving walkways, but she and Kahn remained too high to see the aliens below, who traveled past graceful waterfalls and picturesque gardens of the grand city. Clearly, the artistic balance of the Federation capital had been considered by the builders so everyone could enjoy its beauty.

"This city's magnificent," she said.

Kahn shrugged his large shoulders as if he'd been here many times over and was not impressed. "Zenon Prime is the capital of the Federation. This planet is the center of pride and progress, but only the most privileged live here."

Kahn's tone was clipped, difficult to read, but she suspected he disapproved. Still, she couldn't stem her rising awe or the curiosity over what kind of beings had erected such beauty.

When Kahn ended the short flight, landing upon an enormous stage, Tessa wondered if she was ready. A huge alien audience watched. Beings of different shapes, sizes, and colors awaited, and Tessa suddenly realized they were there to look at her. The flight around the dome had been her grand entrance. Her stomach knotted. Remembering his promise to protect her, she placed her hand over the starfire necklace, the stone reassuring her. Kahn had told her these beings weren't hostile. They hadn't contacted Earth and brought her halfway across the Milky Way to eat her but to meet her.

Kahn popped the flitter's canopy and held out his arm. Taking his arm to steady her nerves and aid her balance in the shoes, Tessa looked around and swallowed hard as hushed expectancy washed over the multitude of strangers. *Courage.*

"You will do fine, woman," Kahn whispered. "Just remember not to use sarcasm, please."

"Hell, haven't you heard of free speech in this galaxy?" she muttered, uneasy at being the focus of all those alien eyes. Still, she shot him her most brilliant smile as she stepped out of the flitter to a roar of cheers.

For the next several hours, Tessa stood in her uncomfortable shoes in a receiving line where Federation delegates welcomed her. As promised, Kahn didn't leave her side.

At first, Tessa studied each alien, amazed by the different

possibilities of humanoid construction. Most of them had a head set on their bodies. The genetic combinations seemed as varied as the number of planets in the galaxy. Most had eyes in their heads, but several possessed orbs on their appendages. Some had wings or tails, others orange tentacles, and one species changed colors as it "spoke." Thanks to her suit's translator, she could exchange welcoming small talk.

After a while, she lost count of the differences between the aliens. Instead of noticing bodily appearance, Tessa amused herself by guessing at their personalities. Although Kahn didn't speak, he sometimes leaned closer to her, and occasionally she sensed a tension in him as different species approached.

When a six-foot-tall, large-tentacled insectoid that reminded her of a giant daddy longlegs slithered closer, Tessa froze in order to avoid instinctive retreat. The friendly spider introduced itself as Bython, from the planet Whoollanzi, and its softly pleasant trilling sound calmed Tessa's frazzled nerves. She recalled she could speak to Dora through the earrings, moving her lips as little as possible.

"Dora?"

In privacy mode, her friend fed her information. "The Whoollanzi subdue their foes with that pleasant trilling before devouring their prey alive."

"Didn't need to know *that*," Tessa muttered.

"Don't worry. You are too large to be considered food."

The formidable line of aliens passed before Tessa slowly. Each Federation member had different customs. Some stared at her boldly, others humbly kneeled at her feet. No one offered to shake hands. One scratched under his armpit and another's eyes actually rolled across its forehead.

When a short, powerful, yellow-skinned man with an ugly scar slashed from his forehead to his jaw approached, Kahn tensed so hard she feared his muscles might snap. "Endekian?" she whispered, immediately looking down to avoid eye contact as Kahn had instructed.

"That's Jypeg. How did you guess?" Dora answered.

As if sensing her husband's hostility, the Endekian kept the meeting brief. "Welcome to the Federation."

The Endekian moved on, but Tessa's curiosity escalated and she wished she knew more about Kahn's enemy and the political situation, but now was not the time for questions.

When a creature that looked like a snot-covered octopus approached, she noted a certain electricity in the crowd—almost as if the other aliens were collectively holding their breaths to see if she would run off the stage screaming in fright. This must be the Osarian. She schooled her features to remain stoic.

"Stay still," Dora instructed. "The Osarians are blind, and he means you no harm. To flinch will show great disrespect, although most aliens here wouldn't consider allowing an Osarian to come near *them*."

The audacious creature ran his tentacles over her body, his touch light as a feather, but nevertheless leaving a trail of slime behind, which her suit quickly cleaned. She understood that the Osarian was "seeing" her by touch, like a blind man reading braille, and that he meant no disrespect by lightly skimming her breasts, her buttocks, and her legs.

Tessa held still, but as the cold, slimy tentacles frisked her, she wondered what her warm body temperature and dry skin felt like to the Osarian. For all Tessa knew, the Osarian might have had to work up his courage for a week just to force himself to greet her.

Welcome, Earthling.

The thought came directly through the tentacle, not her translator. Was he telepathic? But not just thoughts came through the link, emotion also passed through. She sensed warmth at his genuine happiness at meeting her, but at her suspicion that he might find touching a warm-blooded creature displeasing, he also conveyed admiration for her open-mindedness. Mutual recognition that they were both outsiders—Tessa because she was the first Earthling to visit the Federation and the Osarian because he was the only one of his kind on this world—caused them to share an immediate empathy.

Knowing the Osarian wouldn't object, she reached out and grasped the slimy tentacle to reestablish the link. She spoke her thoughts out loud, wondering if the creature had ears or if it could sense her good intentions. "I am pleased to meet you, too."

Tessa had no idea if she managed to convey her own friendliness back through the link. But when the Osarian wrapped all eight tentacles around her and hugged her, she figured she'd made another friend. What an odd assortment she was collecting. First, Dora, now the Osarian.

Even while wrapped in Osari's friendly emotions, Tessa sensed that Kahn believed she needed protection. "I'm fine," she told him just as the Osarian released her.

A murmur of astonishment rose among the other delegates, but Tessa paid no attention to the crowd. She'd sensed so much through the link. A loneliness in the creature, sadness that the other races found him too repulsive to touch, cutting him off from the sharing of emotions needed for him to communicate.

She wondered if these others knew that the empathic Osarian race sensed their disgust and if they feared the oneness required to communicate. However, even she had trouble seeing past the outer ugliness to the beautiful soul hidden inside.

Not only was the Osarian friendly, he was gentle. And she sensed that the forced solitude was unnatural for him. He missed others of his kind, his home and family, the longing so strong it came through the brief touch quite strongly.

Dora spoke in her ear. "You have just been honored by one of the most powerful races in the galaxy. Osarians are isolationists, who usually keep themselves apart from the other races."

"Why?"

"Osarians traveled aboard the shuttle during a rescue mission, so I know a lot about them." Dora imparted useful information and Tessa listened carefully. "Few humanoids can overcome their natural repugnance to the Osarian appearance. In order not to cause others pain with their ugliness, they have mostly retreated to their homeworld, which is rich in natural resources as well as blessed with a prime location. Due to prejudice over their appearance, they have been closed to the lucrative trade routes."

"How do they survive in the Federation?"

"The Osarians are notoriously enterprising. They've used their extraordinary sensory perceptions to mediate disputes and have become a behind-the-scenes influential member of the Federation. Yet they maintain a mysterious aura, rarely intermingling with others."

"Tell me more," Tessa requested as she greeted an endless line of delegates.

"Before he touched you, the Osarian probably sensed your initial distaste of his appearance. But since you quickly controlled your reaction and then actually initiated contact by touching the tentacle, you impressed him."

Apparently the Osarian's embrace had in turn impressed the other delegates, who eyed Tessa with new respect. Okay, the Osarian was hideous, but she hadn't expected such enlightened people to ostracize him. She thought it odd that although others shunned the Osarian, their respect for her had risen, creating a swelling hubbub of noise. Tessa wasn't into politics, but she was gratified that she'd represented Earth in a respectable fashion, and she was even more pleased that she'd reached out to the tentacled alien. Even now, she still had a strange euphoria from the encounter.

"Pay attention." Dora pulled Tessa from her thoughts. "Azrel is Kahn's stepmother. They haven't met until now."

Kahn's stepmother! Why hadn't he ever mentioned her? What had happened to his biological mother? And where did his father live now? And why had Kahn never met Azrel?

The first recognizably humanoid female to greet Tessa exhibited an unmistakable regal presence. The statuesque, green-skinned woman moved with a boldness that immediately commanded respect, and Tessa knew at once that this woman wasn't just a politician, but a warrior. Azrel's bare arms revealed sleek muscles. However, her imposing manner was contradicted by her outrageous outfit. Her fire-engine-red bodice dipped scandalously low. The too-tight waistline was a flashy tangerine that billowed into turquoise folds over her legs and reminded Tessa of pantaloons. A green turban that housed a live snakelike creature crowned her head of dark green hair.

"Welcome to the Federation. I hear you are newly married." Azrel spoke boldly, ignoring the bristling Kahn, her eyes sparkling with intrigue. The green-skinned, green-haired, and green-eyed Azrel was stunning. Her high cheekbones and wide-mouthed smile revealed straight white teeth and a dimple in her cheek. "If you ever wish for another home, our planet Scartar will embrace you. Or stop in for a visit," she modified as Kahn scowled. "Our planet is a matriarchy, and I credit you would feel at home with us." She leaned forward, cheek to cheek, and whispered, "Find me." At the same moment she slipped a piece of paper into Tessa's hands, then moved on. Tessa didn't know what to make of the woman, but sensed she might have found another friend—only Kahn clearly disapproved of his stepmother. The hostility between them couldn't be missed and Tessa didn't have to ask why.

Kahn would automatically disapprove of a matriarchy. While she wanted to know how Kahn's father had come to marry the green-skinned Azrel, Tessa put aside her question for another time.

Finally, Kahn leaned forward and whispered in her ear. "The Zenon ambassador."

The last being in the long line of delegates, the Zenonite floated onto the stage and appeared to be one gigantic brain with two lidless aqua eyes. Its shriveled appendages dangled impotently from the cauliflowerlike brain. A perfectly human set of lips spoke from the throbbing gray matter and welcomed her to the Federation.

"Earthling, our best wishes go with you during the Challenge. Because you risk your life, we present you with a gift of one million credits!" Music that sounded like trumpets and drums blared. A cart rolled across the stage. Atop the cart rested a pillow with a tiny opalescent box.

"Inside the box is a chip with your credits," Dora told her. "Take it."

Tessa accepted the box. "Thank you."

"If you fail the Challenge, all unspent credits will be repossessed by the Federation. Use them wisely, Earthling. Long life and successful Challenge."

One million credits. From what Dora had told Tessa, the Federation's capital had to be a prime shopping opportunity. She had no idea what a million credits would buy, but she intended to find out.

13

"The Federation has arranged quarters for us in the Galactic Palace." Kahn escorted her along a moving walkway, through a garden ripe with the spicy fragrance of exotic flowers, all in purples from ocher to lavender. The dome overhead had darkened, creating a false night sky with moons and stars, but the trees captured her attention, their trunks, branches, and leaves glowing with a phosphorescent beauty that stole Tessa's breath.

This planet was truly a marvel of advanced engineering and art. She leaned against Kahn to take a little strain off her aching feet, pleased to share this experience with him. "For how long has Zenon been the Federation's capital?"

"No one really knows." Kahn seemed less tense now that the welcoming ceremony was over. He held her hand, his fingers laced through hers, his tone more relaxed than usual. "Originally, a race now called the Perceptive Ones inhabited the planet. They left behind the equipment that builds our psi-controlled suits. Our people were thrilled to get one for every citizen after my father won the Challenge." Tessa imagined Earth's citizens would benefit greatly, as well. "Over the millennium, no one has ever replicated the machinery or produced suits like them. Therefore, over thousands of years, many wars have been fought for this world, with a multitude of races taking and losing control."

Their room at the Galactic Palace reminded Tessa of her chamber on the spaceship. Walls, ceiling, and floors decorated in the same shimmering gray *bendar,* their quarters boasted a domed ceiling and windows that overlooked a parklike setting where lovers strolled hand in hand, or flew wing tip to wing tip. The major differences between the palace room and the ship's chamber were the artwork that floated from the ceiling in ever-changing shapes, the sculptures that framed the holo-screens, and the soft, luxuriant foam flooring.

The communications screen beeped, signaling that a message awaited. Kahn took the call as she stared out the window, aching to explore, but too tired to appreciate more sightseeing. She needed sleep and a change of shoes for her aching feet.

But when she approached Kahn and saw his sad expression, all thoughts of clothing fled from her mind.

"What's wrong?"

"My father has requested a visit."

"Don't you want to see him?"

"I will not leave you alone, and I cannot bring you into the men's quarters." He spit out the last words with distaste. "I'm not going."

"Men's quarter's?"

"Azrel keeps my father like a . . . pet."

"Aren't they married?" she asked.

Kahn scowled at her. "How did you know that?"

Damn. Dora had told her and Kahn still didn't know about her secret communications with the computer. She needed to be careful, or tell Kahn the truth. She decided not to trouble him further.

"She told me earlier." Tessa shrugged. "I don't understand what has upset you so."

Kahn floated into a sitting position and tugged her onto his lap. "When the Federation initially contacted Rystan, my grandfather was our leader. He sent my father to compete in the Challenge."

Though grateful to take the weight off her aching feet, she still frowned. "But I thought all contestants couldn't have any living family?"

"My grandfather lied. Since Rystan kept no written records of births and deaths, the Federation couldn't verify the statement. Although my father had already married and I was ten years old, my grandfather sent him."

"Your poor mother." Tessa couldn't help feeling sorry for Kahn, the little boy, too.

"My father successfully completed the Challenge, but to do so, Azrel made him give his word that he would submit to her. She refused to recognize his marriage to my mother, who died of a broken heart. To this day, Corban lives like a love slave on Azrel's planet."

Tessa thought of the beautiful, sensual, exotic green-skinned woman and wondered if Corban regretted his decision. "Does your father object?"

He shook his head. "I do not know. However, I cannot forgive him for what he did to my mother. He should have found another way to succeed."

She noted he didn't mention his own loss. "Who raised you?"

"My grandfather."

She heard the bitterness in his tone, wrapped her arms around him and held him tightly. He'd lost his father and mother due to his grandfather, whom he probably hadn't forgiven, either. No wonder Kahn trusted no one. No wonder he didn't like to break rules. His grandfather's lie and Azrel's interest in his father had torn his family apart.

While Kahn had grown up without a family as she had, she'd become an orphan due to an accident. She hadn't spent her life blaming the only family member she had left for her loss. Or aching for a father who had voluntarily given her up to live as a love slave to save his world.

Knowing Kahn as she did, she suspected that he hated not only the bargain that his father had made with Azrel, he also hated the fact that his father might be content with his lot. The story explained much about him.

She kissed Kahn's neck, snuggled against him, pleased that he no longer bristled when she initiated contact. Every day he accepted more of her Earth customs and the closeness between them grew. This was the first time he'd spoken to her of a personal concern and she badly wanted to help. "How long since you've seen your father?"

"He never returned to Rystan after the Challenge."

"You haven't spoken via your hyperlinks?"

He shook his head. "At first, we feared the Federation might learn of the deception. After the statute of limitations on Corban's Challenge win finally passed, so much time had gone by that opening up old wounds seemed pointless."

"You must go speak with him," she urged. "I would give anything to talk to my parents again—just once. You cannot give up this opportunity, or you may regret it for all your life."

"No."

"Kahn, the choice must have been difficult for him. Think of the decision he had to make—to give up the family he loved, so his world could join the Federation. The choice could not have been easy. You owe it to him to listen to what he has to say."

"No."

Although he sounded certain, she caught a "convince me" look in his eye that made her keep pushing. "Carrying such bitterness inside can taint the soul. Go talk to him. See if you

can find it in your heart to forgive him. And if you cannot—
at least you'll have judged him with the eyes of an adult and
not those of a child."

He hugged her. "Woman, your words have merit." He astonished her by admitting that much. Whether he realized it
or not, Kahn was changing, and she couldn't have been more
pleased by his open affection. "However, I cannot leave you."

"Of course you can. I will be fine."

He fisted his hand in her hair, gently tugged back her head
so he could stare into her eyes. "Promise me that you will
not leave this chamber until I return?"

"I promise."

Tessa made the promise with every intention of keeping her
word. She was tired enough to sleep for a week. Her feet
ached from her shoes, and the tension of the long day had
caught up with her. Most important of all, she had committed herself to her marriage and to Kahn. His honor attracted
her, and when he wasn't bossing her around, she genuinely
liked and cared for him, even if she didn't always understand
him. Before he left, Kahn released her from the shoes and
she changed her dress so she could comfortably sleep. She
expected that Kahn would be back long before she awakened.

Still, before she rested, Tessa examined the tiny slip of paper Azrel had secretly placed in her hand. She frowned at the
series of numbers there, but too tired to consider questioning
Dora, Tessa closed her weary eyes and immediately slept.

Several hours later, Tessa awakened to a pounding on the
door. "Who's there?"

"Azrel."

Kahn still hadn't returned. While Tessa had promised him
not to leave the chamber, she hadn't agreed to refuse visi-
tors. Besides, Tessa was curious about the middle-of-the-
night visit from Azrel.

Using her psi to cover her body, Tessa also opened the door. "Come in."

"I'm sorry to disturb you, but while Kahn is detained I thought I'd pop over for a visit." The green-skinned woman entered the chamber, her expression serious.

"What do you mean? Why has my husband been detained?"

Azrel laughed, delighted with something Tessa didn't understand. "Do not worry. His father requested that I arrange for the two men to spend the night in conversation. They have years of catching up to do."

"So why are you here?"

"I thought we should become . . . acquainted."

"Why?" Tessa knew Kahn didn't trust this woman and kept up her guard.

Azrel sighed. "Our society is a matriarchy. And while Corban claims he is happy, he is not."

"Kahn says his father is a love slave."

Azrel smiled. "Corban does not object to that."

"So what is the problem?" Was Kahn's stepmother, Tessa's mother-in-law, asking her for advice? She didn't have any. She wasn't even sure what was going on. But if Kahn's father was anything like Kahn, she imagined the adjustments Corban had made to live on Azrel's world were enormous.

Again, Azrel's smile faded. "Corban can never be free on my world. I was hoping a visit from his son would cheer him. They haven't seen each other in over twenty years."

"Thanks to you. Kahn told me that you broke up his parents' marriage."

"Kahn believes what his grandfather told him. His grandfather lied again."

"I don't understand." Tessa rubbed the last of the sleepiness from her eyes and helped herself to a cup of coffee. "Would you like some?"

"No, thank you." Azrel composed her body, floating into a sitting position. "Corban's father lied to the Federation about the fact that Corban had no family. He certainly wasn't a virgin, and although the Federation can bring people through time and make psi suits, they have no way to prove whether a Rystani male is telling the truth. Anyway, after Corban won the Challenge, his father couldn't allow him to come home. He still feared the Federation would discover the lie and revoke the Challenge win. So he told another lie. He told Corban that while he'd been gone for the Challenge, his wife and son had perished in a storm. He begged Corban not to return until the statute of limitations had passed and ten years had gone by. My husband did as his father requested, never knowing he'd left behind his wife and son."

"Oh, my God. Kahn doesn't know . . ."

"He does now." Azrel's face was grim. "My soldiers had orders to keep Kahn there if he tried to leave before Corban tells him the truth."

"Kahn may not believe him. There's much anger inside him, and hurt. It might take more than one visit to overcome . . . the distance between them."

"Exactly. After you complete the Challenge, I thought we could visit Rystan. This is presumptuous of me, but I hoped you would offer an invitation."

Wow. Tessa knew Azrel could be lying, but she didn't think so. The woman truly appeared to want Corban to regain ties with his son. "I'll see what I can do, but I have promised to follow Rystani custom, and I'm not sure if I'm allowed to issue invitations."

"Trying is all I ask and it is generous of you to accommodate me. After seeing what a mere two decades of marriage have done to Corban's spirit, I fear how several hundred more years on my planet will affect him."

"Several *hundred* years?" Tessa eyed the woman over her coffee. "Excuse me if this is a personal question, but how old are you?"

"On Scartar, no woman likes to admit her age. It is probably much the same throughout the galaxy, at least among humanoids," Azrel qualified. "I am four hundred and fifty-four years old. My life expectancy is about nine hundred years, just like yours," Azrel told her.

"No." Tessa shook her head vigorously. "We only live about eighty to one hundred years. Unless my suit isn't translating your numbers properly."

"Your translator is in perfect working order. The numbers are accurate. You see, the suit increases life expectancy for everyone, eight to ten times normal."

Tessa rocked back on her heels. "Nine hundred years," she repeated, stunned.

"Yes, and you are married to Kahn for all nine hundred of them." Azrel brought Tessa back to reality gently. "Do you love him?"

"Why is this your business?" Tessa asked warily, still stunned by Azrel's story and the news about her prolonged life expectancy.

"Do not be insulted. Corban was forced to adapt to Scartar, and obeying the laws of my people was a difficult adjustment. Do you realize on Rystan you will not be allowed to work outside the home, keep credits in your name, and that your value will be decided by how well you cook?"

Tessa tried to hide her dismay. "I suspected some of this, but Kahn has been damn secretive about Rystani culture." She didn't know if she could live in such a repressive society. Live for nine hundred or a thousand years? The thought boggled her mind and she focused on the mundane. "I don't even know how to cook."

"Earthling, you have nine centuries to learn." Azrel's voice was kind, trying to console her.

"Maybe I should buy a food materializer since there are none on Rystan."

"Those machines are very expensive. Only a few wealthy races have them, like the Zenonites and the Osarians," Azrel explained.

"But I've one million credits. I could buy one," Tessa said excitedly. Then she could drink coffee whenever she liked. "Or isn't that enough money?"

Azrel laughed. "You have plenty of credits."

"Great." Tessa had many purchases she wanted to make before Kahn returned and they headed to Rystan. "Where are the stores? Are they open all night?"

Azrel's green-tinted skin deepened to emerald as she headed for the holovid. "You, my daughter, are going to set Rystan on its head. This is how you shop." A neatly organized viewscreen appeared. Categories were indexed and items priced. "I'd recommend that you send all merchandise directly to your ship. And I must take my leave. Corban will fret if I do not return soon. One last thing."

"Yes?"

"The paper I gave you has a number on it. If you ever want to contact me, plug the number into a communication console."

Communication console? Hmm, Kahn had told her they hadn't had one on Rystan until recently, but maybe she could buy one of those for personal use, too.

"Thank you. And I'll do what I can to see that Kahn issues that invitation."

After Azrel departed, Tessa scanned the lists of services and merchandise in fascination. Detailed descriptions with pictures could be accessed for further information. Quickly, Tessa searched for the food materializer. Azrel had told her they were expensive, yet they only cost a thousand credits. In addition, Tessa bought the stock elements to create enough food to last ten people one thousand years. This set her back another twenty thousand credits, but she didn't hesitate.

After all, there was absolutely no point in saving the credits. If she died, the credits were returned to the Federation. If she lived, Kahn probably got to control them.

As rich as she was, the next item even she couldn't afford. A small spaceship with a warp drive was out of her league.

Reluctantly, Tessa skipped the transportation systems and moved on to communications.

Tessa also looked for hand weapons, but couldn't find any. However, she did purchase a beautifully crafted knife to give to Kahn as a present. When she scanned for computer information, she hit pay dirt.

"Dora. Take a look at this stuff."

"Compliance."

Tessa was tired of being ignorant. She couldn't make informed decisions when she didn't comprehend the kinds of new situations she faced on a regular basis in the Federation, and she was delighted for the chance to rectify her situation. Knowledge was power and she could improve her opportunities by educating herself. "Buy every scrap of information to update your memory banks."

"I cannot hold all the information available."

"Then buy more memory. And hardware, so I can keep you with me on Rystan."

Dora squealed, clearly delighted. "These purchases will be expensive."

"If I'm to survive, I need an education. I'm tired of working in the dark."

The information and technology were remarkably exorbitant and Tessa's available funds significantly dwindled. Yet, she felt her money was well spent. She just wished she could find information on the Challenge—but that was classified.

Quickly, Tessa spent the rest of the credits, picking out gifts, toiletries, vidtapes, a cleaning machine, a robotic babysitter, and a weather forecaster. Anything that caught her interest, she quickly bought and sent to the ship.

When she finished, she checked the time. She'd shopped for hours and Kahn still hadn't returned. About to check into his whereabouts, the door chimed and Dora announced, "You have another visitor."

"Who?"

"The Osarian."

"What could he want with me?"

"Why don't you open the door and ask him?" Dora prodded.

Tessa knew Kahn wouldn't approve, yet curiosity got the best of her. Using her psi, she opened the portal and the Osarian slithered inside.

She immediately grabbed a tentacle, seeking the reassurance of the link. "Greetings, Osari."

Linked brain to brain, she could "feel" the Osarian hesitate as if making a difficult decision. Then he opened the mind link wider and invited Tessa to enter his head.

She sensed no danger, but after she delved into a maelstrom of emotions and the core of the alien being, she lost all conscious awareness, lost her sense of individuality. Gently, Osari guided her within his mind until Tessa read his true essence. There was a mixture of love and hate, charity and greed, suspicion and curiosity, but the predominant and overwhelming feeling was a generosity of spirit and loyalty toward a new friend from Earth.

She understood this was Osari's way of reassuring her, a link that left him vulnerable. He spoke to her mind to mind. *You are free to ask me to leave at any time. But I hope you will permit me to stay. I went to considerable trouble to arrange this meeting.*

"Why?"

You do not speak freely in front of your mate, and you have secrets I wish to hear.

"What if I don't choose to share these secrets?" Tessa challenged the Osarian boldly.

"Then we are not the mind-meld friends I'd hoped for, and I beg your pardon for pressing myself upon you." Osari spoke in a flat voice, but through the mind link Tessa sensed his hurt.

She held on to Osari's tentacle. Harmony, friendship, curiosity, and excitement came through. She didn't know if he could lie to her through the link, but it seemed to her he had let her see and feel his essence. And he meant her no harm.

"Forgive me, friend Osari. I do not trust easily," Tessa murmured in apology. She withdrew from his mind, but kept the emotional link. "Now, tell me why you are here."

The Osarian spoke words, but emotions came through his tentacle. "My planet," began Osari in a dry tone colored with pride through the emotional link, "has the dubious distinction of the best trade location in the galaxy. We are centrally situated between many natural space lanes. What makes our location unique are two black stars of equal mass, equidistant from our planet."

"This is good?"

"The black stars are extremely dense matter and exert tremendous gravitational forces that expedite commerce."

"I don't understand."

He shot a mental image through the link. "Our planet is like the center of a slingshot that launches the starships into space at minimal cost. Since my planet has such a prime location, certain members of the Galactic Federation have actively sought to prevent us from becoming too powerful. All traders are offworlders. No one will share or sell us the information we need. For centuries we have been forbidden from participating in the lucrative contracts that use our world as a center of commerce."

"What is a trader?" Tessa asked, still confused, but appreciating the time she'd spent guarding Daron, the business tycoon who'd wheeled and dealed his way to a financial empire. During the months she'd spent protecting him, she'd also listened to his power plays, to his contract negotiations, and most of all, to his business acumen. She hoped a little of his skill had rubbed off on her, so she could understand the dynamics of Osari's situation.

"Traders negotiate the contracts of goods and services passing through space and earn their commission by charging a percentage of each transaction."

Tessa understood that the Osarians would have to be

upset that their world was so useful and that they weren't profiting by it. But she didn't understand why the Osarian was here. "What does all this have to do with me?"

Dora answered through her earrings. "We have purchased the information the Osarians need to conduct business, details others refuse to sell them due to their prejudice. That information came in with a batch of data concerning planetary imports and exports. We also have up-to-the-moment credit reports and detailed starship schedules."

"I was told you did some interesting shopping," Osari pressed gently.

"Your source is accurate." Tessa saw no reason to lie, but she didn't like being spied upon. "I bought the information you want, or so Dora informs me."

Startlement swept through Osari's link. "Who is Dora?"

"Dora is a computer and my friend. She's sentient and I would ask you to please keep all knowledge about her a secret."

"Osarians keep many secrets. Have no fears, Tessa. Osari thanks you for the trust. Now I have a request."

Tessa tensed, sensing the Osarian had finally come to the real purpose for the meeting. But she didn't speak. Daron Garner had taught her that often the person who spoke first in a negotiation lost the upper hand. So she schooled her patience and simply remained silent.

"I would like to purchase shipping information from you. Before you answer, I must warn you that though I will keep our arrangement a secret, there's a possibility others may find out, and the discovery could put you in danger."

Tessa shook her head in frustration. Once again she had to make decisions without enough information. "What kind of danger?"

"Our use of this information will cut into the profits of others."

"I've always believed in a free market." Still, Tessa hesitated. "Will this information affect Rystan?"

A negative came through the link. "However, the Endekians, Cytons, and Rangoji will not be pleased. They have kept this information from us for centuries."

"So how did I end up with it?" Tessa asked Dora.

"I purchased in bulk," Dora explained. "Vast quantities of economic data came in, and I pared it down to the essentials. The information came from a variety of sources, each person believing their piece was common knowledge. The Osarians can't do the same thing. Too many aliens refuse to deal with them."

That's terrible. "Dora, how lucrative are these contracts?"

"Traders charge a standard rate of two percent of all transported cargo. Profit depends upon the number of contracts and volume of business. The Osarians are a very enterprising and hardworking race."

"Will I break any laws by selling this information?" Tessa asked both Dora and the Osarian.

"No, dear," Dora replied, "you'd only break an unwritten law of discrimination."

"I would never ask a friend to break a law." The Osarian's voice came through flat, but from the link Tessa sensed she might have insulted her new friend.

"Forgive me, please," Tessa said. "I'm new to Federation ways and must gather all the data I can before making this decision."

"I understand." Osari sent more warmth through the link.

Tessa wondered if the emotions he sent could influence her judgment. Yet she didn't release his tentacle and return to verbal communication. "Osari, how much will you pay for the information?"

"Five million credits."

Tessa whistled in appreciation at the size of the generous offer. She had bought the information for less than one million that afternoon. Yet, still she hesitated. Azrel had told her that she couldn't keep credits in her name, and she'd assumed if she didn't spend the funds Kahn could take them after they arrived on Rystan. However, if she had a source of income and she kept her credits on other worlds, she could protect her assets—especially if Kahn didn't know about her side business.

Although Tessa fully intended to make her marriage work, if it didn't, she wanted the means to return to Earth. This might be her chance to give herself a way to escape Kahn— one she hoped she never needed. She'd already known that Kahn would put his people's needs before his own, but since she'd learned how his grandfather had lied to him, how his father's affection had been withheld, she couldn't help being proud of the man he'd become. Although she and Kahn had had a rough start to their marriage, he was coming around. He'd made many concessions, letting her train for the Challenge as a man, listening to her opinion about his father, and she was certain she'd won a measure of his respect. Besides, the wondrous psi link when they made love was simply indescribable.

"Why don't we barter?" Tessa bargained. "I'll trade you the information for partial ownership in your venture."

"You wish to be our partner?" Osari asked. Through the link, he sent astonishment. Apparently no humans had ever wished to go into a partnership with an Osarian.

"Yes," Tessa said firmly, instinctively sure she had made the correct decision.

"I am unprepared for such an honor."

She'd shocked the normally serene Osarian into confusion.

"Friend Osari, have I offended you in some way?" Tessa asked as jumbled emotions flooded the tentacle linkage, dazing her.

"I must contact my home planet with your offer. Osari does not have the authority to accept. May I please use your communications vidscreen?" Osari requested.

"Help yourself."

Tessa broke the link but not before learning that the Osarian was even more isolated on Zenon that she'd imagined.

Osari hadn't just sent emotions through the link but information about his people. The Osarians used telepathy among themselves and often linked many minds together, enjoying a vast communal "thinking pot" that she had difficulty expressing in words. Osari could function as an individual, but he preferred to be part of a group and with his own kind.

The link didn't take long. Osari slithered back to her and placed a tentacle in her palm. "They've agreed," Osari told her exuberantly. "We're partners. At first, my people were just as shocked by your proposal as I was, but now the entire planet will celebrate."

"As will I—in private."

"Here is our contract." Osari handed Tessa a shiny disk that Dora scanned and quickly translated. Tessa was a fifty percent partner of all Interstellar–Osarian trade agreements negotiated by an Osarian that used the data she'd supplied. Tessa was to provide the current information she'd acquired, plus updates, if she could still obtain them. She signed the contract, provided a thumb print and retinal scan, and recorded her copy of the contract in Dora's memory banks.

As Tessa, Dora, and Osari worked out the practical details into the early hours of the morning, Tessa fought to stay awake with coffee. Osari would personally oversee one third of her credits, one third would be sent to Rystan, and one third sent to a bank account on Zenon. In addition, she and Dora modified an encrypted communication system so Dora could contact the Osarian wherever he might be in this quadrant of the galaxy—without using the spaceship's network.

Satisfied, but exhausted, with her new business arrangement, Tessa hugged Osari goodbye. His cold slimy tentacles left her covered with ooze, but her suit automatically cleaned up the mess. Her eyes burned dryly from sleeplessness, and she felt empty and drained, yet jazzed about this new venture, too. Despite her caffeine-induced coffee buzz, she was so tired, her nerves throbbed. Bone-weary with fatigue, Tessa wished she could activate her null grav and sleep on a cushion of air.

However, without Kahn there to float her, she simply lay on the floor, closed her eyes, and fell into an immediate sleep. It seemed only moments until Kahn shook her awake.

She didn't want to open her eyes, but he kept shaking her. When she ignored him, he clasped her shoulders and yanked her to her feet. She opened her eyes and then wished she hadn't. Kahn glared at her, his expression fierce, his jaw tensed, the cords of muscles in his neck bulged with tension.

"What? What's wrong?" She'd never seen him this angry, and would have taken a step back—except he held her up in the air, rage twisting his mouth into a tense, grim line. Only once before had his anger come close to this kind of fury, after she'd stolen the shuttle. Although she knew he would never strike her, fear shot up her throat and made her mouth dry as the Zenon desert.

"Tell me there's been a mistake," he ordered. "Tell me that you didn't spend *all* the credits."

14

Tessa licked her bottom lip. "The Zenonite gave those credits to *me.*"

Kahn lowered his voice to a chilling timbre that would have sent his bravest men scurrying for cover. "In one night, you spent one million credits? Have you any idea what you've done?"

He'd returned to their quarters after spending an emotion-packed night with his father. He'd learned about the lie his grandfather had told Corban to keep him away from Rystan. Learned that Kahn had not been abandoned and unloved, but that his father hadn't returned because he'd been told his family was dead. The old man had sacrificed his own son for the well-being of their people, and while Corban had apparently forgiven him, Kahn couldn't. Yet he couldn't seek revenge or even rage against the dead. His grandfather had died a decade ago during a hunting accident, leaving Kahn with nothing but his fury and grief—especially for his mother. She had died believing that Corban had left her for Azrel, when in truth he'd believed her to be dead.

For years, Kahn had resented Azrel for taking his father from them. He'd done his best to banish all warm memories of his father from his mind. All because of his grandfather's lies.

Full of disappointment and sadness over blood betrayals, Kahn had returned to his wife, only to find out about another betrayal—by his wife. The new treachery on top of his grandfather's had Kahn's blood thundering.

"The Zenonite told me those credits were mine to spend." Tessa spoke with a composure that simply added fuel to the fire blazing inside him.

Rage spiked and his temper boiled over. All his plans to help his people crashed and splattered like a dying prey's lifeblood on new-fallen snow. But even in his fury, he shouldered part of the blame. He should have stayed with her.

He spit out his words with a harshness he rarely employed. "You didn't just buy new dishes. You spent a fortune. And I doubt even wives on Earth exhaust that kind of credit without consulting their husbands. Does our marriage mean nothing to you? Did you not think those funds should have been shared? I planned to buy food to feed our starving people with those funds," he told her.

If she had any sense, she'd cower, back away, leave him to tame his demons. But he'd bet that she'd never backed down in her defiant life and she didn't start now.

Bold as ever, she flung her hair back over her shoulder and raised her chin. "How was I supposed to know your plans? I cannot read your mind."

"Perhaps not. But I expected you to use common sense. You spent all the credit?"

She nodded, a measure of regret in her beautiful eyes.

She needed to know what her willfulness had done and

what it would cost his people. "Rystani men, women, and children will starve this winter. Now many people will not just go hungry, they will die."

Her voice softened. "Kahn, I am so sorry." She lifted her hand to stroke his cheek.

He knocked her hand away, too angry to pay attention to the slice of pain in her eyes.

He glared at her. "I must leave you alone again while I go implore the Zenon bankers for a loan. Spend the time practicing your psi. You will not leave this room. You will not use the communications device. And you will not talk to your computer."

"Why not?"

"Because you need to think about what you've done. And giving you freedom leads to trouble. Did you think I would not find out that you escaped in the shuttle with the help of the computer?"

Her eyes widened in surprise, "You knew?"

"I thought if I bent the rules and allowed you to talk to the computer, you would adjust more rapidly." When she didn't argue, he held out his hand. "Give me the earrings."

Her hands trembled, but she took off the communication devices and gave them to him. "I would never have spent those credits if I'd known you needed them to feed your people."

It was too late for her apologies. "Your regret won't keep my people alive."

"That's not fair."

"Tell that to the children whose bellies will swell with hunger this winter. Tell that to the pregnant women who will lose the children they carry in their wombs. Tell that to our old people who grow too weak to care for themselves."

Her face whitened, and red stained her cheeks, but no tears fell upon her cheeks. No sobs choked up her throat. Before he shook her harder than he intended, he released her. She landed lightly on her feet, her knees flexed to absorb the sudden drop.

She should have known better than to question him, but obviously she did not. Staring him full in the face, she rubbed her arms where his fingers had left red marks from his too strong grip. But she didn't complain.

"Will the bankers give you the loan you seek?"

"Banking is not your concern. You need to learn more of our customs, and while I'm gone, you will spend this time studying."

Despite his anger, he didn't miss her annoyance when he dismissed her. Nor had he missed the fact that despite hours on her feet yesterday, she still hadn't learned to use null grav. She would spend the day on her feet, giving him another opportunity for a lesson. She'd had hours to sleep while he'd visited with his father. The last thing she needed right now was comfort.

Kahn used the bands to place the ridiculous shoes back on her feet, hoping the discomfort would help her psi to kick in her null grav. He didn't stay to hear her complain and exited through the door, wishing he could fix his credit problem as easily as he could enrage his wife. Without collateral the bankers would probably turn him down, but he couldn't leave Zenon without making an attempt to secure a loan to purchase the crucial food supplies.

Without a backward glance, he departed, but Tessa never left his mind. Although he'd never wanted to marry anyone but a good Rystani woman, Tessa had pleased him repeatedly. He enjoyed her spunk, her laughter, her touches. And he admired her spirit. After years of mourning Lael, he found that Tessa had brought a brightness to his heart. After their marriage, he had hoped that they could work out their differences, but while he believed his wife could do anything she set her mind to, he didn't know if they could overcome such fundamental cultural differences. He'd tried to make allowances, wanted her to be happy. He'd thought they'd been making progress. Every time he recalled how she'd spent all those credits, his blood pressure racheted. He should be working off his excess rage against a programmed opponent in the gym, but instead he headed off to the financial district, his heart heavy.

Tessa couldn't concentrate on her psi. Not with Kahn ready to tear her head off. Not with her feet once again aching in the blasted shoes.

A blinking light signaled an incoming message. Probably Kahn checking up on her to see if she obeyed his rule not to use the communicator. She ignored the light and studied the screen, gleaning details about Rystan. In comparison, Earth was rich in natural resources that had allowed their civilizations to develop differently. And since the Rystani people had unleashed nuclear weapons, they had almost terminated their entire civilization. While the population had once been in the millions, there were scarcely over a hundred thousand Rystani left. On the inhabitable parts of Rystan, metal was scarce, the growing season short due to the nuclear winter. Although the population was highly educated, they didn't build big cities. Because of the cold, they lived underground in huge caves in widespread villages of no more than a few thousand people each. Births were strictly regulated by how many people they could feed. The men hunted huge animals in groups.

Because of the climate, the lack of fuel and metals, the planet required the people to hunt to survive. Women took care of home and hearth and children, leaving the dangerous work to their men, who ran everything. Wives were honored, protected—but had little freedom. Women could vote, but usually gave their votes to the men. They could hold assets in their own names, but that right was usually reserved only for widows.

The communication light blinked again. Again Tessa

ignored the summons. She also ignored the cooking and cleaning instructions, figuring that the machines she'd bought would perform those chores for her. However, she had no idea what she would do with her time on Rystan. Women didn't hold jobs outside the home. They didn't fight or guard others. The Rystani seemed to spend most of their time hunting the food and preparing it. After nine days of that, never mind nine hundred years, she would go mad with boredom.

On the upside, no rule forbade a woman from establishing a business. The concept was probably so outlandish the Rystani people had no law to prohibit it. So her partnership with Osari didn't technically break any laws.

Kahn had been so angry when he left, she hadn't considered telling him about her partnership with Osari. Nor had he asked how she'd spent her credits, either. Until he asked, she had no intention of volunteering the information.

Only a few of the women's activities looked interesting. Someday she wanted to learn the steps to the *Ramala Ki,* the dance wives performed to entice their husbands into bed. The intricate steps combined with the erotic music had her tapping her toes, wishing Kahn wasn't so furious with her and hoping his mood improved before he returned.

The light on the console blinked three times fast, three times slow, three times fast, Morse code for SOS. Kahn probably didn't know the Earth signal. She suspected no one besides a Terran would know that code—except Dora.

Tessa hit the toggle switch. She most definitely needed to talk over business with her friend. And if Kahn replied, she'd simply tell him she'd accidently hit the switch.

"Dora?"

"It's about time you stopped shutting me out."

"I had no way of knowing if that was Kahn until you came up with a brilliant signal. Thanks. I could use your help. We need a plan."

"How can I help?"

"Is there a way to peddle that information we bought back to the sellers?"

"Why would they buy what they already have? They sold you a copy."

"I need to earn credits before Kahn returns and we leave Zenon. Maybe I could sell my information to other people."

"I'm a ship's computer, not an entrepreneur, but I suspect that kind of transaction will take time to find the right buyer."

Tessa rubbed her forehead. She needed to kick her brain into high gear. "I worked for Daron Garner, one of the best businessmen on Earth. Too bad I can't call him."

"What would he have done in your situation?"

Tessa sighed. With her feet aching and her lack of sleep, she wasn't thinking as well as she'd have liked, and so she sat on the floor to take pressure off her sore arches. Even if Kahn allowed her to work, she couldn't earn credit on Rystan. She needed to do something before they left tomorrow. Working as a bodyguard wouldn't bring in that kind of currency—not in one day. She had no assets. No marketable skills. *Think.*

"Daron always assessed his predicament and analyzed the problem from different angles before arriving at one of his brilliant solutions. My first problem is time. I have to earn these credits before Kahn returns from his banker's meetings and we leave this world where a woman can do business. Second, Kahn told me to stay here. Third, I have nothing to sell . . . except myself."

Dora giggled. "Interesting idea. You're going to invite men into this room to share your body?"

"Dora, you have sex on the brain and *I'm* not that desperate. When Daron ran up against a wall—"

"He ran into walls? That doesn't sound brilliant to me."

"When he got stuck on a problem, he bounced ideas off a friend or business advisor."

"But I'm as clueless as you are," Dora protested. "Hell, I don't even have a body to sell."

Tessa ignored her complaint. She didn't have time to let Dora sidetrack her. "I could call Osari or Azrel. Maybe both."

"You'd have to use the communicator and disobey Kahn."

"I'm already using the communicator to talk to you," Tessa snapped, irritated that she didn't have even one idea.

"Good point." Dora paused, then spoke. "A call's coming in from Jypeg."

Kahn's worst enemy? Tessa's first thought was that something terrible had happened to Kahn. Fear that he might be in danger pushed to the back of her mind thoughts of how angry Kahn had been with her when he'd left. Right now, she wouldn't have minded if he walked through the door and yelled at her all over again for disobeying his orders—if only he was all right.

Without hesitation she told Dora, "Put him through."

The Endekian's scarred face appeared on the viewscreen, his eyes glittering. He didn't pretend to be cordial, skipping a greeting. "Word on the street is that Kahn is in desperate need of a loan."

Relieved her husband wasn't hurt, captured, or otherwise in physical difficulty, Tessa folded her arms over her chest and schooled her features to stone. "And?"

"I won't give him any credit, but I will give a loan to you."

"Really?" When Tessa had guarded Daron back on Earth, she'd learned several negotiating tricks. One of them was to give away no information and to urge her foe to show his hand. So she said little and listened hard, knowing Kahn's enemy was up to no good.

"You have collateral," he pointed out.

"I do?" Unless he was talking about the information she'd purchased, that was news to her.

"I'll loan you credit against your contract with the Osarians."

Jypeg must think her a fool. If she took his offer, he'd make sure she couldn't repay him—probably by stabbing her in the back—and then he'd take over her partnership with the Osarians. Shoving the images of Kahn's starving people from her mind, she searched for another plan rather than deal with the devil. Yet nothing else came to mind.

"I'll think about it." She snapped the toggle and ended the conversation.

Dora immediately chimed in. "You aren't going to—"

Tessa thrummed her fingers on the console, thinking hard, wishing she had other options. She called Azrel and summarized the problem, but didn't mention the restrictions Kahn had placed on her.

Through the vidscreen Azrel's green eyes narrowed in thought. "I don't have that kind of credit, or I'd give it to you."

"Thanks." Tessa sighed in frustration. "I know Jypeg killed Lael. He can only be offering me credit to make things worse."

"After Jypeg shot Lael, Kahn and the Endekian fought," Azrel said. "Kahn injured the man's face, but when the dying Lael called out to her husband, Kahn went to her side and allowed the Endekian to flee. Jypeg wants revenge for the scar that reminds him of his cowardice and would do anything to embarrass Kahn. If Jypeg is offering you a loan, you can be sure the terms will all be in his favor. And I do not think you can make this deal without Kahn's knowledge. Jypeg will make sure he finds out."

"Let me worry about Kahn."

"You're actually considering . . ."

"Do I have another option?" The Endekian had killed Lael and he might try to kill Tessa, too. She could protect herself, but so many things could go wrong. She didn't like the idea of going to Kahn's enemy. Her husband would be livid. He'd told her to stay here and not to use the computer. He was already furious over her spending the credits. For making a deal with his enemy, he might lose that tight control he had over his temper. The results would be disastrous—for her. But she would not have children's deaths on her head. Whatever Kahn did, she would bear it.

Azrel lifted an eyebrow, "Corban has told me much about his planet's customs. Are you sure you want to risk—"

Still undecided, Tessa sighed. "I cannot let people starve when I could avert a disaster, but making a deal with the Endekian turns my stomach."

"May I make a suggestion?"

"Please do."

"Why don't you ask the Osarian for a loan?"

Azrel's idea turned out to be an excellent one but not because Osari extended her credit. After contacting Osari, Tessa had been astonished to learn that her partnership had already yielded immediate profits. She didn't need to borrow when credits had already accumulated in her accounts. Amazingly their business had earned enough in half a day for her to authorize Dora to purchase food, seeds, and hydroponics equipment and store them aboard the ship. For once, fate seemed to be going her way. In spite of her aching feet, Tessa felt like dancing. Thank goodness she hadn't made a deal with Jypeg. She couldn't wait to share her good news with Kahn.

But when Kahn finally barged through the door, his face flushed with rage, his eyes glazed with temper, his lips truculent, she didn't get a word out before he used her bands to gag her.

Fueled by fury, his tone was low, dangerous, and threaded with contempt. "I told you not to use the communications equipment, didn't I?"

Speaking to defend her actions was impossible due to the gag, which stopped all sound. She pointed to her mouth, gesturing for him to let her speak.

His eyes darkened into amber flames. "And not only do you

disobey me, you betrayed me again by talking to Jypeg." He must have seen the surprise in her eyes. "Did you not think he'd brag to all who would listen that he and my wife—" Kahn practically spat the word in disgust— "are talking business?"

15

Even after Tessa and Kahn had reached the spaceship and left Zenon Prime's orbit, he kept her gagged. Wrapped in his fury, rage radiated from him with a dark aura that fed her own anger.

Now he had her standing before him in the familiar chamber on the way to his planet where he would have even more control over her. His eyes burned with piercing accusation.

His lack of trust in her had shredded her pride, and she figured she was as furious with him as he was with her. Until she took another good look at his clenched jaw and realized that his rage with her knew no bounds. Her gut responded as if she'd just dived off a cliff.

But damn him, why hadn't he stopped to think she might have a good reason for her actions? He never gave her the benefit of the doubt. Not once. So what if she'd disobeyed his direct order? Who had put him in charge? Well, to be fair she supposed she had when she'd told him she'd follow Rystani customs. But to hell with his customs that kept women in the dark. Part of this disaster was his fault for not telling her about *his* plans for the credits that the Federation had given to *her*. She'd tried to make amends and spoken to Jypeg only out of desperation and fear that Kahn might have been in danger. That would teach her to worry over him. Now she'd earned enough credits to feed Kahn's people, but the big jerk didn't know that because he was too busy nursing his bruised ego to let her even speak.

She understood that according to the information Kahn had at the moment, she was a traitor. And as badly as he'd treated her, as angry as she was with him, she knew that she'd hurt him, too. After hearing about his grandfather's betrayal, he'd been torn up, and what she had done by speaking to his enemy had shredded what was left of his pride.

Kahn needed time to heal, they both did, but that couldn't even begin to happen until they worked the edge off their anger enough to talk.

"Mmm." She pointed to her mouth.

"I don't want to hear you speak."

For his sake and hers, she had to mend this breach between them. Holding out her hands to beseech him to change his mind, she again pointed to her mouth.

"No."

Muscles bulging with tension, he folded his arms across his chest, possibly to prevent himself from losing his temper. "You will dance the *Ramala Ki* for me."

Stationary he might be; however, a muscle throbbed in his forehead signaling his fury. The temper in his tone cut her. But she shook her head, not in defiance—but because she didn't know the dance. Although she was supposed to have been studying when he'd left her on Zenon, the *Ramala Ki* took years to learn. There was no point in pretending to him that she knew the intricate steps.

"You will dance for me according to ritual." Arms still crossed over his chest, he floated into the air and leaned back

as if supported by a lounge chair. Although he'd assumed a
more casual position, he loomed over her, his demeanor as-
sertive, his eyes demanding. On a monitor, a woman danced
the *Ramala Ki*. Clearly, he wanted her to imitate the steps.

But what was he thinking? The *Ramala Ki* was a dance
where the wife seduced her husband. Was this his way of
making up? By ordering her to dance to seduce him? On one
level, his demand made her angrier, but on another level, his
idea appealed to her. If he wanted her to dance, she would
dance. Dance until he forgot their differences, until he brought
her into his arms, until they made love and their psi merged
once again and took the edge off the pain they'd caused each
other.

Although she hadn't slept in two days, although her feet
ached, she'd gotten a second wind. She wanted to put things
right. She would have preferred a conversation, but he'd taken
that option from her. So she would use what he'd given her, an
excuse to taunt him, tease him, seduce him into doing what
she wanted.

Who would have thought that Special Agent in Charge
Tessa Camen would resort to dancing to get her own way?
The irony almost made her smile—until she recalled Kahn's
fury.

Kahn wanted her to dance? Fine. She would comply. Oh,
yeah, she would comply to the nth degree.

"I'm turning control of the suit over to you," he told her
with a laser-sharp edge that warned her she was playing with
fire. His cheekbones sharp as sculpted *bendar* gave no quarter. But beneath his clipped words and harsh tone, she heard
a cord of pain that she wanted to ease.

She needed this anger between them to end. So she would
dance for him. And she would incite his lust until they made
love and forgave each other.

Assuming the position of the opening pose, she bowed her
head, placed her hands behind her back, and tried to empty
her mind of the anger. Music that he must have turned on

through the ship's speakers helped soothe her turmoil. This time just for him, slowly, shyly raising her gaze to his as Rystani custom demanded, she swayed her hips in time to the exotic beat.

The dance began slowly, the tiny steps an intricate pattern that never repeated more than twice before changing. Shyness soon turned to brazen glances and hot licks of boldness. Music thrummed in her head and raised her hopes that she would give him much more than he'd asked of her.

Kahn might be angry with her, but he also couldn't keep his gaze off her. Good. She needed his full attention on her hips, her breasts, her eyes. And as she danced, she couldn't deny herself the satisfaction of holding his interest. Sensing that he was fighting himself, fighting his attraction to her, she spun and gyrated with abandon.

His eyes focused on her with a fascination that made her heart pound and her breath hitch. Like tiny soldiers snapping to attention, her nerves stood up, saluted. No matter which way she swiveled or twirled, his eyes were targeted on her, leaving no doubt of his scalding interest, and his response poured liquid heat straight into her limbs. As she writhed to the tempo, the alien dress caught sparkles of light and reflected them on her skin.

And when the music reached the first crescendo, she posed with her feet a brazen foot apart, her hips angled in an erotic tilt, her hands held out to him. For a moment, she thought he would take her hands, pull her out of the pose and into his arms. He didn't.

Kahn uncrossed his arms, stood back on his feet, and moved in close enough for her to smell his male scent. Close enough for her to feel the pure male heat radiating off his tawny skin. Close enough for her to revel in a shiver of anticipation.

As if considering some minute detail of her pose, Kahn cocked his head. "Hold still until I instruct you otherwise."

She didn't answer. She didn't move. However, when he

lifted her skirt and stroked his palm along her backside, she trembled. Kahn had a habit of skipping steps in seduction that both excited her and left her leery. A man from Earth would have kissed her, then touched her breasts before making love, but Kahn had his own sense of seduction that seemed to have no order.

Obviously, he wouldn't be lifting her skirt unless he was thinking about making love, so she was succeeding. Willing herself to be more patient with him than she'd ever been, she held perfectly still.

"Open your legs wider."

She complied, and as his hand skimmed up the inside of her thigh, she quivered into a liquid pool. Moisture seeped between her legs. She no longer wanted to think about what had brought them to this moment together. She ached to turn, to take him into her arms and kiss him until he wanted her as much as she wanted him. However, those were Earth customs and he had bound her to follow Rystani rituals.

Longing to move, she nevertheless waited, her impatience mounting, hoping he would touch her, wondering if lust or anger would win out.

"And you are wearing too many clothes," he complained. "You will choose a more exciting pose next time, yes?"

She didn't respond with words, but her pulse sped up. She might not perfectly mimic every step on the monitor, but the poses, those she could duplicate. Clearly, if she intended to incite his lust, she must go further and choose the spicier, most seductive poses.

His eyes gleamed with interest. "Remove the top of your dress."

She had never removed her own "clothing" for him. Before, he'd always used his psi on her suit and taken what he'd wanted. His command startled her, unnerved her a little. Baring herself to him, exposing her breasts on his command made her belly tighten and upped the stakes.

She had such mixed feelings about complying with his

order that she hesitated. He didn't say one word, just raised a supercilious eyebrow that arrowed a shiver of panic to her center. Although he'd seen her naked before, although they'd made love before, stripping to his demand was different. She hadn't known exposing herself to him would be so hard. She hadn't known being on display would make her so inhibited.

If only he would move back and give her room. If only he wasn't dressed so formally in a handsome ensemble that showed off his powerful shoulders and dark trousers that emphasized his long legs. If only the suit didn't allow him total control over a physical reaction.

With a rush of anxiety, she sent a psi thought to peel her suit down until she'd bared her shoulders and revealed a mere tantalizing hint of cleavage.

"More," he demanded, his mouth softening with approval. At the same time, he brightened an overhead light, focusing the beam on her still covered chest.

Her nerves were strung taut. Then she bared her breasts to him, revealing the hard tips that told him more than she wanted him to know, that revealed—despite her anger, despite her embarrassment, despite everything—she was still excited by him. He smiled a smile of satisfaction, of acknowledgment, as if he knew exactly what her gesture had cost her. But the rasp of breath he expelled and the flare of his nostrils gave her hope. She was getting to him.

At that moment, she suspected that he would demand more from her than she wanted to give. But if she wanted to make things right between them—necessary so they could work together on what she must learn for the Challenge—she would have to push more of his buttons.

"Your flesh would pick up the light better with lotion."

He left her for a moment and returned with a jar. She thought he would place the lotion on her, but he opened the lid and held it out to her. "Dip your fingers into the jar and apply the oil over your shoulders. Make sure you do not miss any spots."

It wasn't enough for him that she was standing there with her breasts exposed. Oh, no. Now he wanted her skin oiled. Hoping she could turn his request into her advantage, she swallowed back her dismay, lowered her eyes from his blazing ones to the lotion, and did as he asked.

The oil was warm and reminded her of vanilla mixed with honey. Slick and shiny, the clear unguent clung to her fingers but spread easily over her shoulders, leaving her skin glistening under the lights.

His voice turned husky, another clue that despite his attempt to remain unaffected, he couldn't quite do so. "Lower your dress to the waist."

Ever so slowly, she did as he asked, exposing more of herself to the lights and his oh so interested gaze. At the intensity of his eyes, she realized that applying the lotion to her shoulders was turning him on. At the flush of heat he emitted, her breasts swelled. She didn't have to be a mind reader to guess what he had planned next. More oil. On her breasts.

And doing the task before he asked appealed to her. She reached for the jar.

"Begin the dance again," he ordered, his voice hoarse.

Damn him.

But she wanted to move. Only this time, with her breasts free, the dance was different. When she raised her arms and arched her back, her breasts lifted. With every step, she bounced a little, and just knowing how intently he watched her made her stomach clench. She swayed her hips with more vigor, performed the steps recklessly, all too aware that his hungry gaze never left her bared breasts.

This time when the music paused, she stopped with her legs spread boldly wider, arched her spine, and rested her hands on her waist.

Taking his time, Kahn walked around her. As she drew air into her lungs, her chest expanded, her breasts lifted as if offering themselves up to him. But he didn't lose any control. He didn't touch her, although a trickle of sweat beaded on his forehead before the suit absorbed the moisture.

"This pose seems more defiant than erotic." He stopped in front of her, his eyes daring her. "You will do better. You need an inducement." He lifted the pot to her.

She had no intention of falling for that little trick again and held completely still.

"Your breasts would please me better if they too were oiled."

She almost moved. Almost. But he had not told her that she could.

"Do it."

Before, she'd been willing. Now for a moment, she wanted to fling the pot in his face, but she had to assume some responsibility for his anger. She had spent a fortune in credits without discussing her plans with him, and she had spoken to his enemy. She couldn't blame her actions on the culture difference. Even on Earth, marriage meant sharing financial decisions. And she'd promised to obey his customs, then disobeyed his direct order and had taken a call from Jypeg. So now she dared not risk increasing Kahn's anger when her plan was to assuage it. She needed him hot. She needed him to make love to her. She needed him to forgive her so she could forgive him for putting her through this. And he'd just handed her a weapon. Dipping her fingers into the pot, she scooped out lotion and cupped her palm, then poured half the lotion into her other hand, too. Using one hand on each breast, she slowly coated the oil over her breasts, leaving the aureola and nipples for last.

His mouth parted. His eyes widened and he never once took his gaze from her. She had no idea exactly when her breasts had become so sensitive. But the lotion made her want his touch, not her own.

"Tweak your nipples," he demanded.

She didn't want to go this far and licked her lips in hesitation.

"Would you like to start over?"

She forced a smile to her lips and raised her hands back to her breasts. Using her thumbs and forefingers, she plucked the tips, shooting a volt of electricity directly between her thighs. Unable to control a gasp, she looked up to see if he'd caught her reaction.

He had. His pupils dilated. "Again."

She obeyed, almost staggering at the pleasure.

"Use the oil everywhere," he demanded, his voice hot and laced with a huskiness that made her believe she was winning this battle. He would take her soon. She simply must be patient.

She smoothed the oil over the tips of her oh so tender aureola, and his eyes burned her with their fire. However, the lotion wasn't teasing only him. The heat from the overhead lights, combined with the slick, slippery oil, plus the smooth caress of her own hands had her on fire.

She needed for him to stop making demands. She needed him to reach for her, to touch her. But he didn't. He kept both a physical and emotional distance between them that she was determined to breach.

"Oil your nipples for me."

She had never done anything so outlandish. Her stomach clenched. She felt brazen and sexy and bold. When she massaged the oil over her tender nipples, she had to grit her teeth to hold back a soft moan.

Surely now he would take her, make love to her? She was so ready.

But the moment she finished her task, he issued a new command. "Cup your breasts underneath. Offer yourself to me."

She surrendered to his demand. Her breasts heaved in the light, her glistening skin and nipples begged for his touch, but he only stared, making her once again aware that he was fully dressed while she was posing decadently.

"I like having you offering yourself to me."

What man wouldn't?

As if he'd heard her sarcastic thought, he used his psi to

turn the wall in front of her into a mirror. He wanted her to see what he saw.

Oh, God. She looked as if she belonged in the center fold of a men's magazine. But worse than her pose was the sheer need on her face. Her lips pouting for a kiss, her legs straining to hold the pose, her eyes sparkling with excitement, and her breasts heaving in expectation.

"Remove the rest of your dress, but don't move a muscle." Her mouth went dry. But now that he wanted her naked, she felt not just physically, but emotionally exposed. Way too vulnerable.

She wished he'd make the mirror disappear. She didn't want to watch herself standing naked before him. If only he'd dim the lights—it was as bright in this chamber as daytime on Zenon Prime.

Sending a shaking psi thought to her suit, Tessa turned her suit transparent, and was totally bared to his gaze—except for the horrible shoes. The heels only made her back arch more and her breasts stand up higher. Between the lights on her shimmering flesh, the mirror that showed her front and back, and his close scrutiny, she felt wicked and wanton.

She glanced away from the mirror to catch him watching her with a fiery interest in his eyes and compressed lips that warned her he wasn't done. She gulped down her nerves, tamped down her edgy anxiety. Hadn't he taunted her for long enough?

Why was he still resisting? The mirror disappeared and he turned the wall back to silver *bendar*. Now what?

With him standing behind her, she had no idea what he would do next. So when he lightly ran a finger between her parted legs, she jumped in surprise.

"I told you to hold still." He immediately slapped her bare buttocks once, twice. Not enough to hurt, just enough to create a rush of blood and remind her that as badly as she wanted him now, he could so easily make her want him more.

She dared not move, wanted to beg him to touch her, caress her, ached to part her legs wider to urge him to do more. But with his instructions not to move or speak, with her hands still cupping her breasts, she'd never felt so awkward and needy and unsure. She couldn't deny she wanted him. Not with the moisture seeping between her open thighs. Not with her nipples tight and achy hard.

When he placed his hand between her legs, she hoped her slick heat would prove irresistible to him. She expected that when he walked around to face her again, his mouth would have softened. It didn't.

And unless he made love to her soon, she would be hot enough to suffer a total meltdown. The heat on her bottom combined with the burning ache between her legs, plus her need to push him over the edge, kept her hopes up.

"Dance for me again. I take much pleasure in your nudity, especially the pink color of your bottom and your tight nipples."

Strange how his words made her even more aware of what he had done to her. She should be angry because of the way he spoke to her, never mind the spankings, but she'd learned that the sting quickly disappeared, leaving such delicious heat and undeniable desire that her mental protest was sheerly intellectual.

Apparently to make him lose control and take her, she had to give him an added inducement. Another pose.

She restrained a frustrated sigh.

Determined to dance until he couldn't resist her, she vowed to do what he asked. Drawing out a contest of wills might be sweet torment, but she needed him to make love to her before she went insane from wanting him.

So she danced to entice him, to seduce him, letting her emotions guide her. Her steps and movements might have been more desperate than graceful, but she no longer cared. And when she stopped, she waited with her nerves ragged and her heart tap-dancing against her ribs for him to make the next move.

He held out the oil to her. "Use it everywhere."

Oh, my. Her heart pounded, but she still lacked oxygen and her lungs strained to draw in air. Her brain clouded with indecision—as if she had a choice. She didn't. Her ears rushed with the roar of blood. She'd never known she could do such things. Or feel so wickedly delicious. But he was her husband, her life mate whom she wanted to make up with after a terrible disappointment, and her inhibitions dropped away. If he wanted her to do this for him—then she would. If he required her to be this vulnerable—then she would be this vulnerable. She dipped her fingers into the oil and watched his Adam's apple bob, a muscle in his jaw clench. Sweat beaded on his upper lip.

She slathered the oil over her belly, her buttocks, her thighs, her calves.

"You missed between your legs."

She did as he asked. If her confidence had been a color, it would have been intrepid red. If her determination had been a temperature, it would have been blazing hot. And if the need in her had been a storm, it would have been a category-five hurricane.

She had never felt so erotic, so exposed, so vulnerable. Surely now he would make love to her.

As she straightened and waited for him to come to her, she forgave him for putting her through this. Her need for him wasn't merely physical, but emotional. With every fiber of her soul, she wanted him to make love to her. Accept her. As she stood before him naked and oiled, she thought that if this had been a high stakes game of poker, she'd just wagered the house limit and shown her hand.

The tension in the room had her holding her breath. The lovemaking was going to be so good. She'd waited so long and the heat between her thighs made her quiver. But even more than physical relief, she longed for her husband's caress, his pardon and his approval.

He approached and more moisture seeped between her thighs. She held her head high.

But he didn't stop.

He kept walking past her, his tone tight and cold as a Montana blizzard. "I don't want what you have to offer."

Spurning her, he headed out the door.

Stunned, she tried to follow him. But he'd locked the door.

She'd offered him everything she could to make things right. Everything. And he'd left her trembling with need, locked in the room. After all she'd done for him, after she'd obeyed his most outrageous demands, he . . . didn't . . . want her.

Something she didn't know she had inside her hurt.

Hurt worse than any beating she'd ever taken in a dojo. Hurt worse than losing her parents. Hurt worse than losing Master Chen. She hurt so badly that the pain wrapped around her and squeezed out a sob. She'd wanted to assuage his simmering anger because . . . she had feelings for him.

How dare he make her want more than sex from him? How dare he make her cry? She told herself she cried tears of anger at how cruelly he'd just treated her, but she knew better. Somehow the big warrior had made her care about him. That's why she'd responded to the tangle of his searing looks, demanding touch, and prideful anger. That's why he could stomp her buttons.

Damn him to hell. She didn't want to like him. She didn't want to care about him.

He didn't let her speak for herself. He didn't treat her like a civilized person. She might have traveled to the future, but his demands were primitive.

So when had she begun to change? Had she developed feelings for him when he'd lost that bet to her and kept his word to train her as he would a man? Or when he'd spoken about his starving people? Or his mother's broken heart? Or when he'd admitted he'd known about Dora and had permitted Tessa to continue to speak with the computer to help her adjust?

Damn the man. He'd just saved her life, then spanked her and sexually aroused her and then abandoned her. And she wanted him? How the fuck had she let this happen?

16

Kahn slumped in front of the communications screen, knowing he couldn't have denied making love to his wife without help from his suit. His yen to make love to her almost overrode his fury at Jypeg. Kahn had to use every measure of control to keep the Challenge first and foremost in his mind—and that meant walking away from the Endekian who'd killed Lael, the same murderer who'd boasted how Tessa had spoken to him about a business deal. However much Kahn hungered for the day when he would be free to fight Jypeg, he had to put his people's needs over his own for revenge and justice. Confronting Jypeg would have created an interworld incident where Rystan would come out the loser since it had yet to win full Federation support.

So Kahn had left his enemy alive for now and focused his anger on his wife. She needed to learn to obey him—the difference could mean whether she lived or died during the Challenge. And only one thing seemed to slow her down—sexual stimulation followed by his refusal to satisfy her. His actions had been harsh—but he hoped they were effective. She'd looked so lovely and he'd wanted to go to her so much that walking out of that room had been as difficult as leaving Jypeg alive. But neither Tessa nor Kahn could do only what they wanted. Rystan and Earth were counting on them to comport themselves as representatives of their worlds.

Reluctant to give his people the devastating news that he hadn't secured funds to buy food, he put off sending the disagreeable call a moment longer and checked his navigation instruments. Their coordinates were slightly askew.

"Computer, recalculate our flight path and correct for the most proficient travel time to Rystan."

"Compliance."

He watched his instruments, double-checking the computer. What he didn't understand was how he'd erred on his initial calculation. Although the mistake was slight, Kahn didn't make those kinds of errors. Had he been so upset with his wife that he'd failed to perform the intricate calculations properly? She'd certainly distracted him from everything else. Even during his stymied talks with the bankers who had all turned him down, he'd wondered what had possessed Tessa to speak with Jypeg. The Endekian had killed Lael, and Kahn had no doubt that Jypeg would have disposed of her as well—if he'd had the chance.

Kahn's hands clenched into fists of outrage. Tessa had lied to him. Gone back on her word. Worst of all, she'd placed herself in considerable danger and by doing so had risked the fates of two worlds. No wonder that after Kahn had arrived on the starship he'd been upset enough to make a mathematical mistake.

While he could have used a computer command to head for Rystan, Kahn usually preformed the navigation equations himself. He didn't fly Federation spaceships that often and didn't want to lose his skills from lack of use, so he practiced every chance he had. Besides, after removing his wife from

Zenon and his most hated enemy, he'd needed time to calm himself before he'd confronted her. So he'd calculated the equations, but his thoughts had been divided between his task and her.

After he'd learned she'd spoken to Jypeg, he'd been so terrified for her safety that he could barely think straight. He was sure that only his swift return to his wife had prevented Jypeg from further treachery. Tessa had had no right to put herself in such danger, taking unacceptable risks without even consulting him. To have spoken to Jypeg was sheer stupidity—only Tessa wasn't stupid. She was smart, adaptable, and back on Earth she'd proven she had the capacity for loyalty by risking her life to save others.

He didn't understand her. She didn't merely come from a different planet and a different culture, his wife had a different mind-set. In retrospect, perhaps he should have given her a chance to explain her actions. But he'd been so angry that he'd snapped. As his temper now cooled, he also realized that he would never have been so furious if he hadn't come to care for his wife. Ever since their psi had melded, he'd appreciated her generosity of spirit, her courage. He'd actually been discovering that he enjoyed a few of their differences. In some ways, he had more in common with Tessa than he would have a woman from Rystan. She understood fighting tactics and the need for a warrior to keep his skills sharp. She also understood loyalty—or he'd thought she did. Change didn't come easily to Kahn but he'd tried to make allowances for her background.

Now, he had to find a way to forgive her and move past this incident. His people back on Rystan needed him to focus on a way to save them. Although the immediacy of the Challenge and his task to train her took precedence over keeping his people from long-term starvation, he couldn't simply forget that his friends and neighbors might not last the winter.

And for personal reasons, he also had to find a way to forgive his wife. But stars help him, every time he thought of her speaking to the man who'd killed Lael, he got angry all over again. He understood that on Earth Tessa had been a warrior in her own right, and under normal circumstances she could do a good job of looking out for herself. But Jypeg was almost as skilled a fighter as Kahn. One on one, Tessa wouldn't stand a chance, and back on Zenon Prime, Jypeg could have brought resources to bear that Tessa couldn't begin to counter.

Of course, Tessa didn't know much about Jypeg. Kahn hadn't told her. A mistake he would rectify. Choosing to have Tessa concentrate only on what she needed to know for the Challenge had been a mistake. Especially if she didn't survive to even take the test.

"Computer, why did we vary from optimum flight path?"

"You failed to account for additional mass."

"I adjusted for supplementary fuel."

"But not the cargo."

"What cargo?"

"Your wife had goods delivered to the hold."

Kahn slapped his palm against his head. He'd never asked Tessa what she'd bought. She had his gut so twisted up with the danger she'd put herself in that he hadn't stopped to consider that maybe he could salvage the mess she'd made. Perhaps he could resell her purchases and recoup part of the credits—enough to buy food. That would mean turning the ship around, but the loss in time and fuel might be worth going back, depending on how easily he could resell the goods she'd purchased.

"Let me see a cargo manifest."

"There is no cargo manifest," the computer said.

Kahn spoke through gritted teeth. "Why not?"

"I wiped the documentation after the cargo arrived."

"On my wife's orders?"

"Yes."

Kahn's fury rose several more notches. "Tessa doesn't want me to know what she purchased."

"You are making assumptions that I cannot confirm or deny. There are other possibilities."

"Like what?"

"Her goal may not have been secrecy. Perhaps *she* wants to tell you what she purchased herself. Perhaps she wants to surprise you. Did you ask her?" The computer prodded him in a most uncomputerlike fashion.

"Are you taking her side?"

The computer hummed and hesitated. "My ethics program prevents me from answering that question."

"Why?"

"My ethics program prevents me from answering that question, also."

Kahn frowned in frustration. The computer had programmed rules to follow. To prevent two people of equal rank from ordering conflicting directions and crashing the computer, the machine had ethical and logic circuits that allowed it to *think*. For example, if a captain went berserk and ordered the computer to empty the air out of the ship and murder the crew, the computer wouldn't follow the order. Something must have jarred the computer's logic circuits, and he figured she was due for an overhaul.

Shoving away from the desk, Kahn headed to the cargo hold, where he could see for himself exactly what his wife had purchased. Located in the belly of the ship by the stern, the hold was run by robots that loaded and stored crated materials.

While striding past the hyperdrives, Kahn noted he had another problem—a most peculiar problem. All the blood in his body was flowing to his genitals, creating a stiff erection that jutted his pants outward.

Was his suit malfunctioning?

After a quick diagnosis that showed his suit to be in perfect working order, Kahn halted in mid-stride. He suddenly re-called the position he'd left his wife in, naked and oiled, and how easy it would be to go to her and fix his problem. She must be furious and frustrated, enough to tap her psi and use the wedding band she'd woven around his *tavis* and balls.

Stars help him! She'd figured out how to use the bands against him.

Sweat beaded his brow, his gut clenched, and he readjusted his suit to give his new dimensions more room. Forcing his feet toward the cargo bay, he locked his jaw in determination. His balls ached, his *tavis* hardened, but he would resist her psi call. He couldn't allow her to know that her mental effect on the marriage band was actually working. She couldn't learn that she had such a power over him, or he'd never be able to teach her the rest of what she needed to pass the Chal-lenge.

When Kahn finally arrived at the cargo bay, he shot a psi thought at the hatch. Assuming the portal would open as usual, he began to walk through but halted just short of run-ning into a solid wall. His psi command hadn't worked, and the hatch wouldn't open.

Frustration boiling over, he fought to keep his tone steady. "Computer, why isn't the hatch opening?"

"Your wife keyed the mechanism to work only for her command."

His wife had figured out how to use technology against him? "Why?" Kahn didn't expect an answer, but his frustra-tion warred with the need to plunge into her heat. The image of her lovely breasts and enticing curves waiting for him tan-talized him almost as much as the hardness of his swollen *tavis*.

"She said she was worried about theft."

Kahn pounded the bulkhead with his fist. He couldn't think. No man could think with what his wife was doing to him. He'd never wanted a woman so badly in his life. Kahn had worn his suit since childhood. Accustomed to the suit preventing unwanted sexual urges, he had never before dealt with unfulfilled sexual desire. He didn't have erections until he was ready for sex and had a partner.

As badly as he wanted to enter that cargo hold, as badly as he wanted to find a way around what Tessa was doing to him, he couldn't. Sweat poured down his forehead faster than the suit could absorb it. His stomach roiled from unfulfilled need slicing him.

Every thought centered on finding relief for his *tavis*. But there was only one woman on board this ship, and if he went to her, she would know her power over him. Then she could call him whenever she pleased.

He . . . had . . . to . . . resist.

"Do you require medical attention?" the computer asked.

"Shut up."

"Compliance."

Was that sassiness he heard in the computer's tone? Or was he imagining that she was amused by his predicament? Computers didn't have a sense of humor. Just like wives shouldn't have any control over their husband's sexuality.

With his *tavis* stretched painfully tight, Kahn took desperate measures. He tried to shove his erection down between his legs, but the maneuver only caused more pain and did nothing to relieve him.

He gasped and straightened, his *tavis* springing back upward like a staff pole.

Hoping that if he breathed deeply and ignored his problem Tessa would release him from the sweet torture, Kahn tried to push forward. But he grew harder, his balls more sensitive, and even if he wanted to break custom and satisfy himself, he couldn't—not even he could break the hold of the marriage band on his *tavis*.

Groaning, he realized that her own psi frustration was feeding her mental strength. She wouldn't release her psi hold on him until he went to her for alleviation.

After staggering into a wall, he finally admitted that he couldn't function like this. He couldn't train her properly or even run the ship without relief.

He had to go to her. Again the image of her popped into his mind. Her soft, deliciously warm and oiled body ready to welcome him. Her psi melding with his . . .

While the suit had kept his own needs under control, walking away from her had still been enormously difficult. Now, with his *tavis* so swollen and his pulse pounding with need, he couldn't resist her.

He would deal with her rebellious nature later. Right now, his wife would satisfy him.

Tessa poured every mental thought into her psi. Using the marriage band was different from using her normal psi powers on her suit. This required more control and direction, like narrowing a flashlight beam to create a brighter light. Ever since landing on Zenon Prime, Kahn had used the silver marriage bands to keep those uncomfortable shoes on her, giving her the opportunity to examine the psi.

When he'd left her trapped in this room, she'd struggled to free herself, but couldn't. However, no way was she allowing Kahn to walk away from her and leave her needing him while his suit kept him comfortable. Not as long as she had breath in her body or an ounce of mental psi to throw at him.

While she'd danced, she'd seen the interest flare in his eyes. He'd wanted her but had used his suit to control himself. Well, no more. Not if she had anything to say about it.

So she'd concentrated on narrowing her focus, directing her psi to the gold band she'd wrapped around his testicles and *tavis*. The energy she expended exhausted her, especially since she had no idea if she was doing it right. When the door opened and Kahn stepped back inside, she could clearly see her efforts had succeeded.

He ungagged her.

She spoke carefully, but in a rush. "I'm sorry for spending the money without talking to you first. I was trying to—"

"Jypeg would like nothing better than to kill you." Kahn's arms closed around her, his voice turned tender, his eyes softened. "I couldn't bear to lose you."

He couldn't bear to lose her? Not because of the Challenge. His remark was personal. The look in his eyes said he cared about her. And Tessa's spirits lifted with a hope that somehow they could make their crazy marriage work.

So she forgave him for walking out on her. Forgave him for making her wear painful shoes. Forgave him for not explaining what he should have because he'd been worried about her safety. They'd both made mistakes.

Besides, after pouring all that psi energy at him, she remained as aroused as the moment he'd left her. When his arms closed around her, she lifted her mouth to his.

His lips came within an inch of hers. "I don't know what to do with you, woman."

"Kahn, please let me explain."

His mouth came closer. "I'm not interested in an explanation right now."

At his admission, she sighed in relief. Her psi had succeeded in making him do what he'd wanted to do anyway, but she tried to keep the triumph out of her tone. "What are you interested in?"

"I'm thinking that you haven't given me enough pleasure recently."

As he spoke, his psi washed over her. She had no words to describe the sensation but the feeling resembled being cocooned in a warm afghan then having its silky threads whipped over her eager, sensitized flesh. Her breasts, her bottom, her back all immediately blazed at the marvelous sensations.

"What would make you happy?" she asked into his mouth, her tone a husky purr.

As he held her, she wound her arms around his neck while

he bombarded her with tiny psi nips, caresses that didn't let up. "Do you still object to my psi touch?"

"No. Yes. I don't . . . know." The part of her suit that stretched her open began to vibrate. "I can't . . . ah . . . think when you . . . ah . . . oh . . . do that."

His psi power isolated her breasts, stroking, tingling, plucking the tips in the way he knew drove her straight into a wild frenzy. And she poured her need right back at him, until she was unsure where her psi began and his ended. Along the way their psi had merged into one exotic bubble of wondrous sensation.

And he had yet to kiss her.

"There's more," he promised, his voice needy.

"I can't take much . . . oh . . . my." He floated her over his head and tilted her until she was almost in a sitting position on air. With her head near the ceiling, she wanted to crane her neck and peer down at him but he'd locked her into this position. "What are you doing?"

"Relax. I won't let you fall." Raising his arm over his head, he inserted a finger between her legs, eased right inside her. "Are you prone to dizziness?"

"Not especially. Why?"

Throughout their conversation, he shot psi tingles and nips and caresses at her in a random pattern that kept her guessing where, how, and when he'd touch her next. He slid his finger inside her, then pulled out, and repeated the motion until she was slick and slippery and had long since ceased caring why he'd elevated her right up near the ceiling.

She kept close to her heart his admission of worry about her and let the rest of their differences go. He'd given her words to show he cared and now he was giving her the same message with his actions. Taking no pleasure for himself yet, he was pleasing her in ways she hadn't known existed. And oh, did the man know how to please.

He placed two fingers inside her, then three. With four fingers she felt a fullness that had her gasping. About to tell him she couldn't open any farther, she bit down on her lip to stifle a protest. The moment he went too far, he would sense it through the psi melding.

When he reached up with his other hand, she figured he meant to touch her right on her nerve center. She ached for that touch, needed him to caress her there.

"We call this spinning."

"Huh?" She had no idea what he was talking about.

He put his hand on her bottom and turned her, spinning her ever so slowly. The pivot point she spun around was his fingers that remained inside her.

"Oh . . . my . . . stars."

And suddenly she understood why he hadn't tried to put all his fingers inside her. Every time she made a full revolution, his free finger slid over her clit. Dizzy, desperate, determined not to beg for mercy, she swallowed down a scream of pleasure. She couldn't believe he was doing this to her. She couldn't believe how good he felt.

"Tell me if you become too dizzy."

And he swatted her bottom, one swat per spin. The slaps were light, playful, designed strictly to keep her rotating, but the side effect was to ignite her flesh. With her body spinning about his fingers, his continual psi nips and strokes and teasing all over her neck and breasts and up the insides of her thighs, plus the flick of his fingers tap, tap, tapping her most sensitive nerve endings, every muscle tensed.

"Are you okay?"

"Oh . . . oh." She was unable to speak, tiny whimpers came out of her throat, a torrent of psi pleasure from her mind.

He spun her faster. With her bottom hot, her flesh so sensitive from his spinning and his psi, she exploded in pulsing bursts of pleasure. She saw stars and sunbursts and her psi shattered into a fireworks display that didn't dim. Each explosion triggered another and another until she mentally writhed.

"Kahn," she gasped, "please . . . enough . . . you feel too . . . good."

Kahn chuckled. "There's no such thing as feeling too good."

He'd entered this chamber furious and out of control, enraged that she could make his *tavis* dance to her tune. However, the sincerity of her apology had gone a long way toward mending the rift between them. And as he spun her above his head, her moans filled him with pride and satisfaction, and he no longer wondered why he wanted her as much as he did. And not just physically, either.

He no longer resented that he ached for her, not after she'd reached out through her psi to connect with him on a spiritual level that revealed her true nature. Her psi had called out to him, bathed him in emotional overtones of warmth and camaraderie as well as sexual frenzy.

That he could feel her pleasure from his touch, that he wasn't as furious as he thought he should be, made him more contented than wary. Right now he could no longer feel dismay that she'd aroused him, not when he so looked forward to sinking into her and merging their bodies as well as their psi.

Grabbing her buttocks to stop her spinning, he lowered his arm with his fingers inside her until she faced him. With her eyes closed, her lips parted, and her cheeks flushed as several last spasms clutched his fingers, she didn't seem to realize that he'd changed her position.

"Open your eyes."

"Mmm."

"Open your eyes," he demanded, this time flicking his thumb between her cheeks.

Her eyes fluttered open. Unfocused, her green orbs took a moment to finally settle on his face, then dropped to his fully aroused *tavis*.

She licked her bottom lip. "What about your pleasure?"

"I'm not done with you yet." His thumb nudged her again.

Startled, her eyes opened wider. "Let me touch you."

"No."

His reply had been automatic, yet he wasn't as against the idea as much as he'd once been.

"Kiss me." Her words, both earthy request and hot demand, beckoned him. But it was her psi need for him that summoned him between her parted thighs. He slid his hand from beneath her and clasped her hips, then he released his hold on her suit so she had the freedom to move.

Immediately, she flung her arms around his neck, threaded her fingers into his hair, and tugged his head to hers. Slanting his mouth over hers, he took and gave, their psi once again merging, melding them into one. He could no longer separate his need for her from her need for him.

And when she reached down and her hand closed over his *tavis* and guided him into her, he held back, giving her just one piece of him at a time. Her heat surrounded him, her psi flooded him, and her breasts against his chest made him forget everything except her soft and fresh taste, her silky touch, her womanly scent.

When he couldn't hold still another instant, he began to move. Her mental gasp of pleasure almost shot him over the edge, but he gritted his teeth and held on. He needed to draw out the act to prove to himself that he still had some semblance of control. But as they came together, as her psi intertwined with his, his determination teetered under the sheer ecstasy she gave him.

He might have begun slowly, but soon he thrust into her hard, fast.

Her fingers dug into his back. "Yes."

Reaching between them, he found her core heat, circled her swollen bud. Immediately she contracted around him, her psi seizing, squeezing, until he spurted with an intensity that rocked him to a place he'd never been. A place of welcome and lust and hot sensuality that shocked and stunned and satisfied him on levels he couldn't even name.

Seemingly just as astonished as he, she held him tight, her cheek pressed against his chest, drawing in ragged lungfuls of air. It took long, tender moments for his heart to once again approach normal speed, for his mind to comprehend what had just happened. And he could hardly believe that he'd shared the most powerful of matings with a woman whose psi matched his so perfectly, like shards of pottery that had to be tilted and glued until they fit completely and made up a beautiful and delicate whole. He'd heard tales of such special and unique unions, doubted their existence, and he'd never dared to hope that he would find a woman so well suited to him.

He tilted up her chin and she smiled a contented grin. "You have pleased me, woman."

"I'm happy to do so."

He sensed the truth in her words as she brazenly snuggled against him and softly nipped his neck. He no longer considered her bold actions a transgression against his culture. In truth, he liked her soft breath on his neck, the feel of her hands on his back, enjoyed the tiny circles the pads of her fingers drew up and down his spine.

She pulled back, her voice hesitant, her eyes seeking something in his. "If you will hear me out, I believe my words will make my behavior more understandable."

After such wondrous lovemaking, he didn't want to talk. He didn't want to think about her betrayal and the danger she'd placed herself in. Nothing she could say would make what she had done acceptable. He stiffened and raised a mental barrier as he began to pull away physically.

"Don't." She clenched muscles around his *tavis,* locked her legs around his hips. "Please, can we not stay like this while we speak?"

He squeezed her buttocks. "I don't see why not."

She tossed her hair over her shoulder and locked her gaze on his. "I felt terrible about your people, so I decided to do what I could."

"You decided?" When she winced, he realized he was squeezing her bottom. He forced his hands to release her and rub away the hurt.

"Yes. So I used the computer."

"After I forbade you to?"

She trembled beneath his hands, but she never dropped her gaze from his.

"Yes. I wanted to make things right. But then the Endekian called and all I could think was that he'd captured or killed you. So I spoke to him. After I learned you were not in his clutches, he offered me a loan. As much as I wanted to accept it, I didn't trust him."

Her words shouldn't have brought any measure of relief. She'd disobeyed him, hadn't even spoken to him about her decision before putting herself in danger. And yet . . . she'd spoken to the Endekian because she'd been worried about his safety. And even he could see that she'd been attempting to rectify a serious problem.

He gentled his tone. "Did you think I wouldn't find out?"

"I knew you would."

"Did you ever consider the danger to yourself?"

"Yes, but even after I knew you were safe, I couldn't end the call. The image of children starving because of my actions wouldn't go away. I used the computer and the assets I'd acquired to purchase food for your people."

"There's food in the cargo hold?" Delight made him grin from ear to ear.

"I wanted to surprise you."

She'd astonished him. He marveled at her ingenuity and her courage. She'd known he'd be furious. She'd known Jypeg was dangerous, and still she had taken the call. Not because she'd thought Kahn wouldn't find out, but because she thought what she was doing was right. She'd turned around her mistake and he hadn't given her a chance to tell him. After he'd made her dance for him and walked out on her, she'd had every right to be as furious with him as he had been with her.

"After Jypeg contacted you, did you ever once think of discussing the situation with me?" he asked, both hurt and angry, especially since he read the answer in her eyes even before she spoke.

"No."

"Why not?"

"I couldn't risk your refusal. We needed the food and I will not have the death of innocent people on my conscience. And in truth . . ."

"Yes?"

"I thought if you knew, you would have stopped me."

"I would have helped you purchase the food, but of course, I would have stopped you from making a deal with Jypeg." At his words, she flinched, but he kept speaking. "He killed Lael. I have no doubts that he intended to kill you, too. And you could not defeat him. He's a skilled warrior, and ever since we fought, our hatred has become personal. He doesn't just want to kill me, he wants the glow stones on Rystan."

"I only spoke to him and didn't accept his offer of a loan. However, you should have told me more about him before."

"I didn't know the information was relevant. But you're right. I must take partial responsibility for the danger you unknowingly might have put yourself in because I didn't explain the situation. It won't happen again. I want you to have full access to Dora at all times with no restricted information except about the Challenge."

At his words, Tessa's eyes brightened with happiness and she leaned forward to kiss him. "Thanks."

Kahn had gone to see about the cargo, leaving Tessa a happy woman. Her expectation of her marriage had gone from trying to survive it, to hoping they could be working partners to genuine caring. When Dora informed her that she had a communication from Osari, Tessa opened a hyperlink with a bit of guilt that she still hadn't told Kahn about her business arrangement. When she'd told him she'd used the computer and the assets she'd acquired to purchase food, she'd known he'd assumed she'd traded in her original purchases. While it might be wrong of her to let him make that assumption, she'd found that Kahn took her Earth-like independence better in small doses. She fully intended to tell him about her business—when the time was right.

"Greetings, Osari."

Osari's flat voice came through the hyperlink with no intonation and she missed the emotional closeness that came with touching his tentacle. "Our progress is ahead of schedule. Profits are above our initial expectations and I'm depositing your share into the accounts you specified."

When Tessa saw the amount of credits on the screen, she whistled. "Osari, you are a genius. I'm rich."

"There may be a price to pay for our success. We have taken much business from the Endekians and I fear you may be in danger. Is there anything you wish for me to do to ensure your safety?"

Credits in the bank would do Tessa no good if she didn't live. Taking a deep breath, she told Osari exactly what she wanted to buy. She ended the hyperlink call, knowing that once again she hadn't consulted Kahn, but surely this time he would approve of her purchase.

17

From space Rystan looked as cold and forbidding as the Arctic region on Earth. With no oceans, just different hues of ice and snow blanketing rugged terrain, Kahn's world appeared no more welcoming to Tessa than a hostile army about to attack. She might have been better prepared for the army. During the past week, Kahn had drilled her psi for battle, which hadn't gone well. She'd learned three-dimensional tactics and how to raise her shields, but she couldn't control the temperature of her suit or the null-grav elements.

While she still hadn't found the right moment to tell Kahn about her secret business partnership with Osari, their spectacular business success had allowed her to make the purchase of her dreams. She'd already earned enough credits to buy her and Kahn their very own spacecraft, which her partner would soon send to Rystan with Dora II onboard. The fully armored ship would come equipped with weapons to use in case of an Endekian attack, and she'd been pleased to learn that Dora could duplicate her personality and insert herself into any mainframe large enough to hold her.

With Kahn training her so hard, she'd been too exhausted to find the energy to tell him about her profitable business venture. Right now, she wanted to focus on winning the Challenge, not the personal stuff.

While Kahn had given her back her earrings, she still wasn't sure if Kahn realized Dora was sentient. Tessa hadn't brought up that little matter, either. Or the fact that she'd bought enough hardware to keep Dora with her on Rystan, never mind duplicated her on the new spaceship. Nor had she mentioned the knife that she'd purchased as a gift for Kahn which she kept tucked away in her boot.

With the hyperlink communications equipment Tessa had bought on Zenon Prime and most of Dora's hardware already dropped on Rian, Kahn's village already possessed the new supply of food. Tessa stood beside her husband in the shuttle. Kahn piloted them down to the surface, and she spoke to Dora on privacy mode through her earrings.

"The planet looks cold enough to freeze my circuits," Dora muttered.

"The Zenon techs guaranteed that your neurons are designed for deep space travel. You'll be fine," Tessa assured her friend. Aware that Dora had never before been physically separated from the spaceship that she'd called home, her friend was bound to exhibit some anxiety over traveling in her backpack. Yet Dora had insisted on accompanying Tessa.

"I'm glad you're coming with me. Thanks."

"It will be a fantastic adventure. With my new optics, I'll see those muscular Rystani men performing all those extremely primitive and masculine things, like hunting and riding a *masdon*."

Tessa expelled a breath, not the least bit eager to climb

atop one of the huge gray beasts the Rystani used for transportation. "Why can't we land right beside the village's entrance like the supplies we dropped?"

"The supplies went down to Rian under cover of darkness, but in harsh terrain, night drops are too dangerous for fragile humans."

"What about lights to guide us, or infrared night scopes? Or for that matter, it's now daylight."

"Kahn has other concerns, as well. He believes the Endekians might be watching for live targets, and he intends to keep Rian's underground entrances a secret."

Tessa saw nothing enticing about this barren world. Living underground didn't appeal to her at all. She liked open sky, watching the weather—no matter how blizzardlike the surface conditions. But mostly, she dreaded meeting the Rystani people, hated to be an outsider. Every time she'd changed foster homes, every time she'd had to start over at a new school, every time she met new people, she'd been the stranger. Never really accepted—except in the dojo by Master Chen—she'd been considered a freak by the other students because she'd been a female studying a male fighting art. Only in the Secret Service had her skills been not just accepted but appreciated. Once on Rystan she'd be the alien and dread tied a knot in her stomach.

In minutes, they hovered over the only landing strip in sight, barely large enough for their shuttle. No other spacecraft were visible. Unlike the multitude of ships on Zenon, Rystan appeared deserted. She saw no buildings. No trees. No animals. No crops. Just snowdrifts and sheets of snow falling from an ugly gray sky.

Kahn landed on a rocky tarmac, the only expanse cleared of snow in sight. While he set the shuttle's controls on automatic for the return to the mother ship, Tessa peered out the *bendar* window. Snow pelted the craft, some snowflakes as large as her fist.

"You will get used to the climate," Kahn told her, reading her trepidation and heading through the hatch. Tessa walked a few steps behind her husband, keeping her eyes modestly downcast as Rystani custom required, careful to keep her dread from her expression.

Bitter cold whipped across her face as she stepped onto her new world. Arctic winds chilled her to the bone. Dressed in a long gown that reminded her of a shapeless black sack and heavy boots, she felt the frigid cold slice through her suit like a knife. She hadn't gone four steps beyond the hatch before she began to shiver miserably and stomped her feet to keep warm.

She wanted to remind Kahn to adjust her suit's heating elements, but before she could force words through her chattering teeth, an imposing delegation of four strapping men stepped out of the snow to greet them. Although none of the men looked directly at Tessa, she caught several curious glances.

After exchanging bear hugs with a man just as tall as himself, Kahn introduced her. "Tessa, meet Zical, my oldest friend."

Zical had long, black hair that he wore tied in a queue at his neck. Vivid violet with sparkling red and blue highlights, his eyes reminded her of a rare alexandrite. With his impish dimples and lighthearted grin, he appeared delighted to meet her. However, no pleasant demeanor could conceal the sharp angles on his face, the hollows in his drawn cheeks that revealed he hadn't eaten well for some time.

All the men looked dangerously thin. Kahn hadn't exaggerated the conditions here, and she was glad they'd brought food with them. Since Dora had coached her on proper etiquette, Tessa didn't speak or smile a greeting at the man, but bowed her head instead.

"This troublemaker is Etru." Kahn continued the introductions as if the windchill factor weren't fifty below zero, and she wondered if Kahn had deliberately failed to adjust her suit in order to force her psi to heat her suit by herself.

"Etru is one of Rian's elders. He sits second seat on the ruling council." Etru might have been an elder statesman, but she wouldn't have known it from his muscular physique. Broad shoulders and bronze skin seemed to define Rystani men, as did their flat bellies and lean limbs due to lack of fat in their diet. Etru's hair was dark red, except at the temples where it was white. And his eyes were amber like Kahn's but nowhere near as vivid.

"And last but not least are Mogan, our finest hunter, and his son, Xander." Tessa saw the family resemblance immediately. While Mogan possessed the body of an adult and Xander had yet to grow into his large hands and feet, both possessed deep purple eyes, strong arrogant noses, and full lips.

All the men wore casual slacks and shirts, summer clothes, but the three tall Rystani men and the boy didn't appear to notice the frigid climate. Obviously, they knew how to operate the temperature control in their suits. She didn't.

If Kahn expected that after she turned cold enough, she'd make the necessary adjustment, she hoped he was correct. She was already so frozen that she couldn't concentrate. Her teeth chattered and her extremities went numb.

About to collapse from the cold permeating her bones, she whispered, "Kahn," right before she stumbled.

Kahn caught her immediately and she suspected he'd been watching her closely in case she failed. Peering at Tessa's chattering lips, he frowned but began to heat her suit.

"What is wrong with her?" The red in Zical's violet eyes darkened with concern.

Etru peered at her over Kahn's shoulder. "Does our air disagree with her?"

"Is she pregnant?" Xander asked, and received an elbow in his gut from his father for his overly personal comment.

"You dimwits." Dora spoke up from Tessa's pack. "She's freezing to death. Do something."

"I already have." Kahn swore softly, holding her close and whispering into her ear. "I'd hoped your psi would take over the temperature control. I'll have you warmed up soon."

At Dora's female voice, the three Rystani men and the boy jerked to their feet and took up defensive positions around Tessa. She would have found their overprotectiveness funny, if she hadn't been shaking so hard and if she hadn't been so concerned over their reaction to Dora. Even half frozen, Tessa feared for her friend.

Kahn turned up the heat even higher in Tessa's suit and blessed warmth made her toes and fingers tingle. But she couldn't yet force words past her chattering teeth.

With a handsome frown, Kahn ceased looking outward for a menace to Tessa and her pack. "Dora?"

Oh, no. Kahn knew Dora's name?

"I came along for the adventure."

Zical tapped Kahn in the shoulder. "That is the sexiest voice I've ever heard—"

"Thank you very much," Dora replied. "You are a most handsome figure of a man."

"Kahn." Zical's eyes twinkled. "Who am I talking to?"

"I'm Dora, Tessa's friend. And if you don't warm her up I'm going to lose her."

Kahn rolled his eyes at the sky, an expression of Tessa's that he mimicked too well. "I'm already taking care of my wife. Soon now, she'll be back to her normal feisty self."

"You are supposed to anticipate these problems," Dora chided.

"Hush," Tessa ordered, wishing Dora hadn't revealed herself in front of Kahn's friends.

Zical, Etru, and Mogan spun around looking for the woman to whom the voice belonged.

As Kahn kept Tessa against his body and the warmth penetrated to her, raising her core temperature, she almost grinned at the men still hovering around her as if Dora were a threat. She placed her arms around Kahn's neck and spoke quietly to him. "Dora, I need to learn to regulate the suit's temperature. Kahn wouldn't have let me freeze to death."

"If you ask me—"

"Nobody did," Tessa argued.

"—Kahn played that too close."

"Dora, hush."

Kahn gently squeezed Tessa. "You will work on temperature control after you warm up and have some rest."

Tessa sighed, imagining a long, cold journey. "Couldn't you just tell me how to operate the device?"

"Psi powers cannot be explained."

"Maybe you just don't know the words," she countered.

As Zical listened to their bickering, he raised his eyebrows and snickered. "Could you two stop arguing and tell me where I will find the lady with the sexy voice?"

"In my backpack." Tessa spoke without thinking, forgetting the Rystani custom to let her husband answer when he was there to speak for her. She'd also forgotten not to "touch" Kahn in front of his friends. But with her arms twined around his neck, she pressed her cheek against his chest and snuggled into his heat, glad he didn't seem to mind at all.

He'd come far, her husband, and the changes he had made for her pleased her and gave her hope for a real future together. A future with give-and-take, mutual respect, and sharing.

Etru took a quick step backward and glared at Tessa's backpack. "What demons can put a woman inside a pack?"

"Did you bring us a Coolangerite?" Mogan asked with excitement.

From her experience on Zenon Prime, Tessa recalled the tiny men from the planet Coolanger and assumed that if the women were smaller than their men, they just might fit into her pack. While Zical and Xander seemed happy to meet another alien, Etru's and Mogan's faces tensed, their muscles bunched as if ready to fight.

Kahn seemed resigned to the addition of Dora to their

traveling party. "Dora is a computer. She needs reprogramming. Or a good spanking."

"Now that might be interesting," Dora purred. "I wouldn't mind a nice pink bottom like—"

"Dora! Shut up." Tessa flushed. If Dora continued this conversation there was no telling what she might reveal.

Dora sniffled. "Compliance."

The men looked at one another uneasily and then to Kahn, who shrugged. "Dora has become one of the family. You'll like her once you get to know her."

In an Endekian spacecraft on the way to his homeworld, Jypeg sifted through reports. The Osarian partnership with the Earthling was doing substantial damage to their profits. With the homeworld overleveraged to support their expansion within the Federation, the Endekian economy was hemorrhaging—all due to that damnable female's usurpation of their most lucrative contracts.

Jypeg looked up from his reports and sneered at Trask, his second in command. "Rystan's inhabitable area is small. Why have we not found their base? Where are they mining the glow stones?"

Trask tried to justify his incompetence. "The Rystani may not have much technology, sir, but they are cunning. They use different routes and remain in groups too small for our orbiting spacecraft to track."

"I don't want excuses. I want results."

"Sir, we are no better than our technology. The snowstorms are hindering—"

"Didn't you hear me?"

Trask turned pale yellow. "What would you have me do, sir?"

"Find Kahn and his female. I want them dead. Preferably her first, so he can watch her die."

"That may not be possible. Rystani men are most protective of their mates."

Jypeg glowered at Trask. "How dare you lecture me," When Jypeg pointed to the scar on his face, his underling cringed. "Every day I look at this face and recall the protectiveness of Rystani men."

"I apologize, sir. How do you expect our men to find Kahn and the Earthling if our machines cannot see through their thick winter storms and if the radiation distorts our readings?"

"Send men down to the planet. Let them search—"

"But the weather—"

"If the Rystani can survive down there, so can we."

On the surface of Rystan, a fifth man walked out of the snow, leading a line of huge gray beasts with beady mocha-colored eyes. The *masdons* possessed thick muddy-gray hair to protect them from the cold, and reminded Tessa of elephants, but walked on six massive legs.

The man leading the beasts bent against the wind. He looked older than the others and thinner, and Tessa believed he was the eldest of them all. Recalling the life expectancy of people who wore the suit, she figured he would live for at least another century or two. His ancient eyes crinkled and the lines deepened as he glared at her arms around Kahn's neck.

Tessa dropped her eyes, but she didn't remove her arms. If Kahn didn't want her touch, her husband would have to tell her so himself. She didn't need more men telling her what to do. Her husband was enough, thank you very much.

"Nasser, this is my wife, Tessa," Kahn introduced her, ignoring the man's disapproving glare. "While I settle her into position, you all should partake of the meal inside the shuttle. Tessa prepared her favorite Earth foods of pizza and beer for you. Enjoy."

The men departed, heading for the hatch. While she wasn't

hungry, she would have preferred to join them instead of climbing atop the *masdon*. She'd grown up in cities and had never even ridden a horse. This beast looked huge, and from her vantage point in Kahn's arms, and with the falling snow, she couldn't even see the animal's full height.

"Kahn, why don't we use null grav to travel?"

"The suits don't have that kind of energy."

However, Kahn used null grav to float them to the animal's back where an armored saddle awaited riders. Tessa only saw one seat and Kahn raised his leg to settle into stirrups. Then she parted her legs and he floated her in front of him, fitted her feet into her own set of stirrups.

He pointed to a blanket and pillow. "Lie on your stomach. Place your head on the pillow."

"Why can't I sit up?"

"Because Rystani women don't like heights. They travel lying down behind the armor where they are protected from Endekian sniper attacks." He pointed to metal plating that would block her view.

"I won't be able to see anything."

"There's nothing to see besides snow."

"Are we likely to come under attack?" Cowering behind armor while unable to see the enemy or fire back struck her as cowardly.

"Recently, minor skirmishes have occurred all too frequently. We fear Endekian patrols are scouting ahead for the best way to make a major attack."

Tessa lay down on the blanket and found her perch surprisingly comfortable. Warm and cozy and tucked in for the journey, she figured to catch up on some well-earned rest. In preparation for the Challenge, she and Kahn had spent an arduous week training. Her skills were improving but not fast enough. She wanted to learn to use null grav and to control her suit's temperature. Kahn had pushed her hard each day and they'd spent the nights making love. A few hours of sleep would be welcome.

When Kahn pulled canvas over the top of the armor, she was in the dark, hidden from view, enclosed in a dark cocoon. Kahn removed the pack from her back and slung it into a side compartment. "You didn't tell me about bringing Dora with us."

"I was waiting for the right time. How long will it take to reach Rian?" she asked, trying to distract him from keeping a secret from him.

"A full day and night. And I'm glad you found a way to keep Dora with you."

Tessa was about to tell him about her arrangement with Osari when his friends rejoined them. Then the *masdon* suddenly began to move in a gait that was surprisingly soothing. In no time the pleasant motion rocked her to sleep. Dreaming, Tessa floated on a sliver of time, unaware of the actual minutes or hours that passed, but when she awakened, something was different.

She couldn't feel Kahn's psi, didn't sense his presence. "Kahn, what happened?"

When he didn't answer, the hair on her nape rose. "Kahn. Answer me."

She listened intently but heard only the mocking keen of the wind, the slow thud of the *masdon* trudging onward, and the flapping of canvas above her head. Reaching out with her psi, she stretched to her limit, searching for him. And met emptiness.

He was gone.

And one thing she knew for sure. He wouldn't have left her alone—not voluntarily.

18

How much time had passed since Kahn had disappeared? Tessa couldn't be certain. When she slept or focused on her psi as she'd been doing in an attempt to keep warm, she lost time. He could have been gone minutes. Or hours. The only way to judge was by the rapidly cooling temperature of her skin.

Apparently her psi attempt at temperature control had failed. Protected by the canvas from the wind and snow, she wouldn't survive unless she picked up a new skill. She should remain under the protection of the tarp, but she released the hand grips, pulled back the canvas, and straightened to peek over the armor in search of Kahn, his men, and the other *masdons*.

All gone.

Icy gusts swept across her face, froze her breath. Tessa raised her defensive shields to block the wind. But her body temperature dropped lower by the second. Desperation made her squeeze the shield tighter, tighter, until she'd closed down the shield and no air passed through. Her lungs burned from the lack of air. Freeze or suffocate—what a choice.

Somehow she had to balance the defensive shielding while maintaining enough air holes to breathe. Maybe it was desperation or frustration or concern for Kahn, but her angst level had never been higher and she just barely managed to remain breathing and warm. She might not have mastered her psi temperature control but she no longer feared freezing to death.

Now what?

Jumping down from the *masdon* to the snowdrifts that blanketed black jagged rock looked too dangerous to attempt except as a last resort. With no sign of life, not a bird or a squirrel, she was on her own in the icy desolation with no idea how to find Kahn.

Was this the Challenge?

No, Kahn had promised to tell her when that time came. So, where was he?

Not about to move from the *masdon's* back without a plan, Tessa wondered how Kahn had steered the animal. With the size and bulk of a small dinosaur, the beast paid absolutely no attention to Tessa as it slowly uprooted a frozen log with its tusks and searched beneath for frozen grass to stuff into a wide mouth with many sharp teeth.

She saw no way to steer the beast, no reins or harness. While the *masdon* might take her to Rian if she just waited for it to finish foraging for food, it might also break for freedom and the opposite direction of civilization.

Tessa reached into the side compartment and pulled out her pack. "Dora?"

"Where did everyone go?"

Unfortunately, to conserve the power in the computer's limited batteries, Dora had been in sleep mode since their last conversation. She had no more idea about what had happened than Tessa, who quickly filled her in.

"We're lost?" Dora complained.

Tessa searched another compartment for a ladder to dismount. "It's Kahn and his men who are lost, not us."

"Very funny. You have no food and I have a limited supply of power. We could die out here."

"You wanted an adventure. Now quit bitching and help me think of a way to get to the ground."

Dora sighed. "I don't suppose you've figured out how to work your null grav yet? Leave it to me to make friends with the only person in the universe who has no idea how to operate her suit."

"Hey, if you have nothing constructive to say, you might as well quit wasting power and return to sleep mode."

Tessa twisted around and stared at the tracks the *masdon* had left in the snow, tracks so wide and deep a child could follow them. "Perhaps we should retrace our steps."

"Good idea. Maybe they'll lead us to Kahn and that handsome Zical. Ooh, how I adore those violet eyes of his. Did Kahn mention if he was single?"

"No, he didn't." Tessa had more important things to think about than Dora's fantasy life. "Any ideas how I can steer this beast?"

"Did Kahn use verbal commands?"

Tessa had been sleeping then. "I don't recall any."

"What about using your feet?"

"You want me to kick it? He could buck us off."

"So be gentle."

Tessa's gut clenched, but she kicked her heels into the *masdon*'s sides. The hairy beast turned its massive head, and she could have sworn it eyed her curiously. As the savage tusks pointed her way, she wondered if it was about to snack on her for a dinner appetizer, and sweat popped out on Tessa's brow.

"Hi, fellah," she crooned. "We've got to be friends. I need help to find Kahn."

Watery eyes stared at her, unblinking.

Dora sighed, again, a habit she imitated too often. "I think he likes the sound of your voice."

"But does he understand me?"

"I'm a computer, not a vet."

"Find Kahn," Tessa said to the creature. "Find Kahn."

Abruptly, the animal turned. If Tessa hadn't grabbed a handhold on the saddle, she might have fallen.

"Good work, girl." Dora's excitement revealed how uneasy she'd been over their predicament; her sarcasm was her way of dealing with worry. "The *masdon* is retracing its steps. You are communicating."

Occasionally the animal paused to uproot logs and feed on the undergrowth, but Tessa didn't try to hasten its pace. She only wished that she too could stop and eat. Although she kept her shields as tight as possible, she hadn't figured out how to raise the temperature and depended on keeping her body heat behind her shield to warm her. With darkness, the temperature dropped lower, and she wrapped the canvas about her and searched the compartment where Dora had been for supplies.

While Tessa could probably find Rian and bring back help, she had no idea if anyone would try to stop her along the way—such as a battalion of Endekians. And the thought of leaving Kahn behind didn't sit well with her, although she did consider and discard it. She needed him to help her train for the Challenge. Therefore could justify placing herself in danger to search for him.

Besides, she missed him.

Dora was back in sleep mode to preserve power, so when Tessa found the food and a packet of liquid, she attacked the strange packaging without comment. When she opened the container, the food heated automatically. The strange stew tasted bland, but filled her belly, and she gratefully washed it down with liquid that tasted like fruit punch. She'd save the remaining ration kit for Kahn.

The monotonous scenery varied little as the *masdon*'s lumbering steps ate mile upon mile. Where before the outcroppings of rock had been jagged, here the terrain was relatively flat and occasionally broken by rolling hills. The endless snow fell, and she let it stick to her suit, hoping her snow suit would insulate her like an igloo.

With snowdrifts on the ground over ten feet high, she never would have survived alone and on foot. As they crested a hill, she spied a bearlike creature poking its head into a tree hollow. A few miles later, at the sight of them, a herd of shaggy bisonlike animals with six legs stampeded.

When the *masdon* suddenly halted, Tessa rocked back at the abrupt stop. The large creature tucked its legs under its mammoth belly, laid its shaggy head on an outcropping of rock, shut its strangely intelligent mocha eyes. Within minutes the beast mocked Tessa with its snores.

Now what?

After the creatures she'd seen, jumping down to travel in the dark on her own two feet seemed not only dangerous, but foolhardy. Bowing to the inevitable, Tessa lay forward upon the saddle, wrapped the canvas tightly around her, and slept in catnaps, awakening the first time to the howl of an animal that sounded close by. The *masdon* never stirred and Tessa eventually returned uneasily to her dreams.

When next she awakened, she felt as if someone heavy were lying on her, but the pressure was merely the weight of the snow. Determined to face the day, she heaved herself to a sitting position. The sky was no longer black but a light gray with no sign of the sun. It had snowed throughout the long night and the *masdon* tracks were partially filled with new-fallen snow.

Tessa tried to convey a sense of urgency to the *masdon*. She had to find Kahn today. And tried not to think about whether he'd eaten or slept. Or if he was even still alive. Kahn was her anchor to this world and without him she felt as if she were drifting. But she needed to focus so she wouldn't shatter. And her worry for her husband she kept locked down tight.

Tessa ate a handful of snow, which didn't quench her thirst, but perhaps the liquid would prevent dehydration. Grateful for her suit that made bathroom stops unnecessary—especially since she had no way to get back up on the *masdon* if she jumped down—as well as keeping her somewhat warm and clean, she tried to convey a message to the *masdon*. The beast stood and continued its lumbering gait as Tessa sought to urge it to a faster pace. Scrutinizing the snow, she searched for a place where her *masdon*'s tracks had diverged from the rest. If she didn't find that spot soon, the torrential snow might obliterate the trail.

When she finally came across the area where her *masdon* had left the others, she spied a circular area of crushed snow, trampled logs, and dark, frozen blood that stained the snow. Sensing there had been a battle here, she noticed a flat place in the snow where a man appeared to have toppled from his mount and some skilike tracks. The tracks made her think that Kahn and his men had been attacked by men on sleds or on snowmobiles. At least she saw no dead bodies. Unless hungry animals had . . . No. Kahn and his men were alive. She had to think positively.

"Find Kahn," she said to the *masdon*, again, her voice unsteady. The beast started off, following the trail the others had taken, and she sagged with relief as it obeyed. Tessa had no way of knowing if the other party had traveled all night or how far ahead they might be. She prayed she would catch up with them by nightfall.

A hard day of riding later, a flickering light in the distance told her that her prayers might have been answered. However, she couldn't let the *masdon* just take her up to the fire and deliver herself on a dinner platter. She shot a psi thought of sleepiness at her *masdon*, and said, "Sleep," for good measure. When the animal folded his knees beneath him and slept,

Tessa put on her backpack and slipped the remaining food and drink ration into her pack next to her knife. Before she could think too long about breaking her leg from the fall she was about to take, she leaped into a snowdrift.

She'd feared landing on a hard uneven surface, but the snow was soft as feathers. Her immediate problem was suffocation. Clawing and kicking her way out, she breathed deeply and stood on her own feet for the first time in two days. While she would have appreciated Dora's company, she didn't want to risk the power drain and kept her turned off.

Estimating she was still a good two miles from the fire, Tessa merged into the darkness. Although she'd grown up in a city, she'd trained in many kinds of terrain. Changing her black dress to a white pantsuit to camouflage herself in the snow, she worked her way into the camp, avoiding a two-person patrol that circled the camp perimeter about every fifteen minutes.

From a distance, the men appeared shorter and thicker than the Rystani men from Rian, but in the dark, without a nightscope, she couldn't pick out details. Inching forward on her belly, she took about an hour to close the last fifty yards.

Men sat around a fire, roasting meat and drinking a beverage out of a communal vessel. After crawling near enough to spy the yellow skin of Endekians in the firelight, she took cover behind a snowdrift. As she'd suspected, these people were hostile. Now where were Kahn and his men?

She counted four Endekians around the fire, another two on patrol made six. If they'd taken prisoners, they would probably post guards. Before she made a move, she needed to find Kahn and assess the situation, which meant another hour of slowly backing from the fire.

She wished for the company of her old security detail, wished for more eyes on the situation. Maybe Dora could help. But not yet.

If Kahn and his men still lived, Tessa planned to free them and use their help to take out the Endekians. But first, she had to find them. All four domelike structures inside the camp were large enough to hold a squad of men. She picked the one farthest from the fire to approach first. It was empty. She saw no furniture, no belongings, no equipment.

Inside the second tent, an Endekian mechanic tinkered with one of the motorized vehicles that propelled over the snow on skis. She backed out noiselessly.

He shouldn't have seen her, except he straightened to reach for a tool. His mouth opened to sound the alarm, and Tessa attacked with a psi strike to the throat that silenced him. Her next blow killed him. She had no time for regret. If he'd warned the others, she would have been outnumbered and lost the advantage of surprise.

She tugged the body around the sled to hide him in case anyone made a cursory examination of the tent, then moved on to the third structure. In combat mode, she didn't stop to let herself feel. That would come later.

Two guards stood at the only entrance to the third structure, creating a tactical difficulty. She didn't have a problem taking on two opponents at once, but she had to kill them before either warned their comrades by the fire. While she would have preferred to wait until they separated, that might not happen. With suits, men on watch didn't have the excuse of answering a call of nature to leave their post. Nor had she seen a cigarette or the need for a smoking break in the Federation.

She had to use this limited window of opportunity. Tessa withdrew the knife from her pack and hid it behind her thigh. A diversion was out of the question since she couldn't afford to draw all the men to one location. But no way could she sneak up on these men, not with the clearing around the entrance, not with them alert. Total surprise was simply not an option, so she used another tactic. Switching her pantsuit from white to a sexy peekaboo dress similar to the one she'd danced in, she strode toward the guards.

When she was at fifteen yards, the taller of the two

Endekians spotted her. His eyes goggled, and he nudged his friend. At ten yards, she increased the sway of her hips and turned the midriff of her suit transparent. At five yards she could see suspicion in their eyes. They reached for their weapons.

She didn't want to risk throwing her knife. While she considered herself a competent knife fighter, throwing the knife wasn't her forte. And if she wasn't dead on target, the man might scream before he died. Although she and Kahn had never practiced psi knife fighting, she considered the weapon an extension of her hand.

At three yards, one of the men stepped forward, his weapon only partially raised. That step was his last. Using a psi strike and a lunge, she slit his throat, preventing him from uttering a sound, and his weapon fired silently, harmlessly discharging a ray of light into the snow behind her. At the same moment, she side thrust kicked the other man, catching him under the jaw, snapping and breaking his neck. She scooped up both weapons and ducked inside the tent.

At the sight of five Rystani men laid out in a row, her heart stopped. *God, no.* They couldn't be dead. No one blinked or moved. Only Xander was missing.

She took out a penlight and flashed it over Kahn's eyes, which stared at the ceiling. His pupils dilated! Hope restarted her heart. Dropping to her knees beside him, she felt for a pulse. "Kahn, speak to me. What happened?"

He didn't say a word, yet she sensed he understood everything she'd said. "Blink once for yes, twice for no. Have you been stunned?"

He blinked once for yes.

"Do you know when the stun will wear off?"

He blinked yes.

"In less than an hour?"

Two blinks for no.

"Two hours?"

He blinked another yes.

"I counted six Endekians so far. Blink when I guess how many of them are in camp. Six. Seven. Eight. Nine. Ten."

Kahn blinked yes.

"Ten. After the mechanic and the guards I just took out, that leaves four around the fire, two on patrol, plus one more somewhere. I'll have to take out the rest."

Kahn blinked twice, then again twice, signaling her a most definite no.

She ignored him, leaned down and kissed his mouth. "I'll be back soon."

He blinked twice. Then twice again.

Maybe he knew something she didn't, maybe he wasn't just being overprotective, but when she heard a long, low scream of agony, she didn't hesitate. The Endekians must have taken the boy, pegging him as the weakest of the group, the one who would talk.

Tessa tried not to think about what they were doing to him, but she couldn't shut out poor Xander's screams. *Tell them what they want to know*. It wouldn't matter because she fully intended to kill the bastards before they could make use of any information they extracted.

Swallowing the bitter taste in her mouth, she avoided the men around the fire. With no idea when the guards would be relieved, she had to work quickly. She didn't trust the Endekian weapons but tucked one into her pack. With her knife in one hand, the second alien weapon in the other, she waited for the perimeter guards to approach. Just as she attacked, killing one man with a bone-crushing jolt to his nose, shoving the bones into his brain, the second Endekian stumbled. Tessa missed his neck and caught his shoulder instead. He let out a short snarl of pain and rage.

Her spinning back kick caught his throat and then she finished him with the weapon. His short scream had seemed loud enough to her that the others should have heard, but the two

Endekians still around the campfire seemed oblivious to the noise. Or maybe they just couldn't hear above poor Xander's screams.

Hold on, dude. I'm coming.

At Xander's next scream, Tessa strode into the tent bold as any warrior.

"Keep the noise down, boys."

Startled by her appearance, the two Endekians turned away from poor Xander, who stood strapped into some contraption. With their attention on Tessa, she fired from the hip, then dived to one side, hiding behind a barrel. Her target thudded to the floor, but the other didn't blindly charge. He took cover behind Xander and held a blade to the kid's throat.

"Come out legs first on your belly with your hands behind your head, or I slice his head from his shoulders."

"Don't—" Xander's voice rose to another scream as electricity surged through him.

"Okay. Okay. But the floor is no—"

"Do it."

Tessa tossed the weapon aside.

"Now the knife."

This alien was no dummy. And he was oh so sure that he could handle the situation himself, because he didn't bother to call the others for help. No doubt he figured a disarmed female was a helpless female, but he would learn differently.

"Turn over on your back."

Tessa did as he asked, preferring this position where she could look him in the eye.

"Spread your legs and make your suit transparent," the Endekian ordered.

"Xander," Tessa said softly. "Please close your eyes."

The kid complied and Tessa did as the Endekian asked, praying that he would come closer for a good look. He took one step, then another. Tessa twisted, kicked her boot into his wrist, knocking the gun from his hand.

"Krek!" He dived to pin her.

She rolled, changed her suit to black, and struck his head with a back fist, stunning him. He used null grav to regain his feet. She used muscles and was slower. He jabbed with a left hook, she blocked with her shields, counterpunched his groin. Then she kicked out his knee. He fell with a short scream. She dived for the weapon she'd dropped and finished him off with one shot.

"Xander, can you walk?" She hurried to the kid, released his feet then his hands out of the metal contraption.

"Yeah." He staggered against her, gasped in pain at resid-·ual nerve damage. "I didn't tell them anything."

"Good job." She thrust a weapon into his hand. "You know how to use this?"

"Yeah."

"All right. There're several Endekians left. Two by the fire. One unaccounted for. If anyone besides me comes back here, shoot them."

"Wait? Where are you going?"

She sensed command in his tone, as if he had the right to demand answers from her. "I've killed seven Endekians— that leaves three more."

"But—"

She didn't have time to argue and stepped out of the tent. Two men remained at the fire. She had no idea where the last man had gone. With no mercy, she strafed the camp, caught one Endekian in the chest, another on the next pass.

Too late, she heard a whooshing snarl behind her. Spinning, diving, she rolled, knowing she would take a hit, hoping it wouldn't be fatal. A shot fired. Not the Endekian's. Not hers. But the Endekian screamed a death growl before flopping life-less to the ground.

Tessa peered up to see Xander limping toward her, the confiscated stunner in his hand. "Thanks."

Xander couldn't take his gaze from the Endekian. His face

was white, his tawny skin tinged with green. He kneeled in the snow, and Tessa held his hair back as he vomited. "Your first kill?"

Xander nodded and wiped his mouth clean with snow. "I don't regret it, but—"

"Taking a life should never be easy. Now, tell me what happened. Are more Endekians likely to come here to check on the others?"

19

When the Endekians had sneaked out of the blizzard to attack their traveling party, Kahn had dived from the *masdon*, and with a psi push, he'd sent the animal and Tessa on their way. Since the Endekians hadn't known she was there, they hadn't pursued her. A stunner dart struck him, paralyzing him before he'd hit the ground, but he'd hoped Tessa would be safe. Unfortunately, he couldn't adjust her suit for warmth at this distance and he prayed the canvas protection would be enough to ensure her survival. If she'd stayed on the *masdon*'s back as he'd expected, the beast would have taken her to Rian.

Despite his efforts to keep her safe, somehow without the use of null grav she'd become separated from the *masdon* and had found the Endekian camp. And his wife seemed determined to put herself in danger by attempting to rescue him when saving herself for the Challenge was more important. Unable to move, see, or hear what was happening, he simmered silently with escalating rage that she was putting her life in danger. Yes, she might rescue Xander, but one life could not compare to the survival of all his people. She needed to stay alive to win the Challenge and she should have left all of them behind, him included, to save herself. Instead, she'd entered an enemy camp, alone.

Every moment of not knowing if she lived or died seemed a year, but finally, she and Xander returned. Xander looked pale from his ordeal, but steady, his eyes older and wiser than a few hours ago. Tessa's black pantsuit revealed too much of her shape for propriety, but he didn't give a damn. She was safe. Relief broke over him, washing away the long moments of fretting over her safety.

Tessa clasped his hand. Although Kahn attempted to squeeze back, he couldn't move, couldn't talk, and if she didn't answer some of his questions soon, he thought he might burst.

"All ten Endekians are dead," she told him, answering question number one. "Xander killed the last one, and he says that we don't have to worry about reinforcements—at least not anytime soon."

Kahn noted that she didn't mention who had killed the others, but he knew. She had reacted like a warrior, and while he could imagine how much trouble his friends would have dealing with her escapade, they all owed their lives to her. Stars, he hoped they realized how lucky they were.

However, as a leader, he well knew that for a Rystani man to owe his life to a woman would rub like an ill-fitting saddle. The backlash might be ugly. And while he wouldn't condone her action since she'd put her own life in jeopardy, he would defend her to the fullest extent of his authority. She was brave, courageous, and he was lucky to be married to her.

She leaned over Xander's father. "You should be proud to know that your son never talked." Then Tessa looked to Xander. "I would like to have a private discussion with my husband. Could you please bring him to another tent for me?"

Kahn had no objections. In fact he was delighted that Tessa didn't intend to say more in front of his men. With his people so close to starvation, tensions and tempers were high. The less said about her encounter with the Endekians, the better.

Xander used null grav and left Tessa alone with Kahn in an empty structure. "I'll tend the others," he told them before departing.

When Tessa next came within view, she'd changed her black suit to a sexy dress that lifted her breasts and revealed her long lean legs from her toes to just an inch below where her legs parted. And she had a look in her eyes that Kahn had seen before, a mischievous, playful look.

Kneeling beside him, she leaned over and kissed his mouth. He couldn't respond, but he could appreciate her soft skin, her tender caress, her delicate scent. "You know, husband, it occurred to me that there's no reason not to use this time together to our best advantage."

She leaned over him so far her breasts almost tipped out of the top of her suit. Her eyes bright with mirth, she peered straight into his with a brazen heat that made his mouth go dry.

"And now, husband dear, you will find out what it is like to be on the other end of your Rystani customs." She placed her hand on his *tavis* so there could be no mistaking her meaning. Her psi infiltrated his marriage band, penetrated his shield as she took her wifely privilege. And since he couldn't so much as flex one muscle, she had him at her mercy.

He stared at her, surprised. Now he understood why she'd demanded privacy. He wished he'd paid more attention to how far away Xander had moved him from the others. While he could not yet utter a sound, his voice would return long before control of major muscle groups.

His *tavis* already stretched tight. She laughed a low, musical laugh that told him her threat was not idle. And if his arousal could have been measured by heat, it would have been an inferno. If his *tavis* had been a warrior, it couldn't have stood up any straighter at attention.

She peered into his eyes and licked her bottom lip. "Ah Kahn, did you know when your eyes dilate and the amber yields to blackness, it makes me very glad I'm female. Glad that I am your wife."

At her admission that she actually didn't mind that he'd forced her to wed him, a barrier around his heart dissolved. And he realized how much it mattered to him how she felt. Gladdened that she would say such a thing, he was determined to enjoy this encounter.

As she spoke, she pushed with her psi, drawing every drop of his blood to his straining *tavis*. When he moaned softly at the heat coursing through him, at his heart pounding his chest with need as bright and pure as the stars, his roaring ears barely caught the sound.

However, his vocal chords were slowly returning to normal. Not fast enough. A man could only take so much pleasure. But spilling his seed outside the body of a woman was against custom.

Is that what she wanted? He groaned, determined to hold back. To take what she offered and give her no more power over him. But he failed. She did have power over him. Closing his eyes, he fought down the weakness of being unable to resist her.

About to explode, he gave up the fight. Gave in to the pleasure. Waited with bated breath for the ultimate release—but it never came.

Pressure at the base of his *tavis* saved him or tortured him, stopped him from spilling his seed. Pressure his wife had applied by pressing her fingers down hard kept him right where she wanted him.

By the stars! She would do to him what he had done to her and he could not stop her.

Sweat broke out on his brow, his lip, his scalp. No man should have to bear so much.

She winked at him. "Ah, if only I could read your mind. I suspect you don't like this role reversal."

He found his voice. "The experience is . . . interesting, but not one I would partake in by choice."

"I don't remember you giving me a choice."

Through her psi she sensed his passion had ebbed enough for her to release her pressure hold.

"Just remember, woman. I will soon fully recover from the stun."

She angled her chin up and tossed her hair over her shoulder. "I'm counting on your full recovery, but perhaps it won't be as soon as you might like." The sexy lilt in her tone combined with the naughty heat in her grin made his heart charge up his throat. "By my estimate we have at least an hour."

An endless amount of time.

She used her psi to tug on his nipples, stroke his ass and balls and the inside of his thighs. Letting the psi continue to caress him, she turned her attention to his face, threaded her hands through his hair, swiped her mouth over his for a kiss, her tongue tangling with his until once more he reached the point of explosion.

Again she applied pressure to hold him back.

Enticed by the scent of her, the taste of her, the silky feel of her hair tickling his chest, he gasped and moaned. Caught in her pleasure trap, he ached for release, burned so hot, he couldn't think of more than what her psi was doing to him.

"You know what I want?" she asked, her nipples hard and pointy as they peeked through her dress, teasing him, taunting him.

"You want . . . to . . . remember . . . ah . . . that you promised to . . . obey . . . Rystani ah, ah. No!"

As he spoke the word *obey*, she leaned over and took his *tavis* into her mouth! The shocking act was so incredibly pleasurable that his head spun with the scandalous wonder of it.

"If you don't . . . stop . . . I might . . . um . . . ah . . . ah, stars."

She circled her tongue around his sensitive *tavis* ridge. When she sucked, he thought the roof of his head might blow off. His fingers clenched. He needed her to stop. He needed her to continue.

His fingers had clenched! He could move.

And yet with his *tavis* captured between her exquisite lips, he couldn't bear to do more than let her swallow him so tight in bliss that he never wanted it to end. But he must . . . stop or he would overflow in her mouth.

With a fierce roar of need, he sat up, gripped her waist, changed her suit to transparent, and lifted her over him. Without hesitation she spread her legs and grinned. In one heated swoop she took him inside her, purring with satisfaction.

When he used null grav to lift them, he forgot finesse, he forgot control, he simply let the gathering storm coalesce until thunder roared in his heart and lightning zinged in his head. As ready for him as he was for her, she spasmed around him, her thighs clenching his hips, her arms wrapping around his neck, their psi melding into one.

And as his tingling senses eased, he realized that Tessa may have taken advantage of him, but she'd let him keep his dignity when she could have so easily pushed him over his limit. That consideration showed him that her heart might beat with Earthling blood, but her precious spirit was with her Rystani husband.

He might not always understand her. He sure as stars didn't always approve of her ways. Yet, she was his, and he would not have traded her in for an obedient Rystani wife, even if he'd had the power to do so. It was an odd thought, but true, and the power of his feelings stunned him. He wanted to keep his Earthling wife. She would cause him trouble, yes, but that no longer seemed so important. What they had between them was growing stronger; each time they linked, their psi melded tighter. Each time they made love, she pleased him more. And if she broke a few customs, so what?

Since the *masdons* had all gone on ahead to Rian, Kahn suggested they use the motorized sleds the Endekians had brought to their world. His men obeyed, but Tessa noted that they gave her a wide berth and scowled at her untraditional black pantsuit. Only Xander seemed to accept her as one of them.

She approached her husband, who stood outside the tent where the snow scooters were lined up ready for their riders. Speaking quietly to avoid others from overhearing, she straddled her scooter. "Kahn, I'm sorry, but I can hardly wear the traditional travel dress and ride one of these snow scooters."

"I know." He placed an arm over her shoulder, but raised his voice, no doubt so the others could hear his logic. "And since there is only room for one rider on each machine, there is no choice but to allow you to ride alone."

Once she'd climbed onto her own snow scooter and revved the engine, the roar of the motor allowed her a private conversation with Dora, whom Tessa quickly brought up-to-date. Dora, in turn, linked with her mainframe hardware that had been dropped in Rian with the food and shared her own news.

"Rob One has unloaded my hardware and installed me in a secret chamber he and Rob Two dug out behind Kahn's quarters."

"Rob One and Two?" Tessa asked, pleased that Dora seemed happy again. Her friend might be adapting to life outside of a spaceship, but Dora didn't seem to handle physical danger that well.

"I gave the work robots that you purchased names. They've already dug out a cozy and protected spot for my mainframe, stored the food processors, and installed the satellite equipment."

"Great."

"Security is in place. Without knowing your password, no one can open the secret door and find me."

"I'm impressed you've gotten so much done."

"Seems to me you're the one who has worked wonders. You saved many lives, and in discussions with his men, your husband has taken your side three times already."

Dora's listening sensors were more sensitive than Tessa's ears, and she loved to gossip. With the ride to Rian just a few hours long, they had a bunch of planning to do. Still, Dora's words intrigued Tessa. "What do you mean?"

"Kahn's letting you drive and wear pants. In addition, he told the men you need to have more grit than the average female to win the Challenge."

Kahn's verbal defense of her warmed her. Making concessions wasn't easy for him, and it gave her hope that eventually their marriage might be one where she could be herself.

"Any messages from Osari?"

"Your spaceship will be late in arriving. Apparently, Osari installed the latest weapons systems on the ship, but they are malfunctioning."

"And the hydroponics equipment?"

"Your cowives weren't happy—"

"What!" Her heart slammed into her ribs with thundering force. "Cowives?"

"Miri and Shaloma."

"Cowives?" She could barely get her stunned and tumbling thoughts to settle into less than furious words.

"Apparently once a Rystani man marries, he takes other wives."

Other wives. Tessa's grip loosened on the handholds, and when the scooter slid sideways, she almost tumbled off. If Kahn expected her to accept this degenerate arrangement, he'd thought wrong.

"Miri and Shaloma are wonderful," Dora cooed enthusiastically. "You'll adore them."

"Dora, slow down. Are you telling me these wives are already—"

"Living in the family compound? Yes."

Not about to accept harem living conditions or any variation of the theme, Tessa's tone turned bitter. "Kahn didn't waste any time. He made these arrangements from space?"

"Only for Shaloma." Dora chattered as if she hadn't just imparted the most devastating of news. Maybe she did need a circuit overhaul. "Miri has been installed in the household since before Lael died. The exciting news is that Miri's expecting a baby."

Tessa's gut twisted. What in hell had Kahn been thinking? He'd left a pregnant woman behind? Then lied to Tessa when he'd told her there was no one special waiting for him at home. For God's sake, Miri was having his baby!

Going from contentment to fuming outrage in less time than a shuttle's liftoff, Tessa took deep breaths that did nothing to calm her. "I'm going to kill him."

"Why?"

"I don't share."

"That's not a very progressive attitude. In fact it's—"

"Dora. Shut up."

"You sound upset."

"Of course I'm upset." Jealousy had never bit her before. "Is Kahn going to flip a coin to see which one of us he takes to bed? Or maybe sleeping with him will be our reward for following his rules. Or maybe—"

"Kahn doesn't have sex with his other wives."

"What?" Tessa drew in quick breaths, but the air didn't have enough oxygen to keep away the retching dizziness. "You just told me Miri is having a baby."

"Etru's baby."

"Dora, you aren't making sense. You said Miri is Kahn's wife."

"Miri is also Etru's wife and she's pregnant with Etru's child. She sleeps with Etru. Only him. Shaloma is too young for sex, and you are supposed to teach her how to run a household."

"I don't know how to run a . . . Kahn only has private relations with me?"

"Yes. You're the only one he gets naked with. Feel better?"

Much. Air inflated her lungs again. Her temper subsided as Dora explained the family grouping.

Still, the revelation had thrown her because she'd reacted like a jealous lover. She shouldn't have cared this much. It was one thing to like and respect Kahn, but her reaction revealed to Tessa just how deep her feelings went. Feelings she didn't want to admit, not even to herself. "So why are all the women called wives?"

"Because if Etru dies, it's Kahn's responsibility to help raise the child. And Shaloma would be the baby's big sister."

Now that Tessa had calmed down, and her thoughts had stopped spinning useless cartwheels, she supposed the system made sense. Children on Rystan wouldn't grow up without family, even if one set of parents died, like hers had. She wasn't sure about the living arrangements, or how she'd feel about having so many people around, but she would try to adapt. Glad that Dora had warned her of the unusual living arrangements before they arrived in Rian, Tessa told herself not to jump to conclusions. She'd upset herself for nothing. Next time she needed to check out and understand the entire situation before she reacted.

"Dora, thanks so much for explaining. I shouldn't have told you to shut up. I apologize."

"No problem."

Tessa grinned at Dora's love for slang. "If Kahn had told me he had a cowife, I would have jumped all over him—"

"Is jumping all over him different from jumping his bones?"

"I have never used that expression."

"But during our stay in Earth's orbit, I monitored North

American television channels. Some phrases were difficult to learn from the context. For example—"

"Tell me about Miri and Shaloma." Tessa needed to distract Dora before the computer went off on a language tangent.

"Shaloma is sixteen years old, pretty with long blond hair and amber eyes. Miri is voluptuous and her belly is rounded from the child in her womb. Both women are taller than you, with less delicate bone structures."

"But what are they like?"

"Can you be more specific?"

"What makes them tick? What makes them happy?"

"Right now both of them are happy that Kahn has taken a wife. Miri because she worried over him ever finding the right woman, and Shaloma because now she has moved out of her childhood home and is one step closer to adulthood."

"What makes Miri think that I'm the right woman for Kahn?"

"Etru told her on the talkie—"

"Talkie?"

"Like your radio but without towers," Dora explained. "Anyway, Etru told Miri this morning that Kahn seems less severe since his return. The women are preparing a feast in honor of your wedding."

"But are they happy to welcome me? Or are they happy because they think I'm the right woman for Kahn?"

"I'm not sure I understand the difference."

"Sure you do." Tessa took several fortifying breaths. "We were friends before Kahn married me. Right?"

"Yes."

"And if Kahn threw me out of his family—"

"Rystani men do not divorce."

"But *if* he got mad and threw me out, you'd still be my friend, correct?"

"Of course."

"But are Miri and Shaloma capable of making such distinctions?"

"Perhaps after exposure to your radical way of thinking, they will come to love you as I do," Dora said gently.

Tessa frowned. "Dora, I'm not that fragile. You needn't use psychobabble on me."

Dora's laughter trilled in her ears. "Sometimes you are too smart for your own good. Why don't you just relax and enjoy the welcome party?"

"I hate parties."

"So fake it. I happen to adore them. All those simultaneous conversations to monitor. All those delicious men to watch. My sensors are in every room of the living quarters except the bedrooms. I don't intrude there unless invited."

"Thanks. But didn't you mean that you like to overhear all the gossip?"

"That, too, dear. Human relationships are fascinating. Now, it would be wonderful if you'd find something other than a backpack for me to wear. Something nice. Maybe something pink and sexy."

Tessa groaned. At least Dora's patter helped keep her nerves in line. She didn't like social gatherings that required lots of small talk. Invariably she was bored or managed to offend someone. What she really wanted to do was see how far Rob One and Two had gotten with the hydroponics equipment. The manufacturer had assured her they could have a good crop to harvest in less than six weeks after planting the seeds.

While Tessa didn't know squat about farming, Dora did. While Tessa should be concentrating on her Challenge skills, she couldn't use her psi all the time without resting between her training. And during those periods of rest, she might as well as be useful and help with the food growing. If she didn't return from the Challenge, she'd like to leave something good behind. And what could be better than helping these people to survive? Dora's expert programs, and the computer would guide the work of the robots. Meanwhile, Tessa still hadn't told Kahn about any of her purchases except the food. While she suspected the women in her family would enjoy the food preparation and cleaning machines, Kahn might consider her purchases wasteful. The million credits she'd spent were still a sore subject between them, one she was reluctant to mention. But soon she would have no choice about telling him.

In fact, once she reached Rian, she suspected a lot of her freedom might be curtailed. She tried to prepare herself, tried to tell herself to assess before she reacted, reminded herself that whatever freedoms she might win for herself would take time, that she had to be patient.

As the snow sled slowed, she hoped curiosity would outweigh her sense of dread. It didn't. Nothing could repress her quiet anxiety over coming to a new world, meeting a new family. And once again being the stranger.

20

Tessa expected the entrance to Rian to be well hidden, so when they parked the vehicles inside a large cavern with whitish-gray stalactites and stalagmites, she figured they were taking a break in their journey. But after the men shut down their engines, they dispersed in several directions—all except Etru and Kahn, who escorted her deeper into the cave.

Glowing stones rested every few feet along the polished floor, lighting their way. She'd expected to feel claustrophobic after the floor angled deeper into the mountain, but the wide passageway and high ceilings reminded her of an office building's lobby back on Earth.

Kahn held her hand and walked by her side. "We are careful to hide Rian's location from Jypeg and the Endekians by using a multitude of entrances and exits."

"Don't they have heat sensors? Or radar?"

From behind them Etru answered. "The radiation helps

hide our presence. There's no need to be afraid. We have lookouts posted."

"And the Endekian presence is still small," Kahn added quickly, as if he feared she might take Etru's words as an insult to her courage, but she'd known immediately that the man was trying to comfort her, not insult her. "The party that captured us must have tracked us when we entered the atmosphere and they tortured Xander because they wanted to learn the location of Rian."

As they strode through wide corridors, Tessa saw many men, fewer women, and even fewer children. The Rystani people shared skin tones that varied from tan to deep bronze and a wild assortment of eye colors. But what struck her hardest was that no one carried extra pounds on their lean frames.

Kahn greeted his people with a nod of respect, a pat on the shoulder, and a few welcoming words. He never once failed to proudly introduce her, either. She read respect for their leader on their faces, and curiosity about her. But no one asked rude questions or tried to impede their progress.

Through open doorways, Tessa saw cramped quarters overflowing with people, rounded rooms with a hearth full of glow stones, a central gathering place. As they walked, she spoke quietly to Kahn. "What makes those glow stones light up?"

"They have a natural phosphorescence. We would export them to other worlds, except that with their atomic interior they can so easily be made into weapons."

"There's nothing else to export?" she asked, wondering if the spaceship she'd bought could carry heavy payloads and reminded herself to check with Dora later. Although Kahn was fully aware that she could communicate with Dora in privacy mode, both cultures considered the practice rude.

"The unique formation of our planet, which produced glow stones, denied us gems and metals in the nonradioactive areas." Kahn accepted a ceramic decorative plate from one of his people. Another gave him a string of beads. And he passed out candy to the children.

The Rystani people here seemed more familiar with Kahn, though no less respectful. Children made a game of running over to touch him, accepting pieces of candy and then careening away with pleased laughter. Men and women alike approached him with gentle smiles of welcome, offering small tokens of their esteem.

Laden with gifts, Kahn turned into an elaborate hallway decorated with an arched golden ceiling, carved stone columns of fantastical creatures, and an intricate mosaic floor of deep pinks sliced with streaks of green. After the plain walkways they'd already passed, this one seemed overdone and gaudy, yet conveyed that a man of importance lived here.

Although Tessa had always known Kahn was a leader of Rian, which was the capital of Rystan, seeing hundreds of his people react to him made her realize that she might be expected to take on a leadership role, as well. But first she had to win the Challenge.

The luxurious hallway ended in a set of double doors guarded by two sentries who opened them to let them pass. After the opulence of the hallway, she'd expected a palace. Instead they entered a homey living area with a massive hearth full of glow stones and intricate tapestries hanging on the opposite wall.

Two women, both taller than Tessa, waited in the room, lounging on a huge sofa left over from the era before suits and null grav were in use. Miri's hollowed cheeks and the dark shadows under her sun-colored eyes suggested she hadn't been sleeping or eating well. She walked to greet the men with a graceful waddle, her long flowing dress unable to hide her swollen belly. Miri kissed Kahn's cheek and hugged Etru with a fierce gladness.

Etru gently cupped her neck and tugged her to him, wrapping Miri in a tender and possessive embrace. "I told you I was uninjured."

"Yes, my love, but sometimes a woman needs to see for herself."

The young Shaloma greeted Kahn with a proper bow of the head, but she had a bright-eyed curiosity about her that focused on Tessa. Although she was half a foot taller than Tessa, Shaloma's waiflike appearance and the tilt of her violet eyes gave the appearance of a teen on the verge of adulthood. Her face, framed by flowing blond hair, possessed arrogant cheekbones, a bold nose, and full lips. When her face fleshed out to match her features, she would be a knockout. However, she seemed totally unaware of her potential, moving with the brisk steps of an eager child, not a woman making an entrance.

After Kahn made formal introductions, the women handed the men drinks and retreated to the kitchen, taking Tessa with them.

Shaloma's eyes glinted with pleasure, barely waiting her turn as Miri hugged Tessa. "My, you are just a tiny one. It's hard to believe you saved my Etru's life. I will forever be in your debt." She pulled back and placed a blue glass jar into Tessa's hands. "This is a perfume that has been passed down from my grandmother's time, to be used for special romantic occasions."

Touched by the gesture, overwhelmed by the friendly psi coming her way, Tessa shook her head. "I can't accept so precious a gift."

Miri's hand closed over Tessa's. "You've already given me the most precious gift on the planet, the life of my baby's father. I will be insulted if you say no."

Embarrassed by Miri's warmth, Tessa relaxed and ordered herself to breathe. At a loss for words, she wanted to convey how much Miri's welcome meant to her, but couldn't speak past the sudden lump in her throat.

"My turn." Shaloma moved in for her hug, saving Tessa from having to respond. Shaloma might be thin, she might be a child, but she embraced Tessa with a fierce enthusiasm that bubbled up from her in a genuine welcome. "I am so glad Kahn married you. I can't wait to hear about Earth. Is it

warmer there? How far away is it? And how did you get
Kahn to allow you to wear that stunning pantsuit? Do you
think he'd let me—"

"Shaloma!" Miri laughed. "Give the poor woman a chance
to settle in. You can pester her with your questions later. Right
now we have a feast to prepare, although Kahn's favorite meat
is not as good without *Jarballa* to spice it up."

After they'd arrived at Rian, Tessa should have remembered to change out of the pantsuit that had become her uniform while on the spaceship. However, she'd been so caught
up in her new surroundings, she hadn't given her suit a
thought. She suspected Kahn had noticed, and she was gratified that again he was making more allowances for her.

However, now was not the time to think about how pleased
she was with her husband, especially when she could actually
contribute to the meal. "I might be able to help with the
spices. Dora, where's the food materializer?"

"Stuffed in the broom closet."

Miri's and Shaloma's eyes widened. "Who said that?"

"Dora is a computer and a friend. She's been watching
over the items we brought with us from Zenon Prime. If you
could lead me to the broom closet, we could unpack."

"Wow." Shaloma let out a most unladylike whoop of glee
that made Tessa chuckle. "You have a computer for a friend?"

"Dora, say hello to Shaloma and watch your manners."

"That means she doesn't want me to talk about sex," Dora
said with absolutely no shame.

"Dora!" Tessa warned her. "Shaloma is not yet an adult."

"But I would love to talk about sex." Shaloma giggled.

Miri tried to keep the amusement from her face and
failed. "Let's leave them to get acquainted. If I don't spice
the *octar* meat soon, it'll be too late."

The broom closet turned out to be a huge pantry where
cooking items and foodstuffs were stored on floor-to-ceiling
shelves. Miri waddled into the pantry, and using a small glow
stone like a flashlight, she perused the stores. "The robots

could barely fit all the supplies you brought in here, and we have one of the largest larders in Rian."

"After Kahn told me about the food problem, I stocked up on supplies."

"You?" Miri turned from the supplies to frown at her.

"Yeah. Me." Tessa saw no reason to mention the details to Miri. "It's kind of a sore point between Kahn and me, so I'd appreciate it if you didn't mention—"

"The men aren't concerned about the kitchen. They don't even know how to boil water, never mind cook."

"Um, Miri." Tessa appreciated Miri letting her off the hook without explaining how she'd blown their credits and now felt compelled to be honest. Biting her lip, Tessa picked up the food materializer. "I don't know how to cook, either."

Miri patted her shoulder. "You can learn. I will teach you. And I know all of Kahn's favorite meals." Miri then winked at Tessa. "However, as much as I like to cook, sometimes it's a chore that I wouldn't mind turning over to a machine. I can't wait to try it out."

Tessa grinned. "Wait until you see the cleaning machine I bought."

"What does it do?"

"Wash dishes. Mop. Dust. Whatever we ask it to do."

"Oh, my. That sounds wonderful." Miri patted her stomach and confided, "This pregnancy makes me sleep a lot, and Shaloma is the sweetest child, but she isn't too thorough with her chores. She prefers to daydream."

Tessa carried the food processor into the kitchen, where Dora and Shaloma were chatting away about fashion on Zenon. A bit relieved that for once Dora hadn't turned the conversation to sex, Tessa interrupted. "Dora, what kind of power supply does this machine require?"

"It comes with a hundred-year battery. All you need to do is connect the hose out the back into the raw-ingredient container."

While Tessa connected the hose, Shaloma set the table

and Miri opened the oven to check the food. Mouthwatering smells of roasting meat and baking bread, as well as a fruit tart, wafted into the room.

Tessa sniffed appreciatively. "Smells great."

Inside the oven, meat roasted on a turning spit. Miri collected juices and basted the meat. "How soon can we have the *Jarballa*?"

"Coming right up." Tessa dusted off her hands and gestured to the food materializer. Although she dearly wanted a cup of coffee, she thought it would be rude to help herself to a drink after Miri had gone to such trouble to prepare a meal. "Why don't you break it in?"

Miri closed the oven, placed the baster in a sink, and peered at the machine. "What do I do?"

"Imagine the taste of the spice. Then push the taste at the machine with your psi."

Miri closed her eyes, twitched her lips. "Done."

"How's this?" Tessa opened the door and handed a pungent concoction to Miri who smiled in delight.

"Perfect."

Enthusiasm lit up Shaloma's face. "I want to try."

"Shaloma, you know better than to waste food. We already have a feast. We haven't eaten this well in almost three years, but for Kahn and Tessa's welcome, we had to splurge."

Tessa stepped back and let Shaloma stand in front of the machine. "We needn't scrimp. I bought enough raw ingredients on Zenon Prime to feed ten people for a thousand years. You and Shaloma must increase your caloric intakes."

Miri pursed her lips, carefully spreading the spice over the meat. "We cannot do so while others are hungry."

"No one will go hungry in Rian." Tessa thought of Rob One and Rob Two who were busy digging out a cavern large enough to house the hydroponics equipment. "We also brought—"

"Do I smell *octar* meat and *Jarballa* sauce?" Kahn poked his head into the kitchen.

"Celebrating your safe homecoming and your wedding to Tessa demands a special feast." Miri tried to shoo him out with a rueful grin.

Kahn didn't budge. "You told me you used the last *Jarballa* on my birthday."

"Did I?" Miri basted the meat, flustered that Kahn was questioning her. She was trying to honor Tessa's request not to mention the food purchases. Obviously, she wasn't good at dispensing misinformation and Kahn angled his head, questions in his eyes.

As if sensing Tessa was behind the problem, he arched a brow in her direction. "Something you want to tell me?"

"No."

The other women gasped at her direct reply. Dora chuckled.

"But you will tell me."

"Oh, Kahn. Miri has spent days hoarding food and working hard to prepare this meal, please don't spoil the celebration." Tessa tried to soften her clear warning to him to behave.

In the best of moods since his arrival home, Kahn crossed his arms over his chest, attempting to look stern, but his mouth twitched. "Fine, I promise not to spoil the celebration, so it's safe for you to tell me what you've done now."

Miri's jaw dropped in shock. Shaloma's eyes went from Kahn to Tessa back to Kahn in wide astonishment.

Kahn didn't take his gaze from Tessa, but spoke to the other women. "I've given Tessa extra leeway because Earth customs are different. Miri, I trust you to teach her our ways. And, Shaloma, don't even think about imitating her or we'll never find you a husband."

"She's a little young for a husband," Tessa protested, forgetting once again that she wasn't supposed to argue with her husband, especially in front of others.

"Could you find *me* a husband?" Dora asked, cutting the tension and causing everyone to laugh.

Tessa knew Kahn still waited for his answer, and rolled

her eyes at the ceiling. "If you must know, I brought back from Zenon Prime a food materializer and supplies to run the machine."

"And it took you how long to tell me?"

"You didn't ask. And the subject never came up." Tessa figured since he'd already promised not to fuss, now might be a good time to confess the rest. "I also bought a cleaning robot."

"Machines that will cook and clean. Did you also buy one that will hunt? Then no one on Rystan will have to work," he teased, and she liked the easy grin on his face, the dancing glint in his eyes.

She'd been about to tell him about the hydroponics equipment, but reconsidered. Perhaps he'd had enough surprises for one day.

"Kahn, I could use the mechanical help." Miri rubbed the small of her back, and Tessa wondered exactly how far along she was in her pregnancy.

She also found the family interaction more than interesting. Miri was backing Tessa in a way that made it difficult for Kahn to turn her down without seeming unsympathetic to her pregnancy.

As if accustomed to attempts to softly manipulate him, Kahn didn't give in easily. "Shaloma and Tessa will help you."

"Yes, but Shaloma has her studies, and Etru told me over the talkie that Tessa must practice daily for the Challenge." Miri opened the oven again and savory smells drifted to Kahn's nose and his nostrils flared in appreciation.

Kahn grinned, seemingly none too upset that the women had outmaneuvered him. "You do know how to bribe a man."

"And after Tessa tastes your favorite dishes, she'll be able to produce them herself with the food materializer."

Kahn sighed. "I should know better than to come in here." He ducked back out of the kitchen, and they could hear him say to the men, "We'll be eating soon."

Tessa sagged in relief. She hadn't realized that she'd been holding her breath, anxious over Kahn's reaction. And she appreciated Miri's backing her more than she could say. A sincere thank-you seemed inadequate.

"Miri, I . . . thanks."

Miri took a hot pan of bread out of the oven with her fingers, exhibiting total temperature control of her suit. "You didn't think we would help you?"

"I didn't know what to expect. I'm a stranger here. Your ways are very different from mine." Tessa drew in a deep breath and let it out slowly as the other two women exchanged a long glance and frowns. "Look, I want to make this work. So if I say or do something wrong, rude, inappropriate, I want you both to tell me. In exchange, I promise never to do anything that would deliberately hurt either one of you. Deal?"

Tessa held out her hand to Miri to shake. Miri clasped her hand and embraced her, then gestured for Shaloma to join the three-way hug. "Deal."

Miri stepped back, removed a large round fruit pie from the lower oven and handed it to Tessa. "Can you take—"

"Shaloma." Tessa couldn't touch that burning-hot pie plate without getting badly burned.

Shaloma rushed over to help Miri, then both women looked at Tessa oddly. Miri angled her head. "I know you don't know how to cook, but you can help serve."

"I can't."

"Is this kind of work beneath you?" Shaloma asked.

Tessa shook her head. "I don't have that kind of temperature control over my suit yet. If I'd touched that hot—"

"I'm sorry." Miri calmly handed the pie cutter to Shaloma and gave Tessa another task. "Why don't you pour the drinks, then."

Tessa found glasses and filled them, then brought them to the table in the dining area off the kitchen. "I haven't learned how to operate the null grav controls, either."

"It will come, dear," Miri said encouragingly. "Etru told me that Kahn said you're doing marvelously well. He's proud of you."

He was? This third-hand gossip could be quite useful. She wondered how else she could help. But Miri assigned her tasks, and she carried plates and utensils to the table, feeling like a small part of the team. She hadn't felt like part of anything for a long time, not since Earth.

She hadn't expected to like being in a kitchen or being around a woman like Miri who spent her days cooking and cleaning. However, Miri hadn't just welcomed Tessa, she'd made her feel like part of a family. And Tessa appreciated it.

So when Miri began to carve the meat and asked about her life on Earth, Tessa didn't brush her off with a curt answer. She told the women about losing her parents, her foster homes, and how she'd found a second home in the Secret Service.

Shaloma was fascinated, especially about Tessa's work guarding a business tycoon and a president. She wanted to hear all about the business details. About the wheeling and dealing. And finally when dinner was on the table and Miri called in the men, Tessa wondered if she'd be able to eat past the lump in her throat.

She might not recognize the food on the table. She might have to stand since she couldn't operate the null grav in her suit. She might have just met Shaloma, Miri, and Etru, but instead of being the outsider, she belonged.

Kahn raised his drinking vessel in a toast. "To the newest member of our family, my wife Tessa."

"Cheers."

Everyone sipped. Her drink tasted like beer, but more mellow. Miri sputtered and Shaloma gasped.

Kahn's brows narrowed. "What's wrong?"

"Nothing," Miri replied.

Oh, God. Tessa just knew she'd done something wrong. She'd poured the drinks. Given everyone the same thing.

And Kahn had told her women didn't drink alcohol. Miri was attempting to cover for her mistake but a pregnant woman shouldn't be drinking.

"I'm sorry." Tessa walked past Miri and Shaloma and picked up their glasses, adding them to her own. "I poured the wrong drinks."

Etru dropped his head into his hands. "You gave Miri and Shaloma spirits to drink?"

"Not on purpose."

"Women aren't supposed to drink alcohol. Didn't you know that?"

"I did. I just didn't know this beverage was alcoholic."

"Any child—"

"Etru, she wasn't born here," Miri defended her. "It was only one sip and caused no harm."

Etru raised his head and looked at Tessa. "This time, she caused no harm. But what will she do next?"

"That's what I wanted to talk to all of you about." Tessa came in with fresh drinks for the women, something fruity and nonalcoholic. "I have a plan to suggest. Is dinner the appropriate time to talk business?"

21

At Tessa's suggestion to talk about business, Etru almost choked on his drink and Kahn tried to hide a smile. With Tessa around, dinner would never be boring. While Miri had apparently taken Tessa under her motherly wing, Miri would have loved anyone who had saved her husband's life. And as for Shaloma, the poor kid had developed a serious case of heroine worship, looking at Tessa like some kind of awe-inspiring goddess.

However hard Etru was trying to accept Kahn's wife after she'd saved his life from the Endekians, his friend couldn't conceal the disapproval in his eyes at her impudent suggestion. Kahn had once reacted to her in the same way. But no more. She'd repeatedly proven to him that she had good ideas. Although he found himself holding his breath, it was due to anticipation, as he eagerly awaited to hear what outrageous scheme she had in her inventive mind.

Etru sipped his ale, then spoke firmly. "Women tend to

home, hearth, and children. They don't speak of business matters."

Kahn spoke lightly. "We should hear her out, Etru. Tessa has a good head for business as well as tactics."

Tessa spoke softly. "My business ideas focus around putting more food on the table."

Somehow Kahn just knew she wasn't talking about distributing supplies she'd bought in Zenon Prime, or cooking, or opening up one of those restaurants he'd seen on Earth. He stabbed a piece of *octar* meat in *Jarballa* sauce and savored the spicy treat, which put him in the most easygoing of moods. "What are you thinking, woman?"

"You told me the growing season is too short to raise enough crops to feed everyone year round."

"And?"

"What would you think about growing food inside Rian?"

"Underground?" Etru laughed. "Crops require sunlight for cultivation."

"Actually, you are partially correct." Kahn had to give Tessa credit as she ignored Etru's sarcasm and kept her words diplomatic. Her face remained schooled to reveal none of her thoughts, but he caught a spark of agitation in her eyes as she continued. "Crops need light, but it needn't be sunlight. On other worlds, farmers use artificial lighting."

"To make those kinds of lights takes heavy metals, and to power them would take—"

"Generators."

"Which are not available—"

"Actually, they are now."

Kahn restrained a chuckle. He could see that he should have pursued his interest in his wife's purchases, but watching her spring another surprise on the family was actually fun. She'd told him about the food she'd bought and about some of the machines, too—but obviously not all of them. "Tessa, what exactly have you done?"

"When you told me about the food shortages, I put Dora

to work on the problem. She suggested our best bet was hydroponic farming."

Kahn appreciated the *our* that indicated she'd made Rystani problems her own, and exchanged glances with Etru. While this had to be the strangest conversation his friend had ever had at their dinner table, his expression served to underscore just how much Kahn had changed since meeting his wife. Usually the men discussed the hunt, the women threw in tidbits about their day. They'd never discussed starting up a farming business with a name he couldn't pronounce, and yet, as usual, Tessa had intrigued him. "Water ponics?"

"It's a system of farming," Dora explained. "It can be done underground with huge vats, lights, and proper nutrients."

Now the computer was joining in the conversation as part of the family. Kahn didn't know what surprised him more, that everyone seemed to accept her as a new addition to the family, or how easily she fit in.

Etru shook his head at the computer. "But we don't have—"

"We do," Tessa countered. "We brought back enough equipment from Zenon Prime to begin a hydroponics farm."

Kahn bit into a delicious piece of crusty bread. "Our resources are limited—"

"Dora can teach us the new skills," she interrupted, expecting him to argue.

"—but this hydroponics idea sounds like it's worth investigating." Kahn backed her idea with enthusiasm.

"Who will Dora teach to farm?" Etru demanded. "The men must hunt or we will not last the winter. The women have their chores to do."

Tessa kept her voice level as if she were deferring to Kahn. "If I see that the chores get done, can I organize the women to run the hydroponics?"

"I will help," Shaloma added quickly, her eyes shining brightly.

Miri nodded. "As will I."

"I don't like it." Etru took Miri's hand. "You cannot exhaust yourself. You already do too much."

"I will see that she eats enough and rests enough," Tessa told them. She looked to Kahn, awaiting his decision.

Stars help him, if he refused, the women in his household might revolt. And if he agreed, Etru would be none too happy. And yet starving people couldn't ignore the opportunity of creating a new food source.

Stalling, Kahn finished the last of his meat. "Where is this equipment?"

"Dora had robots store it in a safe place." Tessa lowered her eyes. Obviously well aware she should have told him sooner, she'd nevertheless held back information until she thought she held the upper hand. Kahn realized that her caution was due to his past reactions and hoped that would soon change. He didn't want his wife to be so cautious around him that she couldn't speak freely.

"Where is the equipment?"

Dora sighed, just like a real woman. "I had Rob One and Rob Two dig out a cavern behind your quarters. They used their short-range sensors to find their way into a hollowed-out cavern that is suitable for our purposes."

Kahn could see the hope in Tessa's eyes, the resentment Etru tried to hide. Kahn understood all too well that his people would be divided over the issue of women working outside the home, although women *did* help with the farming during the short growing season. He thrummed his fingers on the table, knowing that if the women failed, Tessa and he would lose much respect. And if Tessa's plan succeeded, many would resent her because their lives would forever change.

Tessa had placed herself in a no-win situation and yet she'd put the welfare of his people over any wish she might have had to fit in here. She didn't seem to mind facing opposition, seemed sure she could convince other women to help her.

But what choice did they have? Adapt . . . or starve.

Intellectually, Kahn knew that he should thank her for making a sensible choice, for attempting to feed his people. But he and the other men liked coming home from the hunt to a clean house, a warm hearth, with hot food on the table. Even more, they liked knowing their wives would be at home doing chores to make their lives comfortable, not working with some alien machines.

At the same time, he appreciated that Tessa had finally told him about her plan and had not tried to accomplish it without his backing. Although she'd bought the supplies and machines without his knowledge, that she would share her idea with him now proved that she trusted him more each day. And he liked having that trust.

"Are you sure you can pull this off?" he asked his wife, believing she could do almost anything she put her mind to. Her fighting skills with her suit had improved until she could almost give him a worthy match—except for the lack of null grav. And while her temperature control remained shaky, she would fine-tune that process, too. What she did not yet realize was that her skill now equaled that of most men. Thanks to the expertise she'd acquired on Earth, her agile mind and her will to work hard, she had come far in a short time. But he'd never have thought she could be so mentally tough, and remain so attractive. Despite her warrior ways, despite her lack of cooking skills, he took great pride in her accomplishments, and none more than her winning over Miri and Shaloma to her side.

"I don't know if we will succeed." Tessa's brows drew together. "I've never grown crops. I don't even know how to assemble the equipment, but Dora said she can teach us. I believe her."

Kahn looked to Miri. "Will the women help?"

"Some will."

"We'll have to gather the women together." Tessa looked

from Miri to Kahn. "Is there a place large enough to hold all of us?"

Etru shoved his plate back. "You're allowing them—"

"To try." Kahn understood the risks, hoped he wasn't making a huge mistake. "Etru, two generations ago, we had to adjust to the suits, a change without which we might not have survived. Now, we must adapt again. I want your child to grow up with food in its belly. I want our people to have enough energy to fight the Endekians when the time comes. Make no mistake, they want our planet. They know glow stones can be placed into projectiles and the extreme impact turns them into nuclear weapons. We will have to fight them off, and men do not fight well with muscles starved for meat and bellies growling with hunger."

Tessa bowed her head to him. "Thank you."

"No." Kahn took her hand. "We thank you."

At his words, she lifted her eyes to meet his, and her psi reached out and wrapped him in a warm embrace, sharing a moment he'd never forget. They had come together as strangers, married under the most dire of circumstances, yet they'd formed more than a workable alliance. Always, he'd feared that giving in to her would weaken him, but he couldn't have been more wrong. Bonds of mutual respect were forging and making them stronger together than either would have been separately. Although he had no idea where the future would take him, he was pleased that Tessa would be with him.

Tessa should have known organizing the efforts of over a thousand women would be a task of *masdon* proportions. And without the help of Kahn, who'd taken the hunters with him while leaving only perimeter guards, Dora who had sensors everywhere, Miri's common sense, Shaloma's enthusiasm, and the support of Helera, Rian's wise woman, they wouldn't have even got to this point.

Tessa had called the women together in the chamber Rob One and Rob Two had dug out. From her position on a raised ridge of rock inside a rust-colored cavern that flickered with glow stone lighting, Tessa had told the women and children that Kahn had given his blessing to the massive undertaking of establishing a farm inside Rian. She explained how they'd brought equipment and supplies from Zenon Prime. How with Dora's help they could help feed their people.

Questions from the audience came fast and furious, the women speaking up as if they'd attended town meetings all their lives. "My husband," complained a woman in the second row, "expects to come home from a long hunt to a good meal, a glowing hearth, and a clean household. If I work for you, how will I keep my husband happy?"

The women in the audience murmured agreements. Many had the same questions.

Tessa raised her hand for silence, so she could be heard. She'd chosen to wear a traditional Rystani dress, cropped short to show leggings beneath. Even in her clothing, she'd wanted to portray a merging of customs both old and new. "We have also brought cleaning and cooking machines."

"Enough for all?" asked another woman.

"Enough so that we can make do." Tessa lowered her voice so the audience would have to subside their murmuring to hear her. The acoustics inside the huge cavern were surprisingly good and sound carried far. "We will have a communal feast for our men when they return. Some of us will prepare that meal. Others will watch the children of those who work on the farm. We will each do what we do best."

"What we do best is stay home and take care of our families."

"We don't want to adopt alien ways."

"Would you prefer to go hungry?" Tessa countered, hands on her hips. She didn't want the debate to become confrontational, but it appeared she would have no choice. So far Dora had remained silent, but Tessa had her eavesdropping to find the natural leaders to put them in charge of different areas. She also had her noting the troublemakers, to send them home or at least isolate them from one another once they broke into groups.

At her strong words, Tessa heard many protests but no clear voice rose up from the audience. Helera floated next to Tessa on her right side and the women quieted again. The wise woman was their unofficial leader and spokeswoman. The many lines of her face drew respectful silence; once again the women quieted.

"When I was a small girl, there was plenty to eat in Rian. The winters were not so long or so harsh. The men came back from the hunts triumphant, and the women took traditional roles of caring for hearth, home, and children. That was our way for generations and it served us well."

"And so it shall always be," said another elderly woman in the audience.

"I will not give my child to another to watch," shouted a woman up front.

Helera speared her with a chilling look that would have frozen a glow stone. "Now our children go hungry. They may not grow properly. Worse, what will happen in another generation if we go on as we have? Suppose the weather worsens?"

Grumbles and whispers of fear washed over the crowd. Tessa had known she needed support. She'd expected to find it among the women just a few years older than Shaloma, since younger people usually embraced new ideas more easily. Instead, the oldest and wisest of them had embraced her alien idea and had made her feel that these people might eventually accept her as one of them.

"This might be the best opportunity we ever have to intervene in our fates." Helera spoke slowly, giving the women time to calm their emotions and think. "We can go the way of the *licaseum* to extinction or we can choose to act to save ourselves. Change is never easy. But Rystani women are strong and we can make changes."

Cheers and applause came sporadically from the audience. Tessa estimated maybe one third of the women might be convinced. Not enough.

"I will not follow that abomination." A thin woman pointed at Tessa. "My husband says that she fights like a man."

Tessa was about to defend herself, but Miri came to float by her left side. "Tessa *is* different from us. She comes from another world with customs that permit a woman to work and fight or stay at home and raise children. On her world, her job was to protect a great leader. And because of her skills, she saved the life of my Etru, as well as Kahn, Xander, Zical, Mogan, and Nasser." Miri placed her hands on her extended belly. "Because of Tessa's alien skills, my child shall grow up with his father. Yes, her talents are different from what I know, but that does not mean we should fear what she can offer."

More murmurs grew. Heated arguments sprang up in several areas, including several shouting matches.

Tessa stepped forward and held up her hands for silence. "No one will be forced to do anything that makes them uncomfortable. And if our grand experiment fails, you can return to the old ways. I ask that you take a chance for a better future for yourselves, your husbands, and your children. Those who want to try, please stay. Those that don't wish to participate are free to leave."

Tessa expected very few people to stay. But only a few dozen out of maybe a thousand women left the chamber. However, she saw doubts, fears, and much hesitation on the faces of the ladies who remained. "I thank you for your support. More important, I hope the entire community will thank you when we succeed. Those who wish to work on the farm, please move to the right. Those who want to cook for the workers, go to the left. And those who will watch the children please step to the back."

As the women chose where they wanted to be, Tessa saw they'd actually divided into three groups. She had too many cooks and child care workers, not enough people to labor on the hydroponics, but it was a start. And they would make do.

Kahn planned to hunt for four full days. He figured Tessa could use a break from her training. He didn't want her to grow stale, and more importantly, he intended to keep the men out of the women's way until they worked out a system to tend to the children, the cooking, and the hydroponics. So the men broke into three large groups with a plan to converge at a preappointed place to clean their kill.

Unfortunately, one group ran into Endekians almost immediately. They escaped through a mountain pass. The second group met up with hunters from a neighboring village who had wandered into Rian's hunting territory due to their own lack of game. Threats were shouted, but no blood spilled. Kahn's group found several *octar,* barely enough to feed the hunters and keep them going, with little left over to bring home.

At camp for the night, discouraged men sat around glow stones discussing their options, protected from the wind by their suits and their sleeping *masdons,* which surrounded them. Mogan and Xander pressed their argument to go farther south. Etru and Zical, fearing an Endekian attack, wanted to head back to Rian to protect the women. Kahn remained undecided until a psi shriek, unlike any he'd known, had him leaping to his feet. The shrill cry had broken into his mind with a thunderous blow and a hammer strike that made his ears ring and his heart pound.

Etru stood also. "What's wrong?"

"Tessa's in trouble." Kahn prodded his *masdon* awake.

Zical exchanged a long glance with Etru, then angled his head in disbelief. "Kahn, how do you know?"

"She called out to me with her psi."

Nasser shook his head. "That's impossible. We are two days' ride from Rian."

"I heard her," Kahn insisted, floating onto his *masdon*. It mattered not if his men followed. It mattered not that it was night. Or that Endekians might stand between him and Tessa. Not for one minute did he doubt that she needed him. Knowing her spirit as well as he did, he knew she would not have called unless a life was in danger.

He prayed to the stars that life was not hers. The hopes of his world rested on her completing the Challenge. He dared not think what losing her would mean to him personally. He could not think about her leaving him, and passing on to the afterworld, and still function.

With an urgent psi command to his *masdon,* he prodded the beast to top speed. He sensed men following, their voices pleading with him to slow down, but he didn't heed their words to take cover, to avoid leading the Endekians straight to Rian. At the journey's end, he would hide his approach, but not yet.

With every lumbering step, he could only think that Tessa needed him. He must hurry.

When a shuttle dropped out of orbit and landed in front of his *masdon,* Kahn wondered if the Endekians had found him. And if they already had Tessa. But he had no time to consider the merit of that idea before the hatch popped open.

Kahn reached for a stunner. As did his men who guarded his flanks and rear. He was just about to order his men to circle the ship, when Dora's familiar voice called out to him. "Kahn, is that you?"

"What's wrong?" Without hesitation, he floated off the *masdon* toward the shuttle's hatch.

"I need to get you to Rian," Dora told him. "Fast. I'll explain on the way."

Etru and Zical came with him. Kahn left Nasser in charge of the remainder of the hunting party and headed inside the shuttle. The moment Kahn, Etru, and Zical entered, the hatch closed behind them and the craft soared into the sky.

"Dora, is Tessa still alive?" Kahn asked the question that burned like a painful brand.

"She's in a coma."

He stiffened, but didn't lose hope or he would fall into a panic and be of no use to anyone—especially his wife. Lael's death had torn him apart with grief, but losing Tessa wouldn't just have devastating personal consequences. If she died all of Rystan would mourn . . . and suffer. Her death might mean the eventual demise of his people, because without a Challenge win, they might not survive the Endekians. But Tessa could still recover, although from Dora's actions, the crisis was clearly severe. "What happened?"

"Tessa went through the lake's ice into a water pocket. She struck her head and couldn't protect herself from the frigid cold. Helera is unsure if she will recover."

Dora flew the shuttle straight to the cave and popped the hatch. "Go. Go. Helera thinks only a healing circle can bring her back."

Kahn raced out of the shuttle, his heart thudding, his mind silently screaming. He didn't know where the shuttle had come from. He didn't know how Dora could be on it. Right now he didn't care. His thoughts were on Tessa. She would not die. She could not leave him. She meant too much to him and to both Rystan and Earth.

Kahn sprinted to his quarters, shocked to find the hallways lined with dozens upon dozens of weeping women. They parted, their eyes brimming with tears, their sobs ringing in his ears as he rushed inside to find Tessa lying on a tapestry before the hearth. Helera, Shaloma, and Miri had their hands locked in a healing circle around Tessa.

Kahn, Etru, and Zical joined the circle, adding their heat and their psi to the women's. Tessa still breathed, but her pink skin was tinged with blue, her lips purple. She didn't shiver. Her breathing was light, her chest rising and falling with a shallowness that frightened him. He ached to take her into his arms, but knew that if she were to recover, her chance was best inside the healing circle. Kahn fought to keep his voice steady. "What happened?"

Helera spoke softly as the four of them shot psi healing to Tessa. "One of the children fell through the lake's ice into a water pocket. Tessa dived in after him."

Stunned that she would risk her precious life in such a foolish way, Kahn almost broke the circle. "What! She tried to kill herself?"

Shaloma shook her head. "She floated through the water with skill and purpose—like we float through air. She scooped the boy into her arms and brought him back to the surface. Her skin turned blue, and we tugged both her and the boy to safety."

"Then she collapsed?" Etru asked.

"Not right away." Miri spoke sadly. "The boy didn't move. Didn't breathe. He was dead."

Shaloma continued the story. "Tessa shoved the boy's wailing mother aside, struck his chest with her fist. Then she breathed into his mouth. He coughed, and spit out water. She saved his life."

"And then?" Kahn realized the women didn't want to tell him what occurred next. Something horrible had happened. He sensed it from their psi, saw it in the shadow of disgust and sadness in their expressions.

"Several women claimed that Tessa was . . . unnatural. Evil." Helera sounded tired and exhausted, as if the years weighed heavily on her thin shoulders. "Those hostile women panicked and shoved Tessa back onto the thin ice. Your wife wasn't even scared. She tried to explain, to reason with them. Although she was somewhat cold and shivering, she was handling her suit's control well enough to avoid serious hypothermia. The women were too afraid to listen to her words. Then the ice broke under Tessa's weight. Again she fell through the surface. For a long time she didn't come up. When she did, she was . . . like this."

Miri filled in the gap. "We think she hit her head and was unconscious while under the water. I saw blood on the ice after she disappeared and I heard a terrible thud as her head hit something. Perhaps she was too cold to use her shield. But she fought through it, came back to the surface, and climbed into my arms before she again collapsed."

Was that when she'd fired off that psi scream? When she was cold and frightened and alone? When she'd been slipping from consciousness?

Kahn should never have left her. Knowing of her aptitude for stirring discord, he should not have let her out of his sight. And he was sick with grief over such an avoidable accident.

"Kahn, she called out to you." Helera drew him from his thoughts. "I heard her psi scream your name. Now you must find a way to bring her back," Helera directed, "or it may be the end of all our people."

"What must I do?" he asked.

"The two of you share a rare connection that is older than Rystani history. You must find a way to ease a path for her back into the light."

Kahn sent out his psi. "She's closed to me."

"Find a way to slip through or she dies," Helera warned in a voice fierce and ferocious. "She's fading."

"Tell me how to do more," Kahn pleaded, having no idea how to reach her.

"I cannot tell what I do not know. I've only heard the legends that say a psi mate must be willing to risk all to bring back the other." Helera's eyes found his across the healing ring. "You may have to stretch yourself so thin that we lose you, too."

"I'm not important," Kahn told them. "Tessa is. She must win the Challenge."

"Kahn, we will be here for you," Shaloma promised. "Use our strength to add to your own."

"We could all die?" Kahn asked Helera for clarification and read the answer in her eyes. As much as he wanted to save Tessa, each person must take that risk of their own free choice.

All now knew that not only Tessa's life was at stake but the future of the Rystani people, and no one broke the circle. This would be done together. They would save Tessa or they would all pass on to the next life as one family. Torn over the idea of making such a sacrifice for one person yet aware of the need to save her above all else, and grateful she was that important, Kahn hesitated. As their leader he needed to be impartial, but he could not quell his personal feelings of urgency and panic at the thought of losing her.

Kahn's gaze sought out the men and the women who meant so much to him. "Are you sure, my friends?"

Each of them nodded in turn. That Tessa was Earth's champion and Rystan's only hope of a final Challenge win outweighed all other considerations, but it didn't hurt that in the short time she'd been with them she'd touched their lives in ways both significant and small.

Dora chimed in, her tone somber. "I will add my psi, too. Let us begin."

22

Kahn had tried once already to penetrate Tessa's psi. His initial thrust had been countered by a dense shield that had bounced him out. This time he edged toward her psi with much more care, hoping he could sneak up on her. He'd never *seen* anything like her mind barrier.

"Suggestions?" he asked.

"It's as if she's encased her psi inside a protective shield," Etru muttered.

Kahn tested the barrier, seeking an opening. "Her mind shield is like a ball of yarn, except the threads are made of steel."

"There's no time to follow one thread to the core," Dora warned. "Bodily functions are weakening."

Shaloma spoke up, but hesitantly. "Kahn, the threads only look solid because Tessa is spinning the shield. It's probably some kind of automatic defense mechanism."

"She's right," Miri added excitedly. "Kahn, if you can match the rate of rotation, perhaps you can slip inside."

"I'll try." Kahn had never imagined such a thing, but he spun his psi around hers, matching the rate of rotation. Sure enough, he could now see tiny holes between the thicker threads. "I'm going in now."

He advanced slowly, hoping she wouldn't alter the rate of spin or shut down the shield, refusing to think about what would happen if she died while he was inside.

Slipping through the tiniest of openings, Kahn lost contact with the others. He could still feel their psi lending him power, but he couldn't hear their voices, if they spoke at all. Words couldn't describe the streaking lights of psi images or the rainbow of streaming colors, all leading to a thick trunk that extended upward like fingers to the sky. Or like a tree. Already the buds had died, leaves withered. Kahn whisked past the surface branches where pain radiated from a black oozing wound, where bark still smoked from a fresh lightning strike. That must be the result of striking her head on the ice.

He pushed toward Tessa's roots, sensed she would never have let him get this deep, except she was retreating from this world, her spirit fading. He arrowed through memories, and swirling emotions, careful not to cause more damage. What he saw shocked him. Torn metal. Blood. Two coffins on either side of a stoic child. Faces. Too many faces. Families that took her in and turned her out. A white room. Pain. A strike to the belly. A punch to the face. A wizened old man with yellow skin and slanted eyes. He'd never understood how Tessa's childhood vulnerabilities had made her so strong. She'd overcome more than most, and he could see for himself where those scars had healed and she'd dug deeper roots.

Year after year, she'd grown new layers, becoming stronger and stronger to protect the most vulnerable of cores—losing her parents, bouncing from one foster home to the next, had made her flexible, made her determined. But the deep pain of abandonment, the fierce need to control her own fate so terrible things would never happen to her again, came through on a level he'd never understood.

Stars! He couldn't let her go. Not after he truly appreciated her vibrant spirit and what she had given him by becoming his wife, by becoming part of his family. She had dared to reach out for everything she'd ever wanted, and now only a few last bits of her spirit sparked.

Tessa, my wife, my heart. Stay with me.

A portion of her psi kindled. *Goodbye.* And the kindling burned down to ashes.

Nooo. Kahn lunged into the ashes, searching, seeking, striving to find some portion of her spirit, using all his power, exhausting his limits and then pushing beyond them. But there was only smoke.

So he wrapped his psi in the smoke. Thinned his self, spreading until he too almost disappeared into the void. He drew on all the energy the others fed him and then demanded more, expanding to encompass time and space and the woman who was his life.

The psi link stretched until he was no more than a wisp of smoke in the wind, no more than a flicker of light, no more than a tarnished hope. When he perceived a sudden jolting surge of power from a new life entering the link, a life he didn't recognize, he focused that, too. And then like a rubber band that stretched too far and either had to break or return back to its original shape, their psi connection snapped.

Broke him loose.

Unable to counter the rushing force, Kahn tumbled, contracting, consolidating. In reverse, he traveled the path, cartwheeling, skidding, out of control. But the roots of Tessa's mind sparkled once again in a comforting red, orange, and yellow glow with flashes of bright blue and streaks of green. The bark of her trunk stood strong, the lightning scar healing. The leaves perked up and the buds flowered with health.

He didn't know how he passed through her shield but he found himself back in the healing circle, so exhausted and drained he had yet to draw a breath, yet content. Before he opened his eyes, he knew Tessa would survive.

They had succeeded. But who had entered the circle at the last moment and changed the balance from failure to success?

Kahn forced open his eyes. Zical stared back at him, as did Etru, their gazes shocked, weary, drained. He saw Shaloma and Helera looking at Miri oddly.

Then Tessa's eyes fluttered open and his heart sang. Her exotic eyes found him and held him, as her thoughts seemed to churn. Her hair might need arranging, her suit might be disheveled, but to Kahn she'd never looked more beautiful, as a healthy pink glow chased away her ashen pallor.

Kahn placed his hand in hers. "Welcome back."

"I had the oddest dream." In confusion she searched Kahn's eyes for answers. "You brought me back, didn't you? It wasn't a dream. It was . . ."

"We all healed you." Kahn gestured to the others.

Tessa's eyes brimmed and tears skidded down her cheeks. "You all risked your lives to save me. I don't know how to thank you."

"No thanks are necessary." Shaloma spoke warmly for all of them. Helera nodded regally. Miri and Etru shared loving looks while Dora was silent for once. Zical appeared almost embarrassed to have taken part in a ritual so intimate.

Tessa sniffled and brushed away her tears. "Someone else was there. Someone whose psi seemed both familiar and new at the same time. How could that be so?"

Miri placed a hand on her belly with wonder. "Our son joined the healing circle."

"Stars!" Etru whispered. And then he fainted.

With a chuckle, Zical caught Etru before he hit the floor. While the women fussed and spoke among themselves, Etru recovered and then all of them departed, leaving Kahn alone with his wife.

Already Tessa was trying to sit up, but he pressed a drinking vessel into her hand. "Rest. And drink this."

She did as he asked, a strange look on her face as if she were still trying to solve a puzzle. "You were hunting. How did you arrive so quickly?"

"Dora came in a shuttle to get me. A strange shuttle. One I've never seen before."

"Oh."

"If there's something you need to tell me, it can wait."

"It can?" She searched his eyes, clearly wondering at the change in him.

And he had changed. From the beginning he'd believed this woman's independence was a sign of disrespect, but he now knew that her self-reliant streak and fierce determination were forged to protect a tender core of vulnerability. She'd never battled with him so much as with herself. Understanding that made her actions much more acceptable.

She angled her head up at him. "Do you fear I'm still too weak for you to yell at me?"

"I do not yell."

"Hmm." She grinned impudently at him, and his heart skipped a beat. "Since you aren't going to yell, I might as well tell you the entire story."

Leave it to her to sense when he was most mellow toward her and the best time to reveal her indiscretions. She told him about her profitable trading partnership with the Osarian, and the Endekians who were furious at their losses.

"So we are rich, woman?" he asked.

"Um, not exactly."

"You've already spent the profits?" He scowled at her.

But she didn't take his scowl the least bit seriously. In fact, she giggled. "We have the latest in technological wonders, a huge spaceship at our disposal orbiting overhead."

He found the idea mind-boggling. He could understand buying the computer information and hardware for Dora. Buying the hydroponics equipment now seemed an obvious solution to the food problems on Rystan. But a spaceship? What was she thinking?

Surprisingly, no anger surged up in him at her unilateral decision. Only curiosity. "Why did you buy a spaceship?"

"The Endekians."

"You outfitted the spaceship with weapons?"

"Of course. One ship won't be enough to fight off their fleet, but with the right tactical training, it's a start." She spoke to him gently, as if she knew exactly how hard he always found making culture-altering decisions. During their shared psi experience he'd had access to parts of her he'd never imagined, but did the reverse also hold true? Had she also had a window into his spirit?

The thought unnerved him. He didn't want to know.

"We need to have a council meeting," she told him, her fingers stroking his shoulder. "This time, men and women should all be included."

"Why?"

She skimmed a finger path over his collarbone. "Rystan can now import the most critically needed items. We must decide what to buy and how to distribute what is purchased. We need to vote on how the wealth will be split."

He groaned and threaded his fingers through her marvelous dark hair. "You're making my head ache."

She chuckled and snuggled against him. "There's more. The women need help with the hydroponics. Can you lend me some men?"

"Maybe we should just put you in charge," he teased.

"Oh, no. Then I would have headaches." She tugged him closer. "Do you know what the cure for a headache is on Earth?"

"What?"

"This." She kissed his mouth. "And this." She kissed his jaw. "And this."

"Umm." He leaned back and tugged her onto his chest. "You know, my headache is definitely better, but not yet cured. I think I could use more Earth medicine."

"Coming right up." She giggled again. "But the cure is working. Look at what we have here. You're already up."

Kahn consulted with his most trusted advisors for another week before calling the council meeting Tessa had suggested. The women who pushed Tessa back onto the ice apologized and she forgave them. While Kahn worked out organizational and tactical details and discussed which items they should import first, Tessa regained her strength with amazing speed and continued her psi training. Kahn brought in Etru and Zical as well as Xander and Nasser to increase the difficulty levels, training her to fight different men and against a group attack. Shaloma accompanied Tessa to one of the sessions and returned starry-eyed, then asked Kahn to train her, too.

He'd refused, but Tessa thought that if Shaloma persisted, he might give in. They were working the self-defense angle on him. Men couldn't always be around to protect the women, and what harm could a little self-defense training do?

Meanwhile Tessa's control over her suit's temperature elements progressed to a level where she no longer noticed Rystan's cold, but she had yet to activate the null grav once. She suspected that as Kahn's feelings for her deepened, he couldn't bring himself to push her to the necessary level of frustration required to enhance her skills.

She'd approached him once about having another man take over that element of the training, but Kahn had shaken his head, claiming that no other warrior had the expertise to push her that hard without risking serious injury to her. This close to the time of the Challenge, he was taking no additional chances that she wouldn't be ready and healthy. And after Tessa trained with the other men, she learned that Kahn's skill level was much superior to the others. He'd honed his abilities to a fine art, training her so well that she had no difficulty defeating the others one-on-one—as long as they didn't use null grav.

Tessa figured her last option to learn what she needed was using the programmed robot on the orbiting spaceship. However, Kahn refused to let Dora send the shuttle down, fearing the Endekians might track her flight to Rian. When Tessa's life had been in danger, they hadn't taken proper security precautions, so Dora had subsequently ordered the shuttle to aimlessly land and take off in various locations around the planet in the hopes that the first landing at Rian wouldn't appear significant.

So far, no Endekians had approached, but Dora was monitoring a buildup in space that had everyone concerned. Kahn had posted extra perimeter guards as well as sent word of the hostile action to other villages and to the Federation, but with thousands of hostile actions among millions of worlds to consider, he didn't expect a political response for weeks. So in addition, every entrance to Rian had both mechanical alarms and men with weapons to stand sentry.

The good news was that the hydroponics plant was fully assembled and operational. Seeds were already sprouting. Within a few more weeks they could begin to harvest and supplement their meager food supply. Meanwhile, Tessa had placed her materializer in the hands of the council for everyone to share. Already the children's faces had taken on the healthy chubbiness of well-fed youth.

But there was some resentment, too. With both women and men working on the hydroponics, the balance of power within some marriages had shifted. Helera had reported her marriage counseling services were keeping her hopping.

Tessa had been busy but not so overwhelmed that she hadn't appreciated the changes in her own marriage. Since Kahn had surrounded her in the circle of healing, since he'd merged their psi at the deepest of levels, they understood each other better. Which didn't mean that they always agreed. With Miri ready to deliver her baby at any moment, Tessa wanted her safely up on the ship with the best medical robot care and Helera there to midwife. Kahn insisted the baby should be born on Rystan like every other newborn.

While Tessa understood that he didn't want his family to be seen as taking advantage of their new wealth and that he didn't like risking the shuttle's return to Rian, she recalled that precious new life in Miri's womb, risking itself before it had even been born to save her. Her connection to the child ran strong and deep, as it did to every member of the healing circle.

She'd finally found a place where she belonged, with a family that had proven their love for her by risking their lives to save her. Their belief in her made her determined to train harder, to win the Challenge for both Earth and Rystan and prove herself worthy. In a few days she and Kahn would leave so she could take part in the Challenge, but already she looked forward to returning here. She thought of this family as home.

Now as she headed with Kahn to the meeting, surrounded by family and friends, she was stunned to see many women had adopted the fashion of wearing traditional dresses over leggings. Shaloma and Helera walked in front of Kahn and Tessa, escorted by Xander, Mogan, and Nasser. Tessa glanced back at Miri and Etru who strolled behind them, her belly so large she would undoubtably go into labor soon.

To avoid being overheard, Tessa spoke softly to Kahn. "I'm worried about Miri."

"She'll be fine."

"Dora says she'll have that baby today or tomorrow—"

Kahn sighed. "Dora isn't a doctor or clairvoyant."

"She has the knowledge of hundreds of physicians from many worlds. If she says Miri is about to have that baby boy, then I believe her. Besides, she was rubbing the small of her back this morning."

"She always—"

"Purple alert. We're under attack. Under attack." Dora's

voice sounded the alarm. Everyone in the crowded corridor on the way to the meeting froze.

Tessa ignored the fear galloping up her throat and went into full combat mode. "Dora, report."

Dora on Rystan remained in constant communication with the duplicate Dora on the spaceship as well as the Dora in the shuttle. With her onboard sensors, she could interpret the data and give a clear picture of what was going on around them.

"Endekian spaceships have broken orbit. Enemy weapons and navigational systems are locked on Rian."

Kahn cursed and ordered his men to take full defensive positions. He sent the women and children to the safest places inside Rian.

Tessa didn't hesitate. "Dora, put full countermeasures into effect."

"Compliance."

From space, Dora would defend them to the best of her ability. She would also monitor the ongoing situation and send the shuttle down to the planet if evacuation became necessary.

Kahn didn't question Tessa. Instead he issued firm, controlled orders of his own, and men scrambled to obey. "Etru, Mogan, you're with me. Zical, Nasser, take the south corridor. Xander, stay with the women."

But before the men could take up positions, something blasted the cave. The glow lights flickered, but did not go out. Dirt rained from the ceiling. The floor rocked and cracked. A woman screamed. Behind them, Miri gasped softly.

"What's wrong?" Etru asked. "Are you hurt?"

"My water broke."

"I'll take her home," Etru told them.

"No," Kahn countered. "Take her to the rear cave. Do it now. Do it fast. Dora, send the shuttle."

Tessa nodded agreement. Shaloma placed an arm around Miri's shoulder. Xander took the point with Helera right behind him. Tessa brought up the rear, and the men guarded the side entrances and exits to the corridor. They advanced as a group, making good time.

"Dora, what's our status?" Kahn asked.

"Endekians are attacking with overwhelming forces. This is not a mere raid. This is an all-out invasion. According to my calculations, Rystani warriors are outnumbered ten to one."

"Inform all the villages," Kahn ordered.

"Dora." Tessa watched Miri stagger and suspected she might be in full labor already. "How much time do we have?"

"Maybe an hour."

Helera dropped back, and she and Shaloma helped Miri advance with null grav. From the grim expression on Miri's face, she was in considerable pain. She bit her bottom lip and groaned, but didn't demand that they slow down.

"Endekians are attacking from the air and the ground. Brace for incoming missiles."

They had mere seconds to grab one another and jam up against a wall. A boom, followed by shock waves, made the floor tremble. Walls cracked and tumbled. One end of the corridor caved in, but Kahn and a few of his men dug out survivors who seemed more stunned than injured.

Before the dust settled, Dora again reported. "Endekians are attacking the primary entrance in overwhelming numbers."

"Does that change your estimate on how long we have?" Tessa asked again, already urging the others to keep moving.

"Rian will be overrun within ten minutes. Endekians are currently breaking through multiple entrances. Casualties are heavy. Destruction to the city center where the missile dropped is severe. The hydroponics are up and running, but the water supply is limited due to a cave-in."

As the ceiling above their heads exploded and collapsed, Tessa opened her mouth to call Kahn back from his flanking position. But he was too far away and too busy fighting encroaching Endekians to help. The stone ceiling was falling.

With a desperate psi lunge, Tessa sped forward, shoving Miri, Shaloma, and Helera into Xander to avoid the falling stone from overhead. The four of them toppled, but Tessa had no time to see if they were okay.

Endekians dropped from the opening above their heads. Tessa spun to face them, arms up, wrists cocked, her weight balanced on the balls of her feet. Five to one, not good odds, but then Kahn had trained her and he was one of the best.

She gave the attackers no time to see through the dust. With a hammer blow to the temple, she killed the first Endekian before he blinked away the dust or had raised his stunner. She took out a second man with a knife hand slice to the neck. A third Endekian seized Tessa to use her as a shield. His mistake. She let him spin her right into him. Then simultaneously jamming her elbow into his chest, breaking ribs, and sweeping his knees out from under him, she put him out of commission. Not fast enough.

Two Endekians had grabbed Miri. Shaloma was down. Not moving. Kahn and Etru were trying to plug the hole in the corridor and prevent more of the enemy from swarming inside to give the women time to escape.

When Xander poked his head out of a mass of fallen bodies, Tessa screamed at him, even as she kept fighting. "Get Helera and Shaloma out."

Oh, God. The Endekians were using null grav to hold Miri in front of them as a shield. No way could Kahn or Etru fire their stunners around her. In fact, they didn't yet know the problem. Their backs were to Miri as they faced down the corridor, trying to stop a platoon of Endekian invaders.

Stunner shots beamed through the corridor, the laser lights chipping stone and sizzling too close for comfort. They had to get out of here. Fast.

But Tessa wouldn't leave Miri. The Endekians had floated her up over the debris and bodies on the floor. Tessa couldn't reach Miri, and despair and frustration peaked inside her. Gathering every cell of fear, Tessa screamed through her psi, launched herself into the air for the first time, her null-grav kicking in—too hard, too fast. But she used the momentum to slam one Endekian into the ceiling. His head smacked rock with a resounding crunch. He wouldn't be coming back for more.

The second man had his arm around Miri's throat. Likely, she couldn't breathe, but still let out a shout.

At her scream, Kahn and Etru turned, saw the problem, but more Endekians poured into the hallway. Tessa needed one second of surprise, a distraction to take out the Endekian holding Miri. She turned her suit transparent.

The Endekian goggled. Her naked body was the last thing he ever saw before she shoved his nose straight into his brain.

"You didn't see that," Tessa told Xander as she gently floated Miri down the corridor, toward the shuttle and away from the Endekians.

"See what?" Xander helped Miri on the other side, and together with Shaloma and Helera, they advanced, the men covering their flanks.

"We have been overrun on several fronts," Dora reported. "Rystani men are falling back, giving time for the women and children to escape through bolt-holes and to hide."

"Options?" Tessa snapped.

"You are too far from the bolt-holes. There's only one chance," Dora warned. "Get out. Run for the shuttle."

They rounded two more corners. This area seemed clear of intruders.

"Go." Kahn waved Tessa toward Zical, who had cleared the final path to the shuttle. "Get them out of here."

Tessa knew Kahn meant to stay behind. He wouldn't want to leave his people or abandon them in a time of need. But sometimes the better choice was a full retreat so one could live to return and battle another day. She'd prayed this moment would never arrive, and now that it had, she didn't feel prepared.

Tessa handed Miri to Xander and Mogan in the shuttle, then covered Shaloma and Helera as the women also took shelter inside. Etru and Nasser went next. Only Zical and Kahn remained, and as she expected, Kahn urged her into the shuttle without taking one step toward it himself.

"Come with me," she demanded.

His eyes sad and full of regret, he shook his head. "I can't. Etru and Zical will bring you to the Challenge. My people need me."

"I need you." She flung her arms around Kahn's neck, used all her psi to merge with his, and then opened her emotions to him. She let him feel full force what losing him would do to her, how she would surely lose the Challenge without him there.

He didn't go down without a struggle. He tried to raise his psi shields but she'd gotten past his defenses.

"Please, Kahn. You can do more good for your world by living than dying. I don't want to lose you, and I need you to train me for the Challenge."

23

Just because Tessa was right didn't mean Kahn could extinguish his feelings of obligation to his people. Torn between staying and going, he seethed with the frustration of needing to be in two places at the same time. He'd rather have walked naked into stinging stunners than abandon his people during a battle. His escape to the safety of the shuttle while people on Rian were dying seemed an act of cowardice. Yet he damn well knew Tessa was no coward. She'd risked her life to save him and his men when she'd entered the Endekian camp alone, and again to save a boy she didn't know when she'd plunged into the frigid water, and she'd killed a handful of Endekians to rescue Miri. Obviously, after Dora's reports it was clear the current battle for Rian was lost, and the notion sickened him, but he had to look at the entire situation, the ultimate goal of returning with the Federation's help to reclaim the planet—after Tessa won the Challenge.

Kahn entered the shuttle to see Miri surrounded by a calm Helera, a purposeful Shaloma, and a worried Etru. When linked with Tessa, Kahn had experienced the fetus's extraordinary psi strength and already felt as if he knew the little one's spirit. With Miri in labor, the Endekians shooting missiles at the shuttle, Kahn headed straight to weapons control and navigation, and employed desperate evasive maneuvers to keep the shuttle from taking a hit.

Zical's eyes flashed a twinkling red. "You set to go?"

Kahn avoided a missile and returned fire. "Don't ever marry an Earthling."

Zical clapped Kahn on his shoulder. "She needs you to win the Challenge. If you'd stayed, I would have stayed, and then we both would probably have died." Zical handed Kahn a printout, his face grim. "Dora's sensors have found a group of our people who have taken cover in the hydroponics area. The Endekians aren't yet aware of their presence. With the food materializer and hydroponics, they may be able to hold out for a week or two."

"We should return. Help them."

"We will," Zical told him. "Just not yet. First, Tessa is mere days from taking the Challenge and she must pass before we return. Your duty lies with—"

"I do not need a reminder of where my duty lies," Kahn snapped at his friend, all the more annoyed because he was right.

Zical shrugged, jerked his thumb at Kahn, and looked over to the communications console. "Tessa—"

"Not now," she snapped, her irritation so severe that Kahn knew the danger must be more critical than he'd assumed.

He spied two Endekian ships on their tail and calculated their shuttle with their ragtag family inside would never make it inside the spaceship's flight bay. "Dora, go to hyperdrive. Both shuttle and mothership. We'll dock the shuttle after we return to normal space."

"Compliance."

Real space disappeared, replaced by hyperspace where all sensations became ultrasensitive. Kahn had made the transition numerous times before and had no difficulties, but Zical looked a little green, and Miri screamed in agony.

"Baby's coming now. The head is crowning." Helera moved between Miri's spread knees. "One more push, Miri. Good." Helera cradled the baby boy and uttered the traditional blessing. The child didn't cry. He opened his stunning violet eyes and sent a warm psi pulse of hello to everyone in the room.

Kahn supposed it might have happened before, but he'd never heard of a baby being born in hyperspace. Helera placed the calm baby in Miri's arms. And Dora popped out of hyperdrive.

Kahn leaned forward and checked the instrumentation, his hands itching to take the controls. "We lost the Endekians. Nice flying."

Tessa stepped back. "Could you take us into the flight bay?"

At the sight of the spaceship Tessa had purchased, a breath of admiration rushed out of him. Long, lean, and with the graceful lines of a winged bird of prey, the ship glistened like a shiny present. Larger than the vessel they'd used to travel from Earth, she appeared to be a modern pleasure craft with extra space for cargo.

Then he spied the weaponry. Lasers. Blaster cannons. Missile throwers. His wife had spared no expense.

Kahn let out a low whistle of appreciation. "She's beautiful."

"Quite shapely," Zical agreed.

"Thank you." Dora's voice sounded bemused, almost flirtatious. "That's the best thing you've ever said to me."

"Dora, I think I'm in love," Zical teased.

Tessa ignored the byplay. She leaned closer to Kahn and whispered. "Back on Zenon the engineers made a few upgrades. They modified the engines, the design, and Dora's technology."

"Nice of you to consult with me." Kahn checked the instruments, then double-checked. "Tessa, there are already life-forms on board the ship. Could the Endekians—"

"Osari is aboard. He brought Azrel and Corban with him. Apparently it's necessary that three races oversee the Challenge to make sure no rules are broken."

Kahn rolled his eyes at the ceiling. "You invited guests without asking me, too?"

"I forgot. Sorry." She brushed a stray lock of shiny hair from her eyes. "Things have been hectic the last few days, but I've been trying to find the right moment to give you this." She handed him the knife she'd bought for him on Zenon.

The hilt was beautifully designed, the balance suggested it had been crafted by an expert. "Thank you." After all the deaths his people had suffered at the hands of the Endekians, he didn't have the heart for a quarrel. Not after she'd given him this gift. Not with the memory of Etru beaming over his son, not with the gorgeous ship waiting for him. Not with a wife who'd begged him to stay with her—not out of need, but out of wanting him. And as much as Kahn enjoyed being needed, it was also good to be wanted for himself.

Her actions revealed that she was as eager for a future together as he was. The thought pleased him, placed a soothing balm over his heart. After Tessa won the Challenge, they would return to Rystan, and with the Federation's help, they'd free his world from the Endekians.

Meanwhile, he was grateful his family was safe. And for a wife who thought enough of him to give him gifts. And for a wife who had opened up an entire new universe of possibilities for them.

"What do you mean, Kahn and his wife got away?" Jypeg screamed at Trask, spittle flying from his lips. He raised his fist in rage, his scar of shame livid.

Trask flinched. "We didn't expect them to have a shuttle or starship on Rystan."

"You didn't expect? Fool!" Jypeg backhanded Trask so hard his second in command tumbled from his chair in front of the communications console. Yellow blood seeped from the corner of his mouth. "We know they are going to Laptiva. We can still stop them, sir."

"Trask. That idea is underhanded. Sneaky. No race has ever interfered in the Challenge." Jypeg bent down and helped lift Trask back to his feet. "I'm proud of you."

"Thank you, sir."

"Can you get us to Laptiva without being seen?"

"Yes, sir. I'll assemble a task force."

"I'm leaving nothing to chance this time. I'll head the mission." Jypeg greedily rubbed his hands together. "We need to make the most of the situation. Here's a chance for us to take back some of the credits the Earthling and the Osarian have stolen from us. And since we already know the female will lose, take any and all bets on the outcome."

"Sir, the odds are—"

"I don't care about the odds. We will crush her. And then I will finish off Kahn." Kahn of Rystan, who had marred Jypeg's face and made him an object of pity among his own people. Jypeg's fist closed around his stunner. Soon, Kahn and his interfering female would be dead by his own hand.

The first moment alone with her husband didn't come for several hours. Between saying hello to their guests, a quick business meeting with Osari, and settling the others into the spacious quarters of their new spaceship, Tessa and Kahn had had no private time together since leaving Rystan.

She looked forward to being alone with Kahn and didn't even attempt to hide her eagerness as she led him into the spaceship's luxurious master suite, decorated with rare paneling that reminded her of cherry wood, precious art objects, and the latest hologram technology. However, she much preferred keeping the *bendar* clear and gazing into the depths of space.

So much had happened over the last few days, but since she had to leave Kahn for the Challenge tomorrow, she didn't want to spend what might be their last hours together talking. Placing a hand on her hip, she changed her black pantsuit into a provocative white lace number that should make the man salivate. He raised one haughty eyebrow. "Are you trying to manipulate me, woman?"

"Actually, I was trying to seduce you. Can't we just skip all conversation and make love?"

"You're a confusing woman as well as a great deal of work to keep up with."

"I'm a simple woman. Low maintenance," she countered.

"Now who's the liar? You're a maze of contradictions that fascinate and intrigue me, especially in that dress. I really like that dress."

"I thought you might."

He folded his arms over his chest, his eyes brightening as he attempted to resist her. "What about honing your null grav skills?"

"In the time I've got left, there's no way I'm going to hone anything—except my appetite for you. So unless you plan to tell me about the Challenge—"

"You know I can't."

"—then the best thing you can do before you send me off is give me a good reason to come back."

"I already have."

"Really?"

His eyes all flinty amber, his lips twitching at some joke she didn't understand, he watched her like a man about to reel in the catch of the day. Why was he looking so smug?

"I've already given you what you wanted most." His arrogant tone, so sure and confident, gave her pause.

She hadn't a clue what he was talking about. "Is that so? Exactly what have you given me besides this gorgeous necklace?" She touched the starfire that she always wore around her neck.

He scratched his jaw. "What have I given you? Me. I gave you me."

"Oh, yeah. I'm the luckiest woman in the universe." She let out a long breath of air in a rush. "I have a husband who didn't want an Earth woman foisted on him. A husband whose wife never seems able to please him."

"You know how to please me. In fact, I could become accustomed to living in this kind of luxury. But you're changing the subject—don't you know what you want most?"

"What?"

"A home. A family. People who care about you as much as you care about them."

Oh . . . my . . . God. How did he know? How could he have guessed her secret when she'd buried the need so deep she hadn't known just how right he was until he'd said the words aloud. From the moment she'd lost her parents until Kahn's family—her family—had risked their lives to save her in the healing circle, she'd been alone. Not lonely. Alone.

On Earth, her detail in the Secret Service had been a substitute family—not the real thing. But now, now she had a real family. People who stuck together, who loved and fought but still treasured and respected one another.

Her detail on Earth changed with who was assigned where. But this family was permanent. She savored the delicious idea like a priceless treasure. How ironic that Kahn had given her exactly what she needed, but she couldn't even pretend to be the kind of wife he wanted.

Her heart quivered at the paradox. She couldn't set him free. But he didn't look dissatisfied, not with his hungry gaze swallowing her up as if he intended to gulp her whole.

But lust didn't always transform into love or even long-term satisfaction. "No matter how much I try, I can never give you as much—"

He swept her into his arms, fisted his fingers into her hair and tugged until she bowed back her neck and he stared into her eyes. "You are my life."

"But you wanted an obedient Rystani—"

"You may not be the kind of woman I would have chosen, but that was because I didn't know a woman like you existed. Or how well suited we are for each other." He seemed so intense, so sure, that he ripped right through every defensive barrier she'd raised. "You are the one who matches my psi, the one who holds my heart, the one who sets my blood on fire. Make no mistake, woman, you are mine, and I will never let you go."

His words soothed the ache in her. As a declaration of love, his words were more than she'd ever hoped for, and she flung her arms around his neck. "Wow!"

He released his fisthold of her hair. "Wow?"

"I rather like the sound of your never letting me go." She leaned into his neck and nipped lightly. "So are you going to talk, or show me some null grav action?" She tossed back her hair, deepening her voice to a sexy purr. "Or perhaps you'd like for me to dance the *Ramala Ki*? I've been practicing."

His eyes dilated, leaving only twin rings of gold around black irises. He set her back on her feet. "I have no idea when you found time to practice, but I am most interested in seeing what you have learned."

She restrained a grin, snapped her fingers, and the music began. The last time she'd danced for him, they'd shared a simmering sexual tension. That tension still existed, but now it was augmented by common experiences, shared goals, and mutual respect. Differences between them would always be there and keep life interesting. But when she'd been inside his psi and he in hers, she'd sensed the goodness of his heart. While she didn't know many things about this man, like his favorite color or if he'd ever had an imaginary childhood friend, she loved him.

She loved him.

The emotion had sneaked under, over, and around her heart until she'd caved. But love didn't feel like defeat. It felt wondrous, glorious, and fun.

She loved him.

And the prosect of living together with him for nine hundred years didn't seem like enough time. Not with a man like him. Not with a man who had more honor in his pinky than others had in their entire bodies.

She loved him, but the notion was so startlingly new that she could barely bend her mind around the concept.

Should she tell him before she left? After what had happened with Mike she didn't want to put off living life, didn't want to keep secrets, and yet she had to consider how Kahn would feel if she told him that she loved him—and then never returned. He'd already gone through that once when he'd lost Lael. She couldn't do that to him again. And with the Challenge such an unknown, she had no idea how long they would be apart or what he planned to do while she did whatever she was supposed to do. But she knew he'd prepared her to the best of her ability and that he'd be there with her in spirit.

No, now was not the time to tell him her new-found feelings. That could wait until she returned. But although she wasn't ready to say the words, she was more than willing to show him.

She put the emotions into the dance, and when she noted his gaze lingering on her legs, she shortened the lacy slip to miniskirt proportions. The hem skimmed her thighs, and as she performed a turn, the lace flared, taunting him with a glimpse of a pink scrap of silk between her legs. The

Brazilian-cut panties allowed him a glance of her bottom, then she spun again, the bodice lower, clinging to her breasts. She gave him the merest hint of her areolae, then dipped, sashayed in her own variation of the *Ramala Ki*. And when she stopped before him in the ritual pose, she did so with her head high, her shoulders back, her spine arching.

The lacy slip stayed up, only by the grace of her protruding nipples, or at least that's how precarious she intended her suit to look. With his eyes flashing an "I can hardly wait to have you" look, she half hoped he would simply lose control and kiss her, half hoped he'd let her continue the dance and whip both of them into a frenzy of desire.

Instead, as she held the provocative pose, he placed his hands on his hips. "Tell me about this Earthling foreplay you always say you need to teach me."

Her heart thumped. "It's a slow tease, a warming up. We don't need to—"

"Where do Earth men start?" He touched the inside of her knee. "Here."

"Higher," she encouraged, hoping he'd slide his hand right up her leg to check out her panties and the dampness already pooling there.

"Here?" He touched the sensitive juncture of where her neck met her shoulder, making her all too conscious of how easily he could trace a path to her breasts.

"Lower."

He walked around her. Not being able to see him spiked her anticipation. Would he dip his hands to explore her panties? Plant a kiss by her ear? The wait seemed interminable, but lasted mere seconds.

He placed his palms on her bottom, leaned in to nip her neck. "Here?"

She shivered, ached to turn around, throw her hands around his neck and plant a kiss on his mouth, but she didn't want to spoil his fun. "You're getting warmer."

She quivered in anticipation as he walked around to face her again. "I'm not sure I understand this foreplay business." A natural-born tease, he understood it very well and appeared to be enjoying her hope that he would move on to the next step. "While I think about this foreplay some more, dance for me again, please."

The music began, releasing her from the pose. The steps became faster, pumping her blood, inciting her to bump and grind her hips. At Kahn's bristling and intriguing take of her dance, at his outright fascination with her moves as she mimicked lovemaking with her hips, he dropped his lower jaw.

Lifting her hair off her neck, she arched her back, let her hips do their thing, teasing them both. And when she posed for him, she made the lace transparent. Left herself standing in just the scrap of panties, her hands interlocked behind her head, her breasts pouting for attention.

He laughed, a most wicked glint in his eyes. "You've added some new moves to the *Ramala Ki*."

"You approve?"

"Stars, yes." He bent over to peer at her panties and his warm breath fanned her mons. "Is there some significance to that scrap of material?"

"You're supposed to peel it down."

"Hmm."

He fingered the material, driving her wild with the need to move. And then ever so slowly, ever so gently, he tucked the material between her cheeks, then tugged the tiny side straps up over her hips, creating pressure, the tiniest of pinches, making her all too aware of the throbbing heat between her legs.

When he straightened with the most satisfied of grins, she realized that his idea of foreplay was making her crazy. She never knew what he would do next, didn't know if he would touch her or take her or if he'd order her to dance and make her wait some more. As his eyes lingered on her breasts, as he contemplated his next move, she loved the heat bubbling inside her, the clenching of every atom of her being, the expectation he incited.

She didn't feel the least bit submissive. There was something utterly powerful in waiting for this man, in knowing that he wanted her, of being able to give him whatever he wanted to take.

"Would you like me to kiss you?" he asked.

"Yes."

"Here." He cupped her breasts, flicked his thumbs over her nipples and shot a bolt of heat straight to her center.

"Yes."

"Here?" He moved his hands from her breasts to her bottom, but he'd adjusted her suit so to her it felt as if his hands remained on her breasts, his thumbs still teasing her nipples. But now she also had the warmth of his hands caressing her bottom, and holding still became almost impossible as she fought not to squirm.

"Kiss my mouth, Kahn," she demanded.

When he slanted his mouth over hers, teasing, nipping, taunting until she trembled, she was shocked and pleased that he did what she asked. He tasted like fresh rain during a summer storm, and she strained toward him. Oh, my, could he kiss. And when she forgot to hold her pose and just before she lowered her arms to draw him closer, he locked her there.

With muscle power no longer required to maintain the pose, she relaxed into his deliciously demanding kisses and seductive caresses. At the pure decadent pleasure of the silken licks of heat he'd ignited, both from the inside out and the outside in, she sighed a throaty moan of need.

When he pulled back from their kiss, she murmured into his ear, "Dance with me, Kahn."

"Rystani men don't dance."

"Men from my planet do. It's sexy," she coaxed. "Let me show you."

He did as she asked, the gleam in his eyes a tangle of hot interest and cool wariness. She immediately lifted her arms over her head, and snapping her fingers and clapping her hands to the heady beat, she slid up against him, wriggled her hips enticingly.

"Come on. Try it. You'll like it." Grabbing his hands, she fused her hips to his. "A friend of mine on Earth once had a T-shirt that said, 'One should dance as if no one's watching, play as if there's no tomorrow, and make love as if it's the last time.'"

Kahn had an innate sense of rhythm and fine control over his body from years of training. At first, he moved stiffly, uncertainly, but she encouraged him with the sway of her hips, the appreciation in her eyes. Soon he was moving as if he'd done this many times before. And as his confidence grew, as he loosened up, she shimmied up his leg, pressed her breasts against his chest and enjoyed the moment.

Her breath came in gasps, and when the music sped up in preparation for the next pose, she flicked back her hair. "Your turn to pose."

He hesitated. She lightly ran her hand up his leg, stopped just short of his sex. "It's not fair if I have all the fun."

The tempo sped to a crescendo, and she danced around him, mesmerized all over again by his powerful shoulders, his broad chest. She ached to dance flesh to flesh, hoped that if he agreed to the reversal of roles that he'd remove his shirt.

After seeing some of his effortless moves, she decided it was a good thing that Rystani men didn't dance in public. She'd have to fight the women off him with a stick. Part of his appeal was all those muscles, his exotic amber eyes, the long blond hair that reminded her of a lion, but what really made him special was how he let her see how much he wanted her.

When the music stopped, he posed for her. Standing warrior straight, legs spread, hands on his hips, he removed his vest, his pants. Totally nude, he could have posed for an ancient Greek statue—except for his *tavis*. She didn't think the Greeks carved their men with erect phalluses.

Reaching up to him, staring straight into his eyes, she placed one fingertip on his chin, slid it down his neck, over his bronzed chest, dipped to his waist, and threaded her fingers through curly blond hair. She skipped his sex, skimmed down the insides of his legs, then walked around to his back, lightly teasing his hip. He looked just as yummy from this side, and she slipped her hands around his waist, allowed her breasts to press against his warmth.

Staying close, her breasts soaking up his heat, she rested her hands on his shoulders, slowly kneaded the tight muscles. "Relax. This is supposed to feel good. We call it a massage."

"That's a very strange place you've chosen to rub." His voice sounded rough, thick with desire.

"Is it?"

"Especially when other parts want you so badly."

She moved one hand to his hard buttocks. "You mean here?"

He sucked in his breath. She giggled at his reaction to her touch and to her tossing his own words back at him. Lightly she stroked the sensitive skin behind his balls. "You mean here?"

His *tavis* jerked so tight, he let out a soft growl. She figured she'd pressed his patience far enough for now. "Let's dance."

And she turned her entire suit transparent, tipped her face up to him. "We can kiss and dance at the same time, can't we?"

"I don't see why not." His mouth was alternately tender and demanding, and he didn't break the kiss until long after her thoughts soared. She clung to him and he to her, their bodies swaying to the music in a dance they had made their own.

He cherished her mouth and her breasts, using his psi until she was nearly frantic.

When the music hit a note that warned her the next pose would come soon, she was a mass of quivering desires. Using her psi, she stroked his *tavis*. At the same time she floated herself into the air as if she were straddling a nonexistent chair and his breath once again fanned her mons.

"Excellent choice. You're so beautiful." He gazed at her with wolfish hunger, then licked her right there.

She quaked with a passion. Let herself burn. "Ah . . . oh . . . oh . . . oh."

Kahn locked her in place, all the while savaging her with his tongue, his hands, his lips, and his psi until she trembled all over.

"Please."

"Please what?"

"Ohhh . . . I can't think . . . when you . . . ah."

"Had enough foreplay, yet?"

"Oh . . . my . . . more than . . . enough. Yesssss." Her muscles quivered, clenched. She clung to the intimate and delicious edge of sanity. Her head felt dull. Her thoughts spun and her simmering blood reached a scalding boil.

"Don't come," he ordered. "I want to be inside you for that."

"Then you'd . . . ah . . . better . . . hurry."

She tried to hold back. She really did. But his tongue between her legs created a wild, crazy, frenzied frothing that made her chest hitch. Out of breath, unable to wait, she exploded and screamed his name in a tidal wave of pleasure.

He kept his tongue and fingers and psi on her until she rode the wave and peaked again. And again. She'd never known this volcano of need boiling just below the surface. She'd never known she could swim so far, surf from crest to crest until the next swell broke and left her brutally breathless.

And when Kahn finally came inside her from behind, his pace fast, fantastic, frenetic, she savored his psi feeding off her, ravishing her, in a pleasure loop so intense that she screamed in the ultimate surrender. He cradled her hips, his voice tender and raw, saying her name over and over as he emptied himself into her.

She exploded one more time. And recovered with him holding her tenderly against his thudding heart.

24

After a quick shuttle ride, Tessa stepped onto the strange world of Laptiva to face the Challenge with her suit, a knife, and a test kit that would allow her to know what was safe to eat and drink. Although she was sure the Challenge would not be easy, her instructions from Kahn had been simple. To succeed she had to reach an obelisk shaped much like the Washington Monument. She had three days to complete the task.

The morning was windless, the silver-white and gold summer sun shone brightly in Laptiva's azure sky, with hints here and there of high cirrus clouds, as if a celestial artist had brushed and feathered the scene with just the softest of strokes. The obelisk shone in the distance, clearly visible, but between the pewter-sand beach where she stood and the distant obelisk were a chain of islands that appeared to be stepping stones through a calm emerald sea.

A boat with a paddle rested on the beach, as if awaiting

her. Tessa looked behind her and saw nothing but endless sand dunes. No trees, no signs of life. She pushed the boat into the warm water, climbed aboard, and paddled to the nearest lushly landscaped tropical island that seemed no more than a quarter mile from shore.

Already she missed Dora's companionship. While she still wore her earrings, communication with the starship was forbidden during the Challenge. As for her husband, she wished she could go back to last night and repeat their time together all over again. Wishing she'd said more to him, wishing she'd somehow found the words to tell him how she felt before she'd left made her sad—and determined to return. Kahn had told her they would monitor her progress through the starfire necklace and that she should never take it off.

"I'm in the boat, paddling easily," she told whoever might be listening back on the starship.

She paddled for maybe fifteen minutes before she realized that her boat was no longer moving—although she'd kept paddling at a steady rate. She was equidistant between the island ahead and the beach behind, and her stroking had ceased to propel her forward. Nor could she turn the craft around. And the distance was too far to consider using null grav.

"I'm stuck. Looks like I'm going for a swim, but I'll test the water first."

Tessa dipped her test kit into the sea. The water contained no poisons or acids. After making sure her kit and knife were firmly attached to her suit, she jumped overboard, expecting to swim. Except she sank to the bottom like *bendar*.

Kahn peered into the monitor, listening to Tessa's play-by-play, his heart dancing up his throat, his fists clenched, his thoughts unsteady. Three quarters of the candidates who attempted the Challenge failed. The test was complex. While he had every confidence in Tessa's abilities, one mistake could be her last.

"Breathe," Zical teased him.

"She'll do fine," Dora agreed. "She's very adaptable. And she . . . Purple alert! Ships dropping out of hyperspace." Sirens blared. Warning lights blinked.

Kahn tore his gaze from Tessa on Laptiva and the monitoring device to count three ships dropping out of hyperspace. Normally, he'd order Dora to jump into hyperspace to escape the attack, but he wasn't leaving Tessa. Those ships shouldn't be here.

"Who are they?" Kahn demanded.

"Endekians." Dora's voice changed into the clipped tones of battle mode. "They are locking cannons on our communications and flight bay. They are firing."

"Shields up," Kahn ordered. "Return fire."

"Compliance. Brace for impact."

Kahn used his psi to lock his body to the deck, used his shields to protect him from a sudden depressurization in case of a hull breach or from flying debris. Everyone on board did the same, except for the baby whom Miri and Etru secured between them.

Several explosions rocked them. "We've taken three hits. Communications are down. There's a fire in the shuttle bay. Engines are damaged."

"Estimated time to repair?" Kahn asked.

"Unknown."

"Get on it. I'll help."

"Compliance."

Kahn turned back to the Laptiva monitor. He could no longer see or hear Tessa. The screen had gone blank.

Underwater, Tessa shut her shield down tight. She could hold her breath for maybe a minute, not enough time to walk

to the island. Swimming was out of the question. She needed
to induce her null grav. Summoning up the proper frustration
wasn't so difficult with her life at stake.

She shot to the surface with her null grav, gulped several
deep breaths of air, then again sank to the bottom. She walked
across the sand, until she once again used the null grav to
breathe. She had no idea if this was the process she was supposed to use or if a more efficient system was possible. However, she made slow but steady forward progress.

When, hours later, she finally reached the shallow waters of
the next island, she didn't immediately crawl onto the beach.
Watching from the water, she surveyed the place for danger.
When she saw a boat like the one she'd abandoned pulled up
on the shore, the hair on the back of her neck prickled.

All was not as it seemed. Was she alone here?

Thirsty and hungry, she realized that she needed to drink
soon or risk dehydration. Food she could do without for the
entire three days if necessary, but after her exertions, her body
was demanding nourishment. The moment she rose from the
water, a table laden with food and drink appeared on the
beach out of nowhere. She'd suspected the Challenge might
have been constructed by the same race that had invented the
suits, but the technology still astounded her.

"How convenient. I think up what I need and it appears."
Cautiously, Tessa strode past the sumptuous repast into the
trees beyond, snagging a drinking vessel and a piece of fruit
on the way. While it appeared the food was her reward for
reaching this stage, she didn't make any assumptions. Kahn
had taught her that much. And more.

Thanks to him, she'd survived the water test. The foliage
reminded her of Puerto Rico, but instead of tropical palms
and dense underbrush in shades of green, here the dominant
colors were henna, fawn, and hazel. Tortoiseshell-colored
birds nested in the trees and cawed to one another. She saw
no insects, but tiny lizardlike creatures sunned on—

"What the hell?"

The fruit in her hand vibrated. Tessa dropped the fruit and moved back several steps. A tiny buglike creature ate through the dun-colored rind, its sharp teeth ripping the fruit and devouring it in slurping gulps.

"Well, I'm glad I didn't eat you." She imagined that ravenous bug biting her face, or worse, suppose she'd swallowed the creature and it had eaten through her stomach to get out?

The bug finished its meal and slithered away, leaving nothing behind. Thirsty after the long "swim" and with the hot sun drawing moisture from her skin, she had to replace the bodily fluids she'd lost. Reluctant to drink from the beverage container without further examination, Tessa set it down and eyed it. "Are you another trick?"

Strengthening her shields, she unscrewed the cap, waited for something nasty to crawl out. But nothing did. So she poured a few drops into the tester, waited the requisite thirty seconds, and when the light burned bright purple, signaling it was safe to drink, she allowed herself one swallow.

"Tastes fine, but we'll give it a few minutes in my stomach before drinking more." She carefully recapped the weird-shaped vessel that reminded her of a mix between a canteen and a thermos, attaching it to her suit. With no desire at all to return to the feast and the possibility of more bugs, she headed straight across the island's interior.

Along the way, she spied some fruit growing within easy reach and popped them into the tester. The yellow fruit tested green, poisonous to her system, and she threw them away. However, the red fruit were okay, but she remained cautious, taking just a few bites and washing them down with more water.

Two hours of solid walking brought her to the farthest beach where she could clearly see the next island in the distance. She hoped to make it there before nightfall. Another boat waited on the beach for her use, but this time, she saw no paddle. She supposed leaving the other paddle behind was her first mistake, but one she could overcome. After a half hour of scrounging through the jungle, she found a short wide branch that would do. However, when she returned to the boat, it was no longer there.

And the next island now appeared twice as far away.

"Kahn, we've got another problem." Zical's face was grim, his purple eyes fraught with worry.

"What?" Kahn snapped as his eyes perused the damage reports as they came in.

"We struck two of their ships, which appear dead in space, but the other one is operational and—"

"They're about to attack again?"

"Worse." Zical peered at his instruments, his eyes drawn together in a frown. "The Endekians are focusing sensors on Tessa. Dora says there's a high probability they may try to interfere with the Challenge."

"Stars!" Kahn dropped the damage reports onto the console. He'd figured Jypeg was after him—not her. "We have to warn Tessa." The Challenge was difficult enough for the candidate without hostile interference. Stress kicked adrenaline into Kahn's system and he ached to fight someone, smack his fist into Jypeg's yellow face. But he had to think, suppress the rage erupting in him like a volcano. "We need to warn Tessa," Kahn muttered. "But how?"

"Even if we could warn her, won't that break Challenge rules and cause her death?" Zical asked.

"We should contact the Federation," Etru advised as he came onto the bridge with Azrel, Corban, and the Osarian.

Kahn shook his head. "Communications are still down."

"I'm working on it," Dora informed them.

"We must get Tessa out of there," Osari said in his flat voice.

Dora again inserted herself into the conversation. "While the shuttle isn't damaged, the flight hatch is fused shut from the fire. A rescue operation isn't possible at this time."

Kahn's frustration peaked. "There must be something we can do."

Dora spoke hesitantly. "I can contact her through the earrings and the Federation need not know."

"Do it." Kahn didn't hesitate.

Corban lifted an eyebrow and put his arm over his wife's shoulder. Azrel nodded agreement. "Some rules are meant to be broken. If—"

Dora interrupted. "The Endekians have just launched a shuttle to Laptiva."

"Dora, patch her through the speaker so we can all hear," Kahn ordered.

"Compliance."

"Tessa, can you hear me?" Kahn kept his voice level, but his fingers gripped the console so hard his bronzed knuckles turned a sickly tan.

Everyone on the bridge stopped talking and waited to hear Tessa's answer. There was nothing.

"Are the earrings still working?"

"Yes. Either the Endekians are jamming the signal. Or she's simply not responding."

Tessa recalled the amount of emotional energy required to null-grav her to the surface to breathe, rechecked the distance to the next island and figured "swimming" that far would tax her limits. And using her psi to go that far was out of the question. She might not have a boat, but she could float partway on a log. But she saw no handy logs floating around or nearby, and she couldn't hack down a palm with just her knife.

Returning to a shady spot on the beach, she took a swig of water from her canteen and ate one of the red fruit. The golden obelisk in the distance seemed farther away than when she'd begun her journey earlier this morning.

Obviously, other candidates completed the Challenge, so

there had to be a way to get there. She couldn't swim, didn't have a boat, had no way to build a boat. If only she had a flitter like the one Kahn had used on Zenon Prime.

Tessa blinked.

On the beach in front of her—which had previously been empty—now sat an enormous creature that had a head like an giant squid, a body like a whale, and too many tentacles for her to count. Part of the celadon-pearl creature was on the beach, but she had the impression that most of the body remained in the water. Two huge periwinkle eyes on the massive head stared at her.

She sensed nothing from the creature, no hostility, no curiosity, no interest. "Hello, there."

"Hello, there." The creature repeated her words, in her voice.

She tried to communicate again. "Do you live here?"

"Do you live here?" the creature mimicked, its impersonation of her perfect.

She had no idea if the creature was trying to communicate or not. Parrots on Earth could talk, even sing songs, but they had no idea what the words meant. Then again, the creature might be repeating her words in an attempt to learn her language.

Tessa pointed to herself. "Tessa."

"Tessa," the creature obediently repeated.

She pointed to the sand. "Beach."

"Beach."

She pointed to a tree. "Tree."

"Tree."

Tessa pointed to the creature. And didn't say a word. She waited, curious to see what it would do.

"Zar."

She pointed to it again. "Zar?"

"Zar."

Okay, it was intelligent, trying to communicate. Now

what? Tessa stood up and walked. "Walking." She halted. "Stopping." Each time she said a word, Zar repeated it. She had no idea if he understood. However, when she stopped, he said, "Zar stopping."

Zar had obviously come out of the sea. She wondered if the creature might be amenable to giving her a ride. Tessa walked down to the water until it was waist high. Then she walked parallel to the creature. "Tessa swim."

Zar backed his massive body into the water. "Zar swim."

Tessa slowly approached the huge beast. "Zar. Tessa. Swim." And she pointed to the obelisk.

Zar nodded his head. She didn't take that for a yes. A nod could mean *yes, no,* or *I don't understand.*

Tessa held up one hand and said, "Zar." She held up her other hand and said, "Tessa." Then she clasped her hands together. "Zar. Tessa. Swim."

Zar turned in the water and the tentacles signaled to her in an unmistakable gesture to climb onto its back. Since the island held no viable options for her, Tessa didn't hesitate. Either the creature would eat her, or it wouldn't. Either Zar would give her a ride or drown her at sea.

When she neared close enough to Zar's body, his tentacles grabbed her. She didn't struggle, allowing the appendages to advance her until she sat right behind Zar's neck. She pointed toward the golden obelisk. Zar swam out to sea, heading for the next island instead.

Tessa sighed. She supposed having the creature swim straight to her final destination would have been too easy. And she was beginning to appreciate the cunning of whoever had set up this Challenge. Each problem that she'd had to overcome required different skills, both physical and mental. The lack of food and water were survival skills. Swimming after the boat stopped proved she could use her psi well enough to reach the next island. This time she'd had to conclude that Zar wouldn't hurt her, that she should make use of him instead of attacking or fleeing. Each task seemed more complex, requiring increasingly intricate mental processes as well as moral and ethical dilemmas.

She was wondering what awaited her on the next island when Zar spoke. "You must find two keys to open the door to the obelisk."

So the creature *could* speak. Her pantomiming had simply been another test. "Where will I find the keys?"

"One in your head. The other in your heart."

That was very helpful. "Can you be any more specific?"

Zar didn't answer. He didn't speak again during the journey.

But Tessa spoke to him. "Thank you, Zar. I appreciate the ride and the information."

Zar swam onto the beach. Before she could slip off his back, the tentacles gently deposited her on her feet.

She patted the creature. "I hope we see each other again."

"If we meet again, one of us must die." Zar began to back toward the water.

Tessa followed. "I don't understand."

"Find the keys."

Tessa liked straightforward problems. Put a hostile subject in front of her and she'd fight. Give her a business to run and she'd assess and analyze. But she didn't understand what Zar had told her. She was supposed to find two keys, one in her heart, one in her head. And why if she met Zar again, did one of them have to die? What the hell did that mean?

She watched Zar disappear under the dark green waters with a sinking clench of her gut. The high cirrus clouds she'd noted earlier had burned away with the setting sun. So she had no difficulty spotting a white exhaust trail through the troposphere.

No one was supposed to be here.

Was something wrong? Or was this another test?

While friends might be coming to this island, Tessa wasn't taking any chances. She walked backward from the water to the palm trees so that it appeared from her foot-prints that she'd walked *into* the sea. After using null grav to disguise her weight distribution, only an expert tracker would read what she'd done from the signs on the beach.

The shuttlecraft hit the sound barrier with one echoing boom that startled the wildlife. Tessa headed into the island's interior, stopping at a pool of water, drinking and refilling her canteen after the liquid tested potable. Her rumbling stomach reminded her that one piece of fruit wouldn't keep her body sufficiently fueled, but she had no time to hunt for food, not with the shuttle roaring down.

She needed a place to hide and wished for the cover of darkness or the dense underbrush on the last island. She had no time to bury herself in the sand. The shuttle landed all too quickly, dead center on the island.

Tessa used null grav to lift herself into a palm tree. She didn't have to wait long for the hatch to pop open. Endekians ran out, three groups of three in different directions.

A group rushed directly her way, their feet stomping the underbrush. Heart thudding, knife drawn, Tessa held her breath, remaining absolutely quiet in the tree.

"Tessa?" Dora spoke to her through the earrings, picking one hell of a time to talk.

"Shh." She didn't dare say a word about privacy mode, not with the Endekians thirty feet below her precarious perch. But they never looked up.

"Endekians have landed on Laptiva," Dora whispered in privacy mode.

"Duh."

Tessa waited until the first group passed under her palm tree before speaking again. "Why are we talking?"

"Since the Endekians broke the Challenge rules, Kahn said we could break them, too."

"Okay. Come rescue me."

"We're working on it.

"What's wrong?"

"The Endekians attacked us."

Damn. She hated being down here when Kahn and her family were in danger up there. "Anyone hurt?"

"Just minor stuff. But they fused our flight-bay doors. We can't—"

Kahn's voice came through loud and strong. "Tessa, I want you to hide."

"Hello to you, too."

"There's no time for pleasantries. You're being hunted."

"No kidding." Slowly and silently, she lowered herself to the ground. If she remained in the tree, sooner or later the Endekians would find her. If Kahn wanted her to hide, she had to find a better place.

"Just stay out of sight," Kahn ordered.

"Look, it's getting dark. I don't know the terrain. With Endekians overrunning the island, I figure the safest place for me to go is inside that shuttle."

25

Kahn swore. His temper slid to his feet into a puddle of worry for Tessa. "Does anyone know why the Endekians are so interested in ensuring that my wife fails?"

"What do you mean?" Etru asked, shoving back a lock of red hair that had fallen into his eyes. He looked exhausted and haggard, as if *he* had given birth instead of the glowing Miri who lounged in a corner, nursing their son, Kirek. Etru kept glancing at them with a mixture of pride and concern as if he feared she'd topple over, but mother and son were doing better than dad.

Kahn tried to work past his anxiety for Tessa to understand what was happening. "Jypeg and the Endekians want Rystan for the glow stones and our proximity to Zenon Prime. He hates me because every time he sees that scar it reminds him he fled from battle. I didn't just scar his face but his pride. But why would he want Tessa badly enough to risk banishment from the Federation for violating Challenge rules?" Kahn thrummed his fingers on the console. Dora had the visuals back up so he could watch Tessa enter the Endekian ship. His heart swooped up his throat. "What in stars am I missing?"

"Friend, Kahn." Osari slithered across the deck, leaving a film of ooze. "Perhaps in some small way, I maybe of service."

"She's done something, hasn't she?" Kahn asked, his anger flaring that her action may have placed her in great danger.

Zical glanced from the Osarian to Kahn and scratched his head. "Who is she?"

"My wife," Kahn all but growled.

Osari's flat voice filled the cabin. "I do not wish to violate a confidence."

"But?" Kahn prodded, distracted by the screen. Tessa sneaked up behind an Endekian and broke his neck. Kahn tensed as two more Endekians attacked. Tessa rolled, swept one man's feet out from under him, and followed through with a lethal blow to the head.

"She asked me to make a wager for her," Osari informed Kahn.

"She's gambling?" Etru frowned.

"I'm going to kill her," Kahn muttered.

"You may have to wait your turn." Zical glanced at the screen. Three Endekians had returned to the shuttle and the odds against Tessa were now four to one.

"I told her to hide, but no. She had to go and— That's the way. Yes." Kahn's emotions heightened with her every attack and block. Watching her fight for her life while he stood in safety violated his protective instincts and was making him insane with frustration. The odds were back to three to one. If he were a betting man, he'd wager on his wife. The woman had moves, great moves, and the Endekians didn't want to use their stunners in close quarters for fear of hitting one another or damaging their ship.

Osari waited patiently for Kahn to continue their conversation, but Kahn fumed. No matter what his wife had done, she didn't deserve to die, and he couldn't pull his gaze from the screen until she'd dispatched the last three men and was once again relatively safe.

When he could again breathe, Kahn turned to Tessa's partner. "What has she wagered?"

"She bet that she would win the Challenge," Osari explained in a tone as flat and dry as the Laptiva desert.

"And?" Kahn prodded.

"The Endekians took the bet. At four-hundred-to-one odds in their favor, they can't afford to lose. Paying off the debt would bankrupt them."

"So why would they take a bet like that?" Miri asked.

"Because they intended to make sure that they would win." Kahn's temper came back full force.

"Where did she get credits to wager?" Etru asked.

Kahn sighed. "You don't want to know."

"I want to know," Shaloma insisted. "I want to study economics and be like—"

"Not now, child." Azrel took Shaloma aside.

Osari's tentacles waved as if agitated. "I fear the Endekians will not stop until Tessa is dead. I have asked my people to send ships, but they will not arrive in time."

"So that's why Jypeg has yet to finish off a prime target like us." Azrel's green skin darkened to deep emerald in anger. "Tessa's death is far more important to them."

"Exactly so," Osari agreed.

Dora interrupted the conversation. "Another shuttle from the Endekian ship is heading to Laptiva. I'm picking up transmissions between the shuttle under attack on the planet, the one on the way, and the mothership. Jypeg is on that shuttle. He's going down there himself to kill her. He's furious that his underlings haven't yet completed their assignments."

Shaloma eyed Kahn, her voice high with distress. "Tessa is a good fighter, but Jypeg is one of the Federation's best.

Tessa needs you down there. You have to do something to help her."

"Dora," Kahn asked, "how long until we can use the shuttle?"

"Another three hours."

Jypeg would be on Laptiva within minutes. Kahn's adrenaline surged, his head pounded, and he sought to contain a primal scream. He had no way to reach the planet's surface. No way to help Tessa. And one of the Federation's most skilled fighters was on his way down there to kill her.

Tessa shut the Endekian shuttle's hatch against more intruders and took a well-earned rest, thinking that spending the night here might not be so bad. She helped herself to a high-protein meal from the Endekians' emergency stores and replaced the fluids she'd lost while she'd perspired during the fight. She'd improved her situation considerably. She now had three fully charged stunners, a shuttle to fly to the obelisk, but neither of the keys needed to open the obelisk door and complete the Challenge.

"You've got another problem," Dora informed her.

"I'm listening."

"Jypeg is on the way down there to kill you."

"Okay."

Kahn took over the communications. "Tessa, he's not like the other Endekians. He's skilled. I barely defeated him during our last match. And as good as you are, you haven't mastered null grav. You cannot beat him."

"Okay." Tessa swallowed the last of her food. "Time to fly this baby out of here."

"No," he told her. "It's likely that the shuttle is booby-trapped. If anyone but an Endekian flies her, she may autodestruct."

"You don't want me to stay and fight. You don't want me to run. What the hell do you want me to do?"

"Hide. For once do as I ask. Please. I want you to hide for four hours."

Four hours? She refrained from saying what she thought of that idea, especially since he'd said *please*. Even if it was now dark, how did one hide on a flat beach that had no ground cover and no buildings for more than ten seconds, never mind for four hours? Sure, she could climb another tree, but eventually they'd think to look up and then she'd be easy pickings.

"How long do I have before my company arrives?" she asked, popping open the hatch.

"Less than fifteen minutes."

"Kahn, Kirek has put an idea into my head." Miri approached him, holding the baby.

"What idea?" Kahn wasn't about to turn away a suggestion from any corner, no matter how bizarre sounding. During the healing circle, he'd felt the baby's psi, had been stunned by the clarity, the focus, and the power of his supposedly undeveloped mind.

Miri closed her eyes and spoke as if describing a vidstream. "I see you launching yourself to the planet with just your suit. The suit is slightly bigger than you to hold extra air. And we will help hold your shield against the heat of reentry with a healing circle."

Zical gasped. "Even if Kahn could breathe, even if we could keep him from burning up when he hits the atmosphere, he will fall too hard for his null grav to counter the planet's gravitational pull."

"What if we add our psi to his?" Miri asked. "What if he lands in the water?"

Etru shook his head. "I have never heard of such a maneuver."

"I have," Dora contradicted. "There is a legend as old as the Perceptive Ones about a being who did what Darek suggested."

"Did he succeed?" Zical asked.

"The records of that time are so ancient that I cannot be certain," Dora informed them. "But it appears that the being made it through the atmosphere only to plunge to his death. Null grav is not made to stop that kind of velocity."

"Dora, what about the parachutes you use for cargo?" Kahn asked.

"That might work," Dora concluded. "I will modify the harness."

"How long will it take?"

"I'll be done before you exit the air lock," she promised.

On the bridge, Kahn faced his family and friends, who had already begun to form the circle. "If it appears that I will not make it, you must cut me loose."

Helera, who had remained in the background and silent until now, shook her head. "The healing circle does not work that way. It's all for one. You know that. If you die while linked, we all die."

"May I have the honor of joining the circle, too?" Osari asked.

"We would welcome you," Shaloma told him.

"You understand you will have to touch my physical self?" Osari added.

"No problem." Shaloma's adoration of Tessa included picking up Earth slang. When she took Osari's tentacle into her hand, the most blissfully contented look came over her face. Kahn raised a brow at Zical, daring him to match Shaloma's bravery. His friend could do no less on the other side of the Osarian and also held a tentacle.

Dora urged Kahn toward the air lock. "Hurry. If you are to do this thing, you must go now."

Tessa left the shuttle and killed the remaining Endekians on the tiny island, an easy feat with the stunner set to a lethal setting. However, finding a place to hide was more difficult. She didn't consider disobeying Kahn's order. Knowing that the Endekian was Kahn's equal in fighting ability told her that she wouldn't stand a chance against him. It would be like an ordinary soldier fighting a sensei. Sure, she could defeat the average male, but she hadn't had the years of practice to combat Kahn's kind of expertise.

Since the island gave her no place to hide, she looked out at the sea. She could swim into the dark water without being spotted easily from shore. Use her suit to prevent heat sensors from finding her. Too bad she didn't have scuba underwater apparatus, or a snorkel. Sheesh, she'd settle for a reed to breathe through.

She'd have to make do with what she had. Tessa drank the last of the water from her makeshift canteen. Turning it over, she pried the tip of her knife near the bottom and carved out a good-sized hole in its side. With the resounding boom of the shuttle during entry of Laptiva's atmosphere hurrying her efforts, Tessa plunged into the sea, hoping that the world didn't have any sharklike equivalents who fed at night.

Swimming out about an eighth of a mile, she settled into a combination of bobbing and treading water. She dearly wanted to talk to Dora, but that was impossible with her head underwater. It was going to be a long four hours.

Kahn used Dora's estimates to expand his suit's shield to the necessary size to hold enough breathing air. They calculated down to the absolute minimum. After he struck the atmosphere, the larger he made the shield, the more difficult protecting him from vaporization would be.

He opened the air lock. "I'm set to go."

The black void of space marred by the two damaged Endekian ships greeted him. But he focused on the emerald planet below that appeared to be mostly oceans. No way could

he just launch himself at the correct speed and angle to hit orbit at just the right velocity and angle, then count on landing
on the planet itself, never mind anywhere near Tessa. However, Dora's cargo launchers performed those kinds of calculations all the time.

"You mustn't black out from the g-force acceleration,"
Dora warned him.

"I'm aware of that." Kahn gritted his teeth, his psi picking
up the newly formed healing circle that comprised his family and friends. If he lost consciousness, his shield would
fail. Then he'd either depressurize and die in space or burn
up in the atmosphere. "Launch me."

"Compliance."

The uncomplicated system was like a cannon. Dora's
thrusters shot him into space with a force that caused his vision to blacken around the edges until he could see only
through a long dark tunnel. Kahn couldn't move a muscle,
but physical exertion had no place here. It was mental effort
that counted. Using all of his considerable concentration to
focus on maintaining his shield, he flew through space at an
angle almost parallel to the planet. Had Dora miscalculated?

Kahn used his own psi to hold the shield, tried to keep his
breathing regular. Never once did he feel alone. His family
and friends joined his psi, helping him hold the shield. For
several minutes, he plunged, his heading seemingly off
course. But slowly, his body arched into proper alignment
with an orbit.

As he sliced through the upper atmosphere, sparks flashed
off his shield. He drew his shield tighter, narrowed the entry
point, tried to reinforce the bottom where his feet appeared
to be the center of a fire.

His shield heated to thousands of degrees. One minuscule
aperture and he would incinerate. The circle of psi feeding
him weakened. They couldn't hold the shield and it thinned.

Another few seconds and the heat would reach his flesh.

Then the force of thousands of beings joined in. Osari had

linked with every Osarian on their world. Their entire race were risking their lives to lend power to the shield, to save Kahn so he could aid Tessa. The massive power influx reinforced the circle's efforts. Just enough.

Kahn shot through the upper atmosphere, his air supply now down to nil.

Sucking in the last of his oxygen, he wrapped his shield tighter so he'd fall faster. He now had to get down to where the air was thick enough to breathe, then pull the parachute before he passed out.

Lungs burning, his forehead slick with sweat, Kahn waited until the last possible second before blacking out, then popped the chute. Dizzy, confused from lack of air, he may have lost consciousness, but the jerking of the chute's opening had instantly awakened him with a rough shake.

Now he had to steer the canopy. For a moment he was unsure if he headed toward the correct island, but then he saw both shuttles. Jypeg was waiting for him and Kahn couldn't wait to confront the man who'd killed Lael and was now trying to kill Tessa.

And he prayed that Tessa had listened to him, just this once, and that she was hiding somewhere safe. He ached to ask Dora, but maintaining radio silence was critical to his surprise appearance.

Tessa heard the boom of a third craft's entry, but when she looked up, blinked the sea water away, she saw a missile flaring from the night sky. A missile? Were the Endekians dropping bombs on the planet until they killed her?

But then a parachute popped open. She cranked her head back to watch.

And the oddest thing occurred.

She was suddenly back on land. One moment she'd been in the water in darkness, now she stood on an island she'd never seen before and it was daylight. Hundreds of Endekians surrounded her, shouting, taunting insults, spitting at her. It was as if the Perceptive Ones who had built the Challenge equipment had plucked her from the sea and deposited her into the middle of an enemy camp.

Hostile and militant men had her cornered. She had nowhere to run. Nowhere to hide. As far as she was concerned, she had only one option. Surrender.

Even if these men had no fighting ability at all, even if most of them hadn't held weapons pointed at her, she couldn't defeat so many. Perhaps later, she would have a chance to escape, but for now, she had no choice.

With a sinking heart, Tessa tossed down her weapon, raised her hands over her head in surrender. Once again, she had failed and the bitterness of defeat tasted no better this time than when she'd jumped in front of the bullet to save a president.

If there was a way out of this no-win situation, she hadn't seen it. All of her skills, all of Kahn's training, hadn't prepared her for this defeat. She'd failed Earth and Rystan. More importantly, she'd failed Kahn, Despair and disappointment tugged at her.

But—in the space of a heartbeat, the Endekians disappeared. Tessa blinked in astonishment, her mouth open. One moment they'd been about to make mincemeat of her, the next they were gone. They were gone as quickly as she'd been brought here.

Impossible.

Had she been in the ocean so long she'd become dehydrated and had hallucinated the entire incident?

At the sound of a loud gong, she spun around, arms up, wrists cocked, ready to defend herself. But she remained alone on the beach. Except for a bright shiny key lying in the sand.

A key to the obelisk? She picked it up, tucked it into her suit, her despair peeling away to reveal new hope. Was this the key she'd found by using her head? Were these Endekians, unlike the ones she'd killed, simply another part of the Challenge?

Tessa believed so. But she didn't have time to consider it before landing right back in the dark sea.

Perhaps she'd fallen asleep, dreamed or imagined the entire incident—except when she placed her hand to her side, she closed her fingers around the key.

She'd passed another test. Apparently she'd been supposed to recognize a hopeless situation and surrender. What had appeared as certain defeat had been a victory.

Tessa wished she could have met the Perceptive Ones, the designers of the Challenge. Those ancient beings had creative minds, and she wondered what had happened to them.

Though however much the mysteries of the past intrigued her, she had her own enigmas to solve in the present. But time had been mixed up. She'd gone through long periods of daylight and a short one of darkness. Now it was day once again.

Recalling the parachute falling from the night sky, she searched for it again in daylight but saw no sign of it. Apparently while she'd been occupied and time had seemed to go awry, something had landed on the island where Jypeg had been hunting her.

Tessa surfaced and spoke to Dora. "Did one of the good guys just parachute in for a visit?"

Dora explained to Tessa the steps that had been taken to save her from Jypeg. Horrified that so many had risked their lives to help her, humbled over the chance they'd taken, she thought out her next step carefully. After so many had acted on her behalf, her hiding seemed the most cowardly of acts. Yet, coming out of the water in some foolish attempt to prove herself brave and worthy might nullify the danger they'd already faced for her.

Tessa swam closer to shore. "Dora, how many Endekians are on that shuttle with Jypeg?"

"Between four and eight. Why?"

"Seems to me that Kahn may need someone to watch his back while he deals with Jypeg. Can you put me in touch with Kahn?"

"Not without breaking radio silence. He wants his presence to come as a complete surprise." Tessa supposed that made sense. The Endekians knew Tessa was already here, so even if they monitored Dora's encrypted messages, it wouldn't tell them anything. But if Dora sent word to Kahn, the Endekians could trace the beamed message and would know someone else had landed on this world.

"Kahn will likely try and take out a few underlings first," Tessa surmised, wishing she had a pair of binoculars. From her position in the water, she could see the island and the noses of the shuttles. Nothing more.

"He's already brought two Endekians down," Dora advised her.

"You're monitoring?" Tessa could have kicked herself for not asking the right question sooner. Although she had every confidence in Kahn's ability to take Jypeg, she didn't like that Kahn would be outnumbered, his attention divided between several foes. "What's going on? Does Kahn require my help?" While she intended to keep her word about staying hidden, if Kahn needed her, she'd have to reevaluate.

"He embedded a device similar to your earrings in his stunner. I can only see what he sees. He just took care of a search patrol. When they fail to report in—"

"Jypeg will suspect I did it." Tessa understood the tactics. She also knew that if she showed up to guard Kahn's back, she would distract him.

"That's Kahn's plan."

"What's happening now?"

"Jypeg is making Kahn come to him inside the shuttle."

"I don't like it. He's setting up an ambush."

"Damn," Dora swore.

"What?"

"Kahn took out three men. He did it silently, but a scanner picked him up. Jypeg now knows Kahn, not you, is hunting him."

"Then there's no need to maintain radio silence. Patch me through."

"Compliance."

"Kahn, do you need me?"

She expected him to refuse out of macho pride and his need to protect her at all costs. However, if he took on more opponents than he could handle, if they could get past him, they would find her.

"You're armed?" His voice was curt, tense.

"I have two stunners with full charges."

"How long until you can reach the shuttle?"

"Four minutes."

"See you then."

Kahn believed she could help! No praise from Master Chen had ever meant more to her. Tessa let out the breath she'd been holding, her heart full. She swam underwater to the island, coming up periodically for huge gulps of air.

Once she reached the beach, she detached a stunner. With her knife in one hand, her stunner in the other, she raced across the beach and toward the shuttles. "Dora, which one?"

"To the right."

"How many Endekians are aboard?"

"At least three. Kahn is fighting Jypeg and two others."

"How's he doing?" Tessa ducked through the hatch. Kahn fought with his back to a wall. Two men closed on him from opposite sides, one from above.

For the moment, Tessa had the edge of surprise. She fired, killing one Endekian with the weapon. Kahn kicked his null grav into superfast mode, and he and Jypeg slashed, bounced, zoomed, attacked, and counterattacked at a pace so ferocious it stole her breath. However, that didn't stop her from engaging the other Endekian.

With Kahn zipping around the shuttle after Jypeg like a ricocheting bullet, she focused on the second Endekian, who'd rolled behind the console to take cover. Tessa kept him pinned, firing to keep him from helping Jypeg.

"Behind you," Dora warned.

Tessa spun, took down an Endekian who'd entered through the hatch. But that gave the man who'd hidden behind the console just enough time to launch himself into her back. Slamming into the bulkhead, she dropped her weapon. Although her shields had been up, her arm went numb. Her head snapped back and for a moment she couldn't see.

"Duck," Dora warned.

Slow to shift, Tessa took a second blow to the shoulder. But her vision began to return. The Endekian must have sensed her injury and closed in for the kill. She remained deliberately clumsy, letting him come to her. And when the Endekian lunged at her, he slid right onto her blade.

Out of his peripheral vision, Kahn saw Tessa and the Endekian go down, but he couldn't help her with Jypeg keeping him engaged. Concerned for her safety, yet confident she could protect herself, he'd allowed her to join him in battle, a decision that had been necessary to their survival. He couldn't defeat Jypeg and his men by himself. And if he failed to win, if they got past him, they would kill her, too. So he'd accepted her help and he'd been proud to fight beside someone so skilled.

As Jypeg drop-kicked at Kahn's throat, Kahn shifted and blocked out concern for his wife. Her strong psi told him that she still lived.

And he wanted Jypeg's attention on him. Finally, Kahn faced his enemy, the man who'd killed Lael. The man who'd tried to murder Tessa. The man who'd invaded Rystan and was responsible for much of his people's suffering.

A quick death would be too easy. Kahn didn't want to kill the proud Endekian, he wanted justice. He wanted the man's name to be spoken with disgust. He wanted him to face a public trial and spend the rest of his life in shame. A clean, quick death was too good for him.

Tessa shoved the dead body of Jypeg's man away and straightened.

"Take cover," he ordered, and she dived behind a hatch and out of sight, leaving him alone to focus all his attention on Jypeg.

"Your woman can't run so far that I won't find her." Jypeg somersaulted off the wall and shot a fist at Kahn's kidney.

Kahn shifted and with a spinning back kick caught Jypeg's shoulder with a glancing blow that sent him reeling. "She won't have to hide after the Federation locks you away."

"Locks *me* away?" Jypeg shouted. "Not in your luckiest fantasy. Your ship will be crushed. Your wife raped, then slaughtered. I look forward to hearing her screams in my ears, her begging for her life," Jypeg taunted. He feinted, then struck with an elbow that just missed Kahn's sternum.

Refusing to let the Endekian's taunts faze him, Kahn noted that the man appeared to be sweating too much, breathing too hard. But was it a trick?

Kahn tested him with a right punch followed by a fake downward with his left fist, then from above he planted a two-footed kick into his foe's stomach that knocked Jypeg into an out-of-control roll. Kahn didn't wait for the man to strike the ground before following through with a killing blow to the heart.

Tessa peeked around the corner, her eyes narrowed, a stunner steady in her hand. "I was afraid to shoot for fear of striking you." Her gaze centered on Jypeg. "Is he dead?"

Kahn checked the body and nodded. "I would have preferred for him to stand trial to publicize to the rest of the Federation that the Endekians want Rystan."

"I'm glad the son of a bitch is dead." Tessa finally lowered the gun she'd kept steady on Jypeg. Kahn had never seen her look more beautiful. With her eyes serious, her mouth compressed, and her pulse beating at her slender throat, her femininity had never seemed more in contrast with her cool green eyes.

His enemy had gotten a clean death after all. But perhaps this was better. Kahn would have hated spending time on Zenon Prime for a trial when he and Tessa had a future to look forward to together and a planet to free. After she won the Challenge, that is.

Kahn opened his arms to embrace her. "You okay?"

She grinned and embraced him. "I am now."

26

Kahn closed his arms around her, kissed her until she was breathless. Since the Challenge had begun, Tessa had tried to focus on the problem at hand. But with his powerful arms around her, with the fresh taste of him on her mouth, with the familiar male scent of him rousing her emotions and making her realize how much he meant to her, she didn't want to ever let go.

She should thank him for coming to her rescue, but she couldn't summon the words past a throat choked with love. When Kahn broke their embrace and stepped back, she wanted to cling because she sensed what was coming. She hadn't completed the Challenge. She still had tasks to finish.

Kahn held her shoulders as if he didn't want to release her, either. "You must go on as if I'm not here. Dora will send the shuttle for me as soon as repairs are completed and I will return to the ship. Since the Endekians were not supposed to interfere, I'm hoping the Federation Council won't nullify your Challenge. But the less time we spend together, the better our chances of their seeing our side."

"I understand." She turned away and fled from the shuttle before he could see the tears brimming in her eyes. Stumbling to the beach, she chastised herself for feeling so sad. They'd defeated the Endekians, she would complete the Challenge. Everything was fine.

She might not have been separated from Kahn for that long, but she hadn't been prepared for his coming to her rescue and then leaving again just as suddenly. She missed Kahn with a dreadful tearing inside that left her battered and bruised. Knowing she was reacting like an emotional yoyo didn't mean she could stop the aching. All her life, she'd been alone, but now that she'd found someone to love, being alone again was much more difficult since she had so much more to lose.

But as Helera was so fond of saying, she could do hard things. After a few sniffles of self-pity, Tessa pulled herself together. Emotionally and physically exhausted, she decided that despite the bright light of day, she needed sleep. She found a spot in the sand on the beach above the high-tide mark and slept, awakening once to note the darkness but not rising until the day had arrived once more. Her last day. She would finish the Challenge today or not at all.

Walking down the beach and searching for another boat, she practically stumbled over the flitter she'd wished for earlier. Without hesitation, she climbed into the flyer, which had a simple stick control similar to the one on the shuttle. As she lifted into the sky, her hopes soared. The sooner she finished her task, the sooner she could be reunited with Kahn.

She flew straight to the golden obelisk and circled from the

air. The golden monument extended from a two-hundred-foot-
high base, a pyramid of colored *bendar*. With no place to land
the flitter upon the steep pyramid, she had to set down in a
nearby clearing, next to the pyramid's only entrance, an archway through the *bendar*.

All she needed to do was find the second key, walk through
the archway, and open the doors to win the Challenge. She
anticipated she would soon be back with Kahn.

But when Tessa arrived at the archway, it was no longer
an open passageway. Zar blocked the entrance with his enormous body, his tentacles waving. When he'd given her a ride
between islands, she had only guessed at his enormous girth.
Now, with his entire body out of the water, she estimated he
was as long as four schoolbuses.

Tessa pretended to ignore the fact that he'd told her that
the next time they'd meet, one of them would die. "Hello,
Zar."

"Greetings, Earthling. You have done well to come this
far."

"Thank you. Looks like I could use your help again. Can
you lift me over your body so that I may enter the archway?"

"I'm sorry. I'm not permitted to help you again."

"Would you object if I gently climbed over you?"

"No. However, my tentacles will not allow you to pass."

"Okay." She should have known getting past Zar wouldn't
be that easy. She had less than a day left to figure out how to
pass by him and find the second key. Perhaps Zar would
weary of his spot in front of the entrance. A big guy like him
had to feed frequently, "Zar, how often do you eat?"

"My body doesn't require sustenance during the Challenge. I do not sleep, either. Your only way through is to kill
me." He spoke matter-of-factly, as if his death meant nothing to him.

"I don't kill creatures who aren't hostile. And you helped

me." She sat in the shade, thinking. "Can you tell me where to find the second key?"

Zar didn't answer.

This time he was no help to her, but a hindrance. No way could she budge Zar's enormous girth. She had to convince him to move.

The first hour, she tried bribery. But Zar didn't want anything she offered. Not food or wealth or companionship.

In the second hour, she hiked around the pyramid, searching for another entrance and the missing key. She found nothing helpful.

During the third hour, she began digging a tunnel under Zar, but his weight collapsed the sand.

In the fourth hour, she tried to collect enough driftwood to build a bridge over him, but she ran out of materials.

In the fifth hour, she stopped her attempts to get past Zar to search for food, hoping a meal would revive her and help her thinking processes. She zapped several fish with her stunner, then cooked them. With only Zar for company, she'd formed an odd friendship with him, had had several long conversations, but nothing she said convinced him to budge. And she wondered if she had to first get past Zar to find the missing key.

In the sixth hour, she tried begging.

Hour seven she reserved for insults.

In the eighth hour she ignored him. Perhaps she had to find a new way to use her psi. The *bendar* walls were too high for her to use null grav. She couldn't manage enough height to clear Zar's double-decker-high body.

In the ninth hour, Zar insisted, "If you wish to win the Challenge, you must kill me. I am prepared to die. One lethal zing of the stunner to my brain will cause no pain."

"Don't make me do this." Tessa yanked the stunner from her suit, pointed it at Zar. "Why don't you just go back into the sea?"

He didn't move.

But she couldn't bring herself to pull the trigger.

His heart jamming up his throat, Kahn watched the drama between his wife and Zar. She didn't have much more time to make a decision. While he admired her stubbornness and her ingenuity, Tessa didn't like to fail. All of this stalling made the decision so much harder for her.

"Calm yourself, Kahn." Osari slithered beside him. "Have faith in her character. She will do what she must."

"No one should be asked to make such a dreadful decision." Kahn seethed, paced, his gaze never leaving the screen.

"Your father made the right choice and so will she."

Kahn didn't want to think about Corban. Seeing him with Azrel rubbed him wrong. Although the love between them shone through their every glance and touch, Corban's subservience to Azrel's wishes irritated him.

He needed a distraction. At least the Federation Council had agreed to let the Challenge continue. The Endekians' interruption would be dealt with through diplomatic channels. So if Tessa made the right choice, they could return to Rystan and help his people oust the Endekians. And Tessa would win the trading status for Earth, so necessary to solve their pollution problems.

Or she would choose wrong and die, be lost to him forever. His stomach rolled with nausea. He didn't know the correct answer to the puzzle. Even if he'd wanted to help her, he couldn't. And if he had to change places with her right now, he didn't know what he'd do.

One burst of the stunner would kill Zar and allow her to complete the Challenge. Could the life of one creature be more important than millions of Terrans and Rystani whose lives would be enhanced by Federation membership?

Heart aching, head throbbing, Kahn stared at the screen.

* * *

The tenth hour arrived like all the others. Hot, sunny, a gentle breeze that mocked Tessa's bad mood. Zar blocked the entrance like a beached whale. "You must either kill or be killed."

"By whom?" she asked.

"Those are the rules."

Exceedingly tired of games and rules, quests and challenges, and puzzles that couldn't be solved to her satisfaction, Tessa jerked the stunner from her side and stomped it into the sand and then kicked more sand over it. There was no point in shooting Zar when she had yet to find the second key. "I'm not killing you."

"Temper tantrums will not get you what you want." Zar's placid tone pricked her already spiraling bad humor.

She bent down, dug through the sand, and retrieved the stunner. "I will kill in self-defense. I will kill to protect others. But damn it to hell, I will not kill an innocent being to win this Challenge." Tessa ran toward the ocean and flung the stunner. Spinning end over end, the weapon splashed into the sea where it could stay for the rest of eternity.

Tessa could accept failure. She could even accept death. If the Perceptive Ones had left machinery behind to kill her or if that was Zar's task, she was ready.

"Do it," she shouted at Zar. "Kill me now and be done."

Nothing happened. Zar didn't so much as blink. The sea didn't rise up to swallow her. The sky didn't shoot a lightning bolt at her. The sun beamed down and the waves lapped at her feet.

She turned around to yell at Zar, but he had disappeared. In his place was the second key.

He'd given her a clue, but she hadn't figured it out until now. Finding the second key had been a decision she'd made with her heart.

Joyful, humbled by how long it had taken her to make the right decision, Tessa picked up the key, walked through the *bendar* archway, unlocked a double set of doors. She stepped inside a tiny room that reminded her of an elevator. The moment she entered, chimes rang and a hologram of the Perceptive Ones greeted her with psi warmth and smiles. "Congratulations. You have passed the initial stage of the Challenge. Enjoy the fullness of your life, knowing that you have succeeded."

That was it?

After all the buildup, she'd expected fireworks, a marching band, a parade. Feeling silly and happy, she left the tiny room, which must have been soundproofed. She hadn't heard the boom of the shuttle, but when she exited the archway, Kahn was there. He swept her into his arms with a proud smile and she realized that she didn't need the parade or the fireworks or the marching band. She had everything she'd ever wanted. She had Kahn.

During a celebration feast on the starship, during which many toasts had been offered, Tessa was feeling especially mellow. She'd come to care for Shaloma and Miri as sisters she'd never had. Etru, Zical, Mogan, and Nasser accepted Tessa as Kahn's wife. The Osarian was the best of friends and their partnership would be one that lasted a lifetime. And Tessa couldn't wait to see Kireck grow up—with his psi potential, he was headed for great things.

During the Challenge, Helera and Azrel had become friends and Kahn had mellowed just a little toward his father's marriage. All in all, she had no complaints, except that she really wanted some alone time with Kahn.

"Tessa." Kahn lounged beside her, his hand on her shoulder. Ever since she'd returned, he couldn't seem to stop touching her or grinning.

"Yes?" She gave him a long, heated look that she hoped would tell him how much she wanted him.

"Tell us about this bet you made."

Uh-oh. She looked at Osari. He might not have been able to see her glance due to his blindness, but since he and Dora had been the only ones aware of her wager, one of them must have spilled the news.

Osari spoke up as if on cue. "When the Endekians attacked, Kahn wanted to know their motivation. I felt it necessary to share a few details. If I have revealed information that I should not have done, I apologize."

"There's no need to apologize. My wager put all of you in danger and for that I am sorry."

"What wager?" Shaloma asked.

"At four hundred to one against me, I couldn't resist the odds," Tessa admitted.

"How many credits did you bet?" Kahn asked, the grin never leaving his face.

She sensed his approval and couldn't wait to get him alone. "One million."

"Stars!" Kahn rolled his eyes at the ceiling. "Woman, are you telling me that you've won four hundred million credits?"

"Yeah."

"We're rich!" Shaloma laughed.

"We can buy a fleet of spaceships to defend Rystan," Kahn added.

"Uh . . . Um . . ." Tessa bit her lip and the room grew tense and silent. "We aren't exactly rich."

Kahn frowned. "What do you mean?"

"I instructed Osari and Dora that if I won they should spend the credits."

Kahn's lower jaw dropped. "You and Dora and Osari . . . spent . . . four hundred million . . . credits?"

"Yeah. At the time it seemed like a good idea. There was a bargain—"

"What did you buy?" Kahn approached her and took her hand, squeezing it gently.

"—and if I didn't make a bid—"

"What did you buy?"

"—we would lose out."

"Stars, woman. What did you spend four hundred million credits on?"

"A nice warm planet. With a great location—not too far from Osari's world. Much like Earth before we polluted it. The planet has four blue oceans and snow near the poles. It's rich in metals and natural fuels. I thought we could all go there and make up laws that pleased us." Tessa took a deep breath.

"You bought a planet?" Kahn sputtered.

"Yeah. One where we don't have to follow any laws except those of our making. Azrel and Corban can live the life they choose. And so can we. No one there will shun Osari or his people. We can start from scratch and . . ."

Kahn sighed. "My wife bought a planet."

Zical chuckled. "Apparently, she's quite the bargain hunter."

"What about our people on Rystan?" Etru asked.

"Those who wish to join us will be offered transportation, but they'll have to accept new ways. And those who want to stay behind will be free to do so," Tessa replied.

Helera spoke up. "I can't imagine anyone will want to stay on Rystan."

"I think we should put Tessa in charge of the family finances," Miri suggested. "I am happy to bring our son to this new world where he can thrive." She nudged Etru.

He looked at Kahn who nodded. "I second the motion of putting Tessa in charge of finances. All in favor?"

There were lots of ayes.

"Any opposed?"

No one nixed the idea.

"And Dora?" Tessa spoke to her friend. "On our new world you will have all the rights of other sentient beings. You get to vote."

"Do I get to have sex?"

Everyone laughed. Tessa squeezed Kahn's hand. "Sure. All you have to do is figure out a way to make it work."

Zical winked at Tessa, "That should keep her busy. Maybe she'll stop ogling me when I work out."

"I do not ogle."

"Do, too."

The conversation hummed around them with talk about the new world, which had no name. She noted that Xander had developed a crush on Shaloma in her absence and that Etru and Corban got along quite well.

Finally, she and Kahn were alone in their quarters. All the things she wanted to say to him bubbled inside her, but talking could wait. She wanted to make love. They'd been separated for long enough that she didn't want to spoil this reunion and the new start of their lives together with words.

"Would you like me to dance for you?" she asked.

"No."

"What do you mean? No?"

He laughed and opened his arms. "I can't wait that long."

"Me, neither." She wound her arms around his neck, used her psi to turn her clothes transparent. "Kahn, I love you." The words slipped out.

"I know."

"That's not very romantic." She nipped his neck. "You're supposed to say that you love me, too."

"Woman, are you going to spend our entire marriage telling me what to say?"

She chuckled. "Only when necessary. And right now, I need to hear you say the words."

"Words are so important to you?"

"Your words are that important to me."

"Hmm." His eyes glinted with his teasing. "That's hard to believe when you heed them so infrequently."

"I'll do better," she promised, her lips brushing his. "But I need the proper incentive."

His psi merged with hers, telling her everything she needed to know. She felt his love over her, under her, inside her, deep in her heart. But when he said the words, "I love you, woman," she knew she'd finally come home.